DEATH'S VALLEY

Predators of Darkness Series: Book Four

LEONARD D. HILLEY II

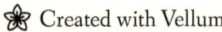

Chapter 1

Salem, Oregon: Midnight

MITCH NILES WALKED SLOWLY along the weathered sidewalk. Fog stirred in gentle wisps, teasing the night as it crept subtlety closer. Three blocks away, a thicker mist swept forward to claim the city until the morning sun melted it away.

He paused at the intersection. Even though the night was still and dead, he waited until the walk signal granted permission to cross. Halfway across the street, he placed his briefcase in his right hand and checked his watch. The Greyhound Bus was scheduled to arrive in less than an hour.

The amber glow of the streetlights dimmed, shrouded by the congealing fog. If Mitch believed in black magic, he'd have thought an evil entity loomed toward him, draped inside a swirling cape of misty vapor.

His weeklong stay in the city had been disappointing. Something evil *was* here, but he had been unable to pinpoint its source. His time to leave had come, but he feared he had outstayed his welcome.

He hated to report his failure to Kat and Lucian. Although this was his first assignment on a trial basis with the Kat Gaddis Agency, he didn't see why they'd keep him on staff. Not after he had failed to produce results. Always a man who loved investigating paranormal activity with great success, Mitch hadn't discovered any useful evidence to keep this particularly eerie case open.

The night air grew colder. Strong wind funneled through the street. As Mitch approached the bus stop, a beautiful young woman seated on the bench looked up and smiled. Surprised to see anyone outside in the depths of darkness, he stopped at the edge of the sidewalk. The last thing he ever expected after the bizarre murders was to find a young lady alone on a dark street after midnight.

Mitch motioned toward the bench. "You mind if I sit?"

"Not at all." She moved her purse to make room. "Go ahead. Are you waiting for the bus, too?"

Mitch nodded.

"Kind of odd to be here during the witching hour, isn't it?" she asked with a smile.

"Wrong Salem for witches, but the atmosphere crafts the mood."

"Where are you headed?"

Mitch studied her attire. She wore a leather jacket with a black fleece hoodie and a short black skirt. Her fishnet stockings were stretched and torn in places. She had a *lot* of facial piercings. A tattoo of a black widow spread across her right cheek. Black lipstick and heavy mascara painted the threat that she wished to convey to the world, but her big brown eyes revealed softness no mask could hide. Within her gaze, he read deeper pain. Past turmoil haunted her. She might fool others with the façade, but not him.

Her pale skin and the black circles under her eyes reminded him of a corpse. He couldn't tell if she wished to portray emo, goth, or punk. He didn't know, and she probably didn't care.

Mitch placed his briefcase on his lap. "I'm traveling back to Jersey."

She smiled. "You're a long way from home."

"Yes, I am." He nodded and offered his hand. "My name's Mitch. You are?"

Staring cautiously at his hand, then to his eyes, she tilted her head with one brow cocked. She accepted his hand with a loose grip. "Sheba."

"Where are you traveling?" he asked.

"I'm not. I'm waiting for some friends."

"This late at night?"

"Yep," Sheba said, sliding her hands into her jacket pockets. "So what brings you across country to this shithole?"

"I'm investigating the strange murders that took place last week."

"Why? Local authorities haven't figured out anything. You with the FBI or something?"

"Or something," Mitch replied.

"Did you discover anything helpful?"

"No, I came up empty. With what has happened, why would you be outside in the dead of night?"

"Darkness doesn't bother me." She paused to light a cigarette. "Few things in this world do."

"You're a brave soul."

"Am I?" She laughed. "If the police listened to me, I could give them the information to solve the murders. But I'm pretty much an outcast."

"You *know* what happened?"

She exhaled a long stream of smoke. "Yeah."

"And the police won't listen to you?"

"No, I'm a social misfit. They don't like me, and they certainly don't give a shit about me."

"Why not?"

Sheba pursed her lips and stared at him for a long moment before turning her attention back to the street. She took another drag from the cigarette, tapped the ash, and crossed her legs. Turning to face him again, a solemn expression claimed her facial features. "Because this has happened before."

Mitch stiffened. "When?"

"Several years ago."

"I never found any reports of it."

"You won't. The police buried it."

"Did they have any suspects?" he asked.

"At first they blamed me."

"You? Why?"

"The girl murdered that night was my friend Gloria. Three of us girls were there when she died. A few months later, what we had seen haunted us so much that Jill committed suicide. She was afraid that what had killed Gloria would come for her, too. Beverly," Sheba shook her head and cleared her throat. "Beverly never spoke again. She's still locked in a padded cell at the mental institution. I visit but she never acknowledges my presence."

"What happened?"

"You wouldn't believe me if I told you."

"Try me."

Sheba flicked the cigarette butt to the street. Glowing ash exploded and faded to black. Folding her arms, she faced him. Her eyes narrowed. "*Whom* do you work for?"

Mitch opened his briefcase and handed her a business card.

"Kat Gaddis Agency?" she said. "Never heard of them. What do they do?"

"Let's just say we investigate unusual circumstances, especially when murder is involved."

"Paranormal shit?"

"No. Not exactly. I wouldn't classify our agency quite like that."

Sheba smiled. "Then you'll never understand what's behind this."

"You believe in the paranormal?"

"With all that's involved, you learn to accept it. If you don't, you'll die quickly."

Mitch nodded. "So what happened to Gloria?"

Sheba looked away. She chewed her bottom lip as her mind carried her back in time. "We were in high school when it happened. What was meant to be a prank ended tragically."

"What kind of prank?"

"Well, I guess you could say that it was more a dare than a prank," she said. "Some boys in our chemistry lab dared us to go to the cemetery after dark. They said that we were too chicken to show up. It was obvious that all they wanted to do was scare the hell out of us. If it had been up to me, we wouldn't have gone."

"Then why did you?"

She sighed. "Gloria. She didn't give us any other option. Being the tomboy in our group, she wasn't about to back down from such a challenge. Instead, she got in Tom's face and swore to him that we'd be there."

Mitch shook his head. "Peer pressure's such a bitch sometimes."

"True. Tom and his friends laughed and told us they'd be at the front gate to witness our bravery. My gut told me differently. I knew they wouldn't be there. They'd be hiding somewhere along the way to jump out and scare us. Boys get a kick out of that spineless crap."

"I assume you were right?"

"Not quite, but almost," Sheba said. "That night we took our flashlights and headed to the cemetery. The fog was so thick; all our lights did was reflect little yellow circles. We couldn't see more than a couple feet ahead, so we turned off the flashlights. Hell, we knew our way there anyway."

"What happened?"

She shook her head. Her hands trembled as she lit another cigarette. "When we got to the gate, the boys weren't there. We didn't hear any snickering in the shrubs surrounding the cemetery gate and that made Gloria furious."

"I bet," he said. "So why didn't you just go home?"

Sheba took a deep breath as if the memories agitated her. "You'd have had to know Gloria. Her fury made her overstep her bounds many times."

"She was a troublemaker?"

"Not intentionally."

Mitch smiled. "How could she cause problems unintentionally?"

"Trouble sought *her* out, but she never tried to sidestep it. She dove headfirst into situations. Her actions always preceded her ability to think first."

"I see," Mitch said. "With poor visibility and them not being there, I don't understand why she didn't turn back. Didn't she have any sense of fear?"

"Not at first," she replied. "Later she did, but by then, it was too late."

"Go on."

"An old rickety manor stands in the center of the cemetery. The place should have been torn down years ago. And Gloria insisted that the boys were hiding there, so she trudged forward. We argued with her to come back, but she refused. Even though we didn't want to go, we also couldn't let her wander into the fog alone. Whether she wanted to accept it or not, she needed us."

"Were the boys there?"

Sheba shook her head. "No."

The cold air nipped at Mitch. Chills ran up his arms and down his spine.

As Sheba shared the grim details of those events, her eyes held a coldness that numbed any bravery a man possessed. Yet, Mitch listened with earnest because Kat and Lucian expected him to gather the necessary information to find out who or what was responsible for these murders. Even if he missed the bus, he had to know the specific details behind what had happened to Gloria that night. Her information might be the missing key they needed to solve the case and direct them to the real source before more people were gruesomely murdered.

"Midway across the cemetery," Sheba said. "The thick clouds broke and the full moon shone down on the manor. The windows looked black. From our distance, we couldn't see inside, but there was this sensation of something watching us from the other side of the glass. Gloria hesitated. She didn't move forward or backwards. She looked scared, pale. I thought, actually I *hoped*, she'd leave. But she didn't."

"Why not?"

"On the ground was a torn flannel shirt soaked with sticky blood. It was one of the boy's shirts. A few feet away lay a flashlight with its light still on. I wanted to run, but my feet wouldn't move."

"What about Gloria?"

"The shirt pissed her off."

"You're kidding?"

"I wish I were. She accused them of killing a rabbit or some other small animal and soaking the shirt with blood to scare us. Whether or not they did that, I'm not certain. I know it scared the shit out of me."

Mitch rubbed his arms against another wave of chills that pimpled his skin. The drifting fog smelled rancid. Paranoia sought to embrace him. He searched the dark corners of the buildings across the street, looking for shadows, for anyone or any creature watching them from an alley or storefront. Nothing presented itself, but he was still unable to shake his uneasiness.

Her eyes revealed that what she told with pure conviction was absolutely true. He doubted any actress had the ability to tell a fictitious account more convincingly. And if so, that person definitely deserved an Oscar on their mantel.

"Seeing the blood didn't deter her?"

"No. For some damn reason she got brave. Too brave. Determined to call them out, she went to the back door to investigate. A deadbolt secured the door, but the knob was so rusted that had it been unlocked, you couldn't have twisted it. She took her flashlight and looked through the windows. I thought she might bust one out, but then she discovered the cellar doors."

"Were they locked?"

Sheba shrugged. "I'm not sure. The wooden doors were weathered and rotten. Painted in red were the words: Keep Out! Gloria stomped the boards until they caved inward. She walked down the earthen steps."

Mitch frowned. "You let her go inside alone?"

"No, we followed. Safety in numbers, so to speak, but we should have grabbed her and carried her out."

"Did you find the boys?"

She shook her head and swallowed hard. "No. We found twelve caskets arranged in a circle. Inside the circle was another casket. It was glossy and free of dust. Curiosity got the best of Gloria. She opened the casket lid."

Sheba's hands shook.

Her lower lip quivered.

Mitch gently patted her arm. "It's okay. Take your time."

She closed her eyes. Tears blackened by mascara trickled down her cheeks. When she reopened them, her expression was distant. "That's just it. I don't remember anything else except Gloria's terrifying, pain-filled screams. I ran so fast that when I stopped I was at the cemetery gate. Beverly and Jill stood beside me. Their faces were shadowed with fear. We were scared and almost unable to breathe."

"And Gloria?"

"We waited for her but she never came. Jill called 9-1-1 on her cellphone. The police arrived a few minutes later. They never found her body."

Mitch's back stiffened. "They didn't find her?"

"No."

"What'd they say about the caskets?"

Sheba laughed until she couldn't catch her breath. Her sudden hysteria alarmed him. After a minute or so, she captured her composure. "They swore they didn't see any coffins. Just a barren dirt floor."

"If they didn't find her body, why'd they accuse you of her murder? Why even think a murder took place?"

She looked at the pavement. "They found her blood. Lots of it. But not her body."

"That doesn't make sense. She couldn't have disappeared that quickly."

"You wouldn't think so. They asked us to go back down there, but we couldn't. After an hour or so, they came out. We mentioned the coffins again and that pissed them off. We were taken to police headquarters and questioned. They showed us pictures of the cellar from all angles. There weren't *any* caskets. Just a big pool of blood in the center of the dirt."

"Didn't they question the boys since they had asked you to go there?"

"How could they? Their parents reported them missing. They've never been seen or heard from again."

Mitch silently thought through the information. "What about the bloody shirt?"

"DNA matched Tom's. Other than that, nothing else was found. Not any evidence that his three friends were ever there, either."

"But the murders last week. Both people were killed rather strangely."

Sheba's dark eyes narrowed. Her jaw tightened. "Yes."

"Their gutted bodies were displayed in ritual-like arrangements."

"That's how the news reported it."

"Do you think these murders are somehow connected to Gloria's and Tom's?"

"That's a far stretch since their bodies were never found."

Mitch glanced at his watch, and then he looked around nervously. "Could you point me in the direction of that cemetery? I'd like to scout around and see if there's anything unusual going on."

"You'll miss your bus."

"I can take the next one."

She stood and adjusted her skirt. When her eyes met his, she smiled. "I can walk you to the gate, but I won't go any farther than that."

"Do you think you can handle going there again?"

She pursed her lips. "Eventually, we have to face our fears, don't we? I will go to the gate. No farther."

"That's kind of you, but what about your friends?"

She shrugged. "Looks like they're not going to show up."

Mitch took his cellphone and nodded. "Thanks. I need to touch base with my boss and inform her that I will take a later bus. Hell, if any new evidence is found, I may be staying another day."

Sheba turned and stood at the edge of the sidewalk while he placed his call. The area was void of life except for them. No headlights appeared from either direction on the street. No vagrants. No animal sounds.

Mitch kept his message brief and faint.

When he stepped beside her, she said, "Did you reach her?"

He shook his head. "Damn voice mail."

"At least you got a signal. Usually you can't get one after the fog rolls in."

"Are you ready?" he asked.

She gave a quick nod, motioning to her right, and then turned and pulled her hoodie over her head. "Follow me."

Chapter 2

New Jersey

KAT'S CELLPHONE vibrated on the nightstand. Rubbing sleep from her eyes with one hand, she patted for the cellular with the other. Mitch's message had recorded to voice mail before she intercepted. She sat up and turned on the bedside lamp.

Lucian stood at the window in his jogging clothes, staring into the night. He seldom slept anymore. Without glancing her direction, he asked, "Who'd be calling at this hour?"

"Mitch," she replied. "Give me a second. I'm listening to his message."

"Maybe he found something that will help solve those murders."

Kat straightened a five-by-eight picture frame on the nightstand. The photo was of her and Lucian with the twins, Paul and Paula, they had rescued from Typhis' hidden laboratory. They got visitation with them one weekend per month as they fought with social services to adopt them.

She clicked off her cell. "Mitch is staying another night in Salem."

"He discovered something?"

"I think so. A girl he met gave him detailed information that the police kept out of the press and to themselves. He's going to check it out."

"Perhaps I had underestimated him during his interview," Lucian said.

"You doubted him?"

"He wasn't quite convincing enough."

"About his psychic power?"

"Yeah."

Kat shrugged. "Kyle vouched for him, and Kyle has abilities that haven't failed us in the past. He can do things most scientists would dismiss as impossible."

"I know. That's why I sent Mitch to investigate this case first. Mainly I want to see what he can uncover without being near Kyle. If he functions well with his psychic hunches, Mitch might prove to be a nice addition to the agency after all."

"It never hurts to work with people that are . . . a bit different," she said with a teasing smile.

Lucian left the window, sat on the edge of the bed, and put on his running shoes. "The information Mitch gathers might be what we need to find the killers."

Kat placed her hand on his shoulder. "What bothers you about these murders? They occurred so far away."

"I'm not exactly certain what troubles me the most, but the brutality the victims suffered was extreme. They were eviscerated and their bodies were left on display in a sadistic manner. Maybe it's to throw people off their trail, but it takes a calloused individual to do something like that. One report indicated animal bites, but I fear it might be something far worse."

"Like what?"

"For one thing, their vital organs were removed. Something bigger is at stake here."

"Nothing like GenTech or TransGenCorp, I hope?"

Lucian offered a slight shrug. "Science never sleeps. Conspiracies never fade."

"I hoped we could stop the majority of these laboratory experimentations."

"Shut down one, but there's still a dozen others. Perhaps more."

"You think so?"

Lucian nodded. "You remember Typhis' sons?"

"Yes."

"They were different than the previous clones I've seen. Much stronger. Had they been seasoned with real life experience and better trained, I couldn't have stopped them. Luckily, they had no idea how powerful they really were."

"You think the murders in Salem are connected?"

"Yes. Because someone's harvesting organs."

"Why do you think that?"

"They're building something or perhaps they're trying to keep someone or something alive."

Kat's eyes widened. "Seriously?"

Lucian shrugged. "Won't know until we see firsthand. But my gut tells me we're dealing with something that isn't exactly human. Typhis' sons looked almost human and with their ears hidden, they passed easily among others without notice."

He leaned over and kissed her. She placed her hands on his cheeks.

"You're burning up, Lucian," Kat said. "You have a fever."

"No, I'm fine."

Kat slipped out of bed and put her hand on his forehead. "No, you're sick. You're covered with sweat."

"Everything's fine."

"Did you take your enhancers?"

Lucian nodded and tapped his watch. "Right on schedule."

Kat hugged him. "Maybe you should take a cold shower to drop your core temperature."

"I'm going for a jog. Be back in a bit."

"A jog? At this hour?"

He smiled. "The cool night air will do me good. You go back to sleep. I won't be long."

"I don't think it's a good idea to run with a fever."

"Kat, you know my metabolism is high. My normal temperature isn't what the medical profession considers *normal*."

"Yes, but you've never flushed with sweats, either."

"I'm okay. You worry over me like a mother does a child."

Kat smiled. "I suppose you're right. It's hard for me to be dependent on someone else. After I allowed myself to open up to you, I fear what we have will sift through my fingers like sand."

"Think of me like the grit that gets caught beneath your fingernails. I'm much harder to get rid of than sand."

"You know what I mean."

Lucian placed his hand to her cheek and smiled. "I understand, but I'm not Tyler. Losses come in life. We can't allow bereavement to keep us from moving forward and loving again."

He kissed her.

"I don't want to lose you, too."

Lucian smiled. "Get some sleep. If Mitch has found helpful information, we'll be flying to Salem."

Kat lay back on the bed. He pulled the blankets up to her chin and turned off the lamp. Quietly, he left her to dream while he dealt with a growing nightmare of his own.

Chapter 3

Salem

SHEBA REMAINED silent for the three blocks they walked to the cemetery. An old, rusted spear-tipped fence enclosed the aged tombstones.
Dead brittle briars roped through the needlepoint holly hedges along the
fence, which added even more deterrents to discourage vandalism.

Mitch followed her in silence.

With her hands in her jacket pockets and her chin pressed against her
chest as she walked, she held the posture of a devout monk. He worried
how she'd fare after returning to the cemetery where her friends had died
and disappeared. Should her boldness succumb to her buried inner fears,
she might never recover from the shock. He'd have a hard time getting her
home.

About a half block later, Sheba stopped and turned. The front gate
was partway open. Her face showed no emotion as she pushed the gate
inward. The hinges wailed mournfully.

Mitch trailed behind her on the gravel path. A sharp wind swirled
around them. Large cedar trees swayed back and forth like giant entities
protecting the dead. Another gust of wind thinned the curtain of fog. The
overhead clouds parted, allowing the full moon to illuminate the old

manor. The windows reflected black and empty. Worn shutters rapped with hollow thuds against the aged boards.

She whispered, "Everything's just like the night Gloria died. Nothing's different."

Mitch stepped beside her. "You don't need to go any further. I can investigate the manor without you."

Her eyes widened as she studied the dark overgrown fence near the gate. She grabbed his arm. "I should go with you."

"But I thought you didn't want to go."

"I don't, but I like the idea of being left alone even less."

Mitch looped his arm around hers. "I wish we had a flashlight."

Sheba dug in her jacket pocket and pulled out a small penlight. "This is all I have," she said, handing it to him.

He shrugged and took it. "Beats nothing at all. If the clouds stay parted, the moon would give us enough light to see our way."

Chapter 4

Lucian jogged about a block and stopped. His head throbbed and everything spun, forcing him to close his eyes. He bent over to catch his breath. The dizzying sensation overwhelmed him and he vomited on the curb. He leaned against a parked car and looked to the sky. The full moon glowed strangely yellow.

After he recovered enough stability to run farther, he took a side street and ran another block. He walked to the steps of an apartment building and scanned the column of occupants until he found Dr. Brockton's name. He pushed a button to page the scientist.

Several minutes passed before Brockton answered. "Who is it?"

"Lucian."

"One second."

A buzzer sounded and the apartment complex door unlocked. Lucian pulled open the door and walked to the elevator. On the third floor, he propped against the wall to keep from falling. The hall spun and grew dark.

Brockton tied his bathrobe, hurried down the hall, and grabbed Lucian's arm. He glanced around. "Where's Kat?"

"She doesn't know I'm here. She thinks I'm jogging."

"What's wrong, Lucian?"

"Get me inside, quick."

Brockton seated Lucian on the couch. Sweat beaded Lucian's brow. His face was pale.

"You look horrible," Brockton said.

"I feel worse than that."

"What's wrong?"

"Not sure. I have a fever. The enhancers aren't working. I think I've lived as long as the drugs will let me."

Brockton put his hand against Lucian's brow. He couldn't hide the worry on his face. "You're burning up. Let me fill the bathtub with cold water."

Lucian's head dropped against the back of the sofa. His heartbeat rang in his ears. Brockton returned a few minutes later and helped Lucian to his feet. In the bathroom Lucian undressed down to his boxers. Brockton coaxed him to slide into the tub.

"Give me a minute," Brockton said. "I have a few bags of ice in the deep freezer. That should slow down your metabolism until we can try something I've been working on."

Lucian gave a weak nod. The chilly water made his jaw quiver.

Brockton brought two twelve-pound bags of ice to the bathroom and ripped them open. He emptied the ice into the cold water at Lucian's feet. Lucian shivered and hugged himself.

"Have you told Kat about this?"

Lucian shook his head. His teeth chattered. "No. Don't say anything to her, either."

"Lucian, she's the closest friend you have. She loves you. You need to tell her."

Lucian shook his head. "She's already lost too much without having to deal with this, too."

"You cannot hide it. You die and she has to deal with the loss anyway."

Lucian nodded. "Yes, but at least she won't have to spend my last days worrying about *when* I'm going to die."

Brockton shook his head. "You're as stubborn as any man."

"What do you expect? Do you think Dr. Helmsby might know why the enhancers are no longer working?"

Brockton shrugged. "Maybe, but I have no idea how to contact him. No one has seen him since he left Grayson Enterprises."

"He went into hiding?"

"I don't know. I have the impression that Grayson's not a man you work for and simply walk away with your life."

"Did Helmsby indicate that Grayson was vengeful?"

"Helmsby and I have seldom talked, although our conversations would be scientifically stimulating. But Grayson is like Idris. He'd kill to keep his secrets secret. He certainly wanted to kill Matthews for betraying him."

"I remember. Grayson didn't hide his hatred for Matthews. You might contact Daniel and see if he's heard anything from Helmsby."

Brockton nodded. "I'll see if I can find him, but until I do, I have a new injection I want to try. I've put it off for a month because I thought the enhancers might still work."

"At this point, I'm willing to try anything."

"You don't have many choices."

Lucian sank into the tub. The icy water washed over his face. He held his breath as the water numbed him. For a few moments, he thought how easy it would be to slip away, to allow death to claim him, but Kat's smiling face entered his mind. He jolted up and took in a deep breath.

"Are you okay?" Brockton asked.

Lucian nodded and wiped water from his eyes.

Brockton took the syringe and pushed out the final air bubbles. He plunged the needle into the thickness of Lucian's left arm.

"Stay in the water another ten minutes. Then I'll help you to the living room."

"Where's Kyle?"

"Asleep. I'll get some blankets and be back in a few minutes."

Lucian closed his eyes. As a genetically enhanced human, he loved the unique abilities Idris had incorporated into his genome, but he hated that the side effect was an approximate three-year lifespan. The enhancer drugs had given him an additional four years beyond his expiration date, but the drugs were no longer capable of extending his life. Worse than the thought of dying was the thought of losing Kat, the only true love he had known during his short life. Love was something he had never expected to experience. Something Idris had never programmed him to seek out.

Tears etched down his cheeks.

Lucian realized there wasn't anything left in the world he wanted to live for if Kat wasn't in it.

Brockton stood at the side of the tub with a towel. "Can you stand without my assistance?"

"I'll try." Lucian grasped the sides of the tub and pushed himself to his feet. He lifted one leg over the side. Brockton wrapped a warm towel around him. Lucian held Brockton's shoulder for added support.

"Sit on the edge of the tub. Don't move around too much yet. The medicine should take effect in about an hour, provided your body chemistry reacts to it, and if it does, it could take several more hours for you to overcome your fatigue."

"And if it doesn't work?"

"We'll figure out something. There has to be a solution. But if this doesn't work, you really need to have a heart-to-heart talk with Kat."

Lucian sighed. "I know I should, but if I do she'll be devastated."

"I understand. I've lost people I love, too."

"She'll grieve over me, but not just that. She really wants to adopt the twins."

"Paul and Paula?"

Lucian nodded.

"I thought the state was denying that."

"Carpenter said that he'd bend a few rules if they continue to block the adoption."

Brockton shook his head. "Why are they preventing you from adopting them?"

"It's not just us, but anyone interested in them are being denied."

"Because of their abilities?"

"I think so. It's horrendous to imagine that the government might be conducting similar tests on these children like Typhis was doing."

"Because of their genetic engineering enhancements?"

Lucian nodded. "They fear they'll be treated like freaks in society."

"Nonsense."

"I know."

"The next time you talk to Carpenter, tell him I'm willing to stand in as a research scientist overseeing their progress. That way, you and Kat can give them the parental attention they need. You know me well enough that I won't harm them in any way."

"I know. I'll tell Kat."

"Yes, and tell her about your condition before it's too late."

"I will."

———————

LUCIAN FELL ASLEEP a few minutes after Brockton helped him to the couch. Lucian had never been in such poor health before. Of course, when Idris had blackmailed Lucian by withholding the enhancers, Lucian plummeted near death. Had Brockton not intervened, Lucian would have died. As a future precaution, Brockton stole enough enhancers to last well over a year, and Lucian never skipped a dose.

Brockton found it extremely hard to understand how Lucian healed from injuries so easily, only to be a victim to his own genetic flaws. He might heal from bodily injury, but his unstable genetics could never repair his DNA blemishes.

As soon as morning came, Brockton would attempt to locate Dr. Helmsby to see if he had any ideas on how to correct the flaws in Lucian's genome. As a scientist, he never opposed cloning because so many benefits came with the knowledge, but now, with Lucian's condition deteriorating, he couldn't ethically support cloning techniques after witnessing the painful side effects firsthand. Science imprisoned clones to short-termed lives. The anguish they suffered was never taken into account. But Idris only wanted short-lived clones to use for assassins, nothing more. No amount of programming brainwashed them into not wanting more out of life, which wasn't even a factor Idris considered. Certainly, it wasn't something he favored.

Brockton feared what would happen once mind control devices were created and scientists worse than Idris obtained them. What would future clones be commanded to carry out?

Chapter 5

Mitch held Sheba's hand as they walked between the two towering cedars. He kept a tight hold on the penlight, but he didn't turn it on. The full moon shone brightly through the briefly parted clouds.

The darkness of the cemetery didn't bother him, but entering the manor without a flashlight frightened him. He wanted to conserve the batteries until they reached the rundown building and only use the light as a last resort. He'd hate to be inside the dark manor and lose light due to weak, dying batteries.

"We should probably wait until morning," she told him.

"We've come this far. We've no reason to turn back."

Sheba stopped walking. "Yeah, but the clouds are getting thicker. The moon will disappear again. It'll become much darker."

"You told me the darkness doesn't bother you."

"Normally, it doesn't."

"But here it does?"

Her wide eyes searched his. "You have to understand what I lost here."

Mitch nodded. She had lost more than just a friend. Part of her courage and her innocence had died as well.

The manor was less than twenty yards away. "I understand, but look at how close we are." He pointed. "Stand here and I'll go check it out. Shouldn't take me more than ten minutes."

"Shit, no! I'm not standing out here by myself."

"Then come with me."

"When it's daylight, I'll go," she said firmly.

The dark makeup and clothing she wore to act tough was a thin shroud over the timid girl hiding beneath them. Her soft eyes revealed the scared child she fought so hard to shelter. The cemetery stripped it all away and he pitied her. He regretted taking her so far into the cemetery.

"I'm sorry," Mitch said. "I've lost family and friends before. Never as brutally as you have, so I can't say I fully understand your loss. But, if we're going to get to the bottom of what really happened here and what happened this past week, we need to go to the source."

Sheba swallowed hard. "You think it's there?"

"Don't you?"

She shrugged her narrow shoulders.

"Had other murders like that occurred before your friends disappeared?"

"Not that I know of."

He pulled her close and hugged her. In spite of not being a close friend and still very much a stranger to her, she melted against him with the tenderness of surrender.

"I promise I'll keep you safe," Mitch said, pulling back and gently lifting her chin. "Let's go as far as the outside of the building. If there's no reason to go inside, we'll leave and come back in the morning."

"How do I know you can protect me?"

"I've been inside worse places. Trust me." He pulled back his jacket and revealed his gun. "Nothing will harm you."

Sheba nodded.

Mitch took her hand and walked to the front of the manor. Water dripped from the metal roof. Fog billowed in wisps that floated like restless ghosts. He clicked on the penlight.

"Where's the cellar door?" he asked.

"On the other side of the building."

Mitch studied the old building as they made their way to the other side. The penlight revealed sagging boards, rusted nails, and the fact that no one had ever worked to restore the manor. The rotten doors to the cellar were collapsed like she said. He could still read faint red letters that once painted a warning for people to stay out. Everything Sheba described was eerily close to detail. He had no reason to doubt her depiction of the events that had occurred. He just feared what they might awaken should the caskets still be in the cellar.

Near the cellar door, large paw prints were pressed in the mud. Some appeared fresh and trailed out the cellar into the cemetery.

"Will you be okay if I leave you here for just a minute?" he asked. "I want to see what's down there."

Her fingers tightened around his. "I'll go, too."

"You don't have to."

"I need to."

Cobwebs hung from the overhead floorboards. The light made a small arc as he peered around the cellar. The floor was loose soil. Dog tracks and smaller rodent tracks littered the dirt. Rusting garden tools were propped along the wall near the cellar door.

"Where are the coffins?" he asked.

She pointed to the left. "That way. Back in the far corner."

Mitch brushed spider webs out of his way as they cautiously stepped farther into the cellar.

"The police told you there weren't any coffins?"

"Yes," she nodded.

He stopped where some of the overhead flooring had collapsed, which blocked the path to the corner. He handed the light to Sheba and pushed several boards aside. Once the boards were cleared, the penlight revealed what she had said existed.

A circle of coffins.

"They didn't see these?"

"That's what they told us."

Mitch took the light. The center coffin was crafted from dark wood, perhaps mahogany. As he came closer, the wood looked freshly polished. Smooth. The outer twelve coffins were covered with thick dust and cobwebs. He slid his hand across the top of the center coffin.

"Should I open it?" he asked.

"No," she replied, shaking her head. "That's what killed Gloria."

Mitch thought about the police denying the existence of any coffins in the cellar. It made sense. The police must somehow be involved in the murders and the cover-up. No wonder they never offered to reveal any information about the two people killed the week before. They wished to conceal the recent murders as well as the past ones.

Opening the caskets might give a clue as to what happened to Gloria and the boys as well as shed light on the two mauled, mutilated victims. The evidence could give Sheba the chance to no longer be a social outcast in Salem. She might have a new life and the city would be safer.

Mitch's curiosity forced his hand to unlatch the lid. As he lifted, he shone the light to where the head should be if someone was inside the casket. The hinge creaked. Raging growls rose behind him. Before he turned, something slammed against him and dragged him to the ground and across the earthen floor.

He turned the light. Claws slashed his chest. He fought to get the creature off, but it was too strong and quickly overpowered him.

"Run, Sheba!" he yelled. "Get out of here. Get help!"

He struggled as he pushed his attacker. Sharp teeth gnashed at his face. The dog tracks, he remembered, outside the cellar entrance. Apparently the cellar housed stray dogs or a den of wolves.

Mitch swung his fist into its gut. It yelped in pain and then angrily growled. With his other hand Mitch flashed the light into the creature's face. He wanted to know how big the dog or wolf was. He gasped in horror when the light revealed his aggressor. The light was knocked from his hand. Sheba tore at him with long claws. She wasn't human. She was part wolf, part human.

The gun.

"I told you not to open it!" she growled.

Mitch yanked the gun from his belt. Fumbling to get his finger on the trigger and releasing the safety, he fired. The bullet missed her and struck the floorboard above. Sheba gnashed her teeth and bit his wrist hard. Blood seeped from the bite marks. He cried in anguish and dropped the gun on the dusty floor. Her strong claws were fierce and lengthened. They shred through his clothes and sliced into his flesh. The fiery wounds bled.

He screamed for help. His panicked voice echoed through the dark cellar. Sheba raised her fist and hammered downward with a solid punch. She struck him harder than any fighter could have hit. Everything turned black.

Chapter 6

Northeast Neighbors
Salem, Oregon: 4 a.m.

CASSANDRA MEEKS ROSE SUDDENLY in her bed. Dogs barked angrily along 18th street. She hurried to the rear window, pulled back the heavy curtains, and peered anxiously into the darkness. Even though she didn't see anything, she sensed their presence.

For the past several weeks she had seen their yellow eyes glaring through the privet row that fenced her small backyard. They monitored her house. She didn't know what they were, but they watched her, keeping tabs on her whereabouts at all times during the night. When they appeared, the neighborhood dogs grew hostile and barked fiercely—just like tonight.

Cassandra considered calling the police but knew they'd be no help. Who'd believe her? She hardly believed it herself.

Tremors shook through her body. She released the curtain and ran across the hall to her daughter's bedroom. She flung open the door. Her heart hammered in her chest.

The window was open and wind ruffled the curtains.

Cassandra always kept the window closed and locked. She flipped on Alicia's bedroom light.

Her ten-year-old daughter was gone.

Cassandra leaned out the open window, hoping to capture sight of her child's abductors, but they weren't anywhere to be seen. They had probably taken Alicia and fled earlier in the night.

She didn't know why, but she looked under the bed and then checked the closet, clinging to the hope that Alicia might have hidden when they forced the window up and crept into her bedroom.

In panic, Cassandra yanked the blankets off the bed. Tears heated her eyes. "Alicia! Where are you?"

She ran downstairs, room-to-room, turning on lights as she went. In the kitchen, she unlocked and flung open the back door. She pushed the screen door open and searched the hedgerow for glowing eyes. They weren't there. She knew without question they'd never return. They had what they wanted. Her daughter.

Cassandra walked into the kitchen, grabbed her cellphone off the countertop, and frantically punched in 9-1-1.

"I need the police." She sobbed and stuttered as she spoke. "Someone's taken my daughter."

When she disconnected the call, she sat at the kitchen table and shook her head. Tears flowed. Her heart ached. Seizing fear consumed her.

Alicia. Her *only* child. Taken in the night by monsters. Creatures she couldn't explain even if she tried. She worried about the outcome. Two people had been brutally murdered a week earlier, and the police still had no leads. She didn't want her daughter to suffer and die like they had. Alicia didn't deserve to die like that. No one did.

As Cassandra waited for the police, she thought about her miracle child.

Several years earlier, her family doctor had told her she was infertile and having a baby was impossible. While married, she and her husband had tried everything other doctors recommended to increase their chances to have a baby.

Nothing had worked.

Fertility drugs hadn't work. Diets never work. They invested nearly thirty thousand dollars for *in vitro* fertilization and that failed as well.

After ten frustrating years, her husband, Douglas, gave up, divorced her, and started a family with another *younger* woman. Cassandra's broken heart drove her to extreme workouts and excessively long runs. Her drive to fitness waned her loss, but doctors insisted her overly lean body prevented her from having a baby due to a drastic decrease in her estrogen levels.

At the age of twenty-nine, Cassandra had finally decided she'd never have a baby, never be a mother. She had lost all hope. That was, until New Horizons Fertility Clinic opened in Salem.

She received a personalized letter with an invitation to talk to their doctors about her condition. Angered, she called her medical doctor demanding to know who had violated her doctor/patient confidentiality, only to discover her records had been kept completely confidential and no one had ever requested any of her medical information. They assured her none of her personal files had been released to anyone. Mystified, she drove to New Horizons to find out more.

Because of all the time and money Cassandra had expended trying to get pregnant, she explained that she didn't have funds to meet their costs. Dr. Randal Shelby told her he'd waive the costs as long as she endorsed them and allowed them to use her image and testimony to promote their industry. She happily agreed.

As she drove home, she felt more blessed than if she'd won a major lottery fortune because for her to have a baby was worth more than all the money in the world.

After six weeks of genetic selection trials, her first pregnancy test came back positive. She was ecstatic.

Cassandra shopped for baby clothes and decorated Alicia's room. New Horizons offered scientific procedures that had allowed her to choose her baby's sex, and the eye and hair color. Gene selection also provided added benefits—cancer and disease resistance. Unknown modifications later revealed themselves and at first, these anomalies didn't concern her.

Alicia appeared in every fashion a normal child, and Alicia's teachers considered her a gifted phenomenon. She read college level texts by age of three. At four years of age, she solved calculus theorems with ease. Her advanced understanding shunned her from ordinary students and alienated her from her peers. In so many aspects she outranked their abilities. The other children noticed Alicia was different and kept their distance.

New Horizons donated funds for personal home tutors. Cassandra protested, saying that she had no way to ever repay them for their contributions. Dr. Shelby explained that the more they invested in Alicia, the further they promoted their science and reputation. The benefits outweighed their costs and at no time would she ever be required to repay the facility.

At age nine, Alicia had completed two years of college in genetics and microbiology. When Alicia turned ten, Cassandra noticed new abilities her daughter possessed and some of these frightened her.

They could never own any pets. Cats hissed and hid from Alicia whenever she came near them. Dogs growled and snarled at her. When Cassandra brought home a puppy, the little thing whimpered and peed on the floor whenever Alicia reached to pet it. Although Alicia loved animals, she was cursed to admire them from afar.

Alicia's hearing was uncanny. Her sense of smell was acute. She perceived her surroundings in ways that defied all logic. On several occasions, she told her mother which routes to avoid during trips. Whenever she took her young daughter's advice, they avoided major accidents. On the one time Cassandra ignored Alicia's warning during a violent thunderstorm, they were almost swept off the highway by floodwaters crossing the road. From that day forward she never took Alicia's premonitions for granted.

The first night Cassandra had seen the glowing-eyed creatures peering through the darkness, terror seized her. She had been washing dishes when she saw movement outside the window in her backyard. Fear prevented her from moving. In stunned silence her curiosity forced her to study them.

The lack of light prevented her from seeing their bodies. Estimating by their glowing, catlike eyes, they were about the size of large dogs. She counted three sets of yellow eyes staring through the hedges. Their silhouettes moved along in a pack. In unison, they slinked closer to the house. Finally able to move, Cassandra stepped away from the sink, locked the back door, and checked on Alicia.

Alicia sat in the living room doing homework. She set down her pencil and sniffed the air. Cocking her head to the side, she listened. Her blue eyes stared straight ahead. Alicia was attuned to their presence, but Cassandra never understood why.

Cassandra sat on the couch beside her daughter and draped an arm across Alicia's shoulder.

"You hear them?" Alicia asked, pulling her long blonde hair back and uncovering her ears.

"Who?"

Alicia frowned. "I don't know. The new people in our neighborhood?"

Cassandra took a deep breath. Her daughter hadn't seen them, but she knew they were outside. She wondered how long Alicia had known about them and *why* she considered them *people*.

Dogs howled all along the street.

"The dogs don't like them," Alicia said. "The dogs hate them."

"Why?"

Alicia thought for a minute. "They don't smell right."

"What do you mean?"

Alicia shrugged. "Their smell is hard to explain. It's unlike anything *I've* smelled before. But, I don't think they mean us any harm."

The azalea bushes rustled outside the front windows.

"They are a curious bunch," Alicia said.

"What do they want?"

"Nothing. Just curious."

Claws scratched the screen. Cassandra feared they'd come through the window. A dog charged from across the street and chased them away. A few minutes later, far in the distance, the dog yelped and squalled in pain.

Alicia winced and shook her head. "It should have known better."

"They killed the dog?"

Alicia pondered for a moment. "No. He'll live, but he'll be more respectful in the future."

Cassandra marveled at how her daughter perceived the injured dog's thoughts. She also wondered if Alicia understood their new neighbors weren't humans but strange, unidentifiable creatures. Could they somehow communicate with her?

Even when the creatures were at the living room window Alicia hadn't shown any fear, which made Cassandra question if they had taken Alicia, or if Alicia had chosen to leave with them willingly and without struggle.

Cassandra stood and walked to the refrigerator. She removed the magnetized frame that enclosed a photo of her daughter. Alicia's wide smile brought fresh, helpless tears to Cassandra's eyes.

"They took you," she whispered. "*What* do they want with you?"

Heavy knocks thudded on the front door. Cassandra hurried and opened it. Blue lights flashed in her driveway, painting the neighboring houses with an eerie shade of flickering blue. A stocky officer stood on her porch.

"I'm Officer Parker. You reported that your daughter is missing?"

Cassandra hesitantly opened the door a bit wider.

"Yes," She nodded, holding out the photo. "This is a picture of her. It was taken about two weeks ago."

Parker took the photo and shook his head. "This is the second child to disappear tonight."

Cassandra's eyes widened. "Another child is missing?"

"Yes, ma'am." He stepped past her and through the door. "I'm afraid so. Do you mind showing me your daughter's room?"

"Of course. This way."

Parker followed her to the stairs. Parker was a muscular man, about six feet tall with brown hair and hazel eyes. His uniform was tight and form-fitted.

When Cassandra looked into his eyes she felt uncomfortable. His hardened facial expression was like a chiseled granite statue. The lines on his face indicated that he seldom smiled. His gruff, callous voice defined an uncaring nature, void of love or compassion.

"Who's the other missing child?" she asked.

"Seth Greaves."

A lump tightened in Cassandra's throat. "Little Seth?"

Parker stopped at the top of the stairs. "Do you know him?"

"Alicia and Seth are close friends. They have the same tutors."

"Interesting," he replied in an even tone.

"Is Deidre okay?" Cassandra asked.

"Deidre?"

"Seth's mother."

"I don't know, ma'am. Officer Reece is at the scene. Your call came in while I was in transit to the Greaves' home."

Parker opened Alicia's door before she told him which bedroom belonged to her daughter. He stepped across the threshold. When she followed, he turned. His brown eyes narrowed with a violent stare that chilled her.

"They came through the window," she said, pointing.

"They?" His cold eyes asserted dominance as he stared into hers. She didn't have enough courage to hold his gaze and quickly looked at the floor.

Cassandra shrugged and nervously finger-combed her hair. "Whoever took her did."

"When did you discover your daughter was missing?"

"About a half hour ago."

"You didn't hear any noises?"

"Just dogs barking in the neighborhood."

Parker wrote the information into his report book. He peered out the window then he closed it. "You really should keep your windows closed."

"I do. It was locked."

He cocked a brow as he looked into her frightened eyes. She looked away.

"Are you certain it was locked?"

Cassandra nodded. "Yes. I check it every night."

"Any suspicious activities happened lately?"

"Like what?"

"Like people calling and hanging up. Strangers standing around outside. Cars parked along the street that you don't recognize?"

She shook her head. "No, nothing like that."

Parker stared at her for a few more seconds before he left the room and walked downstairs. As he headed to the door, he pulled a card from his jacket. "My number is on here. Call me should she get in touch with you by phone or if anyone calls demanding ransom."

"Look around, sir. You can see I don't have much money. Nothing I have would be worth taking Alicia from me."

He shrugged. "Doesn't mean they won't try anyway. Drug addicts do desperate things to get money."

"I don't think addicts are responsible."

"Who do you suspect?"

Cassandra feared telling him about the creatures because he probably wouldn't believe her. But his attitude indicated that he had information he wasn't willing to share. And he also seemed to sense that she was with-holding information.

"I don't know anyone that would have taken her."

Parker nodded. "Then let us do our job. Workers from forensics will come soon. It's best you don't move items in her room until they dust for prints."

"I understand."

"Call us if anyone else contacts you about your daughter."

Cassandra held the doorknob tight as he stepped out onto the porch. She wanted to slam the door shut and lock it. She wanted him out of her house. She didn't understand exactly why he made her feel so uneasy, but he did, in spite of his police uniform and badge.

He held up the picture. "You mind if I keep this until I can get it copied?"

"Sure."

"I'll call once we turn up something."

She closed the door, leaned her back against it, and in a sense felt more at ease when the officer was gone. Breathing became easier. Her chest muscles relaxed after she released a long sigh.

A part of her was angered and insulted at how little he seemed to care. He displayed no sense of urgency and seemed to shrug off his duty. Where was his compassion? Did he not have any children of his own? What would become of Alicia if the police refused to aid her return?

OFFICER PARKER BACKED his patrol car from the driveway and drove down the street with the lights flashing. He grabbed his radio transmitter.

"Just left Cassandra Meeks' house. I suspect she knows too much."

"Don't worry. We'll take care of her."

Chapter 7

Numbness settled over Cassandra as she turned off the downstairs lights and walked slowly upstairs. So many emotions struggled to surface, and she was growing too weak to mentally dam them back.

For years she'd wanted a baby and a child to nurture. Once that wish was granted, fate turned around and ground her dreams into dust.

She stood outside Alicia's room and wept. She wanted to scream. Braving the steps forward she went to Alicia's bed and sat down. She grabbed a teddy bear and hugged it. Somehow she thought by touching the bear it brought her closer to Alicia. It was probably the last thing her daughter held before she was taken. She could smell her daughter's strawberry shampoo in the bear's fur. Her throat tightened. Hot tears burned her eyes.

"I'll find you somehow, Alicia," she whispered. The words hurt as she spoke them. She wanted to say more, but speaking was too difficult and painful.

A few minutes later, Cassandra forced herself to put down the teddy bear and walk to her bedroom closet, picked out a hoodie sweatshirt and sweatpants and quickly dressed. With as little concern as the officer had shown, she decided to search for Alicia herself. At least she knew about the creatures. If she found and followed their tracks, she might find her daughter. It was better than sitting at home worrying and waiting.

She put on running shoes and headed downstairs. Even though sunrise was less than an hour away, she stopped in the kitchen, took a flashlight from the cupboard, and headed out the back door.

The brisk night air formed little clouds each time Cassandra exhaled. When she reached the hedges, she flicked on the light and examined the dirt. As she expected large paw prints littered the soft earth. Unfortunately, so many overlapped that she couldn't find a clear path to follow. Franticly she got on her hands and knees and looked closer.

Her heart jumped when the light washed across Alicia's bare footprints. She rose to her feet and dusted dirt off her sweatpants. She knew which direction to go. Seconds later, tires screeched in front of her house.

Cassandra turned off the flashlight and pressed her back partway into the hedges to hide. The front door of her house crashed open. Lights moved from room to room and finally stopped inside Alicia's room.

The window rose and a man dressed in dark clothes leaned out. From the reflection of his flashlight she could see the gun in his right hand. Somehow, he saw her before he scanned the backyard with his flashlight. He knew exactly where she stood.

"She's in the backyard!" he said.

Cassandra ran.

A zipping whisper sliced the air near her head. The bullet struck the ground ahead of her. Dirt exploded.

She squealed, dropping the flashlight as she turned and tore through the hedges. The sharp branches grabbed and ripped at her clothes, her skin, but she kept moving.

The back door of her house opened. She crossed a neighbor's yard. Two chained dogs leapt and barked at her, but she didn't slow her pace.

Across the next street, she jumped a low chain-linked fence and ran through another yard. When she reached the sidewalk, she turned and sprinted as hard as she dared push. She knew to pace herself to prevent muscle fatigue. Her months of distance running had given her an edge that her pursuers didn't expect. But since she hadn't stretched and warmed up, she feared getting muscle cramps or worse—tearing a muscle, which would slow her progress and inevitably leave her at their mercy. She didn't believe these men were going to negotiate any terms. They had fired without question or hesitation. They wanted her *dead*.

Cassandra glanced over her shoulder. The full moon exposed the two men chasing her. Even though they looked like dark shadows, she could see the moon reflect off the guns in their hands. She passed between two parked cars, ran across the street, and followed the sidewalk. Sweat covered her but she wasn't out of breath. She was just getting warmed up when her adrenaline kicked in.

The back glass of a parked car exploded ahead of her. She cut through a yard, down a long driveway, and hit a dead end. The wooden slat fence towered eight feet tall.

"Dammit!" Cassandra said.

She sprinted back about ten yards, turned and ran as fast and hard as she could to the fence. She jumped and caught the top of the fence with her hands. Hanging for a moment, she pulled herself up.

Gunfire echoed.

She swung her left leg over the fence. Bullets chipped away parts of the board, missing her by inches. She flung herself over and dropped the ground on the other side. More bullets passed through the boards.

Cassandra moved quickly when the men hit the fence. On the next street she changed her direction, hoping to find a place to hide. She needed to stay alive for Alicia's sake. Alicia needed rescued and she was the only family her daughter had. No one else would search for her.

Pain bit her left arm. Her triceps ached. For a moment, she thought she had bruised herself while crossing the fence. But her sleeve dampened. Warm trickling blood leaked down her arm and dripped from her fingers.

She'd been shot.

Cassandra kept jogging and placed her hand over the triceps. Trying to jog with one arm across her chest slowed her momentum. The best she could tell, the bullet had merely grazed her, but she couldn't be certain until she could examine the wound. Although it didn't seem to be a life-threatening injury, she needed to find a way to lose them and hide before their shots became more successful.

She stumbled and tripped over junipers when she left the sidewalk. After rolling, she pushed herself to her feet and found herself outside a cemetery. Long shadows slanted from the gravestones in the moonlight. She jumped the short chain-linked fence and ran to a massive headstone.

When Cassandra reached it, she crept low and hid behind it. The cold granite was smooth like polished ice. She took deep breaths through her mouth as quietly as possible. Sweat dripped from her hair and trickled down her back. As her adrenaline waned, the pain in her triceps steadily increased.

She estimated the men were less than two minutes behind her. Perhaps more if they weren't in shape. While she waited for their approach, she rolled up her sleeve and inspected the gunshot wound. Under the moon's glow the injury was a dark line. The bleeding had stopped but the fiery pain stung when the cold breeze brushed across it.

Two large shadows moved over the chain-linked fence from the far side of the cemetery. The moonlight spotlighted the men well. At least she could see them. By hiding in the shadows she hoped she remained unseen.

Cassandra positioned herself into a sprinter stance as if awaiting the beginning pistol to fire at a track meet. Should the men come too close, she'd tear off as fast as possible, hoping the taller tombstones shielded her from their gunfire.

The men moved slowly, examining each row of tombstones as they went. Her eyes fastened to them, but from the corner of her eye she noticed they weren't the only ones in the cemetery. Smaller shadows edged along the fence line.

Cassandra nearly gasped aloud when the yellow-eyed creatures crept with the growing fog toward the shadows of gravestones.

The men approached from the east about twenty yards from her position and were getting closer. The creatures moved swiftly in her direction from the north. She closed her eyes and shook her head pondering which death would be worse—being shot to death or ripped to shreds by the night creatures?

The two men took quick steps, looking left to right while they walked, hoping to flush her from her hiding place and get her out into the open. Their determined search led her to believe they had discovered her whereabouts. She rose slightly, preparing to dart away, but the creatures had circled around behind her. She was wedged between both groups.

Whispering a quick count of three, Cassandra kicked up sod and sprinted. From her side-glance she watched the men raise their weapons. She ducked and rolled behind a large tombstone.

No bullets fired.

Instead, the men screamed.

She peered over the tombstone. The creatures were atop the men, biting and clawing. The high-pitched screams silenced quickly after the creatures tore into their throats.

Cassandra ran and didn't dare glance back.

Chapter 8

Several blocks away, Cassandra stopped running and leaned against a massive oak tree to catch her breath. She wanted to know who the armed men were and why they were trying to kill her. It didn't take a lot of imagination to conclude that the men were somehow associated with the calloused police officer at her house earlier. Barely ten minutes had passed after Officer Parker left and those men showed up.

But why did they want her dead?

Cassandra examined her arm. A moist scab was hardening. The fleece material seemed to have aided in stopping the bleeding, but the amount of blood on the sleeve would bring questions from anyone she ran into. No doubt the scent of blood would allow those catlike creatures to follow her easier, too.

The creatures she had feared for the past few weeks had rescued her by killing the mysterious men. At least she hoped her pursuers were dead. The men never fired one shot in self-defense after the creatures attacked. Their lives ended within seconds.

She worried that the creatures were stalking her. She wasn't certain that they had attacked simply to protect her. Perhaps they killed the men because they were armed and she wasn't. Either way, she wanted to put some distance between her and the strange beasts with glowing eyes.

With dawn fast approaching, she figured she had time to seek shelter.

She had never seen the beasts during the daylight hours and never before 9 p.m.

After Cassandra caught her breath, she walked briskly down a side street lined with tall hedges on one side and a solid fence wall on the other. She was less than a block from Seth Greaves' home. Perhaps Seth's mother had information that could help them both find their missing children.

The morning light grew brighter but the lingering mist granted a dim gray shroud along the alley. This soothed her, making her believe she was inconspicuous to waking neighbors.

Cassandra stopped at a row of garbage cans. Static bursts and voices echoed over radio transmitters. She peered over the fence.

An ambulance and two squad cars were parked in the Greaves' drive. Their lights flashed.

Chills shot through her. She gasped at what was happening outside the house.

Paramedics rolled a gurney down the driveway toward the ambulance. The sheet was pulled tight and wrapped over the person's head. Someone had died. She feared it was Seth's mother. There wasn't anyone else it could be.

Deidre was like her, a single mother who treasured nothing more in life than her only child. Seeing her lifeless form was a tragedy. Deidre was a wonderful person and a dear friend. With her and Alicia gone, Cassandra had never felt more isolated in the world than ever before.

Cassandra lowered herself and scrunched behind the garbage cans. At eye level she looked through a small gap in the fence where two slats were missing. Two officers stood on the paved drive. She recognized the one as Officer Parker.

Parker motioned the other officer away from the scene and into the section of the lawn closer to the fence.

"Where is Seth, Reece?" Parker asked.

Officer Reece shook his head. "We never found him."

"Did you check under his bed?"

Reece nodded. "Of course. That was the *first* place I looked."

"The closet?"

"We looked everywhere in the house. There's no trace of him."

Parker's face flushed red. "He escaped, too?"

Reece shrugged. "That'd be my guess."

"Dammit."

Reece frowned. "I thought that's what they wanted. We were paid to make certain their disappearances looked like child abductions."

"Yes, they were supposed to be abducted and taken to New Horizons, but that's *not* who has them."

"Are you certain?"

Parker nodded. "Yes. I called Dr. Shelby after Alicia disappeared. He has neither child at the center."

"Damn. Then who took them?"

Parker shrugged. "I have no idea. He doesn't know, either. Men were sent to take care of Alicia's mother. She acted like she knew something about her child's disappearance that she refused to disclose to me."

"You put a hit out for her, too?"

"Yes," Parker said. "I had no choice. Not if we want this to remain secret."

"So we'll have to send an ambulance to her estate as well," Reece said.

"As soon as they contact me, we will."

"I don't feel comfortable with how this is going."

Parker's cellphone rang. He looked at Reece. "Give me a minute."

Parker turned and answered the phone. He spoke quietly and then he disconnected the call.

"Was that them?" Reece asked.

"No," Parker said, shaking his head.

"Who then?"

"It's not important. Just a problem we ran into last night."

"What kind of problem?"

"A visitor that was snooping around."

Reece frowned. "Mitch Niles?"

"You met him?"

"He stopped by the police station asking questions about the murders, but I told him that I wasn't allowed to give out any information since it was an ongoing investigation."

Parker smiled evenly. "Good."

"You think he has anything to do with the children disappearing?"

"Unlikely, but we'll know soon enough."

"How?"

"Let's just say that he's being detained."

"Detained? In the jailhouse?"

"No. We have taken precautions so no one knows that he's still here."

"Why?"

"That's what I've been instructed for now."

"By whom?"

Parker's eyes narrowed. "It's best I don't say more."

"Fine, but where do you have him?"

"You know."

"The Crypt?"

"Where else?" Parker said, crossing his arms.

"Trying to scare the hell out of him?"

"Something like that."

Cassandra's legs burned from sitting back on them after all the running she'd done. The sensation was similar to hundreds of needle pricks stabbing the back of her knees and upper thighs. She wanted to slip away before they noticed her, but curiosity begged her to continue listening. Parker had sent the men to her house to kill her. The answers to Alicia and Seth's disappearances were linked to New Horizons, but not directly.

"Parker, how are we going to explain this to the Chief?" Reece asked, pointing at the gurney as the paramedics shoved it into the rear of the ambulance. "Two missing children and their mothers are dead? Add this to the two people murdered last week and we have to contend with the media to keep things quiet."

"I know. We'll make up something. Perhaps throw some suspicion toward New Horizons."

"No," Reece said nervously. "That's suicide."

"We have to do something to break our ties to them."

Reece frowned. "I'm not sure that you got the same impression from them that I did."

"What's that?"

"They kind of own us now."

"Bullshit."

"Look, Parker, this whole situation's getting out of hand. Maybe we should come clean and tell the Chief what's going on."

"That's the stupidest suggestion you've ever made."

Cassandra legs and feet numbed. She rose slightly to adjust her weight but leaned too far to the right and lost her balance. She crashed backwards and knocked over a trashcan. Several loose aluminum cans clanged and rolled across the pavement.

Parker turned her direction and pointed. His eyes narrowed. "What the hell? Damn, it's Ms. Meeks!"

"How'd she get here?"

"I don't know," Parker said. "Meeks! Stay where you are!"

Cassandra gasped, pushed herself to her feet, and staggered clumsy steps until the numbness in her legs subsided enough for her to run again.

"Reece, get your car and meet me on the side street. I'll try to catch her on foot."

Chapter 9

Cassandra hobbled. The feeling and circulation slowly returned to her legs. Her fatigued muscles were stiff and sore, but she forced herself to keep moving. Her feet stung, which made running even more difficult. Raw blisters were forming on the soles of her feet where her sweat-dampened socks rubbed against her skin.

Officer Parker ran much faster than the two men that had tried to kill her earlier in the morning. His footsteps approached loudly, swiftly.

She winced, forcing her legs to keep moving until the tightness diminished. Half a block later her stamina peaked. She pushed off her toes with each step, adding length to her strides while mentally fighting to ignore the intensifying pain in her legs and feet.

Neighbors leaving their houses looked alarmed to see her running from a police officer on foot while a squad car followed slowly with its lights flashing. She wanted to call for help, but no one would believe the police were the culprits.

Cassandra left the sidewalk and sprinted across a lawn. Parker closed in behind her, leapt forward, and caught her shoulder. She pivoted to the left, lost her footing on the dew-covered grass, and fell forward. She hit the grass face first. Before he could straddle her back to handcuff her, she rolled. His knee struck the ground. He growled from the pain. He reached for her, but she rolled again, but not quite fast enough.

Parker grabbed her wrists and jerked. She tugged and tried to use her feet against the ground for leverage to pull free, but his strength was more than she could fight. She was weak, tired, and almost ready to give up.

Officer Reece parked the squad car halfway on the sidewalk and halfway on the lawn. He flung open the door and rushed to aid Parker.

Parker clenched her wrists together with one hand and yanked Cassandra to her feet. He reached back to retrieve his cuffs. Before he grabbed them, she freed his handheld Taser from his belt, clicked the switch, and rammed it against his stomach. He quickly released her. He dropped to his knees and fell on his back, writhing.

Cassandra turned.

"Don't move!" Reece said. "I don't want to shoot you."

Tears burned her eyes. She faced him, pleading. "All I want to do is to find my daughter. Alicia. She's missing. I've not done anything wrong."

Reece's young face softened with pity and remorse. He wasn't anything like Parker.

"Keep your hands where I can see them." He steadied the gun. His nervous eyes glanced between her and his partner on the ground.

"Please, sir. Alicia is in trouble. She needs me. Some men tried to kill me. Please, let me find my daughter."

He lowered the gun.

"Don't you dare let her get away," Parker seethed through clenched teeth. His body was still incapacitated. His eyes were wide and his brow tightened as he shook all over, fighting to gain his composure, struggling to rise to his feet.

Reece looked at Parker and shook his head. "She's not done anything wrong."

"Reece!" Parker said. His voice was growing stronger, angrier. His eyes looked dark and cold like an animal. He pushed himself up into a sitting position on the wet grass, but he was still shaking. "You can't let her go."

"We can't kill everyone, either. It's time we told the Chief what's going on."

"Reece, I'm warning you." Spittle flew from Parker's lips.

Reece slid his gun into its holster. He gave a slight nod as he said, "Go."

Cassandra tossed the Taser to the grass. "Thank you."

She crossed the lawn and returned her pace to a slow trot. A few minutes later she was more than a couple of blocks away. She was scared but relieved that Reece had granted her freedom.

A gunshot broke the early morning silence. She glanced over her shoulder for a second before she hurried into a full sprint. She wasn't certain who had been shot, but she guessed Parker had probably killed his partner. If she didn't hurry and hide, she suspected she'd be dead, too.

Cassandra found a large evergreen tree with large branches that spiraled to the ground. The needles clutched together with enough thickness that she could squeeze between the limbs and not be seen from the street. She pried a branch from its stiff position and edged her way closer to the tree trunk. When she released the branch, it swiftly returned to its position. She felt safe, hidden like a baby chick huddled beneath its mother's fanned wings.

She sat on the dead needles, exhausted. Her feet throbbed and ached. She wanted to take off her shoes and examine her soles but feared if she took that chance Parker would find her and she'd have to try to get away on bare feet.

Sweat covered her and soaked through her jogging suit. Heat radiated off her body. Pressing her back against the tree trunk, she closed her eyes. She felt faint and shook uncontrollably. Nausea pressed the back of her throat. Expending all her energy on an empty stomach had finally caught up with her. She needed food and felt so tired. Should she sit much longer, she believed she'd fall asleep.

With her closed eyes, she pictured Alicia's face. She worried about what might have happened to her daughter. New Horizons wanted Alicia and Seth, but why? And if they weren't the ones behind their abductions, who took them? Were the children okay? She wanted to cry, but her maternal instincts prevented her from completely caving in. If she was to find her daughter alive, she needed to maintain full control of her emotions.

A car approached slowly on the street. It crept at a pace she could easily out walk. Blue lights flashed. The officer searched the side of the road as he drove. When she saw his face, fear assaulted her. His eyes were strange, shadowy. Shimmering silver flashed across his pupils. She held her breath, afraid that the slightest noise would give away her position.

Officer Parker.

The gunshot. Reece?

Reece was dead. He had to be. She wondered what control New Horizons held over Parker to possess him to turn on his own partner. And if she had heard Reece correctly, their Chief was not involved, but she doubted she could get to him without Parker finding her first.

Due to the thickness of the lower tree branches, Parker drove past without noticing her.

Cassandra closed her eyes and released a long sigh.

She waited several minutes before crawling to the edge of the branches to see if the road was clear. Not seeing the patrol car anywhere in sight, she eased out of the tree branches.

Running was out of the question. She was too tired. Her feet hurt. Even though she was only a couple blocks from her house, she understood the danger of returning there. Parker was certain to keep check on her house, and even more so once the men's bodies at the cemetery were discovered. She couldn't return home.

The safest place she could hide was at the Greaves' house. With Seth missing and Deidre dead, she could hide there until sunset if necessary.

Chapter 10

Cassandra sneaked through a thick line of pines behind Deidre's house. From the rear of the house, she wasn't able to see the driveway to know whether any official vehicles were still parked there or not. She pried open the basement window and slinked inside. The basement was dank, dark, and the air smelled of earth and mildew. Although she had visited Deidre many times, she had never been in her basement.

She placed her hands before her like a blind woman, reaching and patting for solid objects to guide her until she found a light switch. Several times she struck her shins against old furniture and discarded appliances. When she reached the bottom of the stairs, she placed her hand on the guardrail and headed up.

She opened the door slowly, listening for any movement or voices, just in case forensic scientists were still investigating the murder and Seth's abduction. Satisfied that she was alone in the house; she swung open the door and stepped into the kitchen.

Cassandra raided the refrigerator of its orange juice and two yogurts. After she finished the second cup of yogurt, she pressed her foot on the garbage can pedal. The lid popped up and two envelopes caught her attention immediately. The familiar New Horizons logo was on each envelope. She took them and tossed the empty yogurt containers into the garbage can. She opened the first one and pulled out the enclosed letter.

The message indicated that Seth needed to come to the clinic for more updated evaluations. Apparently Deidre had not followed through for any tests during the past three months as she had previously agreed to do. The second letter warned her *not* to move from the area because Seth's condition required their medical attention frequently. Moving him to another state placed his life in jeopardy and violated any funded monies New Horizons donated to Seth.

If Deidre had planned to move, she never indicated such to Cassandra. But the tone of the letter was more a threat than a request not to move.

Cassandra thought about what the two officers had discussed before she clumsily gave away her position. New Horizons had paid someone to abduct Seth and Alicia.

But why Alicia?

Cassandra never considered moving. She loved Salem. She had never received any letters vaguely resembling those Deidre had received.

Cassandra had always punctually taken Alicia for evaluations anytime New Horizons requested. She was so thankful to finally have a daughter that she didn't mind letting them keep track of Alicia's progress. In fact, she was proud of her daughter and all her testing accomplishments. For some reason, that wasn't enough. They wanted her daughter permanently, and they wanted Cassandra dead.

She tucked the letters under her arm and walked into the living room. Peering through the blinds, she was relieved that no vehicles were outside. She was alone . . . for the moment.

Cassandra returned to the kitchen and noticed the New Horizons' magnet on the refrigerator. It listed Dr. Randal Shelby's phone number and the clinic's address. For a moment she considered calling the doctor. She had never seen a violent or sinister side of this man. Contrary to what the police officers had said, Dr. Randal came across as one of the kindest-hearted people she had ever met.

Upon their first meeting, when he explained that her years of conception failure was an issue of the past, his demeanor was so caring, so passionate. With his gentle voice and bedside manner, she read his charisma as a genuine trait that few people ever possessed. He was a noble man with an agenda to help infertile women have children and become mothers. He was a miracle worker, at least in her mind.

The evaluations and tests Alicia underwent with Dr. Randal's guidance were pleasant. Never had she endured one unkind word or expression from the doctor, nor had she ever felt uncomfortable or that she couldn't discuss anything with him. *Until now.*

Cassandra wanted to call him and ask why her daughter was missing and why someone had tried to kill her, but with everything that had unfolded during that past few hours, calling the clinic would be a lethal mistake. She wanted answers, but for her safety and Alicia's welfare, Cassandra would have to wait or find someone that was capable of getting the information for her.

She walked back into the living room. The television remote was on the coffee table. She picked it up, clicked on the television, and turned down the volume. The local morning news had her picture posted under a *Wanted for Murder* caption.

Cassandra sat down on the edge of the couch, stunned.

"Cassandra Meeks is wanted for questioning in connection with the double homicide of Officer Reece Campbell and Deidre Greaves. She's believed to be armed and dangerous. Should you see her, call the number on your screen and notify the authorities immediately."

"Bullshit," Cassandra said.

The television anchor added, "Here's a live feed from the police station with Officer Parker, who witnessed Cassandra Meeks murder Officer Campbell."

"It all happened so quickly," Parker said to the camera. "I was attempting to handcuff her when she used my hand Taser against me, took my gun and shot Reece. He died before I was able to call for help."

Disgusted, Cassandra turned the television off. Parker had killed his partner because Reece was compassionate enough to allow her to run. Regardless of where she attempted to go, she was wanted for murder. There were few people she could confide in before these events had taken place, but now she had nowhere to turn. New Horizons held no refuge for her. If she were to believe what Parker had told Reece, New Horizons was seeking to abduct the two children they had genetically helped create.

She went to Seth's room. Nothing looked out of the ordinary. His bed was made. The window was shut. His little toy soldiers were set for battle on a small table. A chess set was in progression on his desk where he had played against Alicia once before. The game ended in a stalemate because it seemed each predicted the other's next move ahead of time.

Deidre's room was a disaster. The blankets were strewn. The bedside lamp lay on the carpet. There was no blood, but an obvious struggle had taken place.

Moving closer to the bed, Deidre's body outline remained pressed against the sheet. Cassandra flipped over a pillow and found traces of makeup that formed a face. Deidre had been smothered to death.

Cassandra turned and left the bedroom. She leaned against the wall for support. She was nauseated, faint. Perhaps staying in the house wasn't the best idea. Whoever killed Deidre might come back to destroy the evidence.

She returned to the kitchen, grabbed Deidre's key ring from a hook, and opened the side door into the quiet, dark garage. She crept to the van and opened the driver-side door and got inside. After starting the ignition, she pressed a button and the console. The garage door rose.

Cassandra backed out, turned in the L-shaped drive, and faced the street. As she pulled into the street, a sense of relief and freedom settled over her.

At the next intersection, she looked into the rearview mirror. Officer Parker's police car was right behind her. A lump swelled in her throat, making it difficult to breathe.

She coasted through the green light while watching the police cruiser in the rearview mirror. Her hands were slick with nervous sweat. Her heart raced, fearing that any second his lights and siren would come on, and she'd be forced to pull over or flee.

The van's windows were tinted, which gave her concealment, but Parker had been at Deidre's house. He might recognize the vehicle and suspect she had taken it. All it took was a few seconds for him to run the plate, and her chance for escape ended.

She slowed and stopped at the red light at the next intersection. She watched Parker in the rearview mirror. He was speaking into his radio mike, and he didn't seem to be paying any particular attention to the van. But her apprehension continued to build. She took a deep breath as she waited for the light to change. The red light glared for what seemed an eternity. When the signal finally turned green, she eased the acceleration slowly, hoping not to draw attention to herself.

Parker turned left at the intersection. Cassandra released a long sigh of relief. Her hands trembled. She wiped her hands on her sweatpants.

Nervously, she kept checking the mirrors, expecting Parker to return. Her stomach quaked with a sick feeling that she was still being watched, even though the officer was no longer in sight. Somehow, she believed, whoever had killed Deidre knew where she was, and they would come after her and kill her. Soon.

Cassandra kept the van below the speed limit, which seemed horribly slow when her heartbeat demanded her to flee and get away while she could. But she didn't want to risk attracting attention to herself.

Her options to remain in town to find Alicia were few. The longer she searched the streets, the more she chanced being seen and reported to the police. She couldn't stand the thought of running without her daughter but if she was caught, she knew she'd be killed. Alicia had no hope if that occurred.

In between the front seats, Cassandra found Deidre's spare phone plugged into a charger that connected to the van's lighter. She unplugged the phone and dialed a number.

After a few rings, the party answered.

"Yes?" he said.

"Douglas," she replied.

"Cassandra? What the hell have you done?"

Tears filled her eyes and spilled over, rolling down her cheeks. She pulled the van to the curb and wiped her eyes. Even though he had left her for another woman, she loved him nearly as much as she despised him. There was always that silent hope of reconciliation, but she knew what they had had was gone forever. The bridge love had built between them had collapsed. No amount of groveling or regret on his part could repair the damage. Some pain never fully went away. She truly believed death was easier to cope with than divorce.

Cassandra had alleviated most of her hurt, pain, and remorse by excessive physical activity. She ignored the scars of her heart when she was with her daughter, but now that Alicia was gone, the lacerations from past wounds split open.

"Cassandra?" he said. "You still there?"

"Yes. I take it that you've seen the news?"

"Yes."

"Don't believe what they're saying about me."

"They claim to have pretty damning evidence."

"I know, but they don't. That police officer shot his partner. I didn't kill anyone. Deidre was dead *before* the officer was killed. Two men tried to shoot me earlier this morning, too."

"Why would they want to kill you?"

"I really don't know, but I need your help."

His voice lowered to a whisper. "I'm sorry, but I can't help you."

Cassandra closed her eyes, took a deep breath, and her voice cracked. "Because of her?"

"How would it look?"

"Like you have a heart? Like you're human? Do you not realize how difficult it is for me to call you?"

"I imagine I'd be your last resort."

"Just hearing your voice tears my heart apart."

"I never meant to hurt you," he said. "I just wanted a family."

"So did I. Had you been more patient, we would have. You know I have a daughter."

"Yes, I know. I'm proud for you, but Jen and my son are my family now," Douglas said firmly. "She'd never let me live it down if I rushed out to help you."

"How quick you forget."

"What?"

"When you left me for her, you told me that we'd always be friends. And now, when I need your help, you cannot do me one favor."

"Cassandra, please, Jen's in the next room."

"Fine, Douglas, but someone has taken my daughter. She's missing. I believe the people behind Alicia's abduction are the ones framing me for murder and trying to kill me. You know me better than to think I'd ever kill another person. And if you can't do this for me, at least do it for my daughter before it's too late and she's dead."

"I'm sorry. Truly I am."

"Deidre's son was abducted last night, too."

Douglas remained quiet.

"What if that was your son, Doug?"

Silence.

"Doug?"

"What do you need?" he whispered.

"Nothing that requires a lot from you. I need to know if the police are watching my house. That's all."

"You want me to drive by your house and see if they're there?"

"Yes."

"If they are?"

"Whether they are or not, call me at this number."

"Caller ID says this is Deidre's phone?"

"Yes. It's her cellphone."

"Cassandra —"

"No, Douglas, I didn't steal her van. I went to her house to see what I could find out about her murder. I had to have a way to move fast and unnoticed, so I'm using her van until I can get safely out of the city."

"Where will you go?"

"I don't know."

"Give me about a half hour to call. It will take at least that long to reach your house."

"Thank you, Douglas."

"Yeah."

"I'm serious. Thanks."

Chapter 11

Douglas opened the den door and froze. Jen stood on the other side with her arms crossed. The harsh glare in her eyes let him know she had been eavesdropping.

"That was Cassandra, wasn't it?"

Douglas looked away, stepped around her, and made his way to the kitchen.

Jen grabbed his arm and yanked. She glared at him. "Wasn't it?"

"Yes."

"Did you tell her that we know what she's done?"

"She says that she didn't kill anyone."

"Of course she would!"

"I believe her."

Jen nodded. Her eyes narrowed. "Really?"

"I was married to her for ten years. This isn't something she'd do."

"Have you kept tabs on her all this time since *we've* been married?"

Douglas shook his head. "Of course not. I've not driven past her house once since you and I married. This is the first time I've talked to her since we signed the divorce papers."

"How do you know she's innocent then?"

"I suppose I don't know for certain."

"So why'd she call you out of the blue?"

He sighed. "Honestly, I don't know. She sounded desperate. Maybe she has no one else to talk to."

"You need to call the police. There's the chance that she actually killed them."

"I will," he said, taking his car keys from the wall hook beside the garage side door.

"*Now*," she said, handing him her cellphone.

"Jen," Douglas said, glancing at his wristwatch.

"Now, or I will."

He took her phone and stared at the number pad for a moment. Then he tucked it in his back pocket.

"Douglas!"

"I have to make a quick drive. I'll be home by the time John gets off the bus."

"You're meeting her?"

"No. She didn't tell me where she is. I just need to make a quick drive. I'll be right back."

Her narrowed eyes indicated she didn't believe him.

"Why?" She asked. "After all this time you're going to run to her?"

"No. I'm *not* running to her. She needs help. It's the least I could do after what I did to her."

"Meaning me?"

Douglas shook his head. "Jen, I love you, and I'm thankful for what we have. But, to be honest, the way I left hurt her more than I ever imagined."

"And how about the way *I* feel right now?"

"I've never given you a reason to doubt my love for you," he said.

"Until this."

"Jen, this isn't about you. Or us."

"Then what's it about?"

He took a deep breath. "It's about me trying to help her find her daughter."

"Her daughter?"

"Yes, and she's not the only child that was taken last night. So please be here when the bus arrives." He handed her back the phone. "If John doesn't get off the bus, call me immediately."

Jen nodded. "What do you think is going on?"

"I don't know."

Douglas opened the side door to the garage, gave Jen a quick kiss on the lips, and pulled the door closed behind him. He hurried and opened the driver side door of his pickup and climbed in. After the garage door lifted, he looked over his shoulder and backed the truck out.

Once he drove down the street, he felt relieved not to be in the house with Jen. Hearing Cassandra's voice on the phone had stirred emotions that he thought were long buried and forgotten. He worried that Jen could read it in his eyes or perhaps she had and that was what made her suspicious and overly angry.

Douglas still held an infatuation for Cassandra because she had been the best friend he'd ever had. But the frustration of their inability to have children soured him, blinding him to what he stood to lose by leaving her. Only after marrying Jen did he realize that abandoning Cassandra had been a selfish, foolish mistake. And though he could admit his fault, he'd not been able to bring himself to face her since the divorce. He feared she'd never forgive him, and he knew he'd never forgive himself.

His reluctance to help Cassandra wasn't because he didn't want to, but it brought his guilt back to the surface, making him question whether he was crossing a forbidden threshold that Jen might later despise him for. Ultimately, he needed to confront what he kept trying to ignore.

Cassandra never mentioned where she was hiding, which was the safest thing to do should someone have a tap on his phone. But, in a sense, Douglas wished she *had* told him. He'd love the opportunity to apologize to her face to face. He believed he'd matured that much over the years.

His throat tightened as he thought of the possibility of seeing Cassandra again. After their divorce, he and Jen never moved to another town, even when he insisted they should. But during the years, he never imposed upon Cassandra a single phone call or visit because he feared she might take false hope that they'd eventually get back together. But he secretly worried about how she was coping.

Jen wasn't a bad person. She was a good wife, a tad jealous and insecure at times, like now, but personality-wise, she wasn't anything like Cassandra. Jen didn't possess the grace and strength he had seen in his ex-wife, but that didn't diminish his love for her. Regardless of his mixed emotions, he'd never forsake his son and the loving bond that had brought him into the world.

Perhaps Jen's insecurities stemmed from her guilt of being the *other* woman. Douglas wasn't certain, but the psychology behind the idea made logical sense.

Douglas drove down the avenue where Cassandra lived and almost slowed when her mailbox came into view, but then he noticed a red Camaro parked across the street from the house. The car had tinted windows and though he hadn't been in the neighborhood in years, it seemed out of place. He kept his truck at a steady pace and casually glanced toward Cassandra's house.

The front door had been busted open. So she did have a reason to be concerned. Knowing her, Douglas still didn't understand why anyone would deliberately kidnap her daughter and try to frame and kill her. She wasn't a person that made enemies.

He drove past a few more houses and turned into the driveway of an empty house with an overgrown lawn that realtors apparently had problems selling. For a minute he watched the Camaro, hoping to catch a glimpse of someone inside but the window tinting was too dark.

Cassandra's house was visible from where he parked. It resembled nothing of the home he remembered sharing with her. She had painted the outside a dark tan with black shutters, planted lots of roses across the front perimeter, and hung bird feeders from the flowering pear trees in the yard. She didn't seem to want to keep any memories of him, and he didn't blame her. Perhaps she had gotten over him better than he had her.

Douglas turned on his phone and found the number she had called him from. He hit redial and waited.

Chapter 12

Parked at the side of a shaded alley, Cassandra jumped when the cell-phone vibrated. She fumbled with the phone and answered. "Yes?"

"I think you're right," Douglas said.

"Someone's watching my house?"

"Do any of your neighbors drive a new red Camaro?"

"No. Most of them drive older vehicles. Why?"

"There's a car parked across the street from your house, but I can't tell if anyone's inside. The windows are too dark. I could drive past again."

Cassandra replied, "No, don't. Leave in a different direction. It's too risky."

"What do you plan to do now?"

"I don't know."

"Where are you?"

"It's best I don't tell you. Thanks for checking it out for me."

"Don't hang up, Cassandra."

"I need to go."

"Where?"

"I'm not sure yet."

"Wait."

"What is it, Doug? I really need to go."

"Just be safe. Okay?"

"I will."

"Look, I'm truly sorry for how things fell apart between us. I should've handled our situation better."

Cassandra closed her eyes. The fresh tears stung. "What's happened has happened. Nothing changes that."

"I know. But I regret all the pain I've caused you. I'm sorry."

"Don't worry over it. I survived."

"Dammit!"

"Excuse me?"

"No. Sorry. Jen's turning into your driveway."

"What? Your wife?"

"I guess she followed me. I told her to stay home. Our son will be getting off the bus soon."

"Get her away from there, Doug."

"On it."

Over the phone she heard tires squeal and two quick gunshots blasted in the distance. Cassandra's heart raced. Doug had apparently dropped his phone. She heard it bounce on the floorboard. Another shot echoed.

"I've been hit!" Doug shouted. He groaned in pain. He panted hard, wheezing to breathe.

The truck engine revved as metal crashed and crumbled. The horn blared.

Cassandra's hands shook while she listened. She couldn't do anything else. Even if she hurried and drove like a maniac, she'd never get to him in time.

The truck door opened. One more shot fired. Then the horn stopped blaring.

A rustling sound came over the phone. She guessed someone was pulling Doug's body out of the truck.

"Is he dead?" a man asked.

"Yes," another man replied.

"This is him?"

"Yes," a female answered. "He came here to help Cassandra."

"You're certain that was his purpose, Jen?"

"Of course," Jen said. "I caught him talking to her on the phone. I warned him not to come here."

Cassandra put a hand over her mouth. Tears flooded her eyes. But she didn't dare disconnect the call. Something told her that the conspiracy went much deeper than she ever imagined. Jen had helped these men kill her own husband. But why?

"That's Douglas' phone on the truck floor," Jen said.

"Cassandra?" the man asked in the phone.

Cassandra clamped her hand over her mouth even tighter to prevent any sound from emitting.

"We're going to find you," he said in a cold, harsh tone.

Apparently, the man handed the phone to Jen. Her voice came over the phone. "This is all your fault. I want you to know that. Now, my son has no father. I hope they find and kill you soon for what you've done."

With that, Cassandra ended the call.

She started the van and drove. She wiped away tears while trying to keep the vehicle moving at a steady pace and without weaving. She had asked a favor from Douglas and now he was dead.

"Dammit," she whispered. "What the hell is happening?"

She lowered the driver side window, slowed at an open trashcan, and tossed the cellular into it. Once they pinpointed the location of the phone, at least she wouldn't have possession of it. However, she wasn't certain where she should flee. She imagined it wouldn't be much longer before someone discovered she had taken Deidre's van, so she had to find another means of transportation.

Cassandra took a deep breath through her nose and exhaled slowly through her mouth. She drove past the cemetery where she had seen the creatures attack and kill her would be assassins. She wondered where those creatures had disappeared to, and if they had Alicia. She held a bit of reassurance that these beasts weren't going to hurt her daughter, and certainly, they could have killed her if that was their intent. But they hadn't. Instead, they had rescued her.

The oddest thing that occurred to her was how these catlike beings had *known* that people were coming to take her daughter and Seth. And since Seth was also missing, she could only reason that he was with Alicia. But where? Why?

They had protected Cassandra, but for some reason, Deidre wasn't spared.

With Douglas dead and Alicia missing, she never felt more alone.

"I'm going to find you, Alicia," she whispered. She didn't know how she'd keep that promise, but she needed help in order to fulfill it.

Chapter 13

Jen stared in disbelief as the men dragged Doug's limp body down the driveway and dropped his body into the trunk of the Camaro.

"You weren't supposed to kill him, Blake," Jen said. Her eyes narrowed with fury. "That wasn't part of the deal."

"And *you* weren't supposed to follow him," Blake said.

"I had to know," she said.

"Know what?"

"If he was actually meeting Cassandra."

Blake combed his red hair from his face and laughed. "Apparently not, Jen. No one has come or gone from that house since early this morning. My guess is that she's too afraid to come home."

"I did what you asked. I told you when she called and that was all. You never said anything about killing Doug."

"I suggest you get home to your son."

Jen wiped away tears. Spittle flew as she glared at him. "How do I explain to him that his father's dead? Huh?"

With an even smile, Blake replied, "The best way you can."

"You bastard!" she said. She ran at him and started beating his chest with her tight fists.

Blake shoved her to the ground and aimed the gun at her face. "It'd be a shame if your son lost both parents today, don't you think?"

Jen clenched her jaw tightly. Her rage wasn't enough to get past the gun. Without the gun the odds were still greatly set against her. He was twice her size and more callous than she expected.

Breathing hard, she slid back on the paved driveway and surrendered with a defeated nod. But she never took her eyes off him. If a brazen stare could kill, Blake would have engulfed in flames right where he stood.

"That's better," he said, walking toward the Camaro. "Doug didn't have to die, and I wouldn't have had to kill him had you just stayed at home. Once he saw you here, his trust in you would never have been the same."

"Why do you say that?"

"Because of your insecurities. Eventually, he'd wonder if you were part of the scheme as well."

Blake opened the car door and got inside. "Now get home and speak nothing of this to anyone. Understood?"

Jen gave a simple nod and waited until the Camaro was down the street before she stood up and headed to her vehicle in Cassandra's driveway. She needed to hurry home and hope John was okay. She wanted to hug him close and tell him everything was going to be okay, even though she knew her world had fallen apart.

"Dammit, Doug," she whispered. "Why didn't you listen?"

But she knew the truth. Doug still loved Cassandra and never fully let go of that passion. Jen didn't doubt that Doug loved her, too, but not as completely. He loved their son, John, with a genuine fatherly love, but Cassandra still claimed a part of him that Jen had never acquired. Whatever Cassandra possessed must have been too special for Doug to forget.

As Jen recalled her last conversation with Doug, he was only trying to help Cassandra find her missing daughter. The sincerity in his voice proved he wasn't lying. The love and devotion in his eyes were directed solely at Jen when he held to his side of the argument. Her bitterness toward Cassandra had blinded her and allowed her jealousy to get the best of her.

If Jen simply confessed right then and there that someone *was* watching Cassandra's house, he wouldn't have gone. He would've stayed. He'd still be alive. But telling him what she already knew would have brought immediate scrutiny. He'd probe to find out how she knew that information in the first place.

Her confession probably would've caused him to leave her. The last thing he'd have wanted to know was that John wasn't *his* biological son. She couldn't have endured the anguish of seeing the hurt, disappointment, and betrayal on his face after she told him that. Not that she had cheated on him, but like Cassandra and Deidre, she'd sought the help of New Horizons Fertility Clinic to *get* pregnant. As best she knew, Doug was infertile. Or he had such an extremely low sperm count that she or any other woman would never have had children with him.

She glanced at the clock on the dashboard console.

2:55 p.m.

John's bus should be arriving at the house in about ten minutes. She increased the speed because she feared he wasn't safe.

Jen planned to pick up her son and then she'd go find Cassandra to help her find her daughter. It was the last thing that Doug wanted to do, and it was the least she could do in his memory.

Cassandra probably didn't know what Jen looked like, but she'd know Cassandra the moment she saw her. She had driven pass her house many times over the years, always fearful that one day she'd pass and see Doug's truck in the driveway, but that was never the case. He was loyal and faithful, in spite of her mistrust and constant paranoia.

When Jen arrived at her house, a white van was parked in her driveway that she didn't recognize. She pulled beside the van and hurried to the open front door.

John was inside the door. His backpack was still slung over his little shoulders. His face was pale. His lower lip puckered. A man stood beside him.

"Hello, Jen," he said with a grim smile. "Seems like we have a lot to discuss."

"Dr. Shelby?" she asked. "Why are you here?"

Behind him stood Blake with his gun tucked out of John's view.

"Come inside," Dr. Shelby said. "This won't take long."

Chapter 14

Mitch awakened in a dark room with an earthen floor. Water dripped nearby. The air was cool and sour with a pungent, mildewed scent that tightened his throat each time he inhaled.

His arms were tied tight enough above his head to suspend and hold him in a standing position. His head lulled side to side whenever he tried to look around. He couldn't fight the vertigo and became nauseated when he looked straight ahead.

The cool air made the cuts across his face and chest burn.

Mitch's left eye was swollen nearly shut. The last thing he recalled was Sheba punching him in the face, which probably explained the excruciating headache he endured. The pain in his stiff shoulders meant that he had probably been unconscious for several hours or longer.

Shirtless and standing in his boxers, the cold made him shiver. His bare feet touched the cold dirt floor. He dug his toes into the earth; hoping by covering them, they'd get warmer.

As best Mitch could tell, he was alone in the small room. Hardly any light filtered in. He didn't know if it were day or night. The dusty cobwebbed-covered wall possibly meant he was still inside the cemetery manor, but he didn't know for certain. Salem probably had a lot of other rundown buildings, but it was less likely he would be moved closer to town because it risked his abduction being discovered.

Voices carried beyond the wall. A flash of light brightened the outer hallway.

Mitch closed his eyes and lowered his head, feigning sleep.

"Where is he, Sheba?" the man asked in a low, gravelly voice.

"Usual place," Sheba replied.

The flashlight beacon washed over his face.

"You recognize him?" she asked.

"Mitch Niles."

"Yes," she said. "How'd you know?"

"He was asking a lot of questions about the murders, but I was under the impression that he was leaving last night."

"He was. I met him at the bus stop."

"Why didn't you let him catch his bus and leave?"

"Where's the fun in that?" she said playfully. "Besides, I believe he knows more than what you think."

"What makes you think that?"

"This is the business card he handed me. Kat Gaddis Agency. He works with a team that investigates bizarre murders."

The man sighed. "You should have let him leave."

"I was told otherwise."

"Really?"

"Yes."

"I wasn't informed."

Sheba said, "That's not unusual, is it?"

"Damn," he said. "Now, we have to worry about his employer looking for him. No doubt they'll file a missing person's report soon or come looking for him. You should have let him leave."

Mitch dared a peek and was shocked to see Sheba talking to a police officer. He closed his eyes. His mind raced as he tried to understand the situation.

Sheba said that the police had covered up the murders of her friends from years before, and yet, she bound him and brought an officer back. The police were involved in cover-ups, but so was she, which meant she must have had a part in the murders. But why?

Officer Parker shone the flashlight across Mitch's face, and then his bare chest.

"You must have hit him hard," Parker said.

"Yeah, but he's alive. He'll live." she replied.

"Well, it's best we leave for now. Where are his clothes?"

"I had to take them."

"Why?"

"In case he escapes."

Parker flashed the light to the restraints. "He'll never break free of those."

"Just a precaution."

"It's too cold to leave him like this. He'll get sick."

"He won't be like this *long*."

"Let's go."

PARKER STEPPED up the crude earthen steps. Sheba followed him outside.

"You changed?" Parker asked Sheba. "When you attacked him?"

She smiled. "Of course."

"You need to control yourself better than this."

Her eyes narrowed. "I control myself just fine. Want to see?"

Parker studied her fierce eyes for a moment, and then, he looked away.

"Very well," he said. "Keep an eye on him. You might want to put some clothes on him to prevent hyperthermia or build a small fire."

"No fire," she replied. "That manor will burst into flames if I did that."

"Should he die before it's necessary, you know there will be repercussions."

"He'll be okay."

"Make certain that he stays alive."

Sheba frowned. "You given orders now?"

"No. I'm warning you. For your sake and mine, Sheba, he needs to live."

"I told you that he'd be fine. Now you'd best leave before people see you here."

Parker shrugged and walked away. Sheba smiled and looked down the cellar stairs. Her eyes narrowed as she headed back down.

Chapter 15

Dead River Gulch, Nevada

JOSEPH SHADOW-TALKER AWAKENED WITH A START. Cold dry scales slid across his right thigh. He stiffened, realizing a snake crawled beneath his blanket. He opened his eyes and stared at the ceiling.

Swallowing hard, he kept his breathing calm. Not certain whether the snake was venomous or not, he took precaution because rattlesnakes were indigenous to the area.

The snake burrowed between him and his new lady-friend he had brought home from The Waterhole Bar and Grill the night before. He searched his mind to recall her name.

Misty, he remembered. Like the fog drifting through his head.

Joe drank from time to time, but seldom did he overindulge. Last night was an exception. He and Misty were plastered when he brought her home. They staggered down the hall, undressing one another, and collapsed on his bed. The details of what transpired between them remained a mystery. If they made love, he was ashamed to say that he didn't recall it.

He lay still, careful not to make any sudden movements. He scanned his bed from his neck down. The faint morning light shone through the

Venetian blinds. Not much light filtered in, but enough to see a coiled image if one should be there.

He was relieved he didn't see any snakes on top of the blanket. One under the blanket was more than he needed. Not knowing where it hid enhanced their danger. Several minutes passed without any further movement from the reptile. The snake must have found an inconspicuous hiding place near Misty. As long as she remained still, the snake wasn't likely to bite. He decided to peel back the blanket and carefully slide out of bed.

Joe moved the blanket halfway down his chest when he noticed a second snake—a rattler—poised upon his chest. Coiled tightly, its head rose. Its forked tongue flicked. Cold, unforgiving eyes peered into his. The rattles buzzed with vehement disdain. Every muscle in his body tightened.

He didn't fear rattlesnakes. In fact, he often caught them whenever he found them in his yard and gently moved them farther into the wilderness away from his ranch. Several times he had traveled to Texas and participated in the Rattler Roundup. On a dare, he seated himself in a glass tub with twenty rattlers. Not a record-breaking feat by any means, but not something a timid person attempted, either. But this involuntary situation was different. The two snakes in his bed were no accident. They were placed here and were quite agitated. Any sudden movement on his part was certain to make the one on his chest strike.

While the snake kept its attention focused on him, he slid his hand toward Misty and hoped to wake her quietly without disturbing the other snake. His hand met her cold, stiff flesh. No warmth of life greeted his touch.

She was dead.

Sometime during the night she must have moved. She must have been too drunk and asleep to feel the snakebite. The poison flowed through her bloodstream and stopped her heart.

Anguish overcame his need to protect her. She was the first woman he'd dated in three years. He chanced getting close to her, and now, just as quickly, she was gone. He always believed himself to be an isolated spirit, one to venture the path of life alone. Fate seemed to have carved it in granite for him to read.

His telephone rang on the bedside table. The rattler never reacted to the sound.

Its harsh eyes stared at him.

Unable to reach the phone without getting bit, he waited for the answering machine to pick up. After the beep, no one left a message. A long pause of silence waited on the other end. Right before the person hung up, he was certain he heard soft laughter.

The phone call wasn't someone trying to get in touch with him, but a calloused, ruthless person hoping to alarm Misty or Joe into jumping and provoking the rattlesnakes to bite. The caller wanted them dead. He was halfway successful.

Since Misty was already dead, she couldn't have reached for the phone. His failure to answer entertained the caller that perhaps Joe was dead, too.

Joe stared into the snake's cold eyes. It lowered its head and ceased buzzing. Although the snake was alert, it was calming. His ability to remain still diminished his threat to the reptile.

Still holding the blanket at his sides, he tightened his hands into fists around the wool material. The snake didn't detect the slight movement and settled into a more rested position.

Joe held his breath and bit his lower lip. With lightning speed, he looped the blanket up, over, and scooped it beneath the rattler, trapping it inside the blanket before it had a chance to strike. He shoved the captured snake off his chest to the foot of the bed, and then he spun his legs to the edge of the bed. Before his feet touched the floor, he flipped on the bedside lamp.

Along the far edge of the floor, a third rattlesnake was stretched out, crawling away. Joe shook his head. Someone had gone to a lot of trouble to ensure he'd get bitten more than once if he panicked and ran. Clearly, the person responsible didn't know Joe's nature. He lived harmoniously with nature and her creatures.

Joe remained cautious because the house probably contained more than three snakes.

He peered over his shoulder and looked at Misty's nude back. Blonde hair spilled over her shoulders. Her ivory skin had tinted pale blue.

Closing his eyes, he tried to remember what they'd done after they left the bar. He let her drive his old pickup home because she wasn't as drunk as he was. No one followed them along the gravel roads. He didn't recall any car lights on the road behind them, and besides, the new moon prevented anyone from driving with their headlights off. The ditches along the narrow roads were too steep and gullied for someone to risk accidentally running off the road into a ravine.

Joe's head pounded. He rubbed his temples to ease the tension, but a hangover wasn't easy to dismiss.

Opening the nightstand drawer, he pulled out his Ruger 9mm. Rattlesnakes might not be the only danger lurking inside his house. He stood and stepped toward the center of the room. When he moved, a chorus of rattlesnakes buzzed beneath the bed. Their warning was just that. Stay away. He distanced himself from their hiding place and headed to the hallway.

From the open door he could see the living room. He pulled the bedroom door closed as he exited to contain the snakes while he investigated the rest of the house.

Newspapers were strewn across the living room. Books and magazines were ripped from the bookshelves. They wanted something and were more than willing to kill for it.

Joe knew exactly what they wanted. He just didn't know who *they* were.

Easing to the kitchen, he didn't encounter any more snakes. Apparently, the only snakes were those carefully positioned in his bedroom while someone else ransacked the rest of the house.

Joe took the phone from the kitchen wall cradle. All the drawers, cabinets, and pantry contents were dumped on the floor. He needed to call the sheriff to report Misty's death and the invasion of his home. But first, he'd contact his brothers to warn them of the possible threat to his family.

Chapter 16

Lucas turned and stretched to wrap his arm around Lydia, but she wasn't in bed. He rubbed his eyes and looked across the bedroom. The shower in the adjacent bathroom was silent.

He rose to his feet and grabbed his bathrobe. He stretched and arched his back. A series of painful pops ran up his spine. He turned his neck, side to side, to ease the tightness and more popping occurred. Rubbing swollen knuckles, he wondered if all those years of daredevil stunts had finally caught up with him. He ached from joint pain, arthritis, and age. Although he had not made it public, he had retired from racing and stunt driving six months ago when he helped rescue Lydia. However, retirement didn't shun the pain.

Lucas walked slowly to the bedroom window. With two fingers he opened a gap in the Venetian blinds and peered out at the driveway. Lydia's Nighthawk motorcycle was gone.

Two of her dresser drawers were open and empty.

"Damn," Lucas whispered, shaking his head.

He dressed and went to make coffee.

Some mornings Lydia wanted to drive, think, and try to get a grasp of what her life was meant to be. Something in his gut told him that this wasn't one of those mornings. He sensed she had finally left him for good.

Lydia continually struggled with the knowledge of being created in a laboratory, having no family, and she constantly feared she'd kill again. Nothing Lucas told her could convince her otherwise. She reviewed the knowledge over and over in her mind. It ate at her, and her resentment toward her creators and toward him festered.

Over the past two months, Lydia grew more sullen and silent. She kept her distance and whenever he reached out for her, she turned away with tears in her eyes. She'd disappear in the woods for hours or practice shooting her 9mm on their shooting range. She never smiled and always seemed to be deep in thought. At times, her silence frightened him. Eventually, he understood the day would come when she would leave. He tried to ignore it, and he hoped today wasn't that day, but the evidence reinforced his fear because she had packed a lot of her clothes.

Lucas reached for the coffee canister from the cabinet and noticed a piece of paper near the sink. Stepping closer, he recognized the writing to be hers.

Lucas,

I'm sorry to tell you this way, but I cannot say good-bye face to face. You'd convince me to stay. I gave you six months like we agreed, but how I feel inside hasn't changed. Your life will always be in danger as long as I'm with you. I know you love me, and because I love you, I must leave. I cannot live with you because they will kill you to get me. You're safer without me. That's why I'm going to find them and stop them for good. You deserve a better life. You deserve better than me.

Lydia

TEARS BURNED LUCAS' eyes. His chest felt empty, hollow. He glanced to the wall calendar and saw she had circled the date. Indeed, six months had passed more rapidly than he imagined possible. She didn't lie and kept her word to wait out the six months, but he suspected she never had a day she didn't suffer inner turmoil. He felt guilty for trying to hold onto her when it was obvious her mind centered elsewhere. Keeping her close, he reasoned, was a way to protect her and others.

He picked up the phone and hit '1.' The party picked up on the third ring.

"Daniel?" Lucas said.

"Yes."

Lucas sat at the kitchen table with the note in his hand. "She left me."

"Lydia?"

"Yeah. Can't say I'm surprised."

"Any idea where she might have gone?"

"No. I thought she was readjusting and was getting settled. I believed things were getting better."

"She didn't give any hints that she was leaving?"

"Not verbally." Lucas sighed. "She's been very quiet lately. Always deep in thought."

"I'm sorry, Luke. I know how much you love her."

"I'm worried about her, Dan."

Daniel was silent for a minute. "I don't know what to say, but I'm here if you need an ear."

"That's why I called."

"Did she take her Jeep or the Nighthawk?"

"Nighthawk and some clothes."

"She packed light?" Daniel said.

"More clothes than the last few times. But I doubt she'd ever move any furniture. She acts like she wants to roam. With everything I've offered to make her feel like we have a home, she's more inclined to be alone."

"Maybe she wants some time alone for a few days. Maybe after that, she'll come back."

"I don't think so."

"Did she take any weapons?"

"I haven't checked, but knowing her, probably. Her letter indicates she's going after them."

"Who specifically?" Daniel asked.

"I've no clue. She's not mentioned any labs or scientists. She's sullen and silent. Brooding for weeks. Other than that, she's been practicing her marksmanship at targets on our firing range for hours each day. That seems to calm her."

"She has a vendetta."

"Against who? She's mentioned no one."

"Check through the house and your garage for possible maps. Look through the recent history searches on your computer. She's bound to have left a clue somewhere as to what she plans to carry out."

"I'll check, Dan, but she's not one to make notes. She has an excellent memory. A photographic memory is how I'd describe it. She was created that way."

"Damn," Daniel said. "That broadens the search."

"How so?"

"TransGenCorp, Grayson Enterprises, and Desert Labs. She's been inside all of them. All she'd need is to have seen a list of names for other genetic scientists. She may perceive them as enemies and go after any of them."

"I have to find her before she kills anyone."

"Desert Labs is the closest to your location."

"I'll check there first," Lucas said. "After what she did at Desert Labs, I didn't think she'd forgive herself."

"I don't think she has. She's accepted those killings as what she does. Has she ever expressed remorse?"

Lucas shook his head. "In words, yes. I can't say that she said it with sincerity though. Her eyes seemed cold. God, I need to find her."

Lucas carried his phone to the living room and sat on the sofa. He looked at the television and noticed the screen was frozen.

"Have you seen the news this morning?"

"No," Daniel said. "Not yet."

"I think I know who she's going after."

"Who?"

Lucas grabbed the remote and unpaused the screen. "Apparently Steven Matthews escaped custody this morning."

"Crap. You know she'll hunt him down."

"There's no doubt about it."

"Where was he in prison?" Daniel asked.

"A federal prison in New Mexico."

"That's a good drive."

"I know. The problem is finding her."

"There may be one way."

"How?"

"Her Nighthawk has GPS. Go to your computer and activate a tracker on it. She may not be too far away."

"I never thought of that."

"Just hope she hasn't, either, or she's turned it off."

Lucas seated himself at the computer. He searched for the

Nighthawk's tracker number. Once he found it, he typed the code into the GPS tracker service.

"Thanks, Dan. I appreciate your help."

"Anytime."

Lucas started to hang up, but he didn't want to be alone. "Forgive me for being so selfish, Dan. How is everyone?"

"We're fine. Julia had her eight-month pregnancy checkup. Morton and Felicia are well. The rats are always into mischief, but Morton keeps them in line."

Lucas typed in the search command, and the Nighthawk showed on the Oregon map about ten miles away. She hadn't been gone too long, or she had stopped at the side of the road, contemplating which route to take to New Mexico. She might have abandoned the bike altogether.

"I found the Nighthawk, Dan. She's not too far away."

"Good. Go find her."

"Wish me luck."

"I'm certain you won't need it."

Lucas hung up, finished making the coffee, and filled a travel mug. He checked his gun clip, grabbed the coffee mug, and headed for his SUV. His motorcycle would have been his vehicle of choice, but he wasn't awake enough to drive it. Besides, with his nerves on edge from worrying about Lydia, he needed a vehicle with more balance. If the Nighthawk been moving on the GPS map tracker, he'd need to take his bike, especially if she was driving off road.

He wondered why she stopped so close to their house. Was she reconsidering her decision to leave?

For about six months, they lived in Myrtle Creek. After spending a weekend in a rented cabin, she expressed how much she loved the area. Her brief expression of enthusiasm prompted Lucas to research the realty market in the area because he hoped she was ready to make the adjustment of settling down somewhere. They found a modest house set away from town near the forests where they could have privacy and enjoy nature.

But Lydia's joy was short-lived.

Daniel suggested the possibility that Lydia had a vendetta. Steven Matthews had escaped. She hated Matthews for taking her captive and that he planned to use her as a template to clone more genetic warriors. If his project had been successful, she'd have been trapped inside an incubation chamber for the rest of her life. Removing her from the mechanism would have killed her.

Lucas hated Matthews as much as Lydia did.

He hoped she'd come back and ask for his assistance. If it meant she'd stay with him after they ridded the world of Matthews, he'd help her carry out the assassination. Something told him she didn't need his help, and she had stopped for another reason entirely. The mysterious attraction she had succumbed to in Myrtle Creek wasn't something he understood. The place was serene and isolated by thick forests, but she had an ulterior reason for living here that she had never disclosed to him.

On several occasions, he awakened to find her sitting outside in the middle of the night. She sat in silence at the forest's edge in a trancelike stupor, constantly listening to the chorus of insects, birds, and noises he never quite identified. Whatever reason she had for moving here, he knew he needed to hurry and find her before she did something he couldn't undo or repair.

Chapter 17

Lydia parked her Nighthawk at the vacant scenic view parking lot that overlooked a deep, forested ravine. The news of Steven Matthews escaping from prison infuriated her. She berated herself for not killing him when she could have. The proper authorities failed to enact justice, which didn't surprise her. Now she needed to finish what she should have done six months earlier.

She removed her helmet and placed it on the seat. A gentle breeze blew from the ravine and swept upward with the sweetness only nature offered. She inhaled the fragrance deeply and savored the peace of being surrounded by the forest trees.

She peered over the edge as the wind played with her hair.

The more Lydia thought of Matthews, the angrier she became. She was thankful to have had her tracer chip surgically removed. Matthews couldn't find her, but she'd find him. Although her vengeance demanded her to go after Matthews, she first wanted to discover what kept beckoning her to come to this particular ravine. For weeks, an unknown force pulled at her spirit. Today, she located from where the source beckoned.

Checking her Glock 9mm clip and slapping it into the gun, she tucked it behind her belt and headed down the steep, narrow trail. The deeper into the ravine she descended, the darker her surroundings became. The thick canopy of foliage blocked sunlight and gave the moist mossy ground the eerie equivalent to stepping into another dimension.

Although the signs posted at the scenic overlook stated, 'No Hiking,' crumpled beer cans and emptied fast food containers were strewn all along the dirt trail and clearly displayed how rebellious or illiterate visitors were.

Lydia's purpose for ignoring the sign sided with the tinge of rebellion that had been swelling inside her for months. Compelled to stop here, she obeyed. The wilderness called to her, but she never understood why. Perhaps her lust for freedom and isolation called her more, and nature was the only reserve available to satisfy this desire.

Thick moss hedged the gentle creek that flowed over rocks as smooth as glass from years of weathering. Tiny fish darted in pools while water striders skated across the surface. Further down the creek a large, dead branch snapped.

Lydia froze.

Since no vehicles, other than her motorcycle, were parked on the lot above, she reasoned that either another human was in the wooded area, or a large animal, like a bear, stood downstream watching her.

Lydia eased her hand back and pulled her 9mm. The gun held little chance to kill a bear, but a bear wasn't what she feared encountering. Humans were her greatest threat. An ordinary human the gun could stop. Something like Lucian or herself took different means.

Near a large pine, yellow eyes peered from the shadows. Before she got a better view, they were gone. Rapid footsteps fled deeper into the dark forest. Dry nettles and twigs snapped.

Lydia took a step in the direction of her fleeing observer but stopped when a slamming car door echoed from the parking lot above.

"Lydia!" Lucas shouted, peering over the edge. "Where are you?"

Lydia pushed her back against a large pine in the dense shadows and ground her teeth.

"Shit," she said, shaking her head.

Through the overhead branches she saw him, but the shade surrounding her prevented him from seeing her.

Lucas headed down the rugged path, so she sprinted through several rows of saplings, trying to disappear farther into the forest where the yellow-eyed person had run.

Lydia ran, gun held tightly in hand, and pivoted around the next large pine. She slipped on the moist mossy ground, fell forward, rolled, and pushed herself to her feet.

At the bottom of the path near the creek, Lucas looked around, trying to find her.

Another twig snapped. She turned and ducked seconds before a large rock would have struck the back of her head. The rock smacked the tree and dropped with a loud thud on the ground. She aimed her gun in the direction from where the rock was thrown, but she didn't see anyone. Unfortunately, the noise was loud enough for Lucas to locate her.

He jogged toward her, and she aimed a few inches above his head and fired. A thick leafy branch dropped to the ground in front of him. He stopped and stared in disbelief. She stepped around the side of the tree and lowered the gun at his chest.

"Lucas," she said in an even tone. "Go back and leave me alone. Don't force me to shoot you."

His eyes widened. Coldness that matched her icy words glared in her eyes. "Honey, you can't—"

"Leave."

"Lydia, please. We can get some help for you."

"I don't need any help." Her jaw tightened. She pumped another bullet into the chamber and shook her head. Tears shimmered in her eyes. "No, just go, dammit! Go!"

Lucas raised his hands in surrender and took a step forward. She lowered the gun and fired. The bullet struck a thick root on the path ahead of him. Dirt and wood pulp exploded an inch from his foot. He stepped back.

Her hand remained steady as she leveled it at his chest again. "No more warnings, Luke. I swear."

Lucas nodded. He lowered himself to sit back on his heels. "Your anger isn't at me, Lydia."

"Some of it is."

Her answer surprised him.

"Why?"

Her eyes narrowed. "Because you lied to me. You never told me where I came from and that I had been an experiment. I had to find out from

Idris and not you. You were the one person I never thought would betray me."

"I *didn't* betray you," Lucas said. "I didn't tell you because I wanted to protect you."

"It almost killed both of us."

"Lydia, I regret not telling you. I didn't realize the depth of programming they'd done to you. I'm sorry."

"I'd have been better off left inside the incubation chamber."

"No, you wouldn't."

"It'd be better than the chaos storming through my brain."

"Regardless of what they did to you, I love you for who you are. I need you."

She shook her head. "No. You need . . . you *deserve* someone who has a past and family background."

"I need someone to spend my life with right now and in the future. That's you. We can start a family together."

"Do you not realize the risks we'd take?"

"Life is full of risks. Everything is a gamble."

"No, it's not that simple, Lucas. With my genetics, we have no idea what would be birthed or what the child will grow up to be. I have urges to stalk and kill like an animal. I'm predatory and the urge to kill continues to grow inside of me. I cannot drive that urge out of my mind; no matter how hard I try. A child from me could be even more dangerous or become a vicious serial killer. Would you want that on your conscious?"

"No." Lucas ran his hands through his graying hair. "Lydia, I don't want you to leave."

"Luke." Her voice was softer, sad. "What if everything you believed in was a lie? How would *you* handle the truth?"

Lucas shrugged. "I . . . I honestly don't know."

"You knew what I was, and you kept that information from me. That wasn't something you should have kept secret. I have no inner peace. I doubt I ever will."

"I'm sorry. I honestly thought you'd be better off not knowing. I love you and I want you safe."

"I understand," she said. "So please understand I have to do this for myself. I have to sort through this . . . my need for revenge."

"I know Matthews is out."

She smiled evenly. "That's *why* I paused the television screen."

"You plan to kill him?"

"Need you ask?"

"Let me help."

Lydia shook her head. "No. You're innocent of this. His blood will be on my hands, not yours."

"I can't let you do this alone."

Her eyes narrowed. "I don't see that you have any choice."

"You'd really kill me?"

She swallowed hard, her jaw tightened, and she nodded. "Only if you force me to."

Lucas shook his head. "After all we've done together I mean that little to you?"

"I told you. I have to sort through these feelings. The bloodlust, rage, and revenge. That is something I must do without you around."

"Once you're done sorting through your emotions, will you come home?"

"Perhaps."

"Have I ever made you unhappy?" he asked, staring into her eyes.

She looked away.

"We're soulmates. You know it. You feel it."

"Don't Lucas," she said, shaking her head.

"Can you honestly say you don't love me?"

"This isn't about love, Luke. If only it was that easy. I do love you. I told you that in the letter. But my being with you puts your life in extreme danger."

"Let me worry about that."

"No." Lydia shook her head. "I can't."

"In your letter you made mention of 'they.' I know about Matthews, but who are *they*?"

She sighed. "Telling you only adds to your danger."

"I can help you."

"This is my battle, Luke."

"Our battle. Our fight. You married me, so this is ours together."

"Not this. You're in no shape to go against these people."

Hurt hollowed his eyes. "I see. So I've become too old to protect you?"

"I didn't mean it like that, but you have to admit, your past injuries have taken a toll on your body. You're not as agile as you wish yourself to be."

"I'd slow you down."

"They'll kill you. I cannot watch that. I don't want to see you die."

"I'll worry about you."

"I expect you will. But you're not like me. You know what I am. I heal fast. I'm capable of protecting myself."

"The people you're going after are like you?"

"No, but those that protect them are. I have to stop them."

"Where are they?"

Lydia smiled. "Nice try. If I tell you, you'll try to keep an eye out for me. That's sweet. It really is, but I don't need your protection."

"Look—" His cellphone rang, interrupting him. He read the incoming phone number. "It's Joe."

"Answer it."

After several minutes of talking, Lucas disconnected the call. "He needs our help."

"No," she replied. "He needs *your* help."

Lucas stood and extended his hand to her.

Lydia tucked the gun behind her belt and crossed her arms. Her icy stare was frozen wrath. "Go help Joe."

"He asked for both of us."

"Don't try to obligate me to whatever trouble has arisen. I have personal things to take care of. You help our friend."

Lucas lowered his hand. "So there's nothing I can say that will change your mind?"

"No."

His shoulders slumped. His actions showed his defeat. She had won, but she wasn't satisfied with the victory. Her intent wasn't to hurt him, but she didn't know any other way to keep him safe.

"Be careful, Lydia. Again, I'm sorry that I didn't tell you everything in the beginning."

"When you return, I won't be here," she said, ignoring his apology. "The GPS on my Nighthawk will be turned off. I should have turned it off before I left. Don't attempt to find me again. It's the last warning you have. Anyone who approaches me I consider a threat, and I won't hesitate to shoot. That's you, Daniel, Joe, or anyone. I don't shoot to injure. You know that."

"Okay," Lucas replied. "But just because you heal fast and know no pain, don't think you're invincible."

Lydia took a deep breath. "I may not know physical pain, Luke, but I do know what a broken heart feels like. I carry the pain now."

"Then stay."

"I can't. Just go. Joe has always been there for you, so help him. Worry about me later."

Lucas gave a reluctant nod, turned, and ran to the rugged trail that led to the parking lot above. Lydia watched him disappear. At the speed he ran, in spite of his injuries, Joe's situation must be urgent. For a moment, she regretted not following him out of the ravine, but if she did, she'd have to find another way to leave later. It was better Lucas accepted her decision now than cling to any false hope.

Finding Matthews was her top priority. She believed Lucas could help Joe without her assistance. After all, Lucas had survived Pittsburgh and TransGenCorp without her. She'd never seen anyone tougher and more daring than when they had first started dating. She wondered why he acted so helpless now. Had love really made him that vulnerable and soft?

Being on his own should remind him that he was a man capable of making decisions whenever necessary. He didn't need her to rediscover his inner strength. He didn't need to rely on codependence. He could live without her. However, a part of her wondered if *she* could actually live without him.

Lydia wasn't lying about her broken heart. Her decision left her torn inside. Her emotions battled one another and her confusion frayed her rationality, but she knew Lucas was safer without her in his life. She was volatile, unable to control her emotions.

She waited until his SUV roared to life and tires squealed before she headed deeper into the forest. Hiking two hundred or so yards, she entered an area darkened by a dusk-like eeriness. The flowing creek dipped and vanished underground. The water splashed loudly on rocks hidden beneath the earth. She stood atop a massive cave. She felt the strong presence of others beneath her.

Lydia got on her hands and knees and peered down through the dark, narrow crevice. She could squeeze through the opening, but without a long rope and a light source, the danger was too great, even for her. Getting back to the surface would be impossible if she survived the fall, but she didn't know where she could exit. She'd starve to death.

A deep growl came from behind and unsettled her. She rose with her gun and aimed. The wolfish creature gnashed at her and bolted through the trees. As it ran, it arched upward. After several steps, the slender animal transformed unlike anything she'd ever seen in TransGenCorp. The creature abandoned running on four legs and adapted to two. Before it vanished in the thick trees, she was certain the thing had become human.

According to Kat, GenTech was successful with splicing canine genes with humans', so what she witnessed wasn't imaginary or unbelievable. It was a nightmare of deranged scientific technology.

Her main concern was why the creature was here, so far from any biotech laboratory, and what she sensed in the cavern below wasn't a singular being. It was a massive group, possibly dozens of these unique people.

A colony, perhaps? Again, she wondered how they arrived here.

At night Lydia sensed their presence, but until now, she wasn't certain what kept beckoning her late after sunset with their strange howls. Genetically, she wasn't like them, but she could sense their pack-like need to kill. Even though she didn't know what they were, a part of her longed to join them.

She hurried back up the trail to get her Nighthawk. She wanted to be far away before Lucas returned one last time to convince her to help Joe. She didn't expect less than for him to grovel, and she couldn't stomach it if he did.

After her business with Matthews concluded, she'd return to investigate the underground cavern. She hoped by then Lucas would have given up his pursuit and wouldn't expect her to return to the area. But first, more important matters needed dealt with.

Chapter 18

Lucas drove from the scenic view, much like a dog ran with its tail between its legs after losing a fight. His emotions wrestled between severe heartbreak, worry, and fear. The heartbreak he suffered alone, but his worry and fear hovered around Lydia's safety and wellbeing. Although she was strong in many respects, emotionally she teetered on the brink of shattering from the mental pressure of finding where she belonged in the world or if she'd ever find the stability she sought. Like her, he realized her rightful place might never be found.

After Lydia had killed in self-defense she wasn't able to accept that she was anything less than an assassin. And now that she sought to exact justice, she was without limits to what she might do or how many people she'd kill and feel justified by doing so. Her rage couldn't be reined back under control. Lucas feared the news reports he might see over the next few days about an untraceable serial killer. He believed that she could kill without leaving any evidence pointing back to her.

What Joe quickly told him over the phone was nothing compared to his confrontation with Lydia. Never had Lucas felt so distanced from the woman he loved and cherished. Her abduction in Nevada, weighted him with loss and uncertainty, which hurt far more than he could bear. But this —her deliberately telling him not to find her after she ended their relationship—was even worse than he imagined pain could be.

Lucas wanted to drive out the image of her firing the warning shot just inches above his head and the second shot near his foot. But the cold, calloused look in her eyes was fierce, calculated, and chilled him even now as he recalled the darkness in her stare. Her threat wasn't a bluff. When Lydia said that she'd kill him, he had no doubt she'd do it. Perhaps he had foolishly ignored what she kept telling him she was—a ruthless assassin.

It unnerved him that this was the woman he had slept beside for months. He wondered if she ever contemplated killing him during the past six months. Was that part of the reason for why she had left? He wondered if she had considered it. And if so, how often?

What possessed him, after all this time, to believe she was more than an experiment created by Idris? Indeed, viewing her sleeping nude form through the glass incubation chamber at TransGenCorp was enough to bring out the wicked lust in any man. Her face and body radiated perfection in every detail. Lust, however, wasn't the reason he had chosen to be with her.

Early on, after Lydia was released from the chamber and evaluated by physicians at the hospital, she kept him at a distance. He understood she did this primarily because she didn't have any memories or a family history. In fact, she didn't have any history at all, other than what Idris had programmed her brain to believe. Trying to develop a relationship with her might have been a mistake that he still didn't want to accept. He did love her. He wanted the very best for her, but he was beginning to understand he didn't fit into her life. Perhaps no one did or ever would. That she roamed alone saddened him most of all.

As he drove to Joe's house, he thought of her smile, her unfailing laughter when he caught her off guard with a witty joke or observation. But since the abduction, her laughter faded. She brooded within darkness that he feared. She no longer evolved toward being an optimistic person with real dreams and ambitions. She stood at a destined crossroads, but instead of taking a path toward light and love, she veered toward rage and revenge. A path to self-destruction. He couldn't follow her without tarnishing himself for the rest of his life. If he couldn't follow, she placed herself where he had no power to rescue her.

Lucas wiped tears from his cheeks. As he slowly placed his right hand on the steering wheel, the scar across his palm brought back a youthful memory he'd never forget nor forsake.

At summer camp, he had met Joe Shadow-talker. They hit it off from the beginning. At the age of twelve, they became blood brothers. Although just boys, Joe held a wealth of information far beyond his years that Lucas found amazing. Joe was a mystic, the son of a shaman. All aspects of nature were his family. He understood and saw things that Lucas didn't. Even with the tender explanations Joe offered, Lucas only picked up the basics. His ears weren't keen to the spiritual realm Joe visited.

For Joe to ask his help meant something had gone awry. Lucas lived six hours away, but if he pushed it, he could reach Joe's ranch in four.

Chapter 19

Joe stood outside his ranch house with his hands stuffed in his pockets. His brothers leaned against the fence behind him. The sheriff talked to the coroner for a few minutes after Joe and his brothers cleared the house of the rattlesnakes. None of the paramedics or officers set foot inside until the reptiles were captured and removed.

Sheriff Sterling approached Joe.

"Mind if we have a word?" he asked Joe. "In private."

Joe nodded. "Not at all, Sheriff."

Sterling walked up the gravel drive out of earshot of Joe's brothers. The sheriff was sixty-six years old, thin and tall, and with facial wrinkles defined by the sun and his years of wisdom. He rubbed his hand over his stubbled chin. His brow furrowed as he thought. He pushed the tip of his cowboy hat back and looked directly into Joe's eyes. "Who'd you piss off, Joe?"

Joe shrugged. "No one to my knowledge, sir."

"Hell, somebody wants you dead. We found ten rattlers inside your house. *Ten*. Certainly not intended as a house-warming gift, son. I know we have rattlers all over the area, but the damned things don't roam in packs. And from what we can tell, whoever put them there are responsible for the death of your girlfriend."

Joe gave a solemn nod. "I realize that."

"How well did you know her?"

"Misty? I just met her last night. I didn't have much time to get to know her."

"She didn't seem too shy to shack up with you."

Joe gave an embarrassed smile and shook his head. "We were quite drunk."

Sterling rested his hands on his belt and stared at the ground. "How often do you do something like this?"

"First time I've been to a bar in about three years. First woman I've been with during that time, too. I don't go out much."

"Where'd you pick her up? Which bar?"

"The Waterhole Bar and Grill."

Sterling shook his head. "Joe, you know that bar's reputation toward Native Americans."

"That was years ago."

"Granted, son, it was *worse* years ago. That kind of hostility might fade but it never completely goes away. Especially with some of the racist bikers that frequent there."

"I know, but no one gave us a hard time."

"Did you notice anyone at the bar that might have been watching the two of you? Like maybe a jealous ex-boyfriend or something."

"No, not that I noticed. Like I said . . . I was drunk by the time she and I started talking."

"No problems in the parking lot?"

"No, sir."

"Maybe they tailed you home."

Joe shook his head. "I'd remember seeing headlights if anyone followed us. The moon wasn't out, so they couldn't have driven without headlights on."

"Since they tore your house apart looking for something, she might have been an innocent victim. Any idea what they're looking for?"

"No," he lied.

Sterling studied him for several seconds. "You're sure?"

"I live a modest life. I can't think of anything worth taking."

"They want something, and if they didn't find it, they'll be back. You can be certain of that. Your life is in danger."

"I'll be careful."

"Well, think about your situation real hard, Joe. Real hard. I'll be back in a few days once the toxicology report comes in. If you remember something before then, give me a call."

"I will."

"And should you see any suspicious activities or people, call the department. We'll get to the bottom of this. I certainly don't want to find you like Misty."

"I appreciate it, sir."

Sterling nodded, tipped his cowboy hat, and headed to his squad car.

After the sheriff drove away, Joe's brothers surrounded him.

His oldest brother, Owl-hunter, gave Joe a firm stare. "Joe, who did this?"

"I don't know."

"Who was the girl?"

"Misty."

"Misty?"

Joe nodded. "Her last name was Litman."

"She from around here?"

"I honestly don't know. I met her last night."

Owl-hunter looked at their other two brothers. "We need to know more about her. Joe, what did you do with the strange skull at the excavation? You did rebury it?"

Joe looked away.

"Joe," Owl-hunter said with deep disappointment in his voice. "I warned you. It's a bad omen. You should have left it where you found it."

"It's not a bad omen."

Owl-hunter frowned. "Get the skull. We take it back to the excavation and rebury it."

"No. It's far too late for that."

"Why?"

"I believe that's why they tried to kill me. They know I have the skull."

"Then we take it back and let them dig it up."

Joe folded his arms. "If we do that, we're all as good as dead."

"Why do you say that?"

"Once they get it, they'll kill anyone that knows it exists."

"Same type of people who took Lucas' wife?"

Joe shrugged. "That'd be my guess."

Owl-hunter shook his head and gritted his teeth. "Where is it?"

"Somewhere safe."

"While we all live in jeopardy?"

"Let's hope it doesn't come to that."

"It has come to that, brother. Your girlfriend is dead. They'll come again and more relentlessly next time."

"I know."

"Then we bait a trap."

"Where?"

"Back at the pit."

Joe nodded.

"I'll call you later this evening. Tomorrow, we wait for them. Make sure you bring the skull."

"I will."

"Until then, keep your senses keen."

Joe smiled. "I always do."

"Not last night you didn't."

"I know. That won't happen again."

"You might not be so lucky next time, brother. Be safe."

Joe smiled weakly and as they walked away, he said, "You, too."

Chapter 20

Lucas pulled into Joe's driveway. The coroner's van backed onto the main road and drove away.

Joe sat on the porch steps whittling. His hands gently slid the knife across the wood. Spirals of pulp spindled and dropped on the steps between his feet. His eyes were deep in thought while he worked his finishing touches. He turned the sculpture in his fingers, blew away small bits of loose wood dust, and then he admired his creation. From the piece of live oak, he'd carved an impressive bird. A raven.

Lucas stepped from his vehicle and approached the house. Joe met him halfway. They clasped right hands, leaned forward, and clapped one another's back in a fierce brotherly hug.

Joe stepped back and stared into his friend's eyes. "You look as deeply troubled as I am. Is everything all right?"

Lucas sighed and forced a smile.

Joe motioned toward the porch. "Sit. I'll go grab you a beer, and you tell me what's going on."

"You called me for support, but I'm afraid I won't do you much good."

"Nonsense," Joe said. "Your problems are my problems."

Lucas nodded. "The same goes for you, my friend."

"Take a seat. I'll be right back."

Joe hurried back with an open bottle of Budweiser and a bottle of water. He handed the beer to Lucas. Lucas took a long drink and placed the bottle on the step beside him.

"What happened, Luke?"

"Lydia left me."

Joe frowned with concern. His eyes softened. "I'm sorry. Did she give any reason why?"

"Yes."

"Do you think this is temporary?"

"I don't know. I've never seen her like this, Joe."

"What happened?"

"She's never got past killing those men at her farm, or killing the security guard at Desert Labs, even though it was an accident. The guilt has weighed heavier on her."

"Killing a person is difficult to get over, Luke, even in self-defense."

Lucas shook his head, pulled out his cigarettes, and struck a match on the step. "You don't understand. She's going after Matthews to kill him."

"The man she beat to a pulp at Grayson Enterprises? He's in prison, isn't he?"

"He was. He escaped today."

"I see. And if she succeeds? What then?"

"He's not the only target."

Joe frowned. "There are others?"

Lucas nodded.

"Who?"

"She wouldn't tell me."

"You tried to stop her?"

"Yes, but not successfully though. She shot at me, Joe. Twice."

Joe glanced into Lucas' eyes and shook his head. "You're serious?"

"Dead serious. She fired one shot over my head and another at my foot when I stepped closer. She aimed at my chest and warned me to back off. I did."

"You really believe she'd kill you?"

"The cold look in her eyes indicated she would. I have no doubt she'd have killed me had I taken another step. I've never seen her so full of uncontrollable rage."

Joe sipped his water while he thought. A hawk circled and landed on a power line. "I still remember how she looked when she was ready to kill Matthews. You barely coaxed her out of it then."

"I know."

"But, it's like she has a kill switch. You said something right and she snapped out of it."

"I know." Lucas shook his head. "But she's deeper now. She's lost all self-control. She wants all people like Matthews dead."

"Has she acted irrational since you returned home after her abduction?"

"I honestly thought she was healing mentally, that everything was going to be okay. We went to bed last night, and she held me close until I went to sleep. She felt so warm and comforting. Without warning, I awoke and found her note this morning. I tracked her GPS and found her a few miles away. When I approached, she shot at me."

Joe clasped Lucas' shoulder. "She seems to have gotten progressively worse. You mentioned she was a lab project, that she was programmed to kill. Is there no way to reverse what those scientists created her to do?"

"I have no idea."

"It'll work itself out."

"I hope so," Lucas said. "I saw the coroner leaving. What happened?"

Joe explained Misty's death, the ten rattlers, and his house being ransacked.

"Ten rattlesnakes? Damn," Lucas said. "My entire house would have been full of bullet holes."

Joe grinned. "They're more timid than most believe."

"Sure, but they have the fangs to back that up."

"We caught all ten without incident. I'm certain they'll be more satisfied when we release them in a gulch."

"You're returning them to the wild?"

"Of course."

Lucas looked at Joe and changed the subject. "I wasn't aware you were seeing anyone."

Joe shook his head. "No, I had just met her."

"You hit it off that well?"

"Honestly, I wouldn't have taken her home had I not been so drunk and lonely."

"Nothing wrong with finding a partner, even temporarily."

Joe's eyes saddened. "Apparently last night was the wrong night for her. She'd still be alive if I'd not been eager to bed her."

"You think they would have placed the rattlers anyway?"

Joe took a sip of water, set the bottle on the porch, and nodded. "I know they would have. She was in the wrong place and fell victim to their plot."

"Do you have any idea what they're looking for?"

"I know exactly what they want."

"Did you tell the police?"

"No."

"Why not?"

"No sense putting their lives at risk, too."

"I don't understand. How could handing over whatever these people want endanger the police?"

Joe smiled evenly. "What I possess is probably worth as much as Lydia is to the people after her."

"Government officials?"

"That's my guess."

"So these people didn't find it?"

"No. I have it hidden somewhere safe."

Lucas stood and stretched. "Do you mind showing me what's so valuable to these people?"

"I don't have it here."

Joe grabbed Lucas' empty bottle and his and placed them on the porch table. He walked to the rugged fence and leaned on the top slat. Joe's black appaloosa stood in the center of the pasture lot eating dry hay.

Lucas stepped beside Joe. "Did the sheriff's department find any tire tracks around your house that weren't made by your truck?"

"If there were any, they probably were driven over by the patrol cars, the ambulance, and the coroner's van. They spent a lot more time checking for fingerprints and worrying about accidentally finding more rattlers. My guess is that whoever put the snakes inside the house parked their vehicle a good distance away and walked."

"So no signs of forced entry when you arrived home with Misty?"

"No."

Lucas folded his arms. "Care to take a short walk and look for footprints?"

Joe shrugged. "It can't hurt."

"Who knows? We might turn up something useful." Lucas stopped at his vehicle and grabbed his gun from beneath the front seat.

Joe frowned. "Is that necessary?"

"Joe, I truly believe rattlers are the least of your troubles. Besides, they may still be watching your house since they didn't find whatever it is that they are looking for."

"Unfortunately, bro, you're probably right."

"If we don't find any footprints, I'd like you to ride with me to the bar where you were last night. We might be able to question other patrons from yesterday that can provide clues."

Joe clasped Lucas' shoulder. "Well, I'm glad to see you've jumped in with both feet."

"I have to, Joe, or thinking about Lydia will tear me apart."

"I'm glad you came. Things with Lydia will work themselves out."

"I hope so."

"One way or the other, it will be okay. You'll see."

Lucas followed Joe up a narrow gully that had been washed out from the last heavy rain. Creosote bushes with yellow flowers thrived along the dry, rocky path. Several of their branches were bent and broken. Joe inspected them.

"This is the path they took," Joe said. "Looks like they used scrub branches to sweep away their footprints."

At the top of the gulch the terrain leveled off. Lucas pointed. "They drove a heavy four by four through here. Military, perhaps."

Joe gave a solemn nod. "It is as my brothers and I feared."

"What do you have that they want?"

"I'd have to show you. You wouldn't believe me otherwise."

"I know you'd never lied to me."

Joe smiled. "With this, though, seeing is believing."

"We'll take my SUV and follow these tracks."

"Sure, but we go get the relic first."

"No," Lucas said. "Keep it hidden until we find out who is after you. If we find them and you have the item with you, they'll kill us. We need something for leverage."

Chapter 21

Steven Matthews, using the alias Edward DuPont, sat in the chair with his eyes closed. An anesthesiologist checked the I.V. line and monitor at the side of the bed. On a metal tray lay a syringe.

Dr. Mordia stood near the computer monitor. Her dark eyes held depth, mystery. Her thick black hair was pulled back in a tight bun and tucked beneath a blue sterile cap. During their first interview, Matthews noticed she was reserved and somewhat timid. Even then, she kept her hair hidden.

Although Matthews seldom found women infatuating, he imagined how she might look if she let her long, flowing hair down. Applying a dark foundation to her face could make her a seductress, if she chose to be, and overcame her inhibition, but the more he thought about it, any makeup hid her smooth, unblemished complexion. That would be a shame, a crime. No, her true beauty was exactly how she portrayed it with a modest touch of lipstick and eyeliner.

"Mr. DuPont," Dr. Mordia said with her thick Indian accent. "Are you certain you wish to go through with this? You cannot undo this procedure."

Matthews watched her thick lips move as she spoke, and for a moment, he was captivated by her voice and smile.

"Mr. DuPont?" she said, allowing a flattered smile.

He shook his head. "Yes. Sorry."

She was successful in doing two things no other person had before. She made his face flush red from embarrassment and gotten a one-word apology from him.

"Are you completely satisfied with your decision?" she asked.

Matthews looked at the computerized image of what his new face after plastic surgery would be. The new nose and narrower chin altered his appearance enough to keep him unnoticed by the authorities and Grayson. Hiding without a new face wasn't something he'd mentally survive. His scientific projects demanded he be in the public eye to garner financial support and notoriety, but without the plastic surgery he didn't have the freedom to move from place to place. Once recognized, federal agents would quickly apprehend him.

His ego demanded that he receive the proper adoration from the public and the scientific world. His vanity abhorred superficial qualities. He didn't desire his fame to be associated with striking good looks because he didn't covet gracing the cover of *GQ*. He wanted to be famous for his scientific innovations. Intelligence was more appealing than physical attributes. Not to say that he wasn't a handsome man before the surgery. He was. And after the surgery, he'd have no problem attracting women. He made certain the tweaked alterations were still appealing.

Once the surgery scars healed, he'd dye his hair and use contacts to change his eye color.

Finally, Matthews nodded. "I'm ready."

"Any further questions before you go under?"

"How long before the bandages can be removed?"

Mordia smiled. "With today's technology, usually only a few days."

"Good. Proceed."

"Very well, Mr. DuPont," Mordia said.

She nodded at the anesthesiologist. He injected the contents of the syringe into the I.V.

Matthews closed his eyes, took a deep breath, and waited for the medicine to take effect.

Chapter 22

Grayson Enterprises

A SILVER CADILLAC with mirrored windows pulled through the security gate at Grayson Enterprises. The driver eased the car along the winding blacktop to the rear parking lot. The car parked in the space reserved for Senator Ralph Johnson.

The senator stepped from his car and pressed his thumb against the car security panel, which locked the doors and set the alarm. He nervously glanced at his watch and walked up the concrete sidewalk.

Bright orange-red foliage covered the spreading Japanese maples along the lavishly landscaped quad. The curving concrete path meandered through a slender forest of weeping cherry trees, lilacs, palm trees, and hardy junipers.

Johnson wished he could take the time to inhale the beauty of the landscape, but since Grayson owned the property, it was nothing more than the glossy peel of a rotten apple—spectacular to behold, but the core was filled with putrid, runny goo.

He hated visiting Grayson, but his seat in the California Senate depended on appeasing the wealthy entrepreneur and his unusual political demands. To do less abated Grayson's financial support against Johnson's rivals at the upcoming election.

Large polished MarQuebes, each weighing a ton or more, were massive centerpieces in each flowerbed at the building entrances. MarQuebes were the first discovered gems from the exploration of Mars. The stones were ruby-red but direct light revealed an inner purplish hue. The contrasting colors made them a prized stone. Since Grayson was the first and only man to stake a claim on the Martian mining rights, he controlled the market without any fear of competition.

Grayson had invested billions into his Mars excavation projects and reaped one thousand times what he expended. With his endeavors, though no one dared breathe the words aloud, but Grayson *owned* Mars, Deimos, and the crashed remains of Phobos. His status wrought power, numerous friends, and a vast number of jealous enemies.

Johnson despised Grayson as much as he possessed a treasured need to be considered his friend. Grayson's greed ran deep, and Johnson's desire to feast from the table of plenty overwhelmed his rationality to flee and reclaim his soul. Grayson lined Johnson's pockets with money. The senator understood that no one stood in Grayson's way. Opposing Grayson brought painful repercussions, both physically and financially. Sometimes death.

Entering through the front brass doors, two muscled security guards greeted him. These guards were massive muscled men with dark shades and earpieces. They kept their suit jackets open, revealing their guns. Their massive size intimidated Johnson more than the guns. He doubted these men ever needed to use guns.

Johnson stepped through a metal detector. The green light cleared him. He placed his palm against the print scanner. A line of green flashed on the panel.

A computerized voice stated, "Welcome, Senator Johnson."

Johnson turned. A guard escorted him to the elevator. When the silver doors opened, Johnson stepped inside where another guard waited.

After the doors closed, he nervously nodded at the solemn guard. The man ignored his kind gesture and stared straight ahead at the doors. His silence chilled Johnson.

Lately, Johnson entertained the idea of retiring. Anything was better than facing the pressure of visiting Grayson. He imagined the horrendous pain these bodyguards could inflict should he ever piss Grayson off. And knowing Grayson, death wouldn't come quickly.

After the elevator opened, Johnson stepped onto the plush carpeted hall and reluctantly followed another guard. They turned left at the intersecting hallway. They stopped at the secretary's desk.

Without looking up, she said, "Mr. Grayson will see you, Senator Johnson. He's been expecting you."

He looked past her. Large tinted windows opened to the most brilliant view of the blue ocean below. The sensation of being on top of the world ran through him.

"This way, sir," the guard said.

Johnson followed the guard to Grayson's office. The man opened the door and Johnson crossed the room. Grayson stood from behind his desk and extended his hand.

"Good you could make it," Grayson said.

Johnson wrung his hands. His nervousness and frustration built. In exasperation, he blurted, "Sir, what do you need? I have other appointments."

Grayson turned and glared. His tailored Armani suit displayed his muscled arms, chest, back, and shoulders. He was much bigger than his largest guard.

"Do you? Are they as generous in funding your cause as I am?"

Johnson looked at Grayson's feet. "No sir. They're not *that* important."

"Good. I need more prisoners to mine on Mars. The preliminary projects are going well. With more, we'll be able to establish the settlements quicker."

"More? That's not possible. I've freed as many prisoners as I can to prevent more ethical protests from occurring. Besides, training is expensive."

"Since when are you worried about the finances? I've always covered the costs."

"But I just had seventy men released to you last year for your Deimos project."

Grayson nodded. "I know. Something's amiss there."

"What do you mean?"

"I've not received any communication from Dr. Frank Carter in over a week. Perhaps their satellite transmission is on the fritz. I don't know. But I need to train another seventy prisoners, just in case."

"Mr. Grayson, exactly what are you trying to accomplish?"

Grayson frowned.

Johnson cleared his throat. "I thought your goal was to settle Mars and establish a civilization."

"It is."

"Why not start recruiting qualified people to settle Mars instead of more prisoners?"

"We must set the groundwork first. Why endanger decent, honest people with the drudgery required to establish housing and businesses? You know how overpopulated the prison system is. I remove them by employing them on Mars. They are paid excellent wages and deeded land once we've succeeded in settling outside the mines."

"So you're proposing to later settle decent people with the ex-cons inhabiting Mars?" Johnson asked. "I don't believe you'll find too many eager people wanting to neighbor with the criminals doing your groundwork."

"Even the worst of men can be broken through labor," Grayson said.

"Careful," Johnson replied. "I'm already leading the council to believe that you aren't enacting slave labor."

Grayson laughed. "Whatever it takes."

"I'm serious."

"So am I," Grayson said with an intense glare. "Keep me happy, and your seat in Congress remains safe. Understood?"

Johnson stared at his feet. "Yes, sir."

"Now, what help has the CIA been in tracking Matthews?"

"He's off the radar," Johnson replied. "Not a trace of him. But it's highly unlikely that he'd even attempt to infiltrate your organization again."

"Never underestimate an enemy."

Johnson nodded. *I've thought the same thing for years.*

Grayson turned toward the large windows and crossed his arms, watching the ocean waves. "Should they discover Matthews' whereabouts, have them contact me."

"Yes, sir."

Johnson stood a few minutes longer.

"That's all, senator. Contact the state warden and let me know when I can expect the prisoners to prep for the mines."

Johnson turned and exited Grayson's office.

Chapter 23

Matthews awakened in a small room with dim lighting. He touched the bandages on his face. The material was thin, moist, and warm. He was still groggy from the anesthesia, but he didn't feel any pain due to the morphine drip attached to his I.V.

Dr. Mordia stepped into the recovery room and stood at the end of his bed. The anesthesiologist nodded and walked out the door. She folded her hands and rested them at her waist. A slight smile curled her thick lips. She grabbed his chart off the end of the bed and flipped a page upward.

"The surgery went well," she said. "In a few days, the bandages will be off and you can show the world your new face."

Matthews wanted to smile but thought better of it. "Dr. Mordia, what if I told you I possess a medicinal product that heals incisions faster and painlessly, would you venture investing? There's nothing else like it in the world. It's guaranteed to make you a very rich woman."

She held the clipboard to her chest. Her dark eyes beamed with interest and a bit of skepticism. "Maybe. After you've paid the bill for your operation."

"Well," Matthews said softly. "About that. How about you deduct my bill from what you'll need to invest."

Mordia's dark eyes narrowed. Her jaw tightened. "You *can't* pay? You told me that you had more than enough money . . . You promised cash!"

"I have plenty of money. I do. But—"

"But what, Mr. DuPont?"

"My accounts are all currently frozen."

"Frozen!" The clipboard fell to the floor. Her hands balled into tight fists with whitened knuckles. The beauty of her exotic features dimmed beneath her seething anger.

"Calm down, doctor. You're going to get your money. I promise."

"How?"

"Do you own a plane?" he asked.

"No. Why?"

"I have one hundred thousand dollars cash in a safety deposit box."

"Where?"

"San Diego."

Mordia rolled her eyes. Her thick lips quivered as she attempted to rein in her growing anger. "I should've gotten the money up front. I suppose the best thing for me to do is call the police."

Matthews straightened in the bed. "Yes, doctor, by all means you could do that. After all, I'd be inclined to do the same thing if the tables were reversed. But, as it is, I'd advise against it."

She laughed while taking her phone from her jacket pocket. "I imagine you would."

"Fine," he replied evenly. "Call them, and then let's see how well they react when I tell them that you've been doing plastic surgery for quite some time without a valid medical license."

Her eyes widened. "How do you know that?"

"I've been in prison for a while. I got access to computers once a week. I researched you and your background. A couple of bad lawsuits caused the medical board to pull your license. That explains *why* you're operating out of a strip mall cosmetics shop through underground channels. I'm surprised the authorities haven't already come for you. Such a shame, too. From the results I've seen, you're quite good at your profession."

Mordia stooped and picked up the clipboard. Her anger faded and fear took over. "I worry everyday that they'll come arrest me."

"Listen, you help me and you'll never have to worry about that again. You'll have more money than you've ever imagined. I promise."

Mordia sat on the edge of his bed and stared at the floor. Her doe-like eyes were wet with tears. "I'm really good at what I do. The lawsuits came from two people who had bad Botox injections and nearly died. The Botox had been relabeled from a black market supplier. I really didn't know, but I was treated as though I had intentionally bought it illegally."

Matthews leaned forward and patted a gentle hand on her arm. "I know. I read about it."

She frowned. "Is that why you chose me? So you could bribe me into doing the surgery and you could, as people say, weasel out of it?"

"No. I chose you because you're like me."

"Like you?" Mordia said, looking into his eyes. "In what way?"

He nodded. "You and I have lost so much. We've lost our reputations due to mistakes, and you had nothing else to lose. I want to change that."

"How?"

"I want to start this business partnership with you and give you another chance at success."

"What do you need me to do?"

"Can you hire someone with a private jet?" Matthews asked.

"Yes."

"How soon?"

"You really need to wait before traveling," She said.

"How long?"

"A couple days at least."

"Seriously? No sooner?"

"I think you should rest."

Matthews offered a small shrug. "That's why I want a private jet. I can rest aboard one. Flying relaxes me and gives me time to think. An unthinking mind is a dangerous thing, but I suppose the same holds true for anyone who ponders endlessly about ways to better the world. After all, not everyone is on the same page when it comes to what is best for society."

Mordia frowned with confusion. "Whom are you hiding from?"

"Have you not seen the news?"

"No."

"I imagine there's a great manhunt going for me on right now."

"Why? Did you kill someone?"

Matthews shook his head. The bandages made him resemble a mummy. "No, quite the opposite."

"I don't understand."

"I need to make another confession to you."

Her eyes revealed her nervousness. "What?"

"My real name is Steven Matthews. Research that name and you'll know everything I've done and why I was in prison."

Mordia took a deep breath and closed her eyes. Slowly she exhaled and opened her eyes. "You make it difficult for people to trust you."

Matthews chuckled. "I escaped from prison and sought plastic surgery so people won't recognize me. Lying about my name was just a precaution. I came clean so trust has to start somewhere between us. Right?"

"I suppose so."

"Of course I'm right. I didn't even have to tell you, but I need you to engage your full trust in me. So, we have a deal?"

"I take you to San Diego, and you'll give me cash from your safety deposit box to pay for your surgery?"

Matthews nodded.

"You'll pay the sixty thousand you owe from your money?"

"All the cash in the box is yours."

"The full one hundred thousand?"

"Yes."

"What's the catch?"

"No catch."

"You're giving me nearly double what you owe. It seems too good to be true. Situations like that might leave me dead in an alley somewhere. That's a lot of money."

"It's not the cash that I need. It's the other stuff in the deposit box that I want."

"What stuff?"

"Something that will make you and I both wealthier."

"The healing agent?" she asked.

"Yes. But I need you to be the one to go into the bank and gather the contents together for me."

Mordia's eyebrows rose. "Me?"

"I can't exactly go into a bank with all these bandages on my face. That's certain to draw unwanted attention."

She smiled with a slight nod while thinking about the situation. "Yes, that would definitely draw attention."

"Make a call to get us a flight to San Diego. And while you're at it, order us some champagne. We can take some time to celebrate our future success together."

"I will. Right now, you get some rest."

Chapter 24

Mitch's arms ached. The longer his arms remained tied above his head, the worse the pain became. The stabbing sensations reminded him of the one time he braved acupuncture therapy, but that experience was surprisingly pleasant and relaxing, unlike his present situation. He worried that eventually his fatigued muscles would fail to hold him. The strain might tear his muscles or pop his shoulders out of socket.

Of course, his bigger fear was whether he'd survive whatever Sheba and the police officer intended to do with him. The silence around him indicated that he was again alone in the rundown cellar.

The officer recognized him, which meant Mitch's snooping had caught someone's attention. But whose?

From Sheba's brief conversation with the officer, he was willing to allow Mitch to leave Salem and somewhat angry that she took him captive. For some unexplained reason, someone else made Sheba intervene to *prevent* Mitch from leaving. Possibly a powerful and prominent town member viewed him as a threat and wanted him immobilized.

When Mitch had arrived in Salem, his clairvoyance detected a darkness looming in the town, but for the first time in his life, he was unable to narrow down the force's central location or its origin. Whatever it was seemed aware of his presence and successfully blocked his ability to locate it. His sixth sense was often reliable in the past, but he'd never dealt with such an opposing force from someone possessed by a stronger power.

During Mitch's initial interview process with Kat and Lucian, he was impressed and intrigued when he met Kyle. Kyle's ability to speak telepathically was unexpected. At first glance, Mitch thought Kyle suffered from some type of disfiguring birth defect. He was saddened to learn that scientific experimentations and torture were the reasons for his condition. Few people would have had the savvy will to fight and survive the external environmental factors like Kyle had in order to live.

Kyle's determination was enough inspiration for Mitch to maintain hope that he would somehow find a way to escape and survive.

Mitch tried several times to mentally reach out and nudge Kyle's psyche but either the distance was too great or Kyle's psychic powers were still spiraling downward. Kyle slept more than normal and Dr. Brockton kept expressing his concern for Kyle's regression. From what Kat had told Mitch, Kyle had been advancing forward in his mental precognition tests for more than a year. Then his progress halted and his mental strength was swept backwards without any scientific explanation. Mitch wondered if Kyle suffered more from fatigue rather than any actual loss of power. Brockton's eagerness to see how great Kyle's abilities were might have made Kyle rebel and seek to sleep in order to recuperate. Some of the feats Kyle was capable of doing drained vast amounts of energy.

A sharp wind whistled through the weathered building.

Overhead floorboards creaked, whined. Someone was inside the building.

Footsteps thudded softly. The person crossed the room above and then more creaking occurred when the intruder came down the aged steps. The footsteps silenced.

Mitch raised his head and squinted, trying to see through the darkness. The puffiness around his left eye burned. He could barely open it.

He felt so cold and wished was dressed.

His teeth chattered.

The lacerations on his chest burned.

A warm hand suddenly touched his back and his body tightened. Bright light from a flashlight forced him to close his eyes.

"Are you awake?" Sheba ran her hand along his back, across his ribs, and then rested it right over his heart. She smiled. "Good."

Mitch peered at her. Her brown eyes held a wolfish glint as she studied him.

"How do you feel?" she asked.

"I've had better days," he replied softly.

Her hand patted his cheek with gentle slaps before firmly grasping his chin and forcing him to look into her eyes. She held the flashlight for his benefit. With her abilities, he didn't think she had a problem seeing in the dark. Most animals could see even in the darkest of night.

Her eyes held an eerie glow. Mitch was afraid to look into them, but even more afraid to break the connection because looking away might offend her. He didn't want to find out what price he'd pay for angering her. Entertaining her with submissiveness could serve a better purpose—the possibility of escape when she least expected it, but only if he proved himself willing to give her the dominance an alpha wolf desired. That could work provided she sought wolf hierarchy more than accepting her human role.

"I worked you over worse than I thought." Her voice held a slight, cheerful tone. Her fingernail dug into one of the cuts that she had gifted him. He winced and gritted his teeth. "I'm sorry. It's just when I *change*, I tend to lose my self control."

Mitch coughed to clear his dry throat. "You'd have no problem becoming an actress in Hollywood. You know that? Your performance completely fooled me. I actually took pity for you and believed your story."

"Pity?" She huffed but her tone never darkened. Her eyes narrowed. "A good sob story never fails. Especially when a man is trying to impress a woman."

"That's what you thought I was doing? Trying to impress you?"

"Weren't you?" Her eyes searched his. Even with her hard countenance, he still read the hurt in her eyes. She was more fragile than she wished others to know.

"No. I wanted to find out what really happened and why people are being killed with such savagery."

"Yet, you wanted me with you *every* step of the way. To *protect* me because you thought I was weak. Except you became the unknowing victim."

Mitch stared at the smirk on her face and became angry. "No. I kept trying to get you to remain behind. I told you that I wanted to check it out.

So it was all a bunch of *lies*? What you said about Gloria and the boys never even happened?"

Sheba looked away. Her smile disappeared. Her eyes became sad again.

"Of course it happened," she whispered. "I didn't lie. At least not about that."

"Then why did you lead me out here? Just to torture me?"

"You wanted to get information about the murders, right?" she asked.

"Yes."

Sheba sighed. "Well, you'll have all the firsthand information available soon enough. The unfortunate thing is that you won't be able to tell anyone else about it."

With nervous hands she lit a cigarette. She took a quick draw and exhaled a stream of smoke.

"So I'm going to die?" Mitch asked.

"Everyone dies . . . eventually."

Mitch frowned. "I know you want people to believe you're tough, but I know that's not the truth. You're actually a scared little girl."

Sheba's jaws tightened. "Careful. You're getting awfully brave and stupid. You're not really in a good position to needle me. If I had a mirror I could show you how tough I am. The bruises on your face are evidence."

Mitch shook his head. "You didn't do that. What you became did that."

"We're one and the same."

"Are you?"

"Yes."

Even though her voice maintained some aggression, her eyes revealed that she *was* indeed frightened. Mitch tried to read more, but she had a way of shielding her thoughts and emotions. Her psyche fought her inner beast that wished to possess her, which added more walls he needed to penetrate before he could actually reach the scared young woman hiding in her icy palace of turmoil. Mitch's only hope was to chisel away at her hardened exterior. If he could wedge inside, he might discover her true fears and weaknesses.

"And what is it that you become?" he asked.

Sheba crossed her arms and tapped the ash from her cigarette while staring at the dirt floor. "I don't really know."

"Will I become what you are?"

"Why should you?"

Mitch glanced down at the laceration she had reopened with her fingernail. "You cut me and drew blood. Am I contaminated?"

She pursed her lips. "You watch too much television."

"So you cannot make others like yourself?"

Sheba shook her head. "To the best of my knowledge, we don't have the ability to spawn new beasts with our blood or fingernails. Otherwise, there'd be hundreds of us."

"How do you do transform?"

She swallowed hard. "I wish I knew so I could figure out how to stop it."

"Have you always been able to do this?"

"No. I don't think so, but I'm not sure."

"Did you kill Gloria?" he asked in a stern voice.

"No! She was my best friend. I'd never harm her."

Mitch shook his head. "Maybe it was an accident and you've blocked it from memory."

Sheba's eyes narrowed and her voice deepened. "No. I never hurt her and I won't."

Had he managed to inflict the first chink into her aura?

"Won't?" he asked with a gentle smile. "So she's still alive?"

Sheba shifted her feet back and forth. "I meant to say that I *didn't*."

"What about the boys from your class? They weren't your friends. Not really. Did you go into a rage and kill them?"

"I'm not a murderer," she whispered. Her eyes indicated her mind was racing to recall the events of that night. She nervously scratched her cheek with the spider tattoo.

"How can you be certain?" Mitch asked in a soothing tone. "You don't know what you become. Do you remember what you did after you changed back?"

Her eyes flicked to him and she changed the subject. The little girl innocence was suddenly replaced with cold, cruel animalistic hardness. "I remember hitting you and it's tempting to do it again just to shut your mouth."

"And after you hit me? What happened then? I don't remember because your first punch knocked me unconscious."

"I'd say that *that's* pretty tough." She sneered.

"I'm not questioning your strength. Strong people can still be terrified on the inside. You're afraid of something . . . or someone."

"I'm out of here." She turned to walk away.

"Wait!"

"*What* do you want from me?"

"The police officer. Who is he?"

"Officer Parker? He's not the one you should worry about."

Mitch adjusted his feet, trying to alleviate the shoulder strain. "I gathered that much from your conversation."

Her amused smile returned. "So you were awake?"

"Barely."

"I thought you were. Your breathing gave it away."

"You could tell by my breathing?"

"I have the ability to detect a lot of things. I can smell fear in your sweat and hear it in your rapid heartbeat. These are things I can do. And I'm surprised that you fell so quickly into following me to the cemetery. After all, *you're* supposed to be investigating the bizarre and yet, you never recognized me as a danger. Not much is more bizarre than me. Perhaps your interest was more in what was under my skirt?"

Mitch swallowed hard and looked down.

"Just like any man."

"No, I'm not," he whispered.

"I told you that you needed to accept the paranormal in order to understand how things work around here, didn't I?"

He nodded.

"You never tapped into what you think you possess. But I guess you're not as sensitive to the paranormal as you had hoped. Although . . . should you live a while longer, you might discover other strange things about this area you didn't expect."

"I detect lots of smaller forces roaming near us now."

Sheba smiled. "Ghosts have a lot of haunts in Salem."

Mitch frowned. "I also perceived something much darker and powerful in Salem the second I arrived, but I've never been able to track it. If you'd let me, I could try to help you. Maybe even get you out of this town."

"You're no match for him."

"I could be your friend. Your real friend. Perhaps together we could stop this."

Sheba shook her head. "No, I have *enough* friends."

"If that were true, you wouldn't be in this position. If he's holding Gloria and forcing you to do his bidding, let me help you."

She smiled. "I like that you keep blindly stabbing for information, but I've already told you all I'm willing to say. And even if I thought you had a chance to beat him, I can't risk it."

"Who is he? What does he do?"

"You'll meet face to face soon."

"Just let me go."

"Sorry," Sheba said, shaking her head. "Can't."

"At least lower my arms, please? The pain's killing me."

Sheba dropped the cigarette on the dirt floor and twisted it underfoot. She stepped closer, studied the tight restraints fastened to the rafters, and shook her head.

"Your pain will be over before much longer," she said.

"Who are you afraid of? The cop?"

Sheba studied his face for a moment. A smile curled on her thick lips. "No. If anything, *he's* a bit afraid of me."

"Well, he seemed rather upset that you didn't let me leave town."

"He's more upset that he's not in control."

"Is he like you?"

"If he was, he'd have no reason to fear me."

Mitch said, "If the officer isn't in charge, who is?"

"Oh, he's coming, but be prepared," she replied.

"For what?"

"He's not as nice as I am."

Chapter 25

Lucas drove the SUV across the rocky terrain. Following the tracks caused them to leave the main road. "This is a strange path for someone to take."

"I agree, but it makes sense."

"Why?"

"Sheriff Sterling implied that someone must have followed Misty and I back from the bar last night, but I never saw any headlights. I was drunk but not so much that I wouldn't have noticed lights. Few people travel out here after dark. There's not a lot here. Headlights, had I seen them, would have immediately made me suspicious."

Lucas frowned. "And how does that make sense?"

"If the vehicle tracks are indeed from a military truck, these individuals would have access to night-vision goggles, which would explain why I never saw any headlights."

Lucas nodded. "That's true, I suppose."

"Bro, it's the best explanation that makes sense. The rattlesnakes weren't inside my house when we arrived. Someone placed them there *after* we passed out."

"You'd have had to be quite drunk for them to put snakes in your bed."

Joe shrugged. "I'm a sound sleeper. Worse last night though. I doubt I'll drink the hard stuff again."

They topped a steep embankment. The tire tracks they followed cut a clear path down the hillside and up the next ridge.

"These tracks could go for miles," Lucas said.

"Seems that way, bro."

"And this relic you found? Where'd you find it?"

Joe pointed through the driver's side window. "About ten miles or so in that direction. It's near the outer perimeter of our land."

"Not too far out of the way from this road."

"No."

"Might be possible someone noticed you finding it."

Joe nodded. "If they did, I never noticed anyone in the area. That doesn't mean anything though. A good set of binoculars out here and you can see for miles."

Lucas stopped the SUV. "Any need to keep following the tracks?"

Joe shook his head. "I think we're wasting time. Whoever left this direction is long gone."

Lucas turned the vehicle around. "Any idea what is out that way?"

"Government land, but to the best of my knowledge, not military operated."

"Top secret areas and activities are seldom publicized," Lucas said lowly.

"That's true."

Lucas drove about three miles and Joe pointed to the right.

"Turn here," Joe said.

Without question, Lucas slowed and turned. The silt-covered path was covered with hoof prints.

"This is where I ride my horse. Up ahead," Joe said, pointing. "You'll see a natural bridge that crosses overhead. Park beneath it."

Lucas nodded.

When they reached the bridge, Lucas parked and turned off the vehicle. He lowered both windows. The warm breeze flowed through the truck. Birds whistled in the short shrubs.

"It's beautiful out here," Lucas said.

Joe opened his door. "Come on. It's time I show you."

Lucas got out and followed. Joe descended a narrow, winding path that looped deeper into a washed out gulley. Joe left the path and walked through dense, thorny underbrush. He lifted a flat rock that lay flush against the side of the ridge wall, which revealed a hollow opening in the earth. He moved a ball of dried roots, reached his hand farther into the hole, and pulled out the skull.

"What the hell's that?" Lucas asked.

Joe smiled evenly. "Something that's not from our world, bro. Perhaps this is a great ancestor, but it's definitely not earthly in origin."

"And this is what they want?"

"I believe so. There's nothing else I own that's worth all this trouble. Unless—"

"What?"

"The sheriff thinks the snakes could be a hate crime."

"Because you're Navaho? I find that hard to believe."

"It happens more than you're aware. Gangs and bikers travel through this area a lot, but I agree with you. I don't buy that theory. I think *this* is what they want."

"Do your brothers know about the skull?"

Joe nodded. "They're pissed that I kept it."

"So they know about it?"

"They were there when I dug it up. They wanted me to bury it and leave it."

"Why didn't you?"

"Not really sure."

"It's a damn shame Misty died over this."

Joe looked at the ground. "I know. She might have been someone I'd have liked, but now, I'll never know."

"Perhaps we're both destined to be alone."

Joe shook his head. "Lydia will come back."

"You didn't see the look in her eyes, Joe. It was frightening. I believe she's gone for good. And if she does come back after completing her mission, she won't ever be the same."

Joe placed the skull back into the hole, placed the knotted roots over it, and pushed the large rock against the opening.

"If that's what you believe, you might as well accept it now and move on. When hope's dead, there's no resurrecting it." Joe said. "All that produces is anguish and heartache."

"Moving on," Lucas closed his eyes and took a deep breath. "That's not easy for me to do."

"It's never easy for anyone. But wallowing in despair taints your soul."

"In some ways, life was easier when I didn't care."

Joe shrugged and gave a soft smile. "You were much stronger then. You had less fear. Love changes people, and when it vanishes, it makes you question everything. Just don't let this experience harden you to bitterness."

Lucas sighed. "I wanted so much good for Lydia, Joe. I truly did."

"I know."

"The problem's accepting that she's right."

"For leaving you?"

"That and what I did was unfair to her."

"What?"

"When I saw her in TransGenCorp, I didn't see her as an experiment. I saw her as the most beautiful woman in the world who needed to experience the best life offered. I was also blinded by lust, but after that died down, I found myself totally intrigued with her and wanting to do anything to make her happy."

Joe clasped Lucas' shoulder. "You did everything you could."

"I tried, but I never suspected she was genetically created to be a ruthless assassin. After Idris revealed her true nature, I still believed she didn't *have* to be like that. But, Joe, the hardness in her eyes. The coldness in her voice. She's everything she feared becoming. I don't think she can be reined back in this time."

Joe gave him a side-glance. "I take it that you're going to try?"

"I want to."

Joe shook his head. "I don't think that's a good idea."

"Why not?"

"She'll kill you."

"And if I don't stop her, she'll kill Matthews and perhaps others."

Joe put his hands in his pockets. "As much as it pains me to say it, some people deserve to die. Matthews is one. You're not."

"As I recall, you were bent on not letting Grayson get near Matthews. Grayson would probably have killed him."

"He would have, but his would not be justice."

"And Lydia killing him would be?"

"To a degree, yes. If he had placed her in that chamber, wouldn't she have had to stay there?"

Lucas nodded. "That's what the scientist told us. Removing her after she was connected to the computers would have killed her."

"Understand, I always advocate peace, but I also know that this world isn't filled with kind-hearted people. Those filled with corruption and consumed with greed throw off the balance, especially when they are willing to kill innocent people to further their gains. Matthews is one of those people. If I read Grayson correctly, he's possibly worse than Matthews."

"Possibly."

"We should probably head back," Joe said, walking toward the SUV.

"Sure."

They opened the doors and got in. Joe turned and faced Lucas. "Tell me something."

"Anything."

"Was your relationship with Lydia ever truly stable?"

Lucas put the vehicle into gear and frowned. "That's a good question. Early on, when she was trying to cope with her memory loss, which wasn't an actual problem, she relied heavily on me. We developed a closeness and some trust that eventually grew into love."

"Do you remember when that changed?"

"She became volatile over her frustration when she couldn't recall her childhood or memories that weren't there."

"And perhaps that's when you should have told her?"

"Yeah, but I didn't because I wasn't certain how she'd react."

Joe nodded and looked out the side window. "You were more afraid of losing her."

"That, too. But she left anyway."

"Did she show signs of violence during your relationship?"

"Not really violence. She'd get agitated, but I never perceived her as being dangerous toward me. She could be passionate."

"So my guess is those men at her farmhouse triggered her defense mode and awakened whatever was programmed into her."

"That's when she became a different person than I had known."

"I wouldn't take it personally."

"I don't know how else to take it, Joe." Lucas shook his head. "I hate that she hates me."

"You really believe she hates you?"

"I'm sure she does. She hates me because I never told her where I found her and what she is."

"You were trying to protect her."

"She doesn't see it that way."

"No. Probably not."

"I honestly cannot blame her for resenting me."

"For what it's worth, bro, this isn't your fault. Your heart was in the right place because you tried to love and protect her. But it wouldn't matter who tried to help her. She is what she is. So the best information I can offer is for you to say good-bye and make peace within."

"That'll take some time, but I'll do my best."

"Good. Let's head to the bar and look around," Joe said. "Whoever's trying to kill me for the skull might still be around. Your gun is loaded?"

Lucas nodded. "Always. Especially after Lydia was abducted."

"I understand."

Lucas' eyes narrowed as he stared at the rough road. "I guess that's not something I have to worry about anymore."

Joe shrugged. "Let's hope not. But we must get back to my ranch before sundown."

"Why?"

Joe grinned. "My brothers want to set a trap and bait the people responsible for the rattlesnakes."

"You think they can?"

"Probably. Not sure what they have in mind, but if the bait is good, they can draw the people in. Owl-hunter will call me this evening and let me know what we're to do tomorrow."

Lucas grinned. "It shouldn't take long to look around the bar."

"Unless we find the person responsible for Misty's death."

Chapter 26

Washington, D.C.
   FBI Headquarters

FBI DIRECTOR MIKE CARPENTER entered his supervisor's office. Bennie Dunlap was sixty-five and a few weeks from retiring. His age was outlined by the deep wrinkles around his eyes and his mouth. His blue eyes sparkled as vivid as any teenager, which made him look as though youth was somehow trapped inside his weary body. With Parkinson's slowly claiming him, it was painful to listen to his shaky voice.

Bennie stood from behind his desk and offered his shaking hand to Carpenter. Carpenter shook it firmly.

It pained Carpenter to see the man he'd worked with for twenty years succumbing to this devastating disease.

"Good to see you, Mike," Bennie said. "Sit down. How've you been?"

"Fine, Bennie. And you?"

Bennie's eyes weighed with sadness. "Time's caught up with me, I'm afraid. And Parkinson's hasn't done me any favors, either."

"I'm sorry."

Bennie shook a fist in the air. "I'm not seeking sympathy. Life is what it is. You take what's dealt to you. You can't argue with the dealer. He won't reshuffle the deck and deal again. The cards fall as is."

"I know."

"I announced my retirement, as you're aware. I will also be recommending you to fill my position."

Carpenter smiled. "I'm flattered."

"Don't be. For a director like you that loves working the field with an investigation team, this desk might be equivalent to a prison cell. Or death row."

"I said that I'm flattered, but I didn't say I'd take the job."

Bennie smiled. "That's more the answer I expected from you."

"The confines of an office job makes me uneasy. I'd grow restless."

"I give you another ten years and you'll see this office more of a place to settle in. Prison or not, some days I'm thankful to sit in a plush chair. You're still young, but time catches up with everyone sooner or later."

Bennie wiped his mouth with the back of his hand, glanced at Carpenter, and then looked at the files on his desk.

"I take it your retirement isn't the only reason you called me here," Carpenter said.

Bennie nodded.

"What's going on?" Carpenter asked. "Does this have to do with Matthews' escape?"

"It is a concern, but it's not what you're here to discuss."

"Then what?"

Bennie's eyes pierced into Carpenter's. "I noticed early on, after TransGenCorp was shut down, that you pursued Lucas' clone like a vigorous, hungry bloodhound. You were determined to find this man and suddenly, within the past few months, you just don't seem that enthused about bringing him in. Care to explain that?"

Carpenter shifted in his chair. "I became so obsessed with finding him that other cases weren't getting their proper attention, so I backed off to focus on new cases. That's all."

"I see," Bennie said softly. "Has his trail run cold?"

"Somewhat."

"No clue as to where he is?"

"Am I under investigation?" Carpenter asked in a joking manner.

"No, Mike. I'm just trying to find out how close you ever were to finding him."

"I was close several times. Why? Do *you* know where he is?"

"No. But it's time we close his file for good." Bennie patted the manila file folder on his desk.

Carpenter frowned. "After all this time, just close it?"

"Unless you see a reason to keep chasing what seems to be nothing more than a ghost now."

"I'll accept either. If you wish to close the case, I won't give it another thought. And if you want me to find him, I'll assign a new team to the case immediately."

"Consider it closed."

"Very well," Carpenter said with a slight shrug.

Carpenter felt a sense of relief that his assignment to pursue and capture Lucian was over. At least Carpenter didn't have to wrestle with his conscious over letting Lucian stay with Kat or not taking him into custody after Slayton was taken prisoner. But inwardly he continued the moral dilemma of not seeing Lucian brought to justice for the senate murders. With the case closed he had a valid reason to let it go.

"Now, let's discuss something else about this job."

"What's that?"

Bennie stood and walked to a coffee pot near the office sink. "Coffee?"

"Black, please."

Bennie poured two cups. Without looking back, he said, "Secrets, Mike."

Bennie turned and handed a Styrofoam cup to Carpenter. Bennie's eyes narrowed.

"Secrets?" Carpenter replied, taking the cup.

"The art of our duties as investigators. Secrets."

Carpenter studied him with a slight frown, not certain where the conversation was headed.

"Our jobs cover a vast array of duties," Bennie said. "And often, the job requires us to maintain secrets related to our investigations. You have them."

"I'm sure everyone does, in one way or the other."

Bennie smiled and nodded. He gave a shaky wink. "I have them, too."

"Not quite certain what you're getting at? Is there something you wish me to confess or offer? Ask me a question straight out and I'll give you the answer."

Bennie looked more amused. "You misunderstand. It's not what *you* know, but rather, what *I* know."

"Please clue me in. Does it have to do with the clone's case?"

"Very much so."

"If the case is closed, why are we even discussing this?"

"It's time you knew the whole truth."

"That being?"

Bennie pressed the intercom button on his desk phone. "Anna, please send him in."

The office door opened. A man wearing an Armani suit and hat entered and closed the door behind him. He removed his hat and smiled at Carpenter. It took only a moment for the recognition factor to set in. Carpenter's eyes widened.

"No. It's impossible," Carpenter said. "Senator Godfrey? You're alive?"

Chapter 27

Lydia drove her motorcycle at 80 mph. The wind whipped around her helmet, making a slight whistling sound. Her mind raced almost as fast as her bike carried her.

Lydia thought of Lucas with a great deal of remorse. Fear bit at her soul. She had come close to killing him. Her warning wasn't a bluff or an idle threat. She would've pulled the trigger, killed him, and only now, in the afterthought of the moment, did she realize the true loss and regret she'd have suffered if she'd given in to that impulse.

Her ability to remain rational continued to shrink while her lust to kill escalated. Her mind was becoming exactly what Idris had genetically programmed it to become. Her fate was inevitable. The route she took was one way. She wouldn't return to who she was or where she had lived. She'd never see Lucas again. She couldn't.

She headed for New Mexico, where Matthews had escaped from prison, but she knew Matthews was probably states away by now.

A man with his intelligence and determination had probably used a well thought out plan once he was on the outside. Matthews wasn't one to take unnecessary, foolish risks. She figured he had no plans to be discovered, which made her task of finding him all the more difficult.

She needed help and funds to find Matthews.

Lydia gunned the Nighthawk, watching the speed odometer flirt with the 100 mph mark, and smiling, she remembered someone else that hated Matthews with as much passion as she did.

Boyd Grayson.

Chapter 28

Lucas drove the SUV to the far side of The Waterhole Bar and Grill's parking lot. The building resembled a rustic ranch house like in the days of the Old West. The glass doors had painted swinging doors on the outside. A coiled cowboy rope was nailed to the wall. A neon sign flashing, "Yee-haw!" scrolled across a side window.

Black silhouettes of cowboys and sexy cowgirls were fastened to the fencepost railing along the deck.

Lucas frowned, shook his head, and then he gave Joe a strange side-glance. "You actually went in *there*?"

Joe's face flushed red. "Sorry to say it, but yes."

"You'd have a hard time getting *me* to go inside."

"It was already dark when I arrived. Besides, there aren't many choices out here, bro."

"Surely there's something better than this."

Joe shrugged. "Maybe, but I don't plan to search anymore places like this out. I'll get my whisky from a liquor store from now on, *if* I ever decide to drink it again."

The tranquil pinkish purple sky loomed in the west. The sun was an hour or so from setting, and a couple dozen vehicles were parked in the gravel lot. Nothing seemed out of the ordinary.

Lucas turned off the engine. "When you were here last night, what do you remember? Were there a lot of cars or trucks?"

Joe closed his eyes. "It was already dark when I arrived. Let's see. A couple of pickup trucks, a half dozen or more motorcycles, and several big rigs."

"So it wasn't busy?"

"As busy as a ghost town might be. You have to understand, there isn't a lot of traffic out this way. I'd guess the majority of patrons are those already familiar with this area, but again, I never frequented the place."

"So you wouldn't know who was out of place?"

Joe shook his head. "No, but I really don't think the people who placed the rattlers in my house followed us home."

"I don't either."

Two bikers drove into the lot and parked near the front doors. The riders wore leather jackets with a gang emblem sewn across the backs of their jackets.

"How was the bar's atmosphere last night. Anyone give you a hard time or stare at you?"

"Not that I recall. Most were busy talking and drinking. A few were dancing to the live band. No one started any trouble."

A white Dodge Ram pickup roared through the parking lot, swerved sharply, and slung gravel into the air as the driver slammed the brakes and skidded to a stop. Two men stepped out of the truck, both laughing, and each wearing sand-colored fatigues, which immediately caught Lucas' attention.

"Those two look a bit out of place," Lucas said.

"I agree."

"Did you see anyone wearing outfits like that last night?" Lucas asked.

Joe watched the two men as they walked to the doors, then he shook his head. "No. Most wore flannel shirts or leather jackets with blue jeans."

"They look like possible service men."

Lucas opened the truck door and stepped out.

"What are you doing?" Joe asked.

"Shouldn't we at least look around?"

"They might recognize me. There's the slight chance they think I'm dead."

Lucas nodded. "You're right. You stay here. I'll look around."

"Be careful."

"It won't take too long."

Lucas shut the truck door and headed across the parking lot. He walked to the rear of the pickup and glanced into the truck bed. Two snake tongs lay near a wooden crate. It didn't take any deductive reasoning to conclude that these men had captured the rattlesnakes and placed them inside Joe's house, but whom did they work for?

The tag on the truck was registered to an individual and not a government official tag, which made it even harder to make a connection to the people over them. Lucas memorized the tag number, and instead of entering the bar and confronting the men, he thought it best to leave without being seen. He had no idea how many people they were dealing with, either. Besides, he'd know the truck should he see it again.

Lucas hurried back to the SUV and climbed inside. He took a notepad out of the dash compartment and wrote down the tag number before starting the engine.

"You found something?" Joe asked.

"Not much, but enough to narrow down who gifted you with the rattlers."

"Those men?"

"Saw two snake tongs in the truck bed and judging by their clothing, I don't think they're herpetologists."

Joe smiled. "Probably not."

"Let's get out of here," Lucas said, dropping the SUV into reverse and backing up.

"Hey!"

Lucas slammed the brakes. Gravels crunched beneath the sudden stop. In his side view mirror, one of the men in fatigues sprinted toward the SUV.

"I'm talking to you!" the man shouted, tapping the side window.

Lucas lowered the glass. "Yes?"

"You take something out of my truck?" the man asked.

"No. Why?"

"I saw you messing around my truck bed, then you ran off and looks like you're in an awful hurry to leave."

Lucas smiled. "You're mistaken."

The man grabbed the door handle and yanked open the door. "I don't think I am."

Normally, Lucas dismissed hostile approaches in a cordial manner, except when he felt Lydia or a friend was being threatened. Seeing the man's hostile approach and believing Joe's life might be in danger, he didn't hesitate to immediately stand his ground. But, had he time to really think his actions through, he'd probably blame his quick reaction more in response to all the conflict and disruption that was unfolding in his personal life.

Lucas stepped out of the truck and pressed his gun to the man's throat. He released the safety. "I said that you're mistaken."

The man raised his hands and swallowed hard. "S-s-sorry. Easy now. I did overreact. Again, I'm sorry."

"Now that I have your attention," Lucas said. "Why do you have snake collecting gear in your truck?"

"It's a hobby my friend and I have."

"A hobby?" Lucas asked, easing back the gun.

The man nodded. Sweat beaded along his brow. He was more nervous than Lucas expected the man to be.

"Yeah. Snakes, tarantulas, scorpions. We collect them. Sometimes we sell them to other pet enthusiasts."

"How about rattlesnakes? You ever sell any of those?" Lucas asked.

"Yes. Sold ten of them about a week ago."

"To whom?"

The man looked confused but volunteered information anyway. "Don't know who he was exactly. He paid us really good though. Five hundred dollars for less than a couple hours work."

Lucas clicked on the safety and lowered the gun. "What'd he look like?"

The man took a quick step back. His hands shook.

"We never met him in person. His instructions were for us to leave the snakes near a camp's hiking trail. The money was hidden in an envelope that was tucked inside a sign post."

"If you never met him, how'd he hire you to catch the rattlers?"

He shrugged. "He called me out of the blue."

"It's that easy to find someone in your type of business?"

"We also raise rats and mice for pet shops. He might have gotten our number from one of them. Besides, the money he offered was too good to turn down. We thought someone was playing us for fools, too, but the money was where he said it would be."

"And if it hadn't been?"

"I guess we'd have let the snakes go. Why do you want to know?"

"Because whoever you sold them to attempted to use them to kill my friend."

The man stooped and peered into the truck. Seeing Joe in the passenger seat, he said, "Seriously? How?"

Joe explained the snakes and Misty's death. The man stood with an astonished expression on his face. He looked nauseous.

"Hey, guys. Look, I'm truly sorry. I wouldn't have sold them to him had I known he'd do something like that. Honest."

Lucas studied the man for a moment. The fatigues were actually heavy duty hunting pants with thicker material to prevent briars and cacti needles from pricking the skin. He didn't have a handgun holster. "Okay, but you're sure you don't know anything else about him so we can find him?"

"I told you all I know. Here's our card."

The card displayed: Calvin's Herps, Spiders, & Supplies.

"I take it that you're Calvin?"

"Yes."

"Have a nice day, Calvin." Lucas slammed the truck door and started the SUV. "We'll be going, but I suggest that you turn down any future jobs from this man."

"No problem there."

"Thanks for the card. I'm certain the sheriff will want to talk to you."

"We had nothing to do with her death."

"Maybe not directly. Just tell them what you told us."

Lucas backed the truck up.

Joe glanced at Lucas. "Do you really believe he's innocent of Misty's death?"

"Unfortunately, I do. Don't you?"

"I didn't feel any real callousness from him."

"Well, had he been an operative that wanted to kill you, he'd have attempted to take my gun and not spilled his guts so easily."

"He did offer too much information pretty quick."

"I know."

"Night's coming. I wonder what my brothers are planning."

"I'm sure we'll know soon enough."

Lucas drove out of the parking lot and onto the highway. He thought about Lydia and wondered where she was and if she missed him. It would be the first night without her in a long time, and he dreaded when he'd have to go to bed. He'd probably get little sleep because his mind would run so many scenarios, so many pain-filled moments of anguish and wishing he could change her mind. He'd also battle his regret of keeping secrets he wished he had not. But Lydia was about to be the least of his problems.

Barreling down the highway, approaching them at a high rate of speed was a tan camo Jeep with two armed men. Their mission was to take Joe and get the skull—no matter what.

Chapter 29

Godfrey set his hat on the edge of the desk. Carpenter couldn't hide the surprise on his face, which was mixed with a great deal of skepticism. Carpenter looked at Bennie and shook his head.

"How?" Carpenter asked.

Bennie looked at Godfrey. "It's best that the former senator explain."

"My death was staged," Godfrey said.

Carpenter frowned. "Staged? What about the guards and the other senator?"

"They're all fine, too. None of us were killed."

"Why Bennie?" Carpenter asked. "Why keep me out of this loop and demand that I find the clone?"

"It had to look authentic," Bennie said. "Idris had to believe the clone had carried out the assassinations. We needed an FBI team actively pursuing and investigating the murders. So we sent the best person we had. You. And you're such a bullheaded investigator that I knew you'd make your presence known."

Carpenter glanced at Godfrey. "So the clone was working *with* you?"

Godfrey nodded. "Apparently Idris pissed him off about something. Some sort of blackmail if I recall correctly. Lucian contacted me about the assassination threat on my life. To stop Idris we decided to play it out and make it look like he had succeeded."

"Did Lucas know? After all, he was your friend."

Godfrey looked away. "I know. But sadly, it was something I had to keep from him. We didn't have any other choice."

"Dammit, Bennie!" Carpenter said, rising. "I nearly killed the clone. Lucas nearly killed him. And all the while he was working with the FBI?"

"Even if you had shot him, Mike," Godfrey said with a grim smile. "It's unlikely you could have killed him with his healing metabolism and all."

"Do you have any idea how many sleepless nights I've had trying to figure out *where* he was and *how* I might stop him?"

"I understand your frustration," Godfrey said.

Carpenter brushed past him toward the door. "No, you don't understand. You have no idea at all. I was bent on exacting justice for your deaths. That's my job and I'm damn good at it. For over a year, I've felt like a failure for not bringing him in when I should have."

"Do you know where Lucian is?" Bennie asked.

"Why should I reveal anything to you for withholding this from me?" Carpenter asked, grabbing the doorknob.

"Please wait," Godfrey said. "Let me explain."

Carpenter took a deep breath, let go of the doorknob, and released a long sigh of pent-up frustration. "Once Lucian killed Idris, you still remained in hiding. Why?"

"Idris was the forerunner. There are others."

"I know. We shut down Typhis and stopped Matthews before he used Lydia for further cloning."

"There are more."

"More?" Carpenter asked.

Godfrey nodded. "Idris never worked alone."

"Who else worked with him?"

"Actually," Godfrey said. "Idris worked *for* someone else."

"Who?"

"A man who calls himself, 'Alpha.'"

Carpenter glanced at Bennie. "He was the one behind Lydia's abduction, wasn't he?"

Bennie nodded. "From Lydia's debriefing that's who we believe took her at Desert Labs. But we don't have enough information on *who* he actually is."

"In fact," Godfrey said. "Desert Labs is the last known place where he's been seen. He's elusive. A phantom."

"Damn." Carpenter sighed. His eyes searched and widened. "That means Matthews has connections with Alpha."

"Quite possibly."

Carpenter set his coffee cup down on the edge of the sink. "Do you know where Matthews might have gone?"

"We've been searching but we need Lucian's help to find them," Godfrey said. "I assumed he was dead since I've not heard from him in a long while."

"Dead?"

Godfrey nodded. "His genetic makeup only allows him a short life-span. But you seem to believe otherwise. Is he alive?"

Carpenter crossed his arms and looked at Godfrey. "Yes."

"Seems you have some damn big secrets, too," Bennie said with a shrewd smile.

"We all do," Carpenter said softly, walking back to his seat.

Bennie sat in his desk chair. "So explain to me why you've never brought him in when you were so determined justice be served?"

"It's complicated," Carpenter replied.

"As was my situation," Godfrey said.

"Not like this. Lucian has the ability to change his facial features and not *look* like Lucas."

"Wow," Godfrey whispered. "That's news to me."

"You didn't know about that?"

"No, but him not telling me makes sense."

"Why?" Bennie asked.

Godfrey shrugged. "That would allow him to leave without me finding him. He could simply disappear and make me assume he had died since I know about his genetic flaw."

"His morphing ability kept me searching for a long time," Carpenter said, looking at Bennie. "But I finally figured out who Lucian was and I was set to arrest him."

"What stopped you?" Bennie asked.

"He saved my life. Hell, he saved a lot of our lives by helping take Slayton into custody. He even saved Lucas, in spite of how much Lucas hates having a clone. Or was that just a great act, too? Has Lucas been secretly working with Lucian the whole time?"

"No," Godfrey replied. "That hatred is genuine. They've never worked together. Although they were close to working side by side when Lucas went undercover inside TransGenCorp."

"You worked with both of them at the same time?"

"No." Godfrey shook his head. "I never worked with Lucas directly during that time. Otherwise, he'd know I was alive. I worked behind the scenes. It was difficult, at times, for my associates not to confuse one for the other."

"I imagine so."

Bennie folded his shaky hands and set them on his lap. "Do you know how we can make contact with Lucian?"

Carpenter frowned. "You really don't know where he is?"

"No," Godfrey said. "He stopped contacting me, so I assumed he had died. He had explained that there wasn't any cure to reverse the genetic damage he was created with. So, do you mind telling me where he is?"

"He lives with Kat Gaddis."

Bennie's eyes widened, and he straightened in his chair. "Your former team member?"

"Yes."

"And she knows what he really is?"

"Of course." Carpenter said.

"That's odd," Bennie said. "Is that why she stopped being an agent?"

"That's one of the reasons. When Tyler was killed during the shut-down of TGC, something inside her soured. She wanted to pursue her own justice and Lucian stepped in, offering to help her. They're very close. Does Kat know that you're alive?"

Godfrey shrugged. "Only if Lucian told her."

"Mike, has the bulldog inside you mellowed?" Bennie asked. "You've known where he is . . . and yet?"

Carpenter's face flushed red. "Considering Lucian never murdered Godfrey or the others at the senate hearings, apparently there's nothing I've mellowed over. That's what really pisses me off about the entire situation. I compromised my own principles, which I had never done before, when I never should have had to. So you have to pardon me for being resentful for the whole situation. You made me out to be a fool."

"No," Godfrey said.

Carpenter's jaw tightened. His eyes narrowed. "Really? How else would *you* define it? I worked my ass off trying to find Lucian and bring him in, even kill him if I had to, for what I had believed he had done. And with all that, I find out that it was a ruse? The joke was on me, but I'm not laughing."

"That was never our intention," Godfrey said.

"It's exactly how I view it."

Godfrey crossed his arms. "Look. We honestly didn't have any choice back then. Idris had a lot of pull within Congress. His money lined many pockets. He had loyal lobbyists that were nothing less than spies. I was his most outspoken opponent, so my death had to look genuine. If Idris suspected otherwise, there's no telling what he would have done next."

"And how long did you plan to have me play a victim to this charade?"

"After TransGenCorp was shut down, that was when we planned to tell you what was going on," Bennie said. "But Lucian informed us that others had surfaced."

"Typhis' men and Matthews?" Carpenter asked.

"Yes," Godfrey replied.

"Matthews escaped today."

Godfrey nodded. "I know."

"Forgive me for asking," Carpenter said with a wry expression. "But did you have anything to do with his escape?"

"No."

"With all the lack of former information, I thought it best that I asked."

"The cards are all on the table now," Bennie said.

"All of them?" Carpenter asked.

"Everything," Godfrey said. "No more secrets."

Carpenter shook his head. "I wish I could say that makes me feel all warm and fuzzy inside, but it doesn't."

"We need Lucian's help," Godfrey said. "To find Matthews. Alpha may have helped Matthews escape, and if so, finding Matthews is pertinent to capturing Alpha."

"I understand."

"So you'll help?" Bennie asked.

"I'll contact Kat and tell her. The rest is really up to Lucian, isn't it?

There must be a reason why he's not made contact with you. Maybe he feels a bit betrayed about something. I know I do."

Sadness shadowed Bennie's eyes. "Mike, I'm sorry that I couldn't tell you. Truly I am. But this was a matter of national security."

"Yeah, which I am sworn to protect and uphold."

"And you did. You *do*."

"The fewer people who knew about me being alive, the safer I was," Godfrey said. "And it also reduced the chance that Idris might opt other terroristic attacks as well."

"I get that, and I'm very thankful to learn that you're alive. In spite of my feelings, I'm relieved that Lucian's not a cold-blooded killer, but the revelation coming like this, so unexpectedly . . . I will have to deal with it the best I can. That will take some time."

"I understand," Godfrey said. "I hope that after you've had time to think it over, that you will be able to forgive us."

Bennie straightened in his chair. "I hope so, too."

Carpenter offered a bleak smile to Godfrey. "Don't you believe it's about time you revealed your secret to Lucas?"

"That I'm alive?"

"Yes."

Godfrey nodded. "You're right. It's time I do that."

"Good. Because if anyone wants Alpha captured more the Lydia, you, or I, it'd be Lucas."

"I don't doubt that for a second. Once we find and capture Alpha, maybe we can put an end to all this mad science," Godfrey said.

"Perhaps."

"And if you don't mind, could you contact Kat?"

Carpenter stood and headed for the door. "Sure. I need some fresh air anyway."

Chapter 30

Kat's cellphone rang, jostling her awake. Rubbing her eyes, she grabbed the phone and looked at the clock. It was nearly noon. Looking around, she didn't see Lucian.

"Hello?" she said.

"Kat. It's Mike."

"Is everything okay?" she asked, sliding out of bed and grabbing her robe.

"Yes. I need to speak to Lucian. Is he there?"

Kat walked down the hall, through the living room, and into the kitchen. The coffee pot was empty. The television was off.

"No," she said with a frown. "He's not here. Why?"

"I need you to relate a message to him when you see him."

"Sure." Kat turned on the coffee pot.

"Matthews escaped from prison, and we need Lucian's help in locating him."

"Why Lucian?"

"I'm not certain, but higher ups have requested his help."

"Higher ups?"

Carpenter sighed. "Yeah, it came as a major surprise to me, and I wonder if this news is a surprise to you as well."

"What exactly?"

"Lucian never killed Senator Godfrey."

"What?"

"So you didn't know, either?"

"Of course not."

"At least we're in the same company, then."

Kat sat down at the dining table. "If Lucian didn't kill him, who did?"

"No one."

"Wait. You're saying that Godfrey is actually still alive?"

"Alive and well, Kat."

"But the video footage. Our investigation?"

"Yeah, I'm a bit pissed over all that. Godfrey's murder was staged to keep Idris in the dark. *We*, however, were kept entirely out of the loop."

"But why?"

"It's a long story. I'll fill you in later over coffee or something."

"Why do they think Lucian can help find Matthews?"

"That they've not explained yet. But, I told them that I didn't know if Lucian would be interested in helping or not, so leave that decision solely up to him on whether he wants to help with this."

"Okay. I'll tell him."

"Thanks, Kat."

"Sure, no problem."

"And I'm sorry."

"For what?" she said.

"I've kept a lot of resentment toward Lucian all this time even after he saved my life."

"You didn't know. Hell, he didn't even let *me* know."

"I know, but at least you had enough heart to give him a chance."

"Mike, I'm certain Lucian doesn't hold anything against you."

"But he has every right to."

"He's not like that."

"I imagine you'd know that better than anyone. Let me know what he decides."

"I will," Kat said softly.

"And afterwards, I will go buy him a beer. Maybe three or four."

"I'm sure he'd enjoy that opportunity." Kat smiled. "I imagine you're as relieved as I am that Lucian never carried out those assassinations."

"I am, Kat. I truly am. What I don't understand is how you were able to look past all that when we thought he was guilty."

"You know me. When I looked into his eyes, they told me everything, even though he never told me. I never saw a coldblooded killer."

Carpenter chuckled. "You and reading people by their eyes. That has to be a gift."

"It has never failed me. Never."

"Take care of yourself, Kat. Talk to you soon."

"Bye, Mike."

Chapter 31

Kat ended the call with Carpenter and checked to see what messages or calls she had missed while she had overslept.

Disappointment weighed upon her when she didn't find any messages or missed calls from Lucian.

Frustrated, she poured some coffee, added creamer, and took a long sip while walking to the front door. She peered out the side window. Both vehicles were in the drive.

Lucian had gone for a jog early in the morning, which wasn't something he normally did, but he'd never be gone for hours without letting her know, either.

She tried his cell but it went straight to voice mail.

"Dammit," she whispered.

Kat sat on the couch and sipped her coffee. Her worrying nature crept to the surface. When Lucian had headed out for his jog, he had been burning up with fever. Something was wrong. She needed to find him. Her anxiety heightened as she pondered through different possibilities of bad things that might have occurred.

Hurrying to her bedroom to get dressed, she chided herself. Part of her knew she still felt insecure about Tyler's death, and although her love for Lucian had buried that loss, fear kept trying to dig up the pain.

Kat dressed quickly. She hoped Lucian came home soon because she didn't know where to begin searching for him. Due to his fever, she thought the hospital would be the best place to check first but most likely the last place he'd go.

She stepped into the master bath, turned on the light, and stared in the mirror. Her hair was frizzed so she plugged in her curling iron.

Thinking over the information Carpenter had just given her, Kat wondered why Lucian had kept the information from her, too. She thoroughly trusted him, but she couldn't understand why he'd allow her to believe he had killed prominent people. Had she truly been blinded by love that she simply dismissed it. Or, like she had told Carpenter, could she really read in his eyes that he wasn't a coldblooded killer? That had to be why had she allowed her heart and mind to fully trust him.

Kat was grateful Lucian was innocence of those murders, but she remained somewhat confused that he didn't tell her. What other things had he kept to himself?

The first thing she needed to do was find out where he was and that he was okay.

Chapter 32

Carpenter returned to Bennie's office and sat down. He kept his silence while studying Bennie and Godfrey.

"Well?" Bennie asked.

Carpenter shrugged. "She said that she'd tell Lucian. That's all. The decision is on Lucian. I'll not influence him either way."

"Good," Godfrey said. "Do you know how we can get in touch with Dr. Helmsby?"

"No," Carpenter replied, shaking his head. "Why?"

"I need to apologize to him, too."

"You're suddenly getting all conscious-stricken, aren't you? Kept everything all bottled up so tightly all this time and you feel like you're going to explode. Is guilt eating at you that badly?" Carpenter asked.

"Mike," Bennie said, raising a finger.

"No," Godfrey said, looking at Bennie. "No, he's right. I've been over-burdened for some time now. I need to apologize to him."

"What exactly do you owe him an apology for?"

Godfrey shook his head. "For allowing Idris to bully him in TransGen-Corp. I didn't like that Idris held him hostage to perform experiments that went against Helmsby's morals. And I need information from him, too."

"Ahh, the nugget of truth," Carpenter said. "What information?"

"I need to know what Boyd Grayson was having him work on."

Carpenter shrugged. "No one's heard anything from him in a long time."

"I know, and I believe I know why," Godfrey said.

Bennie rose in his chair. "Why?"

"He's probably hiding."

"Why would he be hiding?" Carpenter asked. "He left on amiable terms with Grayson."

Godfrey chuckled. "You don't know Grayson. With the type of research his industries work on, his top-secret projects are strictly kept inside. Few people ever leave his employ and those that have—well, let's just say it didn't end favorable."

Carpenter frowned. "Are you insinuating that Grayson kills ex-employees?"

"We've not been able to prove it. But Helmsby's safety is an issue I'm taking seriously."

"Me, too," Carpenter said.

Bennie took a pen and wrote on a notepad. "I'll start searching for him immediately. Do you really think he's in extreme danger?"

"Hard to say, but we're opening a full investigation into Grayson's Mars projects and his prisoner-transport release programs he's currently engaging in."

"I don't follow," Carpenter said.

"He's been enlisting prisoners from Texas and soon California to work his mines on Mars and after serving so many years, they will be allowed freedom to settle in the Martian cities he's constructing."

"Sounds pretty harmless."

"Maybe," Godfrey said. "But I'd like to gather more information on what's going on there."

"I understand."

"Carpenter, please try to get Lucian to contact me. Bennie will start his search for Dr. Helmsby," Godfrey said.

Carpenter nodded. "Bennie, you might start by contacting Helmsby's friends first. Maybe they'll know something."

Bennie smiled. "I will, but if they've not heard anything from him, I'll post an internal search within our federal offices, CDC, and other research facilities. It's possible he's working with one of them."

"As much as the man loves science, it's probably one of the best places to look," Carpenter said.

Chapter 33

Morton sat at the large bay window, staring at the hollow dead tree at the edge of the street. A city worker stood inside a cherry picker with a chainsaw and sawed off the smallest branch.

Morton's ears backed. His eyes narrowed. Nothing could hide the scowl on his face.

Kip, wearing a leather Ken doll jacket, scurried across the back of the couch and jumped to the windowsill to sit beside Morton. Morton's tail lashed back and forth.

"Still angry about being locked inside the house?" Kip asked.

Morton cocked a brow and looked down at the rat. The cat's eyes tinted red. "What do you think?"

"I'd say that you're not over it."

"Hardly. I'm a cat, a *shifter* cat. It's a bit extreme for me to be grounded and have to stay indoors. Now *they're* cutting down my favorite tree, and there's not anything I can do to stop them."

Kip straightened his whiskers with his forepaws. "Well, what you did caused a great deal of alarm."

"That was weeks ago. It was only a prank, a harmless one at that."

"Not to say that it was one of the funniest things I've ever seen. Sheer genius."

"Thanks."

"Until you nearly gave that old man a heart attack."

"I didn't see him. And he only suffered a *panic* attack. Not a heart attack."

"Well, other than that, it was righteous." Kip smiled.

"Just trying to save the tree," Morton mumbled. "And keep people away."

"It worked. Hiding inside that tree and moaning in pain made people think the tree was haunted. The ASPLUNDH tree-cutters left without starting a chainsaw."

"I know. That was my plan all along. But some of the older people thought they were becoming schizophrenic because they were hearing voices. They even stopped walking on our side of the street, which was an added bonus."

"Beware the *haunted* tree-ee-ee," Kip moaned.

The chainsaw cut through another branch. The deadwood dropped to the ground. Morton shook his head. He was going to miss that tree. By making people believe the tree was possessed gave Morton added privacy when he was outdoors. Even the unruly teenagers that threw rocks at cats and dogs strolled to the other side of the street to stay out of limb distance. That pleased Morton.

When Daniel discovered what Morton had done, he scolded the cat and grounded him, making him stay indoors. Morton understood Daniel's reasoning. He didn't want anyone to discover that he had the ability to talk. Such knowledge endangered Morton and all of their safety. The last thing they needed was more deranged people like Idris or Matthews trying to take the cat for ill-gotten gains.

"Ever wondered how it'd be as a normal cat?" Kip asked.

"That would be such a humiliating downgrade."

"True dat."

Morton eyed Kip, noticing the leather jacket. "Biker wannabe?"

"Don't dis my rappa threads," Kip replied with a wide smile.

Morton frowned. "You *do* realize you're more white-furred than black, don't you?"

"No chiz. But the stripe down my back *is* black."

Morton shook his head in disgust. "MTV will be the death of society yet."

"Chill, fluffy bro."

Morton opened his mouth to reply but sensed another presence.

"Morton," Kyle said telepathically.

The cat stared straight ahead and cocked his head to the right. "Kyle?" he asked aloud.

Kip shook his head. "Not again."

Morton placed a forepaw over Kip's mouth.

Kip jerked free. "Okay, okay."

"What's wrong?" Morton said, focusing his thoughts toward Kyle.

"Lucian is dying."

Morton's eyes widened. "Dying? You sure?"

"Yes. He's in bad shape. His body is shutting down. He came here last night. The enhancers don't work anymore."

"That's bad."

"I know."

"It's been a long time since I heard anything from you," Morton said.

"I've been . . . drained. Brockton's tests have stressed me. I've been too tired to send messages."

"I understand."

"I'm on strike," Kyle said, followed by a small laugh.

"Have you contacted Lydia since she left Lucas?"

"No."

Morton's eyes narrowed. He watched a larger tree branch fall to the ground. His claws dug into the couch cushion. "You were able to sense her before. Can you do that again?"

"I've tried, but she seems to be . . . blocking me."

"According to Daniel, Matthews escaped and Lydia's going after him."

"She'll kill him if she finds him."

Morton gave a slight nod. "He's not a role model citizen."

"No, he's not. He's dangerous, but if she kills him, she will never have hope for redemption. She'll never recover. She'll live out her life as an assassin."

"Like Idris planned." Morton huffed.

"Exactly."

"If you find her, please let me know."

"I will, but even if I locate her, she cannot hear me like you do. I can only hope to pinpoint her position, nothing more."

"Few are gifted like us," Morton said.

"I'd trade all these odd powers for what I was before Idris messed with my genetics."

Morton sensed the bitterness behind those words. "I understand, and for what it's worth, I would have stopped him had I been there."

"I know you would."

"About Lucian," Morton said, shifting the conversation in a different direction.

"Yes?"

"Any possible solutions to fix his genetic flaws?"

"Brockton is trying something that will probably only be a temporary fix. It might give Lucian a couple more weeks. Brockton wants Lucas to donate a blood sample or stem cells and see if he can find a reversal cure."

"He wants Lucas to help his clone?"

"Yes."

"I doubt Lucas would agree to that."

"He might if Daniel persuades him."

Morton nodded. "I will talk to Daniel about it, but it's unlikely Lucas will budge."

"If Lucas refuses, Lucian has no hope left. I'll try to find Lydia and contact you later."

"You have my telepathic number," Morton replied.

Once the conversation ended, Morton looked at Kip.

"Bad news?" Kip asked.

Morton sighed. "It's not good news."

Another large branch dropped from the hollow tree. Morton's ears backed. His teeth grew. He lengthened the claws on his right forepaw. "You know something, Kip?"

"What?"

"I'd love to use that tree-cutter's leg for a scratching post."

Kip laughed. "I bet you would."

"I can't stomach watching this any longer." Morton turned from the window, plopped down onto the couch, and grabbed the television remote. Morton lengthened his paw and turned on the news. Kip stood beside him.

"What are you doing?" Kip asked.

"Looking to see if any new information surfaced on Matthews."

"Why?"

"He needs to be found *before* Lydia finds him. Otherwise, he's dead."

"That's not a bad thing."

"For her, it will be."

Kip straightened his whiskers and frowned. "I never liked him. None of us did. If it's death he gets, he truly deserves it."

"I didn't think he directly supervised your tests."

"Nah, he didn't, but the constant injections were given at his order."

"Those injections gave you the ability to talk."

"Erm, yeah, but I don't credit *that* to him."

Morton smiled. "Then what?"

"Lucky coincidence?"

Morton gave Kip an amused side-glance. "Have you ever wondered what it would be like to be a *normal* rat?"

"I shiver thinking about it."

Morton smiled. "You could be rooting around through old rotten garbage."

"Yeah, maybe," Kip said. "But if I was in India I'd be worshipped."

"But you're *not* in India. You're in America where most people consider rats pests and run away in fear."

Kip frowned. "Not *lab* rats. We're in an order all to ourselves."

"Not necessarily a strong argument when you think of all the experiments scientists have done with rats."

"The side-effects aren't worth the risks, but our sacrifices benefit humans."

"Sometimes," Morton said. "And other times, rats bite the bullet for nothing."

Kip nodded. "That's true, too, but at least the four of us found a good home here with you."

Morton smiled. "Yes. It's good to have other animals to talk to."

"You like us, don't you?" Kip asked. "I knew it."

"You flatter yourself too much. Don't let the myth of *Tom and Jerry* fool you, either. Cats always win over rodents. Always."

Chapter 34

Lucian slept on Brockton's couch and snored. Some color had returned to his face, but dark circles outlined his eyes.

Brockton shook Lucian until he awakened.

Lucian blinked several times and shook his head. "W-w-what?"

"You've been asleep for hours. I hate to wake you, but I need to know how you feel?" Brockton asked.

"My head still aches but not as badly as last night." Lucian sat up and rubbed his eyes. "God, what time is it?"

"A little past five."

"In the afternoon?"

Brockton nodded.

"Dammit!" Lucian said. He tried to stand, wobbled, and Brockton grabbed his arm to steady him.

"Easy, Lucian. You're still very weak."

"Why'd you let me sleep so long? Damn, Kat will be worried sick."

Brockton took a penlight and examined Lucian's eyes. "I'm certain she's probably looking for you."

Brockton's cellphone beeped. "Speaking of which, that's probably her now."

"Don't tell her."

"That you're here? That will only generate more questions and worry from her."

Lucian nodded. "You're right. Tell her I'm here, but don't tell her that I'm sick."

Brockton sighed and shook his head with disappointment. "Very well, but you'd best let her know. She deserves *that* much from you."

"I'll tell her. Just not yet."

On the third beep, Brockton answered, "Hello, Kat! How are you?"

"Is Lucian there?"

"Yes, he is."

"Why hasn't he come home?"

"He's helping me with research," Brockton said. "He'll be home soon. No later than six this evening."

"Why so late? What's going on?"

"Nothing much. He's helping me with one of my experiments."

"Okay, I woke up earlier and was worried because he had a fever last night when he left. Is that normal?"

"A fever?" Brockton said, eyeing Lucian. Lucian looked away. "I suppose even *he* could have one from time to time."

"So it's not something I should worry about?" Kat asked.

"You worry about everything, Kat. You know that."

"I know."

"I'll make sure he's home soon."

"Thanks."

"Not a problem."

Brockton ended the call. "Other than your headache, how do you feel physically?"

Lucian stretched and popped his neck and back. "Somewhat stronger than when I jogged here last night."

"Good. I hoped the injections would help, but again, it's only a temporary remedy. We need to find a way to lengthen your telomeres. Kyle and I discussed some options earlier this morning while you slept."

"And?"

"We need to see if Lucas will help by donating blood or stem cells for you."

Lucian chuckled and shook his head. "Hell would freeze over faster than you finding success with that request."

"You really think he'd deny you life?"

"He's been against my existence from the beginning."

Brockton shrugged. "I can always ask."

"And after that fails?"

"I suggest you see Dr. Helmsby, provided we can locate him."

"You believe he could correct my symptoms better than you?"

"The man's a genius on a different scientific plane than I."

"I will have Kat contact Carpenter. He might know where Helmsby is."

Lucian walked across the room.

"You feel dizzy?" Brockton asked.

"No dizziness. Just tired."

Brockton nodded. "Probably because your body is still recuperating. Run in place for one minute."

"Seriously?"

Brockton cocked a brow and grinned.

"Very well," Lucian said.

He ran in place while Brockton timed him.

After the minute passed, Brockton said, "Stop. How do you feel now? Are you more drained?"

Lucian took a deep breath and smiled. "Actually, I'm feeling much better. Like a sudden adrenaline kick and my energy seems to be increasing. What did you inject me with?"

"Steroids with a high dose of B vitamins and a serum that even if I explained it to you, you wouldn't understand. This will only help you a short time. It is in no way reversing your symptoms. It will mask them, so be careful not to overexert yourself."

"Play it safe?"

"Don't plan to run a marathon or enter the UFC beat down."

Lucian smiled. "I won't today, but maybe tomorrow."

Brockton shook his head. "Let's get you home so Kat will stop worrying."

"Did she sound angry?"

Brockton grabbed his car keys. "No. Just worried."

"I don't know what she'll do if I don't survive this."

Brockton clapped Lucian's shoulder. "We'll find a cure somehow."

"I hope so."

"Kyle!" Brockton yelled. "We're leaving. Want to come along?"

"No," he replied from his room.

Brockton sighed. "I keep hoping he'll get back on track."

"He's not feeling well?"

"Oh, he's fine. Just being a bit lazy."

"Maybe you're overworking him?"

"*Me?* Nonsense."

"You get overly enthusiastic from time to time."

Brockton smiled. "Everyone does."

"Not like you."

"Oh," Brockton said, stopping at the door. "When Kat calls Carpenter, remember that I'll be happy to oversee the twins' medical evaluations if he can hurry the adoption along. I was too busy averting her scorn to remember to tell her myself earlier."

"Thanks. I'll tell her. She'll be thrilled."

Chapter 35

Cassandra parked Deidre's vehicle in a narrow, shaded alley. Thick dense vines clung to the wooden slat fences on both sides of the alley, making the painted graffiti on the boards barely visible.

The sky was dark and deep with heavy, circulating storm clouds. Even though sunset was an hour or so away, it was as dark as nightfall. Thunder rumbled in the distance. Sparse, but large, raindrops clinked the windshield with such force the glass sounded like it might break any second.

Cassandra's hands shook. Her stomach turned with nausea. Doug was dead because he had helped her with a simple errand, which made her question Jen's true motive. It couldn't just be jealousy. Jen was somehow linked to the conspiracy inside New Horizons, provided it was an actual conspiracy. But what else could it be?

"Alicia," she whispered. "Where are you?"

Cassandra recalled Doctor Shelby's gentle smile, the charisma that sweetened his voice, and wondered how such a man like Shelby could inwardly be so evil. How had she been fooled so easily? She knew.

She allowed herself mental blinders to shield what she might have seen because she so desperately wanted a baby and truly wanted to believe that good people existed in the world somewhere. After divorcing Doug, who had been a man she never thought would let her down, she heard the gentleness in Shelby's voice and witnessed the kindness of his demeanor and quickly latched onto her dream-come-true fantasy without hesitation. Focusing on the baby growing inside her allowed her to shunt the pain Doug had dealt by leaving.

Now that Alicia was gone and Doug had been killed, reality burst her dream bubble and exposed all the cracks that had been in the fantasy foundation she had settled her life upon.

She needed to escape Salem, but she refused to leave without Alicia.

Cassandra thought about Officer Parker's argument with Reece. They were holding someone in the cemetery where the creatures had torn her pursuers to shreds. He was being kept inside the crypt.

The crypt?

In a town where she was alone and in danger, she knew what she must do. She needed to find this man and help him escape. Perhaps, since he *knew too much*, he might be able to help find Alicia. It was the least she could do, and possibly the only alternative she had left.

Cassandra took the penlight off the key ring and reluctantly left the safety of Deidre's vehicle and stepped into the alley. Should she encounter Parker or any others pursuing her, she had to flee on foot.

A flash of lightning split the sky, which seemed to have slashed open the clouds and hurled rampaging torrents of raindrops downward. She pulled the hoodie over her head and walked in hurried strides down the alleyway. The hard raindrops were cold, making her shiver to the bone as her clothes captured the rain.

The clouds made the alley darker, made her feel somewhat shielded and hidden, but she'd be more comfortable once sunset passed and the night settled in. Of course, it painted a more horrifying thought of entering the cemetery alone, but she'd face the worst fate in the world if it meant she could save Alicia.

Creeping along back alleys and through the hedgerows, she moved stealthily until she came to the fenced cemetery. The cold rain soaked her. Her teeth chattered. She crossed the fence and with each step sloshed mud onto her sweatpants. Her running shoes sopped up the standing water. She hated when water squished between her toes. Should she be forced to run, the rubbing of her wet shoes and socks against her skin would cause her forming blisters to swell and rupture quicker.

The chill of night edged upon her as she blindly moved through the rows of gravestones. She wondered how she'd find the manor until a bright weaving burst of cloud-to-cloud lightning shimmered overhead, revealing the manor's location at the highest point in the cemetery. When the lightning ceased, the gloomy clouds swallowed the world around her. Wind-blown mists skirted across the terrain, and she paused behind a massive gravestone, listening to the sounds around her.

In the darkness and with the surging storm, she'd never know if anyone or those strange creatures approached. She wiped water from her face and then looked across the cemetery, trying to detect any movement. She saw nothing except the solid, cold tombstones.

The last thing Cassandra needed was to run into Officer Parker. With the phony story he had given the media, she held no doubt that he'd kill her without question. He certainly wouldn't give her the opportunity to surrender into his custody. Crossing his path meant death. She had to avoid him at all cost.

And if she failed to rescue the man inside the manor, her mission to find Alicia was over. She had already outweighed the odds against her by staying in Salem instead of leaving. She would be found eventually, and the streak of bad luck that paved her path meant she was running out of time.

Cassandra moved from gravestone to gravestone after each lightning strike faded. She crept closer to the manor and as best she could tell, she was the only living soul in the cemetery. Finally, after what seemed like hours, she reached the front wall.

Although the cemetery grounds were well kept and mowed, no grounds maintenance had cleared away the thick ivy and weeds that formed a micro-jungle around the aged manor. This seemed more a deterrent than a mere oversight by the owners. The appearance was meant to keep the curious away, and had she not been seeking the only person she hoped could help her, she'd have turned back.

Cassandra slipped her hand around the rusted doorknob, but she couldn't turn it.

Locked.

Lightning flashed.

She peered through the dark window. All the furniture inside was draped with dusty, white sheets.

Cassandra edged around the building perimeter, looking for another door, and when she reached the one on the backside, she found that door locked also. Frustrated and almost ready to abandon her search, she nearly stumbled, but luckily steadied herself before falling face first through the open cellar door.

Her heart pounded. She knew she had to enter the cellar and didn't like the idea at all. Even in full daylight, she'd have second thoughts about entering. Before she took a step, she listened for voices or approaching footsteps but heard nothing other than the distant thunder and the sluicing rain that ran off the roof and dug soft gullies in the earth.

Certain no one else was near, she took a deep breath, clicked on the penlight, and stepped down the earthen steps where the world became even darker, but at least she was out of the rain. But she wondered what she had traded the wet misery for.

SHEBA LEFT her tiny apartment above Officer Parker's garage. She thought about Mitch and what she had done to him. He had been overly kind to her when they had met at the bus stop, and even though she had wanted to think him to be as sleazy as all the other men she had dated, she knew he wasn't. His eyes were caring. He had compassion.

"What have I done?" she thought.

The rain slacked. The thunder and lightning was almost gone.

She loved the sweetness of the night air after a good rain.

Barefoot, Sheba sprinted down the sidewalk and wanted to release her human appearance and allow the beast inside its freedom, but she had to withhold that satisfaction. At least for a while. She wanted to see Mitch's eyes again. Would he really help her?

He had read her well. All the things she resented him for saying were true. He had struck a nerve. She needed to acknowledge that to herself and confess it to him. But, after what she had done, there wasn't any way she could fathom him *wanting* to help her now.

Regret for her overly ambitious need to please Alpha she decided she must convince Mitch that she was wrong and needed his help. After all, it was the only way to get Gloria released.

Sheba crossed the cemetery fence and stopped. She sniffed the air and detected the scent of another human. A female.

She immediately thought of the business card Mitch had handed her.

The Kat Gaddis Agency.

"No," she whispered.

There wasn't any chance that the people he worked for had reached Salem this quickly. But someone was here, and from the direction the wind blew, that person was near the manor. Sheba's eyes narrowed, glinted with gold, and she growled as she sprinted across the cemetery. The change was coming whether she wanted it to or not. She couldn't stop it, but she would kill anyone who tried to take Mitch from the crypt.

Chapter 36

Mordia entered the bank with the safety deposit box key squeezed tightly inside her hand. An armed guard politely smiled as she walked past.

She tried to hide her nervousness, but her increasing heartbeat thundered in her ears. She felt lightheaded and afraid she'd pass out before a teller escorted her to the box.

Suddenly, she wondered if Matthews had lied to her about the money. Coming to San Diego was a gamble, a hope that what he had told her was true and that soon the lifestyle she had lost might be within reach again.

"What if he's lying?" she thought.

She glanced back at the bank door. Would Matthews even be waiting for her? So many scenarios raced through her mind. Had he needed to come to San Diego for other reasons and given her such a tempting story of wealth that he'd abandon her while she was in the bank? The key might not even fit a deposit box at all.

She reached the teller's counter and gripped the rail to keep her balance. She was dizzy, filled with fear and worry that she had been deceived.

"Can I help you?" The teller asked with a broad smile. The name plaque showed her name: Tess Becks.

"I need to open my safety deposit box," Mordia replied.

"One second." Tess picked up the phone. Across the room an assistant manager answered her phone. "I'm sending a lady to you."

Tess hung up the phone. She pointed. "Mrs. Pierce will assist you."

Mordia nodded and smiled modestly. "Thanks."

Mrs. Pierce smiled. "This way."

Mordia followed.

"What box number?" Mrs. Pierce asked.

"Thirteen seventy-four."

Mrs. Pierce led Mordia into a room lined with several thousand secured boxes. She scanned a row of numbers until she stopped at 1374. After they inserted each key, Mordia placed the metal box on a table in the center of the room. She waited until Mrs. Pierce left her alone before she opened the box.

When she lifted the lid, she expected the box to be empty. Instead, several bound stacks of one hundred dollar bills filled three-fourths of the box. A tiny Styrofoam tray took the rest of the space. She popped off the Styrofoam lid. Eight syringes filled with yellow liquid were cushioned inside foam slots. For a moment, she wondered whether the fluid was toxic or actually rejuvenated tissue like Matthews insisted.

After putting the lid over the vials, her attention turned to the stacks of one hundred dollar bills. Her heart raced. Her hands shook. She'd never seen so much cash. Matthews hadn't lied. The money was there just like he had promised.

Mordia opened her purse and pulled out a small box. Carefully, she removed the vials, placed them into the cotton-lined box, and stuffed a thick layer of cotton atop them. She closed the box and put it inside her purse.

She stared at the money.

Mordia had never been a greedy person but seeing such an enormous stack of cash prompted her ambition to make even more money. A part of her feared taking the money Matthews had promised her. Doing so tied her to him, and there was the possibility she couldn't back out should situations arise that further tarnished her morals and her soul.

The money baited a trap ever so seductive. Her sweaty hands trembled as she clutched the first stack of hundreds and tucked them into her purse. She took the other stacks, too, stashing them into her purse. She closed the box. Once she fastened the lid shut, she sighed and tried to stop her hands from trembling. Technically, she hadn't done anything wrong, but she felt guilty and a bit dirty inside.

Whether she liked it or not, Matthews owned her, at least for the time being. She almost felt ashamed that she had a price. She left the box on the table and left the bank. Matthews met her on the sidewalk.

"Satisfied?" he asked. "It's all yours with much more to come."

Mordia failed to hide her enthusiastic smile. Her nervous eyes investigated the streets around her. She half expected law enforcement officers to rush from the shadows and take them into custody. A couple of seconds later, her eyes met his dark gaze that peered through his bandages. Although disturbing at the coldness that swirled within his gaze, she smiled again.

"Let's go," Matthews said. "Now we need to find a pet shop and buy a rat."

"A rat?"

"That's the animal scientists use the most, isn't it?"

"Perhaps, but why do *we* need one?"

"I need to show you what this rejuvenating agent does. This is something you must see to believe. The best-written scientific report would be scoffed at without real video footage to back up the claim."

Mordia gazed at him questioningly.

Matthews smiled. "Trust me. You're on the brink of a new era of science and a wealthier bank account."

He took her hand and tugged earnestly.

Frowning, she replied. "Okay."

They walked several blocks until they found a small pet shop. People noticed his bandaged face but most simply sidestepped or pretended not to see him, which was fine by Matthews. These weren't people he'd hold interest in anyway. They were subpar compared to him.

Matthews pushed the pet shop door partway open and faced her. "Spot me a hundred?"

Mordia smiled and nodded. "Get whatever you need. I'll pay for it."

"Of course you will," he said with a condescending tone and a smile.

Chapter 37

Matthews held the rat in the small cage while Mordia drove the rental car. She seemed more relaxed and happier. Money did that for some people. Matthews never expected to be content during his lifetime. Increased wealth had never satisfied him, nor had his scientific achievements, but these were things he still coveted and would kill to possess.

He thought about Grayson Enterprises and how close he had been to killing Grayson and Dr. Helmsby. Every day since, he had struggled with that failure, constantly plotting ways to rectify his temporary defeat. Getting rid of two elite scientists would have placed Matthews farther up the ladder of recognition within the scientific world. Instead, his failure was headlines around the world and in Internet news articles, forever tarnishing his reputation. No matter what successes he could achieve as a free man, he would never redeem his name, which was why he chose plastic surgery to change his appearance.

"Do you have a preference where to stay while we're in San Diego?" she asked.

"Actually, I have an apartment that I paid a full year's rent before I was sent away."

Mordia gave a side-glance. "A full year?"

"Yes."

"So you had already planned to break out of prison before you were incarcerated?"

"Let's just say that I had hopes to be released early."

"You had help?" she asked.

"A big investor. My prison term hampered what he hopes to achieve."

"So you don't work alone?"

He gave a shrewd smile. "You work with me. So I have business partners."

Mordia followed his directions to his studio apartment building, parked in the garage, and stared at him with curiosity when he stepped out of the rental car with the rat.

"Still don't trust me?" Matthews asked.

"It will take some time. I trust few people."

"But you'll follow the money?"

Mordia chuckled and followed him to the elevator. "That part hasn't let me down yet."

"More to come, my good doctor."

Inside his apartment, Matthews set the cage atop a round table in the dining room. An empty glass ashtray was beside the cage. The curious rat stood on its hind legs and sniffed the air.

"You have the syringes?"

She nodded. "In my bag."

Mordia reached into her purse and took out the Styrofoam box. She set the box on the table. Matthews took a syringe from the box and placed it on the table. He opened the rat cage and stepped closer.

"Watch closely," he said.

The rat eased through the open cage lid and crawled cautiously across the lid. It looked back and forth between Matthews and Mordia. When its courage rose, it dropped off the cage and scurried to the center of the table.

Matthews grabbed the ashtray and slammed it down on the rat, crushing the rodent. The dead rat twisted.

"What the hell did you do that for?" she screamed. "You're insane!"

Mordia bolted for the door.

"Patience, doctor, or you'll miss the miracle."

Confused and yet, curious, she stopped and turned.

Matthews took the syringe and injected the rejuvenation agent into the rat's stomach. "You have a watch. Time this, starting . . . Now!"

With a look of disgust she took her watch and forced herself to walk back to the table. A small pool of blood spread from the rat's mouth and nose. Its tail and hind legs twitched.

Matthews capped the syringe. "You're about to witness a man-made miracle, nothing short of godly."

The rat's nose wrinkled. Its sides expanded as it took a gulp of air. A few seconds later, its breathing regulated. Its eyes opened. The rat got up on all fours and stood.

Mordia frowned and looked from the rat to Matthews. "How?"

"Time?"

She glanced down at the watch in her shaking hands. "Three minutes."

Matthews cocked a brow. "Not bad. Better than I had hoped."

"*How'd* you do this? *How* does it work?"

"We'll discuss the technology later. The benefits of immortality are how we'll market this. Everyone seems to want to live forever. We have something to grant people those dreams."

The rat stood on its hind legs and peered at Mordia. Its red eyes were shadowed by an eerie shade of gray. Although alive, it didn't look exactly the same.

"What effects occur with the resurrected creatures?" she asked.

"I never had the chance to get the results."

"So you don't know?"

"I did test this on lab rats, but they escaped."

Mordia leaned down to look at the rat. Its whiskers twitched as it attempted to get her scent.

"How'd you test this before the rats?"

"I used human corpses."

Her eyes widened. "You were able to bring them to life?"

"Yes."

"Like zombies?"

Matthews chuckled. "Nothing like what you see in those silly movies. They were easily trained with subliminal programming. Quite useful in the field."

"In the field? What did you use them for?"

"Assassins."

"That's morbid and creepy."

"Most would agree with you. But there weren't any true risks of causalities, at least not on *my* end, because they were already dead. Well, technically speaking, they were undead."

Mordia shook her head. "Since you've never used this on living humans, what do you predict will occur when we do?"

"My hope is a much longer lifespan. The tissues of these undead creatures continue to decompose, but at a much slower rate. I believe this concoction, when used on healthy individuals, will extend longevity."

"Possible side-effects?"

Matthews shrugged. "There's always a chance for that. Even the drugs approved by the FDA tend to have far more side-effects than actual benefits."

Mordia winced. "We need to know the risks before we use this on patients."

"I know."

"What do you propose we do?"

"We find volunteers."

Mordia shook her head. "You'll have a hard time getting volunteers for such an experiment."

"Why? I'm not going to bash them over the head like I did the rat. They'll be alive and have the opportunity to have a much longer life. Besides, we're in San Diego, we won't have any shortage of volunteers."

She frowned. "I don't understand."

"Lots of underground vagrants. They venture out after the sun sets."

"That's unethical."

"Getting a conscious *now*?" he asked.

"I never lost mine."

Matthews smiled. "It helps *not* to have one."

"I'm sure it does with whatever you're planning to do."

"A hundred dollars per pop should get some quick volunteers," Matthews said. "How many do you think would make a good drug trial? A couple of dozen?"

She thought for a moment. "At least. If we document everything properly, that would be a good basis to study, but there are other factors that must be considered."

"Such as?"

She wrote on a notepad. "We need people who aren't drug addicts or contaminated with diseases. Otherwise, we won't have positive, conclusive data. Only clean subjects will validate your hypothesis."

"Drug-free vagrants. Our *new* challenge."

"I'm serious."

Matthews nodded. "I know, but considering the odds, finding those will be difficult."

"Plus, there's something else."

"What?"

"The test subjects will have to be people who don't have family actively looking for them."

"You're right but our ability to search databases for such information will be extremely limited. Besides, most vagrants aren't looking to be found. They're too ashamed of their current living conditions and failures in life to want friends and family to know where they are."

"Too bad I don't know people in this country with computer tech abilities."

Matthews frowned and suddenly smiled. "Now that you mention it, I do. And one or two owe me a great deal in favors."

"And they're not afraid that you're wanted by police?"

"They'd be more afraid *not* to do what I request."

Chapter 38

Cassandra trained the penlight on the path ahead of her. Occasionally, when the wind blew, the outside shutters rapped the wall. She swayed the light back and forth, fearful someone or something was in the cellar with her.

Passing the coffins earlier had been unnerving enough, but the added sounds of creaking boards and rapping on the outer walls kept her on edge even more.

Down the narrow hallway, a man moaned. She stopped walking and lowered the light. The thought crossed her mind to head back out. She had no idea how many people were in the hallway.

"Help me," Mitch said softly.

Cassandra held her breath, waiting for someone to answer him.

"Sheba, please," he said. "Just let me go."

Still no one else spoke.

"I know you're out there. I saw your light. Stop playing your games."

He was speaking to her. No one else.

Cassandra stepped timidly toward the side door. She washed the light over Mitch's suspended body. He squinted when the light struck his eyes. The dried blood on his chest outlined his lacerations.

After quickly inspecting the room with the light and seeing no one else around, she hurried to him.

"Is anyone else here?" Cassandra asked.

"No. Just me. Who are you?" he asked weakly.

"I'm here to help you. My name's Cassandra."

"I'm Mitch. How'd you find me?"

She tugged at the restraints but they were thick and tied tightly. "That's not important right now. I have to get you out of here before it's too late."

Cassandra studied the deep cuts across his chest. "Are you okay? These wounds are bad. They look like animal scratches."

"I'll be fine. I'm more cold and hungry than I am in pain. Something to drink would be nice. My throat's dry and hurts."

"We can take care of that after I get you down."

"I'm glad you found me. But really, you should leave. You don't have any idea what kind of people you're dealing with."

"I know much more than what you imagine."

Mitch shook his head. "No. The're coming back to kill me. They'll kill you, too, should they find you."

Cassandra gave a wry smile. She yanked at the restraints without any success. "I'm way ahead of you on their schedule. Dammit! They secured you well."

"Their schedule?"

"They want me dead, too."

"Why?"

"That part I don't understand yet, but they killed my ex-husband earlier. He was trying to help me. They, or someone associated with them, kidnapped my daughter and another boy's missing. His mother was killed."

Mitch frowned. "With all that, why haven't you just run? Why take the time to rescue me?"

"You're the last chance I may have at finding Alicia."

"And how did you arrive at that conclusion?"

"I heard the policemen talking about you and that you knew too much. Of course, that was minutes before the one officer killed his partner and framed me for the murder." She tugged and then pulled herself up, adding her full weight to the leather straps. Exasperated, she dropped to the floor. "Damn. I need something to cut through the leather."

"You should leave before they arrive."

"Not without you. I'll be right back. I have to find something to get you down."

"If you can't find anything, please leave, find a phone, and get help."

"From who? All my options are gone. I don't have any other friends in this area. The last person on earth I'd have called was my ex, and now I regret that. But I certainly can't go to the police."

"Go to the next town and get help."

"No. There isn't time," Cassandra said, shaking her head. "I *will* get you down, and afterwards, I need a favor in return."

"I'll do whatever I can to help you."

Cassandra smiled. "That's all I ask. Now, I'll be right back. I think there were some old garden tools near the cellar entrance."

"Be careful. The girl who tied me here. She's . . . she's *very* dangerous."

Cassandra nodded and hurried into the corridor. She hated to leave him. It was great talking to another person. It helped eliminate the insanity of talking to herself and waiting for an answer.

Mitch had warned her about the girl who had restrained him. The fear in his voice was evident as he mentioned her. But, she wondered about the girl's age and what part she played with New Horizons or the police, if any. So much had happened so quickly.

She came to the end of the corridor, turned, and made her way around the fallen boards where the coffins were. She hurried past them because they reminded her of the absolute power of death, and she didn't want to dwell on dismal thoughts because if she died before she found Alicia . . . She thrust the thought from her mind.

The wind whistled through the cellar door. Rain pelted the grounds outside. Under normal circumstances these sounds would have been relaxing, as she lay in bed, but not tonight, not in the middle of a cemetery. Bright lightning flickered and illuminated the earthen steps.

She edged nearer to the door where she had seen some garden tools propped against the wall. A shovel, an old rake, and a rusted pair of hedge-trimmers rested beneath layers of dust and cobwebs. She took the hedge-trimmers, dusted them off, and noticed a curved handheld sickle. Picking up the sickle she momentarily debated which would work best to cut Mitch down.

Lightning flashed and struck a tree near the manor. The harsh thwack caused her to turn toward the door. In the flickering light, a dark silhouette made her gasp. Glowing golden eyes peered at her. Little metal spikes protruded around its lips and cheeks.

A guttural growl rumbled in its throat as it sprang upward and charged.

Cassandra screamed and in a moment it slashed at her with sharp claws. In a defensive attempt to protect herself, Cassandra swung the sickle. The blade sunk deep into its chest. It whelped and pulled back, taking the blade with it as it limped up the earthen steps.

She grabbed the rusted hedge-trimmers and in the dim light of the penlight, she sprinted through the cellar, around the coffins, and down the corridor until she reached the room where Mitch was tied.

Panting for air, she pulled the handles to open the blades.

"What's wrong?" Mitch asked. "You screamed. Are you okay?"

"We have to hurry," she said, fumbling with the trimmers. "A wolf or creature tried to attack me."

"No," Mitch said. "That's the girl."

"What?"

"Yeah, she transforms into a wolf. She did all this to me."

Cassandra positioned the blades against the leather and squeezed. The blades jammed from the rust and their dull edges.

"I don't need any farfetched stories to go with this nightmarish day."

"It's the truth. She is *whatever* she is."

"No. It's not possible," she said, but then she thought of the catlike creatures. Perhaps it was possible. "It did appear to have facial piercings. And a tattoo of a spider? I thought my mind was playing tricks on me."

"No," Mitch said, shaking his head. "She has piercings. A lot of them. And the tattoo."

Cassandra shook her head and concentrated on the leather restraints. She opened the blades and clamped them shut again, but the leather was too tough. Tears welled in her eyes as her frustration built.

"I wouldn't have thought she could transform, either. But she lured me here, changed into that wolfish creature and took me captive."

Cassandra wiped away tears and frowned. "These aren't working."

"Just go before she comes back."

"No," she said. "We're safer if we stick together."

"I'm not so certain about that."

She gritted her teeth and tried a third time. When the blades shut on the leather, she twisted. The blade didn't cut it, but it was weakening the leather. She figured if she twisted back and forth enough, she might stretch the restraint enough to untie it at his wrists. But how soon before the wolf came back?

Chapter 39

Sheba limped out of the cellar and into the rain. Curling on the wet grass, she panted. As a wolf, her paws couldn't grasp and pull the sickle out, but her pain wasn't as severe as it would be if she were human. Shifting back into human form to yank the blade out, the pain would be horrendous but she would heal.

Closing her eyes, she relaxed, and slowly, steadily, she left her wolf form and returned to her human self. The night air and cold rain made her shiver. The sickle blade stuck about two inches into her ribcage between her breasts. Blood mixed with rain trickled off her nude body.

She growled and gnashed her teeth as she took the wooden handle in her hands. Breathing hard, she prepared for the pain and gritted her teeth. She pulled the blade out and writhed on the ground. She fought hard not to allow her beast form to take over, but the riveting pain shot through her body and she gave in.

Hair sprouted over her. Her body changed. Her wound slowly knitted together.

Sheba lifted to all fours and returned to the cellar stairs. She sniffed the air and descended. Blood dripped from the closing wound. Panting with her tongue hanging out, she lowered and curled at the edge of the door. She'd let the wound heal before she continued her pursuit.

"ANY LUCK?" Mitch asked.

Cassandra twisted and pulled. "Not yet, but at least they're not as tight."

Mitch felt the slack in the restraints and it eased the strain in his shoulders. She opened the trimmers and slammed them shut again and again. As the rust scraped loose of the blades, the trimmers operated a bit better.

Sweat poured off Cassandra. She panted and puffed but she continued cutting the leather. Small tears began forming in the strap and blisters rose on her palms.

She lowered the blades to catch her breath.

"I'd pull but I don't have the strength," he said.

"Give me a second," she replied, leaning over to breath. "I'll see if adding my weight will snap it now."

"Mitch!" Sheba's voice echoed through the cellar.

Mitch looked at Cassandra. "Hurry."

Wide-eyed, she peered toward the corridor. Sheba sounded far away, but Cassandra wasn't sure how badly Sheba's injuries were her. She jumped, grabbed the leather strap, and held tightly. For several seconds she hung there, face-to-face with Mitch, and then the strap snapped. They dropped to the floor.

Mitch groaned in pain while she yanked and tugged at the knots around his wrists.

"I'm afraid you're going have to wear these until after we get out of here. They're tied too tightly for me to unravel."

She helped Mitch to his feet.

"I've never been into the bondage thing," he said with a slight grin. "But this whole ordeal has ensured I'll never consider it."

Cassandra draped his tied arms around her neck to support him. They walked to the door. "Any idea if there's another way out?"

"Nope."

She looked down the corridor that led to the cellar entrance and shook her head. "We'll have to take our chances and hope there is. I can't confront her again."

"She'll kill us either way."

"I'd rather it be while we're running with a slight hope for escape than going head-to-head against her."

Mitch gave a slight nod. "I'm with you."

Cassandra headed farther away from the coffins and into another side room door. On a table her light revealed a pile of clothes and a briefcase.

"Those are mine," he said.

"Anything useful in the briefcase that might cut through the leather?"

"I do keep a Swiss Army knife in there."

"Good. I'll see if I can find it."

"While you're looking, see if my cellphone is in there, too. If it is, we can get help."

"It's here."

Mitch sighed with relief. "I'm surprised she left that behind."

"She probably figured you couldn't get free."

He nodded. "True. Dial this number."

Chapter 40

Kat answered her phone. "Hello? Mitch?"

"Mitch is with me," Cassandra said.

"Who's this?"

"Cassandra Meeks. Mitch was abducted and I helped him escape. He wanted me to call you. They have my daughter."

"Is he okay? Can I speak to him?"

"Sure."

Cassandra placed the phone to Mitch's ear. With her free hand, she used the Swiss Army saw blade to cut through the leather straps. Purple marks encircled his wrists. He rubbed them for a moment and then took the phone from Cassandra.

"Kat," Mitch said. "We need help."

"What's wrong? Who abducted you?"

"The girl I was talking to last night."

"The same one that told you she had information?"

"Yes."

"So she was lying?"

Mitch replied, "No. She knows what has been happening here but for some reason, she baited me and took me hostage."

"Any idea why she did that?"

"Fear."

"What's she afraid of?"

"Whoever is behind these attacks," Mitch said. "And it turns out that she's not exactly human."

"What?"

"Yes. She's like part wolf or something."

"Okay. Lucian is on his way home. We'll be on the next flight out."

"I don't know if we'll survive that long."

"Are you okay?" Kat asked.

"I have some cuts and bruises. But moving fast isn't an option."

"Hang in there and find somewhere to hide."

"The wolf girl, Sheba, she's coming after us."

"Let me talk to Cassandra."

Mitch handed the phone to Cassandra.

"We'll be on our way soon. We're going to help you find your daughter. I promise."

Tears welled in Cassandra's eyes. "Thank you," she whispered.

SHEBA STOOD in human form and leaned against the wall. Although the wound had healed, she was still shaken and weak. She pulled on her wet pants that she had left outside the cellar right before taking the sickle to the chest. She believed she had a better chance persuading Mitch if she approached in human form rather than her aggressive wolf form.

Her fingers traced the vanishing scar on her ribcage. She pulled her shirt over her head quickly. Her pain was minimal.

"Mitch?" she said with a sweet, innocent voice. "Did you really mean what you had said? That you will help me?"

No answer. Sheba moved past the coffins and toward the door.

"If you promise to help me, I will lead you out of here. Please? We can help each other."

"WAIT," Mitch said, stopping.

Cassandra braced herself under his weight. "What?"

"I did promise I'd help her."

180

"Are you serious? Do you really think she's going to help you, especially after what I did?"

"It might buy us some time."

Cassandra shook her head. "Keep dreaming. We have to get out of here and as far from her as possible."

She shone the light against the wall. Near the end of the hallway, several fallen boards appeared to be covering another door.

"There," she said, pointing. "I think that we might be able to get out that way."

"Mitch?" Sheba said. "Talk to me, Mitch. Don't be like this. I'm sorry for hitting you and tying you up. Please? Help me?"

Mitch turned his head. His eyes softened.

"Come on." Cassandra tugged him beside her. "I take it you don't date much."

"Why do you say that?"

"You don't seem to understand that she's trying to prey upon your emotions. She knows you were attracted to her, and it seems that she's playing you."

"Don't be ridiculous," Mitch said.

Cassandra laughed. "Really? Look at how you're acting. You're the victim, but you're allowing her to make you believe she's the victim."

"But, in a sense, she is."

"Nonsense. She's already succeeded in slowing us down. Now come on and move your feet a bit faster. We have to get away from here so I can find Alicia."

When she reached the fallen boards, she helped Mitch lean against the wall. She flashed the light back down the hall. No glowing eyes. Nothing moved toward them.

"We have to move these boards."

Mitch stepped beside her. Even though his wrists and shoulders ached, he pulled and tugged a couple of the boards out of the way. Cassandra took the light and inspected the other side of the doorway.

"Odd."

"What?" he asked.

"It's an underground tunnel."

"Mitch?" Sheba said, from the room where he had been tied.

The tone of her voice had changed from gentle and sweet to

perturbed.

Mitch looked nervous.

"Should we go through the tunnel?" he asked.

"Do we really have a choice?"

"I suppose we don't."

Mitch braced himself against the doorframe and took a step through. "The bad part is we don't know where this tunnel goes or if it's blocked halfway through."

"I thought about that myself. Let's hurry, just in case we have to turn around."

She took his hand and walked beside him through the tunnel. She walked at a pace he could keep. They nearly stopped dead in their tracks when Sheba growled behind them at the tunnel door.

Cassandra looped her arm around his and pulled him along with her.

"Don't fall down," she whispered.

Sheba snarled. Her voice deepened. "You said that you'd help me, and like the others, you're going to abandon me."

"Don't listen to her," Cassandra said. "She's trying to slow you down."

"I realize that now."

"Then keep moving."

Mitch's steps went from stumbling to more surefooted. Apparently fear or determination had set in and he moved steadily down the tunnel. The light Cassandra carried swayed back and forth. The glow washed a narrow path of darkness ahead of them.

Sheba growled and sounded even closer in her pursuit.

Cassandra looked back and shone the light quickly. Sheba was moving fast.

"That doesn't sound promising," she said.

She turned back around, and her light reflected off three sets of eyes.

The catlike creatures.

She pulled Mitch's arm, stopped running, and squeezed against the wall. The creatures' glowing green eyes narrowed. They bore their teeth and hissed.

Sheba's footsteps thudded heavily from behind.

Cassandra closed her eyes. They were trapped in between with nowhere else to run.

No escape.

Chapter 41

"Mitch!" Sheba growled.

Cassandra pressed herself tightly against the wall and Mitch.

"She'll find us if we stay here," Mitch whispered.

"It doesn't matter now."

"Why?"

Cassandra looked at him in the faint glow of the flashlight. "You didn't see the creatures?"

"No, I was too busy focusing on her."

Mitch glanced over Cassandra's shoulder. The emerald green eyes glinted.

"What are they?" he asked.

"Not sure," she whispered. "But I think they took my daughter."

"Mitch! I smell you. I'm coming for you."

The catlike creatures released screeching growls like panthers, stopping Sheba in her tracks. Cassandra glanced back, fearful that she and Mitch were about to be ripped to shreds, but she noted the fear in Sheba's eyes when she stood before the cat threesome.

Sheba took a step back, and then another. She turned and fled. The three cats darted after her.

"What the hell?" Mitch asked.

Cassandra took a deep breath and released it. "I'm not certain, but that's twice they've saved my life."

"Really?"

She nodded and told him about the two men that tried to kill her.

"That's interesting," he said. "And you think these cats took your daughter?"

"I do."

"If so, they may be hiding her to protect her from these other people."

"I'd like to think that, but I still don't know where Alicia is."

Mitch patted her shoulder and pulled her close in a gentle hug. "When Kat and Lucian get here, we'll have better numbers. We'll find her."

"What do we do until then?" she asked.

"We hide until morning."

"Hide?"

"It's the safest way. Besides, those catlike things didn't seem interested in harming either of us."

"Where can we hide?" she asked.

"I say we follow the tunnel out. That's apparently how the cats got in here. When we reach the end, we can decide. But, for what it's worth, I believe Alicia is safe."

"Thanks, but I'll be more comforted once I have her in my arms."

"I understand," he said. "Let's go."

Chapter 42

Lucas drove and glanced at Joe. "That skull is extraterrestrial. Wouldn't you say?"

Joe nodded. "That'd be my guess."

"Probably worth millions to the right person, but why would they kill to get it?"

"Perhaps the party doesn't have that kind of money to offer."

"No. There's more to it than just the money. Where did you find it? Anywhere near Desert Labs?"

"It was near the gulch where Desert Labs had been dumping their waste."

Lucas smiled. "That's probably the most useful information yet."

"You think the laboratory owner is behind it?"

"Maybe. Or perhaps someone had been spying on their operation happened to see you find it."

"That still doesn't give the reason why they want it."

"No," Lucas said, glancing into his side-view mirror. "But the people behind us probably know why."

Joe looked over his shoulder. The tan camo Jeep sped right to their back bumper and tapped it hard.

"Have your gun ready?" Lucas asked.

Joe slipped his revolver from his belt holster and focused on his side view mirror.

Lucas pushed the accelerator to the floor. They drove over a hill that plummeted downward and around a sharp, winding curve.

"Hang on," Lucas said.

Lucas hit the brakes and cut the wheel sharp to hug the curve of the road but he was going too fast. The passenger side tires skidded off the highway, slinging sand and loose gravel. The SUV spun into a tailspin. Lucas attempted to straighten out the vehicle, but the Jeep rammed the rear driver side tire and forced Lucas farther off the road. Glancing toward the edge of the road, Lucas noticed the deep gulley. The uneven jagged drop was probably a good fifty yards to the bottom.

He fought to drive the SUV back onto the road but the Jeep driver increased speed to push the SUV off the road.

"Dammit!" Lucas said, pushing the gas pedal to the floor. "There's no traction."

The SUV tires spun uselessly to hold the heavy vehicle on the ledge. Gravity soon won the tittering battle and the SUV slowly descended.

Gunfire.

Bullets chinked through the windows, one narrowly missing Lucas' head. He stood on the accelerator while Joe fired off a couple rounds.

The man backed the Jeep up, shoved it into first, gunned the engine, and crashed into the SUV's midsection, tilting the vehicle on two wheels.

"Hang on," Lucas seethed through his gritted teeth.

The SUV flipped over onto its side, dropped ten feet down the rocky gulley, and rolled over twice, stopping upside down.

Glass shattered and showered around them. Metal crumpled. Everything was one quick blur. Lucas' head hit the side glass. The window burst and his forehead struck the steering wheel. He didn't move. Limp and lifeless he hung upside down, suspended by his seat belt.

"You okay?" Joe asked.

Lucas didn't answer.

"Luke?" Joe shook Lucas' shoulder.

Silence.

Blood trickled from a cut on Lucas' brow and his nose.

The Jeep doors slammed shut. Joe peered through the windshield. The men headed down the slope with their guns raised. The way the men approached detailed their tactical training. Mercenaries determined to carry out their assignment.

Joe looked for his gun but couldn't find it. After the SUV flipped twice he wasn't certain where the gun went. He and Lucas hung upside down fastened in by their seatbelts.

The men hurried down the hillside. Wind kicked up loose sand in little white clouds around their boots.

Joe unfastened his seatbelt and dropped to the ceiling. He positioned himself beneath Lucas, unsnapped his seatbelt, and caught Lucas across the shoulders and positioned him behind the seat. He checked for a pulse. Lucas' heart beat steadily, but he remained unconscious.

Bullets struck the windshield.

Joe dove over Lucas to protect him from the gunfire and in doing so, he found Lucas' gun. He clicked off the safety, loaded a round into the chamber, and fired several rounds through the windshield.

The men stopped their approach and crouched down, making themselves smaller targets.

Joe aimed carefully and shot at the man closest to the front of the SUV. The bullet flicked sand into the air less than a foot away from the man. His adversary rolled to the side. Joe fired another round.

Although he didn't like guns, he was in a situation where he favored having one.

Joe might hold these men off for a while, but he didn't have that kind of time. Lucas wasn't moving and possibly needed medical attention. Blood streamed down his face from his scalp. It looked like he was losing a lot of blood.

"There's no good way out for you!" one of the men said.

"What do you want?" Joe asked.

"The skull."

"Kill me and you'll never find it," Joe replied.

Joe ripped a long band of cloth from his shirt and wrapped it around the laceration on Lucas' scalp. He whispered a brief blessing while tying the cloth. It would be enough to stop the bleeding. Other than the cut, Lucas seemed to be breathing regularly but still hadn't gained consciousness. He didn't believe Lucas was in a coma, but with the sun setting, sidewinder rattlesnakes would seek warmth after the heat evaporated from the rocks. A human's body temperature was perfect to attract such reptiles. He didn't want Lucas's outcome to be what Misty's had been.

Something buzzed and caught Joe's attention. Lucas' cellphone.

Joe grabbed the phone but didn't answer it.

"All we want is the skull," the man said outside. His voice was closer. "That's it."

"It's not with us."

"Take us to it and we'll consider letting your friend live."

The fact that they knew Lucas was hurt informed Joe that they were watching them with through a scope that was probably attached to a high-powered rifle. They could have already shot and killed Joe and Lucas, which meant they really wanted that skull.

The phone stopped buzzing.

"My friend needs to be taken to a hospital," Joe said loudly. "He's unconscious and bleeding badly."

Joe dialed his brother's number and let it ring.

"You take us to the skull and we'll get an ambulance out here for him."

"I don't trust you," Joe said.

The man laughed. "I believe you'll have to take our word."

Joe's brother answered the phone. "Hello?"

Joe whispered into the phone and explained their situation, where the SUV had gone over the gully, and that armed men were threatening to kill them.

"Lucas needs help," Joe told his brother.

With a firm solemn tone, Owl-hunter replied, "We're on our way. Don't hang up. Keep this line open so we can hear what's going on while we track it."

"I will, but I don't think I can do anything else but leave with them."

"We're coming, brother. Be safe."

Joe didn't end the call, but he took the phone and tucked it overhead between the rear seats.

"Toss out your gun and keep your hands where we can see them. Otherwise we open fire. Skull or no skull."

Joe looked at Lucas and shook his head. "Sorry, bro. Got to leave you."

He squeezed Lucas' shoulder and crawled to the passenger side door. He tossed the gun through the shattered side window. Stone crunched beneath the man's approaching boots.

Joe put both hands out the side window with his fingers spread wide.

Each man gripped one of his wrists and pulled him through the open window. The men wore bulletproof vests and dark sunglasses, even though sunset was less than an hour away. Both were muscular, clean-shaven, with burr cuts. Their hardened countenance let him know immediately that Calvin was nothing like these men. He was an actual hobbyist. These men dealt death. Joe sensed it in their aura.

One man took a pair of plastic tie handcuffs and secured Joe's wrists.

"You going to leave him?" Joe asked.

"Help will come, provided you cooperate."

Joe knew help would come, but it would be his brothers, not medics. All Joe needed to do was leave with the men and let them believe he'd lead them to the alien artifact. But that wasn't going to happen. Joe wasn't going to tell them. Not until he knew Lucas was safe.

Chapter 43

Joe sat in the back seat of the Jeep on the passenger side. He rested his tied hands on his lap. The driver was tanned with a solid muscular jaw. His huge muscled hands held the steering wheel tightly. The man's 9mm lay across his legs.

The man that sat shotgun turned where he could keep an eye on Joe. He held his gun with the safety off.

Joe sat passively. His eyes showed little interest in what they were doing, and he had no look of fear or worry on his face. He remained solemn and solid as a rock.

"What's your name?" the driver asked.

"Joe."

"How do we get to the skull? You want to give the directions the easy way?" he asked.

"Or the hard way," Shotgun rider asked with a wide cackle and bizarre smile. He waved the gun and pointed it at Joe's face.

Joe didn't flinch. "It's not too far from here."

"Doesn't quite narrow it down," the driver said.

"I wasn't finished speaking," Joe said firmly.

The man in the passenger seat swung the butt of the gun at Joe. Joe's tied hands rose quickly and blocked the blow.

"Dammit, Reggie! Stop it!" the driver said.

"You heard his defiant tone, Curt. I'm not about to take that."

"Reg, we *need* the skull. Understand? Knock him unconscious or accidentally kill him, and we ain't going to get it. That won't go over well with our superior, now will it?"

"No." Reggie gritted his teeth and bore a hateful stare at Joe.

Joe grinned.

Reggie turned away.

"You have to excuse his behavior, Joe," Curt said. "We kind of thought we could find the skull at your house last night, but well, it wasn't there."

Joe's gazed at the driver with narrowed eyes. Curt never bothered to glance in Joe's direction. "You placed the rattlers in my house?"

"Yeah," Reggie said with a wide grin. He chattered his strange laugh again. "Damn things should have killed you this morning."

"One did kill Misty," Joe said.

"Sorry about your girlfriend," Curt said. "But, it's good that you lived. Otherwise, we'd never find the skull. Now, we need directions."

"Drive about two more miles straight ahead," Joe said. "Then take a right."

The sun was fading behind the mountain ridges. Darkness was coming.

Joe stared straight ahead. His eyes seemed frozen. His spirit stepped into the Otherworld.

When Curt turned right, he asked, "Now where?"

Joe didn't answer. His eyes were focused, and he never blinked.

"Hey," Reggie said, shaking Joe's shoulder. "Dammit, Curt, he's like a zombie or something."

Curt slowed the Jeep and pulled to the edge of the road. After he shut off the engine, he unbuckled his seatbelt and turned in his seat to face Joe.

"Navaho," Curt said. "Wake up! We need directions."

Joe blinked slowly and seemed to suddenly take to life. He shook his head. "I'm sorry? What?"

Curt cleared his throat. "We made the turn. Now where do we go?"

"Help me out of the Jeep, and I'll walk you there," Joe replied.

Reggie looked at Curt. Curt nodded. "Do it, but keep his hands tied."

Reggie helped Joe out of the Jeep.

"That path," Joe said, nodding ahead. "We must take that path."

Joe stepped ahead of them and started down the winding gulch path.

"You try to make a break for it and I'll shoot you in the back."

Joe didn't reply. In his head, he continued chanting while he took slow, methodical steps forward. Darkness settled around them the farther down the path they walked. They took a sharp turn and headed upward. The natural bridge stood ahead.

"How much further?" Curt asked.

"We're almost there," Joe said.

Night birds chirped. Insects buzzed. Joe chanted. Something rustled and breathed in the brush ahead.

"What the hell's that?" Reggie asked, aiming his gun.

"I don't see anything," Curt replied.

"But you heard it, didn't you?"

"Birds, probably."

From behind them a piercing squall made them turn. A large owl plunged downward and its talons caught Reggie's shoulder, slicing to the bone. He cried out in pain and dropped his gun. The owl fluttered and flogged at Reggie's eyes.

Reggie dropped to the ground, covering his face. Joe stooped and grabbed the gun.

"Put it down, Joe." Curt aimed the gun at the owl. He fired three shots. The owl vaporized into a puff of smoke.

Stunned, Curt looked from the air where the owl had been over to Joe. Joe's right hand rose. A large cougar rushed from the brush behind him and charged Curt. Its hard sharp claws sliced into his flesh and wrestled Curt to the ground. Curt dropped his gun.

Joe took the butt of the gun and struck Reggie hard enough to knock him unconscious. Curt screamed in agony. The large cat pinned him down on the rocky terrain. The cougar hissed and spat at him. Once Joe retrieved Curt's gun, the cougar sprang over the man and disappeared down the trail.

Joe pointed the gun at Curt's face. The anger in Curt's eyes turned to fear when he looked at Joe's face. Light illuminated for a few moments around Joe's head and disappeared like the owl had.

"How? What was that?"

Joe didn't answer.

"Did . . . did you make the owl and mountain lion appear?"

Joe ignored the question.

"Normally, I'm not a violent man," Joe said calmly and without anger. "But knowing that you're responsible for Misty's death angers me with a rage I've never known before. Because of you two, my friend was injured and probably needs medical attention, but you left him behind. So, you're going to give me some answers. We can do it the easy way."

Curt closed his eyes tightly, shedding tears.

Joe released the safety and pressed the gun to Curt's forehead. "Or we can do it this way. Your choice."

Curt swallowed hard. His face was haunted and his eyes hollow. Slowly he raised his hands, never taking his eyes off Joe.

"Why do you want the skull?" Joe asked.

"That's what he's paying us to get. He never told us *why* he wants it. He just does. Apparently bad enough to hire us to kill you."

"Who?"

Sweat beaded on Curt's brow. "Don't know his real name. He goes by Alpha."

"Where can I find him?"

"I don't know."

Joe moved the gun a few inches to the side of Curt's head and fired. The blast echoed and bellowed through the gulch and along the ridges. Curt dropped face first and placed his hands over his ears. His body quaked. For a hired mercenary, the man exhibited more fear than Joe expected.

"I don't know where he is. He used to oversee Desert Labs."

"I know," Joe said. "But where is he now?"

"I swear I don't know."

Joe shook his head. "He has to pay you somehow."

"Direct deposits into our bank accounts. That's it. We never meet him face to face. *Ever.* If we saw his face, I'm certain he'd probably kill us."

"Why?"

"He doesn't want anyone to know who he is."

"That seems reasonable enough." Joe grabbed Curt's cellphone and dialed Owl-hunter's number.

Curt dared a peek up. "You should go ahead and kill us. He will once he discovers our failure."

"What I have planned for you is worse than death," Joe replied.

Chapter 44

Lucas opened his eyes and winced. His head throbbed in pain. Placing his hand to his forehead, he discovered the sticky, blood-covered bandage. He looked around the SUV for Joe but since dusk had settled in, he couldn't see far.

"Joe?" he said.

Lucas pushed himself into a sitting position. His head ached even worse. Afraid that Joe had suffered similar injuries, or worse, Lucas crawled through the broken side window. He used the crumpled door for leverage to pull himself to his feet.

Headlights appeared at the edge of the road at the top of the ravine. Lucas crouched down.

"Joe?" he whispered.

Vehicle doors slammed shut and the shadows of three men stood in the glare of the headlights.

The three men hurried down the ravine to the overturned SUV. Lucas was dizzy and afraid to run.

"Lucas?" Owl-hunter said near the vehicle. "Are you here?"

"Yeah," he replied, rising to stand. "But I can't find Joe."

Owl-hunter clasped Lucas' forearm and held tightly, supporting Lucas' weight and preventing him from falling.

"The men who did this," Owl-hunter said, nodding toward the wreckage. "They took Joe."

"Damn," Lucas replied.

"Oh, we'll find him. He's our brother. And he's strong in ways that most men don't understand. How do you feel? Should we take you to the hospital?"

"I'm shaken up. A little dizzy, but other than that, I believe I'm okay. Let's find Joe first and then if I'm still woozy, a hospital will be good."

Owl-hunter smiled. "We'll help you up the steep hill. I don't think you should attempt that alone."

Lucas stared up the steep, winding path and shook his head. "Probably not."

"Oh," Owl-hunter said, walking back to the SUV. He stooped down and crawled inside the wreckage. A few seconds later, he came back out with a cellphone in his hand. "You might want this later."

Lucas took the phone and nodded. "Thanks."

"Joe left it so we could track it and find it."

"Track it?"

Owl-hunter smiled. "Don't look so surprised. We keep up with modern technology. Smoke signals are long past."

Lucas chuckled and looked for messages. "Damn. Battery's dead."

Owl-hunter's cell rang. "Yes? Okay, Joe. We're on our way."

"Joe's okay?" Lucas asked.

Owl-hunter grinned and nodded. "Come on. You won't want to miss this."

Chapter 45

Morton pranced into Daniel's office and leaped onto the desk.

"Well," Morton huffed. "I hope *you're* satisfied."

Daniel stopped typing on his laptop and faced the cat. "About what?"

"My tree. It's gone. They cut it to the ground. Even removed the stump."

"That dead eyesore?" Daniel returned his attention to the computer. "It had a devaluing appearance for the entire block. It needed cut down years ago."

"The hollow tree was my beloved sanctuary. The only place where I had *some* solitude. *Me* time. The rats follow me everywhere indoors."

"That may be. But the tree was rotten and dangerous. A large branch could have fallen at any time and struck someone. Since Felicia's getting older, she or anyone could have been hurt or killed passing under it."

Morton cocked his head and nodded. "When you put it that way, you're right. But still, I'm going to miss it."

"I'm sorry the tree is gone."

"On a worse note," Morton said.

"Worse?"

"Yep. Kyle contacted me via telepathy-satellite."

"Oh?"

Morton nodded. "Lucian's dying."

"What?" Daniel swiveled his chair around. "What happened?"

"Seems his cloned body has reached its expiration marker."

"Dr. Helmsby believed that would happen. It's surprising Lucian has lived this long."

Morton licked his forepaw and stared at Daniel. "When's the last time you've heard from Helmsby?"

Daniel sighed. "Must be months now. Why?"

"Helmsby might know a solution that might help Lucian."

"He might."

Morton wiped his face with his wet paw. "Brockton thinks there might be a remedy without Helmsby's help, but it would require a favor."

Daniel frowned. "What kind of favor?"

"Kyle wants you to ask Lucas to donate some blood or stem cells."

"How will that help?"

Morton pursed his furry lips. "Lucas is the template from which Lucian was made. I assume Brockton believes stem cells might reverse part of Lucian's genetic flaws."

"Maybe so, but I highly doubt Lucas will agree to help."

"That's what I told Kyle."

Daniel smiled. "But that doesn't mean I *won't* ask. After all, Lucian did save his life. It's the least Lucas could do."

Daniel grabbed his cellphone and dialed Lucas' number. It rang and rang. Daniel's brow furrowed. He disconnected the call.

"What's wrong?" Morton asked.

"No answer."

"Maybe he's out of tower range," Morton said.

"I hope that's all."

"You think it's something worse?"

Daniel sighed. "I don't know. When he called and told me about Lydia leaving, he was at a major low."

"Just because she left?"

"He indicated she's been brooding and target practicing a lot. Since Matthews has escaped, her need to kill has returned. Lucas was going after her when he hung up."

"Do you believe she'd really hurt him?"

"It's difficult to say, but that possibility is strong. Especially since she let him know Matthews is out, she might do drastic things to keep her search alive."

"Should we go look for him?"

"I'd like to, but Julia could go into labor soon."

"I could search for him."

Daniel shook his head. "We don't even know where he's at. I'm sure he'll check in with me soon. When he does, I'll ask him."

"I guess that's the best we can do for now," Morton said with a sad tone.

"You think Lucas should help his clone?"

Morton nodded. "Yes. Lucian isn't a bad person. He certainly isn't what Idris had created him to become."

"I gathered that after Lucian shot and killed Idris and then went his own direction."

"He was nothing but kind with Kat, and when Violet was killed, he showed true remorse because he had failed to protect her. If he were a true assassin at heart, it wouldn't have stirred any regret. He'd have shrugged it off."

"I agree," Daniel said, nodding. "I fear Lydia is everything Idris made her to be."

"I fear that, too. Idris said that she was the prototype. It could be that he kept her in the incubation chamber for everyone's safety."

"That's an extreme theory."

Morton's eyes narrowed. "Not really. Her violence steadily increases. The rage inside her grows. Once it surpasses a certain level, I wonder if anyone can reason with her."

"You've really thought through this."

"Kyle and I discuss a lot of theories. Just not recently. Today's the first day I've heard from him in weeks."

"I see."

Morton rubbed his forepaws together and grinned. "Now, can we discuss releasing me from my confinement?"

"You mean returning you to the wild?"

"Indoor habitats are constraining. And that litter box is an insult. No dignity. No real privacy."

"Okay," Daniel said. "But if we let you back outside, would you mind sticking to the backyard?"

"Might as well since they killed my tree."

"It was *already* dead."

"Minus its animated spirit, it was."

"You mean *you?*"

Morton smiled. "I certainly didn't mean Kip."

"You called?" Kip asked, scurrying up the side of the desk, still wearing the little leather jacket. Standing on his hind legs, he crossed his forelegs, struck a pose, looking back and forth between them. "Sup?"

Morton rolled his eyes and shook his head. "You see what I mean about *no* privacy?"

Daniel smiled. "When I was in college I never thought genetics would venture so far as to grant animals your abilities."

Morton glanced down at Kip. "Sometimes I think it's a psychotic dream."

"Not with you," Daniel said. "You, Kip, and the other rats I can handle. It's the deadly creatures like the shifters and Idris' assassins that trouble me the most. It's what Lydia might become. Or where she might end up and how it all ends."

"I'm afraid it won't end well."

"I feel the same way," Daniel replied.

Chapter 46

Las Vegas

LYDIA PARKED her bike in the parking garage near Twilight Towers. She took the elevator until she reached the 19th floor and exited. She entered the hallway, carrying her black helmet in one hand and a small backpack in the other. The plush beige carpet silenced her footsteps. Her stealth movements flowed without thought. Her eyes looked straight ahead, and when she reached room 1912, she stopped and faced the door.

She knocked.

JOHANNA WAS VACUUMING THE FLOOR. Her long blonde ponytail was pulled tightly back. She wore Spandex shorts and a snug halter-top, neither of which hid her toned, muscular physique. She kept training and expanding her fitness routines and eventually formed her own trade-marked clothing line and health food industries. And since her cable network workout program had gone into syndication, she was able to purchase a condo in Vegas and oversee most of her business from her home. She had more wealth than she ever imagined possible. Things were going phenomenally well for her.

She swayed to the retro music that pulsed through her headset while she pushed the vacuum back and forth across the lavender carpet. She jumped when someone pounded on the door. She set the vacuum upright and turned it off.

She hurried to the door, peered through the peephole, and gasped.

Lydia? Why was she here?

Johanna seldom had visitors, and Lydia was the last person on Earth that she expected to see.

Her heart beat harder. Her mind immediately reflected to Lydia's clone trying to kill her in Pittsburgh. Even though several years had passed, Johanna continued having nightmares about the murderous, heartless clone stalking her in the dark halls and nearly killing her. It took Johanna a moment to remember that the clone was dead. This was the *real* Lydia.

Slowly, she pulled open the door and gave a nervous smile.

"Lydia?" Johanna looked both directions down the hall. "Where's Lucas?"

"Called it quits."

"Quits?" Lydia frowned. "Lucas adores you. He'd never—"

"*I* called it quits," she replied coldly. "Mind if I come in? I've driven for hours."

"Oh, sure," Johanna said, stepping back and opening the door wider. "Sorry. Pardon the mess. Just trying to tidy up."

Lydia brushed past and set her pack beside the couch. She faced Johanna with an even smile. "Care if I bunk on your couch? It'd only be for one night. I'll be gone in the morning and won't cause you any trouble."

"Sure, that's fine. How'd you know where I lived?"

"Your address was on the Christmas card you sent."

Johanna nodded nervously. "Oh yeah, right. Where are you traveling to?"

"Not sure yet."

"I hate to hear about you and Lucas. Really, I am."

"It was bound to happen. He should have expected it."

Johanna beamed a stage smile, trying to hide her nervousness. She picked up on Lydia's cold tone and read the icy hardness in her eyes. She looked more like her evil clone than the woman that had helped Lucas bring down TransGenCorp.

"I hate to pry, but—"

"Then don't."

Johanna swallowed hard, fearful to remain in the apartment with Lydia. If she wasn't in her own home, she'd have left, but as it was, she hoped to coax Lydia into a friendlier manner without further agitating her. She wasn't certain why Lydia was so hostile and even though Johanna was much larger in size, she couldn't possibly win any physical confrontation against Lydia. Luck had won Johanna's battle against Lydia's clone, and she had never credited the victory to herself.

Politely, Johanna asked, "Are you okay?"

"I'm fine. Just . . . very tired."

"Let me make some tea. You like hot tea, don't you?"

Lydia plopped down on the couch and gave a slight, tired nod. Her mind seemed elsewhere. "That would be nice."

"Great!" Johanna said in a strained cheerful tone. She headed to the kitchen. "Give me a few minutes."

"No hurry."

"The remote for the television is on the end table if you'd like to watch anything."

Johanna took a ceramic kettle, filled it with water, and placed it into the microwave. The television volume increased. Stations changed. The evening news came on.

After the microwave beeped, she removed the kettle and dropped teabags into the steaming water. She placed the kettle onto a tray with a teddy bear shaped bottle of honey, a few sweetener packets, and two teacups. Then she hurried to the living room and almost dropped the tray.

Lydia sat on the couch, watching the news. An ongoing manhunt for Matthews scrolled across the screen. The news reporter was interviewing the prison warden. Lydia's eyes narrowed. She held a gun and pointed it at the picture of Matthews on the screen.

Johanna took a deep breath and braved steps to the coffee table. With her hands trembling, she set the tray down and smiled. She was thankful she had maintained enough balance not to shatter the ceramic tea set on the floor.

Johanna eyed the gun and forced a smile. "I brought honey and sweetener, whichever you prefer."

Lydia never blinked, nor did she acknowledge that Johanna was even in the room. She aimed the gun with one eye closed, looking like he might squeeze the trigger at any moment.

Johanna stepped backwards and edged her way to the kitchen. Her heart raced. Her mouth became drier than cotton. She sat down at the kitchen table because her whole body quaked. Her muscled legs no longer held the strength to support her.

Despite Johanna's muscular stature, she remained a timid person, especially whenever she thought about the dark days in Pittsburgh. One of the reasons she had distanced herself from Lucas after he married Lydia was because Johanna had great difficulty separating the Lydia clone memories from the real Lydia. Seeing Lydia made her think of the clone. Those nightmarish memories projected themselves onto the real Lydia, and now she wondered if that had somehow been the correct thing to do. Had her premonitions insisted the real Lydia was no different than the clone? Or perhaps she was worse than the clone?

Lydia's gaze was filled with vengeful determination. The fact she had the gun out meant Johanna was in a volatile situation. Lydia might go into a rampage at any moment.

The worst thing about living on the nineteenth floor was only having one accessible exit. Her door linked to the hallway. Telling Lydia that she needed to excuse herself for a quick errand would, no doubt, arouse suspicion. Johanna wasn't certain how Lydia might react or what Lydia might do should she flee.

Johanna thought about calling the police or Daniel, but she had left her cellphone in the living room.

Leaning back in her chair, she was able to see Lydia seated on the couch. Lydia never blinked when the newscaster said, "Matthews is considered armed and dangerous. His whereabouts are still unknown."

"I'll find you," Lydia said.

Johanna had no idea who Matthews was or why Lydia was bent on finding him. She hadn't talked to Julia or Daniel in months. Seeing Lydia in her current mental state, Johanna wondered if Lucas had recognized the assassin inside Lydia and if that was why they had gone their separate ways.

A ringtone played in the living room. Lydia answered her phone.

Johanna eased to the kitchen door and listened. Lydia whispered into the phone, making it impossible for Johanna to understand anything she said. Lydia's demeanor changed while she talked. Her hostility faded and optimism broadened a smile across her face.

Johanna was puzzled. It was almost like watching someone suffer a complete mental breakdown. She returned to the table. Her mind raced on how she might return to the living room and strike up a conversation without revealing her true fear of Lydia or her suspicions. But the more she thought about it, the less she liked the idea of being in the same room with her. Especially when Lydia seemed overly trigger-happy.

Chapter 47

Lydia's grabbed her cell when the ringtone played.

"Yes?" she said.

"Lydia Ridale?"

"Who is this?"

"Boyd Grayson. You're aware that Matthews has escaped?"

"Yes. I've been looking for him."

Grayson chuckled. "I'd like to hire you."

"To find him?"

"That and as my personal bodyguard. Could you kill Matthews if it becomes necessary?"

"Without hesitation."

"I thought that would be your response."

"Do you know where he is?"

"Not yet. But we're searching. With our technology, we can find him faster than you can. Where are you?"

"In Vegas."

"I can have a team pick you up within the hour, provided you're interested."

"I'm interested. Find Matthews and he will die. I guarantee it."

"Good. Meet at North Town Airport. Davis is the head of my security team. He will meet you and escort you to my jet."

"On my way."

Lydia picked up her pack and bike helmet. She eased to the door, quietly opened it, and exited. She hurried down the hall to the elevator. She found it interesting that Grayson would solicit her help when only a few hours earlier she had considered seeking him out. Together, she had no doubt that they'd locate Matthews, and when they did, his death wouldn't be quick and easy. She had plans to make Matthews suffer in ways he had never imagined before his death. He'd probably beg her to end his life quickly. That was one request she'd deny.

An even smile crossed her lips. Her eyes stared deep in thought. She executed various scenarios in her mind. When the elevator opened to the parking garage, her adrenaline surged. For the first time she thought of murderous revenge without the slightest tinge of remorse. She was free from the bondage of guilt. What she truly was had emerged, and strangely she was excited about carrying out this mission. Although Grayson wanted to hire her, this mission was hers and hers alone. The only benefit of being on his team was quicker maneuvering with better weapons and the use of a jet.

Once Grayson's team found Matthews' location, she'd guarantee Matthews never escaped again. He'd die, and she'd make certain that he died *slowly*.

THE TELEVISION WAS the only noise Johanna detected coming from the living room. She crept to the door and peered in.

Lydia and her belongings were gone.

"Lydia?"

When no reply came, she walked boldly through the living room, to the door, and opened it. Lydia wasn't in the hallway. She was gone.

Johanna grabbed her phone and dialed Daniel's number with a shaky finger. She quaked all over and sat on her couch.

Daniel answered.

"Daniel, what's going on?" she asked.

"What are you talking about?"

"Lydia. She was here and just left."

"Lydia visited you?" he asked.

"Yes."

"What did she want?"

"She wanted to stay the night, and I told her that she could. But then she got a call and left without saying goodbye."

"Any idea who called her?"

"No. I stayed in the kitchen. I didn't want to be near her. She . . . she was very menacing. She had her gun out while watching the news. Who is this Matthews guy?"

"She mentioned him?"

"He was on the news and she said that she was going to find him."

"Matthews was the one behind Lydia's kidnapping a few months ago."

Johanna crossed her legs, leaning back on the couch. "She was kidnapped?"

"Yeah."

"No wonder she's so angry."

"I'm afraid it will go much further than anger. She'll kill him."

Johanna's eyes widened. "You really believe she will."

"Lucas called me early this morning after she left him."

"How is he?"

"He wasn't coping too well when I spoke with him. Do you think he was the one who called Lydia?"

Johanna twirled her ponytail around her finger. "I really don't know. I tried to hear what she was saying but she didn't talk loud enough. I was in a different room."

"At least she's gone and you're safe."

"Yes. I know. How is Julia?"

"Due to have our second child any day now," Daniel said.

"Really?"

"Yes."

"Oh, Daniel, that's fantastic news! I'm so sorry. I've been so busy and tied up with my marketing strategies that I've simply lost touch with you two."

"It's fine."

"No. It's not. I had gotten close to Julia and after all the mess with TransGenCorp, and after my producer was killed—"

"It's okay," Daniel said. "You needed to get your mind off everything. We understand."

"I miss her," she said. "And little Felicia. You call and let me know when Julia goes into labor."

"I will."

"Cause I'm going to be there. Okay?"

"Okay."

"I need to go, but I wanted you to know that Lydia came by."

"Thanks. I'm glad you did. Make certain you lock your door."

Lydia wiped tears from her eyes. "I'll probably barricade it for a couple nights now."

"I don't think she'll return. She's after Matthews. She won't stop until she finds him, either."

"Thanks, Daniel. Tell Julia and Felicia that I love them."

"I will."

"Goodbye."

"Bye, Johanna."

Chapter 48

Matthews sat in the chair while Mordia removed the bandages from his face.

"I still think you should wait until tomorrow to have these removed," she said.

"No," he replied. "There's too much I need to do. The bandages make people shy away from me. I need to find volunteers tonight. Walking around like the mummy isn't a good first impression, now is it?"

"I suppose not. But volunteers? So soon?" Mordia carefully peeled away the lubricated cotton mask around his eyes. "What's the hurry?"

Matthews smiled and winced. "Don't worry about the details. I have an agenda to keep. My focus is on achieving it sooner than later."

"You mind filling me in?"

"It's a need-to-know basis, and at the moment, *you* don't *need* to know."

"I thought we are partners."

"We are. Once these test subjects prove the serum is marketable, you'll be the forerunner."

Mordia frowned. "What do you mean? Forerunner?"

"Back to business for you. Not as a plastic surgeon, but a longevity expert. When word spreads about the miracles you can do, the media will get a hold of the story, and investors will be begging to cut into the market share. *That's* when the money starts rolling in."

"I don't understand."

"What's not to understand?"

She shook her head. "No, I mean why would you want me as the person people see. Don't you want the fame for your technology?"

"I wish to remain in the background for now. Besides you have a beautiful face and an exquisite smile. Much better than my own. Men and women will be drawn to you."

Mordia blushed. "You flatter me, but you don't need me. You changed your name when you came to me. Assume a new identity and accept the recognition for yourself."

"Not interested in that right now. I have other people to tend to first."

She frowned and gently lifted another corner of the mask. "Who?"

Someone knocked on the door.

"How close are you to having these bandages off my face?"

"Almost done."

"Good. You mind getting that?" he asked.

"He's already here?"

"Few people ever keep me waiting."

Mordia set the loose bandage aside and went to the door. She opened it and a tall man stood before her with a leather laptop satchel slung over his shoulder. He was lean with a youthful face and blonde hair. She guessed he was about twenty years old.

"Am I at the right place?" he asked. "Is Steven Matthews here?"

"Yes," Mordia replied. "Come in. He's expecting you."

Nervously, he stepped across the threshold. He lowered the satchel from his shoulder. "Where should I set this up?" he asked.

"Use this table, Jimmy." Matthews pointed.

Jimmy stared questionably at Matthews and studied his face where the bandages had been removed. "Is that really you?"

Matthews nodded. "You like the disguise?"

Jimmy shrugged and set his satchel on the table and unzipped it. He removed his computer with shaking hands. "I remember you said that you'd be out of prison early. But—"

"You didn't expect it so soon?" Matthews asked.

"No, sir."

Matthews laughed. "I doubt anyone expected my freedom so early."

"I can't believe you'd have plastic surgery done."

"Life is full of unexpected changes, Jimmy. Besides too many people want me dead or think I *owe* them something. A new look often changes one's perspective, much like an ugly caterpillar can spend the remainder of its life flying with spectacular wings. Scientists call it metamorphosis, and I've passed to the next stage in mine."

Mordia returned to Matthews and continued removing the bandage around his eyes.

Jimmy cleared his throat and ran his hand through his hair. "How did they treat you in prison?"

Matthews chuckled softly. "Solitary confinement. The guards and warden believed the general prison population was safer not gaining my trust. Money and fame does strange things, even behind bars. Muscled brutes can become the most devoted bodyguards a rich man can have in prison. Their loyalties are bought cheap, kind of like hiring someone in a third world country to work for a quarter of the money a qualified US citizen would earn."

"What exactly are you wanting me to do?" Jimmy asked.

"Nothing yet. But in an hour or so, I'll need you to run background checks on some people to make certain they're not being looked for by family or the law."

"I don't understand."

Mordia removed the last bandage from Matthews' face.

"FBI records, criminal investigations, and missing person reports."

"FBI? You want me to *hack* into their system?"

"If that becomes necessary, yes," Matthews said. "You've done it for me before. Is that a problem?"

Jimmy looked at Matthews' harsh glare and shook his head. "No, sir. Not a problem unless I get caught."

"Caught? I thought you boasted that you're a mastermind at hacking into any security system. Have you gotten so lazy during my absence?"

"No, but I'm on probation now."

"Jimmy? Probation, really?" Matthews shook his head with a disappointed expression. "I thought you were more careful."

Jimmy's face reddened. He shrugged.

Matthews stood and looked into the large mirror on the wall behind his leather couch. He turned his head slightly both directions, admiring his side profile.

"You do such marvelous work, Dr. Mordia," he said. "Such a shame that more folks can no longer benefit from your miracle touch."

She blushed again. "Thanks. After the healing completes, it will become even less noticeable in a day or so."

Matthews nodded. "I imagine it will, my dear. I have no doubts your work."

Mordia smiled modestly.

Matthews gave Jimmy a side-glance. "So you put your hands into the wrong cookie jar and got caught?"

Jimmy nodded.

"Well, that wasn't on my watch. You know I protect my own."

"Yes, sir."

Mordia looked at Jimmy and then to Matthews. "How do you know him?"

"Jimmy worked with me when I was at Grayson Enterprises. Pretended to run errands for me while creatively getting inside information on Boyd Grayson."

"I see."

Matthews extended his hand toward the door. "Now, shall we get started, my dear lady?"

He headed to the door, and she followed.

"Shouldn't take us a couple of hours, Jimmy." Matthews said. He handed Jimmy several twenties. "Order several pizzas and make yourself at home. There are drinks in the kitchen cabinets. Get whatever you need. You'll be staying here a while."

Jimmy took the money and glanced nervously around the apartment.

Chapter 49

Sheba ran through the dark tunnel with the three catlike creatures pursuing her. They were fast, but she was quicker and knew the tunnel better. However, being cats, their hearing was keener and their agility swifter.

She had never seen these beasts before and had no clue anything like them existed. Perhaps one-on-one she could stand her ground and win a confrontation. But against three? No. Even she had her limitations. Their sharp claws could gut her in minutes. Although she could heal from near fatal wounds, some injuries were impossible to recover from. And after the sickle to the chest, she remained weak.

Sheba wished she had approached the situation with Mitch differently. She had bullied him unnecessarily when she should have taken his offer of friendship. But she had refused to accept his kindness because she had been betrayed too many times. Mitch's demeanor had been quite forthcoming and caring. Had she trusted him, he probably could have helped free Gloria. Instead, she remained a slave to the man who kept Gloria locked away.

Sheba rushed through the door, turned down the narrow corridor past the room where she had tied Mitch, and ran into the room of caskets. She hurried to the polished mahogany coffin in the center, lifted the lid, dove inside, and slammed the lid shut. She twisted the latch and locked the lid.

She was safe for the moment. Even if the catlike creatures tracked her scent to the casket, which she was certain they would do, they weren't able to get inside.

She panted, trying to calm herself. Her fear lengthened her claws. She tasted blood because her teeth were expanding, making her gums bleed. She fought the urge to change. Turning into a wolf lessened her ability to think rationally. Foolishly, she might open the lid and try to kill her aggressors. That outcome wasn't in her best interest.

What appeared to be a casket on the outside actually camouflaged a passageway entrance. The lid and sides had been reinforced with steel plates. The inside polyester lining and one-half of the casket bottom had been removed. Only a small portion of the bottom remained. Where the other half had been, a ladder had been constructed and led downward into an underground corridor, which tunneled beneath the cemetery. Following it, she'd exit through a trapdoor into an abandoned warehouse at the edge of town. But the path Mitch and the woman traveled was in the opposite direction, so she'd need to figure out a way to find them later.

Officer Parker had informed her about the passageway so she could wander at night as a wolf and not be seen in public. After last week's murders, she used the tunnel more frequently. She wondered if the cats had killed the people but feared she may have killed them.

Claws scratched the casket lid. The beasts huffed, sniffing the dirt and growling as they paced around the coffin.

Sheba slid to the open end of the casket, placed her feet onto a ladder rung, and slowly made her way to the earthen floor below. She wondered how long the cats would linger near the coffin, waiting for her to emerge.

She walked along the damp corridor with water sloshing beneath her feet. Again she thought of Mitch. A bit of her ached that she had betrayed his trust because he had been the first person she'd ever told about Gloria. After sharing her tragic story she had felt relief, like a huge weight had been lifted, her haunted soul lightened, but by the time they entered the cemetery that relief turned to regret and fear. Somehow she felt like her creator would learn she had given away too much information. His punishment would be severe.

It no longer mattered. Mitch had escaped with this woman. That alone would bring a harsh penalty. She hated to admit it, but Parker had been correct. She should have let Mitch take the bus and leave town.

When Mitch had asked, she had not lied. She didn't remember exactly when she had gained the ability to shape-shift. She guessed that she had always had the ability. The night Gloria and the others came to the cemetery was the first time she *remembered* changing. Everything else was a blur. Her creator, who loved her like a daughter, had to clean up the mess after she revealed what she was, even though it had been accidental.

The boys disappeared.

Gloria was held in isolation.

Beverly was placed into a mental institution where no one believed anything she said. And because she truly had believed what she had seen, none of the staff ever questioned her insanity. Beverly would never recant the occurrences as a mad fictitious dream, so freedom from the ward was never coming. She was stuck there. Her heavy medication kept her mind in a constant veil of dullness and emptiness that prevented her from thinking and having uncontrolled outbursts. Seeing Beverly in a catatonic state pained Sheba. Her friend's body was there, but her mind didn't seem to exist. She worried she'd never see the real Beverly again.

Jill had been the weakest in her circle of friends and committed suicide before her parents had the opportunity to place her into the mental institution with Beverly. Sheba visited her grave every night, apologizing and begging for forgiveness, but without a verbal reply, she never accepted closure.

All these incidents were the nightmares Sheba lived with. That night in the cemetery haunted her. It always would. The guilt weighed upon her more and more each day. She was responsible and blamed herself for destroying their lives. It was why she couldn't bear to trust others or even herself. It was also why she painted her face with morbidly dark colors to match her inward pain and regret. Piercings were self-inflicted pain to make her never forget.

The worst part of it all was that she understood none of her friends would have suffered such agonizing outcomes had she never agreed to be enrolled into the public school system. But her creator had demanded she do so and befriend others. He wanted to know how she'd interact with outsiders, with people who weren't like her.

At first, Sheba had been hesitant, withdrawn, but soon enjoyed having friends her own age. She opened up and loved being in the high school clique where she discovered she could fit in. Tragically, they had come to know and love her and that amity succumbed to devastating outcomes.

The two people killed the week before were not her doing. At least she truly *hoped* she wasn't the one who had killed them. She didn't remember what or where she had been that night, so it left her to suspect herself as the guilty party.

Parker had never questioned her about it. He never even asked. The gruesome murders pressed on her and added another reason to continue doing her creator's bidding. Although his love seemed genuine and fatherly compassionate, she didn't doubt for a moment that her outcome might be like Gloria's if she strayed too far. Or worse, she could become lost like Beverly where she never knew what went on around her.

Now, though, seeing the cats, she had to wonder if they had killed those people. It was worth investigating.

Regardless of what she discovered, Sheba's one hope for redemption and freedom had left with Mitch. No matter how hard she tried to convince him that she needed his help, she didn't believe he'd bother to listen.

She jogged slowly. Water sloshed down the tunnel. She thought about the catlike creatures. Nothing like them existed at her creator's residence or in his labs. He favored canines, not felines. So where had they originated? Why were they roaming the area? And why had they not attacked Mitch and the woman? Instead, they were determined to pursue *her*.

She increased her pace. She needed some answers. Only one person could give her that information.

Her creator.

Alpha.

Sheba couldn't ask him and instinct told her that she mustn't seek him out. Not now. Not ever again.

As much as she wanted answers, she didn't feel comfortable going to him. Once Parker discovered Mitch had escaped, she had no doubt he'd run and tell Alpha in an attempt to gain a higher status with her creator because he despised her strength and Alpha's favoritism. Parker would do almost anything necessary to gain Alpha's blessing and promotion. Even if that meant he must kill her in order to gain it.

Her mistakes and inadequacies placed a barrier in her relationship with Alpha. He wasn't one to forgive or forget. She'd never known of one time he had given anyone a second chance. There was no redemption or pleading her side, her reasons. She was left with only one alternative. One that was destined to failure but she had to risk the attempt.

Sheba had to reach out one last time to Mitch's sympathy and hope that he could have a change of heart and help her like he had promised to do. It was the only chance she had left for redemption. It was the only hope Gloria and Beverly had left.

She had to act fast though. The darkness that possessed Alpha brought fear inside of her. She wouldn't be able to hide long. He'd find her. She knew that. He perceived things in ways humans or animals couldn't. He was the reason she had warned Mitch that if he didn't believe in paranormal aspects, he'd die quickly. And foolishly, she had attacked the only man that might have had the ability to free her from her mental and physical bondage to her creator.

At least Alpha didn't control her mind. Not yet. But he did have the ability to bend one's will, to make them do things they'd otherwise never do. He had never forced her against her will, but she'd never given him a reason to. Until today.

When she didn't report in within a few hours like he expected her to do each night, he would channel his search for her until he linked to her mind. When he did this, she didn't have the mental strength to shield against such an invasion. He'd probe through her thoughts and isolate her location. Once Alpha learned about her plans to help Mitch and the woman, he'd unleash his psionic power and thwart a direct attack into her mind, perhaps crippling her and making her useless—or *worse*, hemorrhage her brain to put her into a coma. Forever.

Racing to the end of the tunnel, she hurried up the ladder to the trapdoor. She needed to find Mitch and the woman and warn them before it was too late. She shoved the door upward and emerged in the basement corner of the abandoned warehouse.

Sheba sniffed the air. Mingled with the dusty, mildewed smell was the scent of sharp cologne she knew all too well.

She turned. Parker stood with a smile on his lips. His dark eyes narrowed with malice. His muscled jaw tightened.

The gun in his hand was leveled right at her face.

Chapter 50

Lucas and Owl-hunter hurried to where Joe stood in the center of a dry, rocky gulch. A small campfire crackled. Smoke rose into gentle puffs of gray.

Seated on the ground, tied back to back, were Curt and Reggie. Joe stood near them and said in a calm, almost prophetic tone, "Tonight is your rite to passage. Things will pass through this valley that you won't understand. You'll wonder which is real and which are from your worst dreams. But when the visions come, the spirits will wander past and assault you. Some attacks will be so harsh that you'll *beg* to die."

Joe walked to Lucas and Owl-hunter. He smiled.

"Shouldn't you gag them?" Lucas asked.

Joe shook his head. "No. The louder they scream, the worse their visions become. For their evil, the reckoning will come."

Joe stepped closer to Lucas and looked him in the eyes. "How are you, bro? You had me worried back there when they forced me to go with them."

"I'm dizzy, but I think I'll manage."

Owl-hunter smiled. "You are a warrior in heart, but like all of us, you're getting older. I think you should be examined at the emergency room."

Joe nodded. "I agree."

"I won't argue with you." Lucas limped and squinted from pain with each slow step he took. "The older I get, the longer it takes for my injuries to heal. Better to be safe than sorry."

"These men," Owl-hunter said to Joe, "Are they the ones who tried to kill you for the skull?"

Joe nodded. "But after tonight, I don't think we'll have to worry about it."

"But you still have it?"

"It's hidden."

"You must get rid of it."

"I will," Joe said.

Lucas looked at the two men. In spite of their muscled size, their widened eyes made their faces resemble little children frightened by ghostly tales around a campfire on a late summer evening.

Lucas and Joe walked back toward the vehicle. "Are you really going to leave them out here to die, Joe?"

Joe chuckled. "You know me better than that, bro."

"I thought so, but that was a pretty convincing speech. It was enough to make me weary of staying out here at night. Gave me chill bumps."

"That's the point. To heighten their anxiety. Every little sound they hear from this moment on will make them wonder what's edging closer."

Lucas shook his head. "I never pictured you being so shrewd."

Joe grinned. "That's just the half of it."

"Oh?"

"Yep. Two of my brothers will stay behind and sneak out here later and really whoop up some strange sounds. By morning, they'll be wanting to live a few states over."

"You're not going to let them go, are you?"

Joe's face became solemn. He shook his head. "No. They killed Misty. The sheriff will get them, and they will face justice. But tonight, we give them *our* kind of justice. One that will haunt them forever."

"I like it," Lucas said with a chuckle. He took two quick steps and stumbled on the rocky path.

Joe grabbed Lucas' elbow and kept him from falling.

"You okay?" Joe asked.

Lucas shook his head and squinted. "Not sure. I'm extremely dizzy."

"Let's get you to the hospital."

Chapter 51

Lucian entered the front door of their house and Kat rushed to him, wrapping her arms around him.

"You had me worried sick," she said.

He kissed her lips and smiled. "I'm sorry. Went for that jog and stopped by Brockton's for a while."

"A while?" she said, placing her hands on her hips in a teasing manner.

"That was the intention, dear," Lucian said with a tired voice. "Honest. I didn't expect him to pull me into helping him."

Kat cocked one brow playfully. "What exactly did he need your help for?"

"I don't feel like telling you right now."

"Not feeling well?" she asked.

"Very drained, but at least I don't have a fever."

Kat smiled. "That's good news, but as it is, we need to get to the airport."

"Why? Did Mitch contact you?"

"Yes," Kat said, pointing toward the living room. "The bags are on the couch. Pack them into the car and I'll explain while I drive."

"So it's urgent?"

She nodded. "More than you think."

KAT DROVE with Lucian leaned back in his seat. He was weak but not as badly as the night before.

"What did Mitch find out?" Lucian asked with a tired voice.

"The girl that was going to give him information took him prisoner."

Lucian chuckled. "She needs a love slave?"

"Hardly," Kat said with a frown. "She can turn into a wolf."

Lucian rose in his seat and looked at her with wide eyes. "What?"

Kat smiled. "I thought *that* would get your attention."

"You're serious?"

"Of course. I wouldn't make that up."

"Then how'd Mitch escape?"

"Here's where it gets interesting."

Lucian cocked a brow and he shook his head. "More interesting than her being a she-wolf?"

Kat shrugged. "Maybe not. But a woman helped Mitch get free and now she wants us to help get her daughter back."

"From whom?"

"That we don't know yet. The wolf girl was pursuing them."

"And we have a flight to Salem?"

"Yes."

"Do we have to leave our weapons behind?" he asked.

"No. I made arrangements with a man who owns a helicopter. He'll fly us there."

"Good. That means less headaches."

Kat looked into Lucian's eyes and smiled. "You still look exhausted."

"I could sleep."

"Then lay back and sleep until we get to the airport, which is about thirty minutes away."

Lucian leaned back and closed his eyes. "Sounds good to me."

Chapter 52

Cassandra hurried along in the narrow path of light the penlight offered. Mitch forced himself to keep up. Although in pain, he wasn't as stiff as he had been when Cassandra freed him from the leather restraints. The more he moved, the better he felt.

Water sloshed underfoot from the shallow puddles. From time to time bats flittered past their heads.

"Do you think those cats will come after us?" Mitch asked.

"I don't know."

"At least they seem to favor you."

"They've watched my house for weeks now."

"Really?" Mitch asked.

"I was afraid of them until tonight. But Alicia," Cassandra choked back tears. "She never seemed concerned about them. I know it sounds odd, but she seemed to be able to read their thoughts or communicate with them in her mind."

"What do you mean?"

"Any time they were near the house, she seemed to know it."

"She mentioned them?"

"Yeah."

The light shone on a small metal door.

"Our exit," she said, sighing with relief. "I don't like being in such a dark place."

"I don't either."

Mitch stepped to the door. He grasped the upright slick metal handle and twisted to the right. The lock mechanism clicked. The door popped ajar. He gently pulled the door toward him and peered out.

"Turn out the light," he said.

She did so. "What do you see?"

"Perhaps the source behind the whole mess."

Cassandra peered through the doorway. She gasped when she read the sign on the iron-barred gate: New Horizons.

She spiraled from the door and moved away, fearing someone might have seen her through the narrow door crack. She shook her head. "I don't believe it."

"What?"

"The cats are from here."

Mitch pushed the door closed.

"Are you certain?" he asked.

"What other explanation is there? I mean they came from this direction. They chased that girl in the other direction."

Mitch took her penlight and turned the light onto the muddy path near the door.

"What are you doing?" she asked.

"Looking at what footprints are here. There aren't any catlike prints. Over here is Sheba's. And it looks like she enters through here often."

"So she's connected with New Horizons?"

"Looks that way."

Cassandra rubbed her eyes. "Then how did those cats get on the other side of us?"

"I'm not sure, but I have a feeling this tunnel has numerous exits. They could have come in somewhere else. And since they chased Sheba that direction, I believe they don't want her coming back here."

"It doesn't make any sense."

"It's starting to."

"How?"

"There was a police officer that came into the room while I was tied, and they thought I was unconscious."

"What did he look like?" she asked.

"Muscular and about Sheba's height. Wasn't a tall man."

Cassandra nodded. "Probably Officer Parker."

"He was mad that she didn't allow me to leave town. He got even angrier when she showed Kat's business card."

"Why?"

"Because they will be coming to help me. Well, us, now. Had I left town, they didn't have to worry about more information getting to the public about the murders."

Cassandra exhaled a frustrated sigh. "Then if we backtracked and searched for side tunnels, we might find Alicia and Seth?"

"That's possible, but we need to find a safe place to hide until morning."

"Why? If there's the chance I can find her—"

"Look. I understand your frustration. But the more we move around in the darkness, the better chance they have of finding us. We can't afford that. Alicia and Seth can't afford that, either. Kat and Lucian should be here in a few hours."

"You honestly believe two more people will be that much help?" Cassandra asked.

"I do. You don't know these two. They are more aggressive than Sheba or that officer."

"Fine," she said, crossing her arms. "So you want to hide in this dark tunnel until morning, wondering if she or those cats will return?"

"No," Mitch replied.

"Then where?"

"New Horizons."

"What? Are you crazy?"

Mitch smiled. "It's the last place they'd look for us."

"Or where your friends find our dead bodies."

"Nonsense," he said, pulling the door open. "Come on."

"Wait," Cassandra said, grabbing his arm.

"What is it?"

"New Horizons is a dangerous place. I believe they're the ones that killed Seth's mother. I can't prove it, but I believe they're the ones trying to kill me."

"What makes you believe that?"

"When I was in her house, I found some discarded letters in the trash from New Horizons. They were threatening her and demanded that she not move away with Seth. Before Officer Parker killed his partner, they discussed how angry their boss would be if they didn't find the children. I don't think we should go inside without your friends or outside authorities. It's too dangerous."

Mitch nodded, weighing the information. "Okay, but we could hide in the hedgerow and check out the place from a distance."

Cassandra peered out the door at the hedges that lined the perimeter. Although the drifting fog wasn't heavy, it still obscured their view. He opened the door, took her hand, and they exited. For some strange reason she didn't believe this was the best place for them to be.

Chapter 53

Sheba stared at the gun. From her peripheral vision she didn't see any other movement in the shadows. She didn't hear any other noises except the light drizzle plinking the metal roof. Parker seemed to have come alone.

Parker smiled. "Alpha has ordered me to take you home."

"Really?" she asked with an amused smile.

"Yes."

"And he sent *you* here alone?"

"Even you aren't bulletproof," Parker replied.

"But you're dumber than I gave you credit for."

Parker's jaw grew rigid. "He didn't say I had to bring you back alive."

Sheba shrugged. "So pull the trigger. I *dare* you. Maybe I'm more bulletproof than you'd expect."

His eyes narrowed. His hand tightened around the gun.

"Why did you do it?" he asked. "I'd like to know before Alpha punishes you."

"What?"

"You killed those two men in the cemetery."

Sheba frowned with confusion. "What are you talking about?"

"The two men I sent after Cassandra. They're dead. Ripped to shreds in the cemetery earlier today. Quite gruesome, even for you."

"I didn't kill them. I don't even know *who* you're talking about."

"Well, you gutted them too badly to salvage any of their internal organs."

Sheba folded her arms and glared at him. "Did your ears stop working? Or are you too stupid to listen. *I didn't kill them.*"

Parker took a deep breath and steadied the gun. "Reece? Did he tell you about them? Where they'd be?"

"No. I never talked to Reece. He's more a pansy than you are."

"You know what pisses me off the most about you?" he asked.

She shrugged. "I haven't a clue and don't really give a damn."

"You mouthing off at me," he said, his voice rising. "You always act like you have authority over me. Tonight that changes, you little bitch."

Before he clicked off the safety, Sheba grabbed his wrist, twisted, and yanked. His eyes widened at how fast she had moved. The bones snapped in his forearm, and the gun skidded across the warehouse floor. Holding his arm tightly, he wailed in pain and dropped to his knees.

Sheba stared down at him. Her eyes glinted with gold. Her inner wolf was attempting to control her. "I have authority over you. Alpha made me a she-alpha."

The rage inside her grew. Her jaws ached. She fought the temptation. She didn't want to change. Not yet. Not now.

Parker clenched his teeth together to stop screaming. His eyes met hers but terror silenced him. She glared at him with her right fist raised above her head. "When you awaken, tell Alpha I'm never coming home. I'm through."

With all her growing anger behind the blow, Sheba struck his chin. His teeth cracked. The impact pivoted him backward. He lay sprawled out on the grimy floor. Blood leaked from his busted lips and bleeding gums. Other than his breathing, he looked dead. She grabbed his gun and tossed it across the room. She sprinted through the warehouse while mentally fighting the inward urge to change.

Outside the warehouse, she opened the door and saw his idling patrol car. She turned off the engine, took the keys, and flung them onto the warehouse roof.

"That should slow you down," she whispered.

Sheba sniffed the night air. She altered her ears, listening to the sounds, hoping to detect the direction she needed to go. She was too far from Mitch to hear him. Then the danger he and the woman were in dawned upon her. They would come out at New Horizons where Alpha resided.

"Dammit!" she said, tearing into a sprint.

Regardless of what she had told Parker, she had no choice but to return to New Horizons. If she didn't, Mitch and the woman would die.

Chapter 54

North Town Airport, Las Vegas

LYDIA SAT on a bench near the check-in counters. The airport bustled with people leaving Vegas and others coming in with gambling eagerness set in their eyes. The lust and greed spilled off them like bad cologne.

Lydia sat with her arms crossed and a glare that told the world she hated everything. In spite of all the activity, she felt alone, isolated, which pleased her a great deal. He didn't need a sidekick and didn't *want* one.

A man approached her. "Are you Lydia?"

"I am," she said. "Who are you?"

"Davis. Boyd Grayson sent me. His plane's down that corridor."

"Don't I need to check in for clearance?"

"Everything's been taken care of."

Lydia grabbed her pack and her helmet and followed the man. She didn't feel comfortable leaving her gun and knives locked inside her bike box, but with airport security, she didn't have a choice. She'd never get past any of the metal detectors.

She still had other means to protect herself without a weapon. And once she met with Grayson she was certain he'd provide her with any weapon she requested as long as she killed Matthews. Grayson hated Matthews that much.

Lydia hated him even more.

MATTHEWS AND MORDIA entered a dark alley. Two filthy vagrants—a man and a woman—stood at a metal drum warming in the fire's glow. They looked at Matthews and Mordia suspiciously.

"What do you want?" the man asked, sliding a hand into his jacket pocket as if reaching for a weapon.

Matthews raised his hands calmly. "Easy. No need to panic. We don't mean you any harm. We're just here to help."

"Help?" the man laughed with a coarse bellow, which quickly turned into a hacking cough. "How you plan to help us?"

"How does food and shelter sound?" Mordia asked.

Matthews beamed a slight warm smile. "And a nice place where you don't need an outdoor roaring fire."

The woman brushed her greasy matted hair from her scraggly face and stared at them. Interest beamed in her hungered eyes. "You with the church shelter?"

"Not *that* kind of shelter," Matthews said. "But we offer you food, a hot shower, fresh clothes, and a place to bunk for a few days. Does that interest you?"

"What's the catch?" the man asked, growing less defensive. He scratched at his thin beard.

"A few tests?" Matthews said.

"Tests?" he asked.

"What kind of tests?" the woman asked.

"We're conducting tests for new drugs."

The man eyed Matthews shrewdly. "The kind that make you high or strung out?"

"Nothing like that," Matthews said. "I assure you."

"Well, hell, boy, you had me interested for a moment there."

Matthews pulled a wad of hundreds from his jacket pocket. "But we have money to boot? Lots of money in exchange for your help."

The man's eyes widened. He nodded, salivating at the money. "Sure. Works for me. You said that we get food and a shower, too?"

"Yes," Mordia said.

The man stared at his woman friend. "What about you, Beth?"

She smiled and nodded. "A night inside would be nice for a change. A shower even better. Right, Eric?"

"Been a long time. You guys are lifesavers," Eric said.

"You don't know how right you are," Matthews whispered.

LYDIA SAT on Grayson's Learjet and stared out the window, admiring the glow of the Vegas city lights in the distance. She focused on her hatred for Matthews. She hoped Grayson could track him down as he promised.

Lucas never entered her mind. She had progressed to the next level of her genetic programming buried deep within and forsaken her compassion in exchange for her cold-hearted prowess to track down her enemy. Her intense priority was the hunt, the kill. Nothing else mattered.

SHEBA RAN FASTER than she had ever moved. Knowing Salem, she knew which properties to cross to reduce the amount of time necessary to get to New Horizons. But even as fast as she moved, she knew Mitch and Cassandra would emerge from the underground tunnel well before she even got to them. With odds set against her, she didn't slow her pace. She ran, leapt over fences, through hedgerows, and down dark alleys.

Panting, her sides ached but she hoped her unyielding effort might enable her to plead her case to Mitch and let him know that she had gone to great lengths to rescue and protect them. With everything she was doing, she understood that it didn't guarantee forgiveness from either of them. Should that be the outcome, she'd face Alpha alone. Once that confrontation came, only one of them would survive, and if she died, she didn't care anymore. What else in this life did she have anyway?

Thinking through the situation, she must defeat Alpha. She must win. Otherwise, Gloria and Beverly would never be freed from their prisons of misery.

Growling, Sheba ran harder, faster. She was only a few minutes from New Horizons but she didn't think she's get to them in time.

Chapter 55

Mitch and Cassandra crouched near New Horizons' tall fence. Thin veils of fog drifted across the massive estate yard. Although the swelling around his left eye had diminished somewhat, his vision remained blurry. At times the concrete statues looked like real people that slightly moved, which kept him on edge. Mitch sensed they weren't alone, but he didn't see anyone.

Cassandra studied the inside yard and gasped.

"What is it?" he asked. "Do you see something?"

She grabbed his arm and tugged him to the ground.

A gunshot echoed from the other side of the fence, and a second later, Mitch noticed the dark shadow of a guard running from his spot beside one statue and heading in their direction. He raised the gun again as he ran.

Cassandra covered her mouth. Mitch grabbed her hand and yanked her to her feet.

"Hurry!" he whispered harshly.

They ran through the hedgerow and headed for the door that led to the underground tunnel. Both stopped moving almost instantly. Between them and the door stood Sheba. Her teeth and eyes had transformed and were eerie to behold.

"Oh, God," Cassandra said.

"Please," Sheba said in an oddly deep voice. "I want to help you."

"Riiight," Cassandra whispered. She pulled Mitch's hand and tried to run to the right.

"No," Mitch said. He projected his mental thoughts toward her, sensing her emotion through her plea and gestures. "Wait. She means it."

"Are you serious?" Cassandra stared at him with surprise in her eyes. "You really need some quality dating experience. Look at her. She's changing."

"No, she's reverting to her human form."

"How can you know that?"

Mitch shrugged. "She's fighting the monster inside her."

"I—," Cassandra began.

"We don't have time to argue," Mitch said.

Another gunshot broke the silent night air. This one was nearer the gate.

"Move!" Sheba she bolted toward them. "Get inside the tunnel and wait for me!"

She ran past them. They sprinted for the door.

The armed man came through the opening metal gate. Sheba rushed straight at him. Before he raised his weapon to fire, she disarmed him and knocked him unconscious. She put her hands over her ears and dropped to her knees. Her face contorted from pain.

Cassandra opened the door. "Come on, Mitch."

"No, not yet."

"What are you doing?"

"Helping her."

Mitch sprinted toward Sheba.

Sheba's eyes turned. Her jaws crackled and elongated.

"You can't!" Cassandra warned. "Something's wrong with her. She's changing."

"Yeah, but she's not doing it voluntarily. Someone's making her change."

"Who?"

"My guess is whoever made her."

"Get back!" Sheba growled. Spittle frothed from her mouth. "Run! Get away before it's too late!"

Mitch approached cautiously.

"I won't abandon you," he said.

"Please go," Sheba said. "It's Alpha. He's taking control of my mind."

The closer Mitch came to Sheba, the stronger the dark presence increased. He recognized it as the force that continued eluding him when he first arrived in Salem. Now he was closer to the evil source than he'd ever been. The power was greater than anything he had ever encountered, and it was channeled directly at Sheba.

Mitch thrust his energy along the telepathic conduit toward the man controlling Sheba. Although he wasn't as powerful as the man attacking Sheba's mind shield, Mitch struck hard enough to surprise and jar Alpha's hold on her. It was about as effective as a midget smacking a giant. Mitch hadn't inflicted any pain on Alpha, but snapped Alpha's attention off her and diverted it toward Mitch. Mitch's repercussion for interfering would bring a swift counter that might level Mitch to the ground in excruciating pain.

Mitch grabbed Sheba's arm.

"No!" she said. "Go. He's too powerful."

"I sense that, but come with us into the tunnel. I have an idea."

She interlocked her arm with his and rushed to Cassandra at the open door.

Mitch let Sheba enter the door first. He paused to see the frightened expression on Cassandra's face.

"I hope you know what you're doing," Cassandra said.

Mitch led Sheba past Cassandra and nodded. "Me, too. Hurry and get her farther inside."

"What are you going to do?"

"I'll be there in a few seconds."

Cassandra looked worried. Sheba's facial hair was getting thicker. Her teeth grew longer. She writhed in pain while fighting the internal urges to change. She growled and rolled on the earthen floor.

Mitch nodded at Cassandra with the assurance that he was going to be okay.

Cassandra reached for Sheba's long-clawed hand and hesitated. Sheba looked at Cassandra's offer to help with slight skepticism. After a few seconds Sheba took Cassandra's hand, and they disappeared into the darkness. She feared Sheba wouldn't be able to prevent changing and the she-wolf would turn on her and kill her before Mitch came to rescue her.

Mitch held the door handle and braced himself. He expected Alpha to attack, but he had never thought the initial assault to be so subtle. Alpha's attempt to tap into Mitch's mind had been mild but once his mental tendril crept past Mitch's guard, Alpha pulsed a quick jab that brought agonizing pain, much like a massive migraine, and then Alpha relaxed his hold.

"You should've left town," Alpha said angrily in Mitch's mind.

"I tried," Mitch said, wincing, trying to break Alpha's hold. Veins swelled on Mitch's forehead. His face flushed red. He held the door handle tighter to prevent his knees from buckling and collapsing. "Sheba prevented me from leaving."

"I know. She gets out of hand once in a while. Even from me. Leave her with me and I'll make certain she receives the appropriate punishment."

Mitch shook his head. "No."

"Even after what she did to you, you'd still try to take her from my grasp?"

"Yes."

"You're foolish. You actually trust her *not* to kill you?"

Mitch strained to keep breathing. "Yes. She needs help. Freedom from your hold."

"I'll make her tear you and Cassandra to shreds."

"Where's Cassandra's daughter?" Mitch asked.

"That's something I'd like to know."

"You don't have her?"

"No. But Alicia isn't *her* daughter. I created Alicia and molded her mind. She's mine. Cassandra was only a surrogate. Nothing more."

"If that is true, then why did you try to kill her?"

"She knows too much," Alpha said. "She so desperately wanted a daughter. She'll never stop looking for Alicia."

"Alicia *is* her daughter. She birthed her and raised her. I'm certain DNA would prove that."

Alpha laughed with a mocking tone. "DNA would prove *far* more than that."

"We're going to find Alicia and after we do, we're coming for you."

"You can try, but your power is weak compared to mine."

Alpha thrust his full dark power at Mitch. Mitch howled in pain, dropped to his knees, but he refused to lessen his tight hold on the door handle. Never had he endured such reeling pain. He attempted to parry it but wasn't able. He swung the heavy metal door toward himself and dropped backwards, rolling down the steps.

Cassandra rushed to him with her penlight on. "Mitch? Are you okay?"

"Shut the door," he whispered in little gasps.

She did so. While lying on his back, Mitch pushed himself into the dark tunnel with his feet. The farther from the door he moved, the less noticeable the pain.

"What happened?" Cassandra asked, helping Mitch sit up.

Sheba crouched beside them. "Alpha attacked him."

"From where?" Cassandra asked.

"From within," Sheba said, tapping her finger to her head.

Cassandra looked from Sheba to Mitch. "How?"

Sweat dripped from Mitch's hair, down his face, and he gasped to breath for a minute or so. "He has full psionic powers. Stronger than anyone I've met or ever been exposed to."

"Meaning what exactly?" Cassandra asked.

"It means he can thrust his will over yours if he gets inside your mind. That's why he was able to make Sheba change."

"Then why you?" Cassandra asked.

"That was his punishment for my interfering. Had I not dropped into the tunnel, he'd probably have killed me. The steel door acts like a barrier."

Sheba was now fully human in appearance. She placed her hand on his cheek. Tears were in her eyes. She gave a gentle kiss to his swollen left eye.

"I'm so sorry, Mitch," Sheba said. "I never wanted to hurt you. After I told you everything at the bus stop, I knew I had said too much. I was afraid that you'd return with others and Alpha would kill me."

Cassandra gave Sheba an icy stare. "His friends *are* coming."

"That's good," Sheba said. "We're going to need all the help we can get."

Mitch rubbed his eyes with the palms of his hands. "How are you feeling, Sheba?"

"Okay, why?"

"No, mentally. Do you sense Alpha trying to get inside your head?"

She shook her head. "No."

"Good. I think we're out of his control here," Mitch said, trying to stand.

"Why?" Cassandra asked. "How?"

Mitch stood and wobbled to maintain balance. He took the penlight and shone it toward the tunnel ceiling. "The heavy door, for one. The ceiling is metal and looks like underground telephone and power cables run through the tunnel, too. The electrical currents interfere with his mental reach."

Cassandra braced herself against Mitch to steady him. "How does he do that? Get inside people's heads?"

"Fewer than a tenth of one percent of people in the world have that ability," Mitch said. "But most that do, don't even know they can do it."

"And you've met others?" she asked.

"Yes, I have the ability too," he replied. "I'm also an empath."

Sheba studied his face. "That's how you knew my thoughts when I had you bound?"

Mitch nodded. "Yes."

"Why didn't you know I was setting you up?" Sheba asked.

"I let my guard down," he said.

Cassandra shook her head. "No, he *likes* you and was trying to impress you."

Sheba's eyes widened. She blushed and smiled. "Sure . . ."

Mitch surrendered a meek nod. "It's true. But it's something I'm sharply reconsidering."

Sheba's eyes saddened. "I'm sorry."

Cassandra helped Mitch walk to the wall. He placed his back against it, attempting to regain his strength.

"So you think we're safe down here?" Cassandra asked.

"From his reach, yes," Mitch said. "But if he comes down here, nothing we do will stop him. He's much more powerful than I am. We need a place to hide until morning. Once my colleagues get here, we go after Alpha."

Sheba frowned. "I know a place where you'll be safe until tomorrow, but I don't think it's a good idea to try to take Alpha down. He'll kill without hesitation. You've only felt a sliver of what he's capable of imposing."

"I know," Mitch said. "But you haven't met my friends yet, either."

"I hope you're right. Follow me. I'll show you where we can hide. It's where I go to get away from everything."

Mitch took Cassandra's hand. "I don't know if it's good or bad news."

"What?" she asked.

"Alpha doesn't have Alicia."

"What?"

He shrugged. "That's what he told me."

"He's lying," Cassandra replied. "He has to be."

"From what I detected, he's telling the truth."

"Then who has her?"

"I don't know. But Kat and Lucian will help us find her."

Mitch and Cassandra followed Sheba through the tunnel. Mitch trained the light on the path ahead of them. About midway back to where Sheba had held him prisoner, she turned to the right and pulled aside a black curtain. Behind it was another tunnel. They would have needed a larger flashlight to notice that cloth divider in the darkness.

Sheba paused and listened before she took a step past the curtain.

"Something wrong?" Mitch asked.

"No. I don't think so," Sheba replied. "Just want to make certain those cats aren't in there."

"Do the cats come from where you did?" Cassandra asked.

Sheba shook her head. "No."

"They're not from New Horizons?" Mitch asked. He squeezed Cassandra's hand. "See? That's a good sign that Alpha was telling the truth if those cats aren't his."

"No, they're not," Sheba said. "Alpha works with canine gene splicing. Never seen a cat anywhere on his properties. That would be total chaos."

Cassandra cleared her throat. "So he really doesn't have my daughter?"

"No," Mitch said. "But he's looking for her."

"At least I have the hope we can find her."

"We'll give the search everything we have," Mitch said.

Cassandra glanced at him in the faint glow of light. "Thanks."

"Don't mention it," Mitch said. "But I know Alpha's pissed that he doesn't have Alicia."

"Why does he want her in the first place?" Cassandra asked.

Mitch faced her. "He implied that she is his creation. Alicia is a scientific project and you were only needed as the surrogate."

"Damn him!" Cassandra said, fuming.

"Agreed," Sheba said. "What I want to know is why those cats came after me and didn't bother you."

"They must have Alicia," Cassandra replied. "They were protecting us from you."

"Why would they take your daughter?"

"I'm not sure, but apparently they don't want her or Seth taken by Alpha. I wonder where they are keeping them."

Sheba shrugged. "I have no idea. Tonight's the first time I've ever seen those cats."

"They've watched my house for months."

"Really?" Sheba asked.

"Yes."

Sheba smiled at Cassandra. "That seems a good thing."

"I hope so."

Chapter 56

Grayson sat behind his mahogany desk when the intercom beeped. His secretary said, "Mr. Grayson, he's on the line."

Grayson tapped his earphone. "Have you found Matthews?"

"Yes."

"Where is he?"

"San Diego."

Grayson smiled. "So he's come back for revenge?"

"Probably."

"Perfect. I'm getting a team together."

"There's something you should know."

Grayson frowned. "What's that?"

"He doesn't look the same."

"Prison does that," Grayson said with a broad smile.

"No. He's had plastic surgery."

The smile faded from Grayson's face. "Send me a picture immediately."

"I can't yet."

Grayson's huge hands balled into tight veined fists. "Why not?"

"If I had taken his photo, he'd have killed me. It would be too obvious."

"Okay." Grayson nodded. "When can you send me one?"

"As soon as he returns. He should be back soon. But he's not alone."

"Oh?" Grayson said. "Who's with him?"

"A woman."

"Name?"

"I don't know that yet, but she might've been the doctor that did his surgery. At least Matthews implied it."

"Good to know. Get a picture of him and email it to me."

"I will."

"Great job, Jimmy. Soon he won't be a problem for any of us."

"I'm setting up everything right now—cameras, mikes, and if I'm able, I'll place trackers on their clothes so you can lock in on their location."

"Keep up the good work," Grayson said. "The most important thing is getting us a clear image of his new face, in case you cannot use trackers or he discovers them."

"Getting right on it."

Grayson tapped his earphone and disconnected their connection. A broad grin spread across his face.

He wished he had killed Matthews in New York, but that would have taken the fun out of the hunting game set before him. Grayson liked challenges. He couldn't wait to see the smugness stamped out of Matthews forever. Matthews would get what was coming to him.

———

MATTHEWS AND MORDIA led the homeless couple through the dark filthy alley and across a couple of streets. When they stopped outside the fancy apartment building, Eric looked at Beth and smiled.

"Ritzy place, eh?" Eric said.

She smiled with tears forming in her eyes. "Yes."

Matthews opened the front glass door. Mordia and Beth entered before him. Eric paused at the open door and faced Matthews. "How long will these tests last?"

"A few days. Maybe longer," Matthews replied.

"I hope much, much longer," Eric said, entering the building. "Once you've completed the tests, I'd be available to work for you if you need me."

Matthews nodded. "Let's not get ahead of ourselves. One step at a time."

MATTHEWS UNLOCKED THE APARTMENT DOOR. The smell of pizza drifted on the air.

Matthews let Eric and Beth inside. He pointed toward the table. "Sorry, but all we have tonight is pizza, but I promise you'll have even better meals tomorrow."

"Are you kidding? Pizza is divine when you've not eaten much in days," Eric said.

"Help yourselves," Matthews said.

Beth and Eric grabbed slices of pizza with their grimy hands and ate as fast as they could.

Matthews shook his head. "Easy, folks. Take the time to enjoy the taste of the pizza. No one's going to steal it from you. If we run out, I promise we can order more. After you eaten your fill, take a long shower and clean up. Dr. Mordia and I will get the paperwork started."

Eric's mouth bulged. "Thank you, sir."

Beth nodded. "Bless you."

Matthews acquiesced a nod and turned toward Jimmy. "Everything okay?"

Jimmy gave a nervous nod. "Everything's fine."

Matthews approached the desk where Jimmy had set up his laptop and other devices. "What have you got going here?"

"I have a new type of camera on the laptop that taps directly into the FBI database." Jimmy grinned. "Well, it does now since I hacked into their system."

"Already?"

"Yes."

Matthews nodded. "I'm impressed."

"When you mentioned you might want me to research identifications through their database, I thought I could show you this. If you could indulge me?"

"What do you need?"

"Just a quick photo."

Matthews' eyes narrowed, and he crossed his arms. "Why?"

"We scan your facial profile and compare you with the FBI database."

"They won't find me since my face has changed."

"I know," Jimmy said. "But then I'll run a scan on one of your . . . research participants there."

Matthews stared at Jimmy in silence for several long seconds.

"It was just an idea," Jimmy said. "I thought you might want to make certain that their technology didn't probe any farther and detect who you are."

"And how could they possibly do that?"

"I'm not certain if their technology can also recognize eye shape or even somehow read eye retina recognition through a photo. Should they have that ability, I'd stay off the streets and never enter any bank or government building where these recognition cameras are set up."

"You think they can do that?" Matthews asked with a skeptical gaze.

Jimmy shrugged. "Their programs are state of the art, but I really can't say unless I check firsthand."

At first Matthews looked suspicious, but after a few seconds, his growing paranoia got the best of him. He looked nervous. Sweat beaded his brow.

"Ah, hell, where do I stand?" Matthews asked.

Jimmy motioned him until the camera captured Matthews' face. He typed a command and it froze Matthews' new image onto a small corner of the computer screen. Before Matthews got around the desk, Jimmy clicked another button, which sent a copy of the Matthews' face to Grayson.

"So how's this scan work?"

Jimmy typed several key codes into the computer, and the FBI database scrolled through dozens of faces, trying to match one to it.

"Like I said," Jimmy replied. "There probably won't be anything show up, but I'll let it run for a couple of hours in case they do check eye matches, too."

Matthews said, "Let me know what you find."

"I will."

Mordia entered the room with a stack of towels and washcloths in her hands. She set them on the table close to the pizza boxes. She looked at Beth. "When you're ready, I'll show you where you can shower."

Beth nodded.

"After you two are all cleaned up," Matthews said. "We'll start with your first injection. Then you can sleep. We'll begin evaluations in the morning after a hearty breakfast of course. And coffee. Do you two like coffee?"

They nodded, still stuffing pizza into their mouths.

"Good. Enjoy!"

Chapter 57

Alicia sat on a worn couch with her legs crossed. Seth lay on the other end in a near fetal position. His eyes were red from crying. Alicia hummed a pleasant tune, trying to soothe him, and at least he had stopped sobbing.

The room was small, hardly larger than a prison cell. There weren't any bars, but there wasn't a single window, either. The walls were metal. The only light came from the single hanging bulb overhead. She guessed the place had been a large vault at some point in history, but she wasn't certain.

The tunnels the catlike creatures had led her through were too dark for her to know exactly where they had taken her. Seth came a few hours later.

"Why are we here?" he whispered.

"To keep us safe," she replied.

"From who?" He sat up and wiped his flushed cheeks.

"I don't know."

"I want my Momma."

Alicia nodded. "I know. So do I. We'll see them soon."

"No," Seth said. "I won't. Momma's dead."

Alicia took a deep breath. "You're sure?"

"Uh-huh. I heard the people break down the front door. She started screaming in her bedroom and then became very quiet."

"How'd you escape?"

"Those cats. I followed them through the basement and out the little window into the yard."

"They'll keep us safe," Alicia whispered.

"I hope so."

Alicia smiled at Seth. "If they meant us harm, they'd have killed us already."

"Is your Momma okay?"

Alicia thought for a few moments, closed her eyes, and slowly nodded. "Yes. She's trying to find us."

"I wish she'd hurry."

"Me, too, Seth. Close your eyes and try to sleep. It's late. Maybe things will be a lot better in the morning."

"Okay," Seth said, closing his eyes. Tears slowly crept down his cheeks. His breathing was hampered with occasional sharp breaths. A few minutes later he was asleep.

Alicia uncrossed her legs and looked at the pile of toys in the floor. None of them interested her. They were for children much younger than her or Seth. She was startled that Seth was acting half his age, but she understood why. His mother was dead. Gone. And his shock reverted him to childlike actions as a defensive mechanism. Once his shock subsided, she believed he'd adjust in a few days.

She wasn't affected in the same manner because she sensed her mother was somehow still alive. Her mother was tough and resourceful. She was a runner and that sport required focused determination. Although her mother didn't speak much of her ex-husband, Alicia was aware of the internal strain the failed relationship had imposed on her Mom. The lines and creases around her eyes and lips showed the weathering her soul had endured. Her mother was a survivor, a fighter, and the only time she had shown any fear around Alicia was when the cats were outside the house.

Alicia had known about the catlike creatures for months. She watched them from her bedroom window for a few nights before they finally came for her. They fascinated her because they were the first animals that didn't fear her. They let her pet them. She loved that they trusted her, so she trusted them in return.

Their fur was soft like silk. Their gentle purrs soothed her whenever she petted them and wrapped her arms around their necks. They nuzzled her affectionately, and last night, when they had come, she sensed that they wanted her to leave with them. She read it in their eyes. She didn't understand why she knew this was what they wanted, but her instincts hadn't been wrong. They led her through the alleyways. Their ears and eyes were always alert. They sensed someone was coming. They kept her close, and she never felt afraid.

Alicia worried about her mother. Although she didn't have telepathic abilities, she did detect her mother's determination to find her. She was alive, of that she felt certain.

She didn't want to believe Seth's mother was dead, as he had just told her, but her gut told her that what he had heard was probably the last brutal moments of her life.

Alicia wondered why the creatures had chosen to take her and Seth but not their mothers. Her mother knew about the large cats and feared them. Perhaps that was why they didn't try to persuade her mother to follow. Alicia's curiosity about the creatures was greater than any fear she should have held for them. They were larger than most dogs but gentler than kittens, at least around her and Seth.

Three cats came to her window, but she passed at least a half dozen more when she reached the small room. In the dark hall outside the door, a larger catlike creature sat in a defensive stance. Although these cats were protecting her and Seth, they weren't allowed her or Seth to leave. The one time she walked to the door, the cat guardian turned with narrowed eyes and hissed at her. She stepped back without hesitation.

Another cat entered and nuzzled its head against her hands in a reassuring manner. They didn't want to harm her, but they weren't about to allow her outside. She gathered that something dangerous lurked in Salem. Someone had sent the cats to protect her and Seth, but who?

On a small table beside the couch were several bags of chips, cookies, and jerky. These were different items the catlike creatures had brought to them to eat but none appealed to her.

Alicia took the small blanket from the floor and gently draped it over Seth before she curled into her corner of the couch and rested her head on the armrest. She closed her eyes and hoped that she and her mother would be together soon. Until then, she'd search for her mother in her dreams.

A FEW MINUTES AFTER MIDNIGHT, Lydia entered Grayson's office with Davis. Grayson sat behind his desk with his large hands folded tightly together. Even at the late hour, Grayson wore one of his best suits without having loosened his tie. When he saw her enter, a bold smile spread across his serious face.

Lydia offered a narrowed, cold stare when her eyes met Grayson's.

"Have you found him?" she asked.

Grayson chuckled and shook his head. "Straight to the point. I like that."

Lydia placed her hands on her hips. "Well?"

"As a matter of fact, we now know what he looks like."

Lydia frowned. "What do you mean?"

Grayson nodded. "He underwent plastic surgery. Apparently he knew we'd want to find him."

"Location?" she asked.

"San Diego."

Lydia's eyebrows rose. "Why would he come here?"

"My guess is that he plans to do what he began at my New York facility. He wants me dead, my technology data, and would possibly go after you if he succeeded in achieving those goals."

"He won't have time to pursue either or us. I'm going after him now."

Lydia turned and headed for the door.

"Easy," Grayson said. "Not yet."

Lydia stopped and glanced over her shoulder. "Why not?"

"I have a man on the inside. You rush in right now, and he's dead."

Lydia turned and frowned. "I doubt Matthews will stick around too long before he heads here. It's best we catch him off guard."

Grayson nodded. "That's my intention. But I know he's in no hurry to leave."

"What makes you so certain?"

"The apartment complex where he's at. He paid a year's rent ahead on it. So whatever he's up to, he's going to be working on it there."

Lydia looked from Grayson to Davis.

Davis nodded. "He's right. We did some investigating after our contact showed up. We have proof this is Matthews' residence and has been even though he was imprisoned."

"The plastic surgery isn't something I expected he'd do," Grayson said. "I believed his vanity flowed vigorously from his soul. And as much as he has lusted for notoriety, I assumed he'd also want people to recognize him immediately. So he's in stealth mode, but he won't suspect that we know where he is or what he looks like."

"How soon before I can get him?" Lydia asked.

Grayson smiled and looked at Davis. Davis shook his head and chuckled.

"She's set a vindictive mission," Davis said.

"I see that," Grayson said, nodding. He looked at Lydia. "Within a few hours Jimmy will leave after Matthews has gone to sleep. After he's safe, he'll contact me. Then you move in."

Lydia glanced at Davis. "I need weapons."

"We have an arsenal of weapons you can choose from."

Lydia smiled. "Then let's get started."

Chapter 58

Jimmy sat at the table, working at his laptop. Matthews stood beside Mordia at the edge of the hallway. They whispered, but not so low that Jimmy couldn't hear.

"There's only two," Matthews said. "That won't be enough to gather data."

"It's a start, though. A male and female test subject. So we will see how the serum works based on gender."

"That's true. Good observation."

"Other than being hungry and dirty, I think they are good subjects to begin with," she said. "Don't you?"

"They seem healthy enough, but Eric hinted about drug use."

"I know."

"The good thing is that he doesn't exhibit any signs of withdrawal. So he could be clean."

"Do you think they'll still be willing to cooperate in the morning?" Mordia asked.

"They had best."

"And if they don't?"

Matthews offered a grim smile. "Let's hope it doesn't come to that."

SHEBA LED Mitch and Cassandra to an old mechanic shop on the edge of town. The windows were boarded up. Rusted car bodies and parts lay scattered on the ground. Ivy and briars clung to the paint-peeled walls. The old chain-link fence towered eight feet. Sheba pulled back part of the fence where the links had been cut. With no streetlights brightening the night, it was difficult to see what was enclosed inside the fence.

Cassandra felt blind. Mitch held her hand, following behind her. She doubted Mitch could see any better than herself. She could only guess that Sheba must be blessed with night vision like some animals possess. For all she knew, Sheba could be luring them into another trap, but Cassandra had run out of options, at least until Mitch's friends arrived. She had to begin trusting others eventually, but that was still difficult under current circumstances.

"You stay here?" Cassandra asked.

Sheba stopped inside the fence. "No, I only come to visit."

"Why such a rundown place?" Mitch asked.

"No one comes here. It's quiet."

Sheba led them to the side of the garage and pushed aside a large piece of tin. She listened for a moment before entering.

"Come on," she said.

Cassandra followed. Her mind raced with every possible thing she might encounter. Snakes, spiders, and other nasty creepy crawlers brought chill bumps down her arms and behind her neck. She stopped walking when she worried that there might actually be others like Sheba waiting inside the garage. Or, the cats might lurk in the darkness, which might actually be a good thing.

Mitch bumped into her.

"Sorry," he said. "What's wrong? Why'd you stop walking?"

"It's nothing," she replied.

"It's safe here," Sheba said from across the room.

A light flickered and brightened. Sheba struck a long kitchen match. She lit an oil lantern and shook the match until its flame died. Adjusting the wick, the light intensified and chased away the darkness. A couple of old cars were parked with flat tires. Layers of dust coated them. Wrenches, screwdrivers, and assorted tools hung on the walls above workbenches.

Sheba carried the lantern and placed it on a table. Her voice rose with a pleasant eagerness that was unfamiliar to her nature. "Come look."

Cassandra and Mitch walked to the table. Cassandra studied Sheba's face in the glow of the lantern. All the piercings, the tattoos, and her running dark mascara seemed contrary to how she was acting now. She sounded like an excited child that had found a toy.

Sheba wiped a thin layer of dust off the cover of the large binder. She opened the book and smiled. "These are the reasons I come here."

Mitch looked over Cassandra's shoulder and frowned. "Photos?"

Sheba nodded. "Yes. You see? This is Gloria and I at the park. Beverly had taken that one. Here's one of Beverly and Jill on the rickety old seesaw. Then here's one of us all at Gloria's last birthday party *before* the incident that changed our lives. Her mother had taken this one."

Cassandra glanced at Mitch with uncertainty. He nodded reassuringly and mouthed, "It's okay."

"So you come here to look at them?" Mitch asked.

Sheba smiled. "These and other things. I have Gloria's teddy bear and a few of Jill's dolls. Some other toys we played with, too."

Mitch frowned. "Alpha has Gloria?"

"Yes."

"You're positive she's still alive?" he asked.

"Yes. I know she is. He won't let me see her."

Cassandra shook her head. "Why is he keeping her?"

"To make me do what he wants."

"Have you ever called his bluff?" Cassandra asked.

"No. He'd hurt her. I know he would."

Mitch looked at Sheba. "Has he ever let you see her since that night she went missing?"

"Once. So I know he has her."

"Inside New Horizons?" Mitch asked.

"Maybe," she said.

Mitch stared at Gloria's face in the picture. "Where else might he be keeping her?"

Sheba's lower lip puckered. "The asylum."

"With Beverly?"

Sheba nodded and gently ran a finger across Gloria's picture. Tears welled in her eyes. Mitch stepped beside her, placed his hand over hers, and squeezed.

"Listen," Mitch said. "When my friends get here, we'll find her. You'll get to be with her again, but we need to hide until morning."

"We can stay here," Sheba said. "There's an old mattress over in that corner. You two sleep and I'll keep watch."

Cassandra sighed. "I'm exhausted, and as much as I appreciate the offer, I honestly don't think I'd sleep a wink here."

Mitch placed a hand on her shoulder. "We could at least try. If nothing else, we can rest."

"I need some rest. I've been running full speed all day. Food would be nice, too."

Sheba said, "I have some food. Dry cereal and pastries. A few bottles of water if you're thirsty."

"Right now, anything sounds great," Cassandra said.

Sheba turned and pulled open a filing cabinet drawer.

Mitch's cellphone vibrated. "It's Kat. Her text says that they're on the plane and will be here by sunrise."

"Good," Cassandra said. "Maybe this will be over tomorrow."

"I hope so," Mitch said.

"Stopping Alpha won't be an easy task," Sheba said.

"I know," Mitch replied.

Sheba placed food and water on the workbench. "You felt his power when you risked your life for me."

"Yes."

"Magnify that by one hundred when you get within his sight. You were at a distance. The closer you get to him, the stronger his power."

"Damn," Mitch said softly.

"I wanted to give you the heads up on that. You've not tasted his full strength. No one has ever survived it."

Mitch and Cassandra grabbed something to eat and a bottle of water. Mitch sat on the mattress and patted a spot beside him. Cassandra plopped down next to him. A small cloud of dust puffed upward. She coughed and waved away the dust.

Mitch drank the water and scooted back against the wall. Cassandra did the same. After she finished eating, she leaned and rested her head against his shoulder. She thought of Alicia for a few moments before her heavy eyelids closed and she surrendered to sleep. Mitch did the same.

Chapter 59

Officer Parker awoke with a quick start. He shook his head and instantly felt woozy. He ran his tongue across his shattered teeth and his anger boiled.

"Damn bitch!" He rose to his feet and wiped blood from his lip and spit tooth fragments on the dusty warehouse floor. "I'll kill you for this!"

Parker attempted to stand, stumbled, and caught himself inches before his face smashed against the concrete. He pushed off from the ground, much like doing a pushup, and steadied himself. He shook his head. Everything appeared blurry. For a young lady, she had one hell of a punch.

He turned on his flashlight and staggered across the floor. Seeing his gun reflect in the light, he made his way toward it. Sharp pain pulsed through his jaws and stabbed into his brain. He avoided breathing through his mouth because the cool air coming across his broken teeth increased the pain.

Parker knelt at the gun and picked it up. He didn't rise too quickly because he knew he was close to losing consciousness again. He rose and the room shifted. Nausea churned inside his stomach.

"Steady," he told himself. He holstered the gun.

One carefully took one step at a time. He'd have joked about failing his own sobriety test had he not hurt so badly.

In a couple of intense minutes, he made his way to the door, opened it, and leaned against the frame. All the lights on his patrol car were flashing, but the engine wasn't running.

"Dammit!" He didn't have to look to know that she had taken his car keys.

He wobbled to the car and opened the door. He got on his radio and called dispatch.

"Send someone out to Dirsch's Warehouse. I need my spare set of car keys."

"Roger that," came back over the radio.

Silver shimmered across his eyes. He growled with delight. His pain diminished and renewed strength flowed through his body.

"You're going to suffer for this, Sheba," Parker said. "This time I'm going to kill you."

ALICIA SLEPT QUIETLY, dreaming of her mother's loving smile. In her dream, she reached to hug her mother but felt a presence in the room.

Voices in the small room awakened her. She bolted up and looked around. Seth was still asleep on the other end of the couch. The large cat remained rigid and alert outside the door with its back to her.

"Sorry that I've awakened you," he said.

Alicia turned quickly. The man stood in the corner across the room. A large cat sat at his feet, and he rubbed between its ears. He smiled when her eyes met his.

"Who are you?" she asked.

"Does a name really matter? It won't make you know me any better."

Her eyes narrowed. "Why am I here? Why are *we* here?"

"You are being protected."

"From whom?"

"It's too complicated to explain, but I assure you, you'll be released very soon. Once those who wish you harm are taken out of the way, you're free to go."

Alicia studied the man. He had blonde hair and brilliant blue eyes. His skin was tan, and although he was muscular, he wasn't a massive person.

"Is my mother alive?" she asked.

He nodded. "She's fine."

"And Seth's?"

He looked away and his shoulders sagged. "Regrettably, we weren't able to get to her in time."

Sadness filled Alicia's eyes. "Why would anyone want to kill her? She was a wonderful person."

"I know. But greed has a hand in this."

"Why haven't you brought my mother here?"

"We're working on it."

"Really?" she asked, staring at him with skepticism.

"Yes."

"But the people who killed Deidre might kill her."

The man nodded and smiled. "We've been protecting her day and night. You'll be with her soon. You have my word."

Alicia pondered the man's statements. "This is an odd place to keep us."

He shrugged. "It's the safest place in Salem for you. These old steel walls . . . they keep the intruder out. He cannot find you here. And trust me, he wants to find you. He's looking for you now."

"Does he want to kill me, too?"

"No. Perhaps much worse."

Alicia gave a shrewd stare. "What's worse than death?"

"Many things, I'm afraid. Loss of freedom. Loss of love. Those are two things I think are worse than death."

"I suppose."

"Do you not feel them now?" he asked. "You're temporarily isolated from your mother and held here in this room. How does that make you feel?"

"Lonely. And I hurt inside because I miss her, and I'm worried about her."

"See?"

"I understand."

He smiled. "No, not really. You see, this is temporary. If he gets you, this type of isolation will be the remainder of your life. Only not in *this* room. In his laboratory or a cage. You and Seth are very special and have unique abilities that he wants to use for his own gain. I won't allow it. And he will be stopped. Soon."

"How will you do that?"

"In due time, young lady. In due time."

———————

JIMMY SAT at the desk and quietly disassembled his computer setup. More than an hour had passed since Beth and Eric had taken their showers, eaten more pizza, and Mordia showed them to their rooms to sleep.

Mordia slept on the foldout couch. Matthews chose the room nearest the bathroom and hadn't come out for quite some time.

Jimmy thought it odd that Matthews hadn't invited Mordia to his room. She was a very attractive woman with a great figure, but Matthews had expressed no sexual interest in her at all, in spite of his constant praises toward her beauty and intellect. When it came to work, Matthews always presented everything in a stiff, professional business manner.

Jimmy tucked several computer attachments into the laptop case and slid the laptop into its compartment. He didn't attempt to zip each compartment closed because the sound was certain to awaken Mordia. He held the handles together and tiptoed to the apartment door.

He slowly unlocked each deadbolt as quietly as possible. Each quick *click* caused him to close his eyes and hold his breath. They seemed strangely loud. After the fifth turned, he grabbed the doorknob and turned it silently. Pulling the door toward him, he took a slight step backwards. Cold metal pressed beneath his right ear.

"Going somewhere?" Matthews asked with a broad smile.

Jimmy took a quick breath and swallowed hard.

Matthews shut the door and with a nod, he motioned Jimmy toward the desk.

"Mordia!" Matthews said.

She rolled over on the couch and blinked with surprise.

"What's going on?" she asked.

"I need your help."

Mordia pulled off her blankets and walked toward them. "What do you need?"

"Sedate him."

Mordia looked at him questionably. "Why?"

"He was attempting to leave."

Mordia frowned. "You mean he *has* to stay?"

"He was sneaking out with all his stuff." Matthews glared at Jimmy. "What was the photo for earlier?"

"I told you."

Matthews shook his head. "No, a better question. Whom did you send that photo to?"

"No one. I swear."

Matthews stepped closer to Jimmy and stared him in the eyes. Jimmy looked away.

"See? You're lying. I can tell."

Matthews held the gun on Jimmy. Mordia grabbed a syringe from her bag, thumped it twice, looking for air bubbles, and then she inserted the needle into Jimmy's hip.

The room began to spin. Jimmy dropped his computer case and grabbed a chair to keep from collapsing to the floor.

Matthews smiled at Mordia. "Looks like we have a third participant in this project."

Jimmy felt his body numbing. He tried to hold himself up, but the drug was too powerful. He released his grip on the chair and fell forward on the floor.

Matthews leaned down and turned Jimmy onto his back. Matthews grinned. "Was it worth it, old friend?"

Jimmy lost consciousness.

MORDIA LOOKED AT MATTHEWS. "NOW WHAT?"

"We start the project."

"While they're asleep?"

"Why not? No protest if they change their minds."

Mordia shook her head. "You're more shrewd than I imagined."

He smiled. "You've never seen me when I *don't* get my way."

Mordia grabbed her medical bag. "Well, I don't intend to start now. Let's go."

Chapter 60

Joe returned to where Curt and Reggie remained tied. The sun was rising over the horizon. The vivid yellow, orange, and red pastel colors mixed the sky above the mountain peaks. He walked to where Curt and Reggie remained tied. Fear haunted their eyes. Anyone could tell upon first examination that neither man had slept overnight.

"How did the night treat you?" Joe asked with a firm gaze. "Did the spirits visit as I said they would? If they didn't bestow you with their presences, perhaps I should leave you one more night."

"I'd rather die than stay here another night," Reggie said. His face was pale. His lips trembled.

Curt pleaded, "Cut us loose. We can't stay here anymore."

Joe smiled. "Cut you loose? After what you did to Misty and myself? You shouldn't expect to get off *that* easily. You left my friend behind to die. He's in the hospital. Had he died, your outcome would be far worse. But for what you've done, you have no reason to ask for mercy. You certainly shouldn't expect any."

"Then kill us!" Curt said. "Get your redemption for your girlfriend. I suppose you deserve that much. Just end this torture."

Joe shook his head. "Death's too easy for you. Where you're going, you'll wish everyday that the spirits had taken your lives last night. You'll have a long time to think about what you did. Your loyalty to this *Alpha* has cost your freedom and tarnished your soul."

Reggie struggled with the ropes behind his back.

"The knots are no more loose now than after I tied them," Joe said.

"Where are you going to take us?"

"Me?" Joe said. "Nowhere."

Joe whistled a sharp piercing note. His two brothers rose from thick brush on both sides of the gully where the men sat. Broad smiles covered their faces.

Curt shook his head. "They've been there all night?"

Joe nodded.

"What are you going to do to us?" Reggie asked.

The old sheriff came down the steep dusty trail with slow, steady steps. When he got to the level area near Joe, he studied the two men for a moment, and then looked at Joe.

"These two are responsible for Misty's death?" Sheriff Sterling asked.

"Yes."

"They put the rattlesnakes in your house?"

"Yes, sir," Joe replied.

"How long have they been out here?"

"All night."

"All night? You abducted them? What gives you that right?" Sterling asked.

"They confessed to me and Lucas yesterday. You heard them just now."

"Joe, I understand your anger, but you can't exact your own justice. It's not allowed."

Joe smiled. "No harm came to them."

"Ah, Joe, I think you should come back to town with me."

"Sorry, Sheriff Sterling, but no."

"I wasn't exactly asking," Sterling said.

Joe shook his head. "And I don't have any reason to go."

"They may wish to press charges against you," the sheriff said.

Joe eyed Curt, and then Reggie. He stared into their eyes with a bold gaze. Both men shook their heads.

"No," Curt said. "We won't be. Just get us out of here."

"Joe?" the sheriff said. "At least come and help us file the report.

"Not right now," Joe replied. "I have things I must do. I need to check on my friend."

Joe walked up the path and met Owl-hunter while their two brothers stayed behind to help the sheriff with the men.

"Mind if I borrow your motorcycle?" Joe asked.

"Not at all. Going to get the skull?"

Joe nodded. "It's time."

"Good. If you need our help, let me know."

"Of course."

AFTER JOE RODE to the gulch where he had hidden the alien skull, he drove another hour along winding, dusty paths until he reached his great uncle's hogan.

The vivid, beautifully colored ridges and red colored buttes and plateaus were so spectacular that Joe wondered how anyone in the world could be as coldhearted and ruthless as Curt and Reggie were. How in the vastness of such tranquility could evil root its way to the surface and poison an otherwise magnificent world?

Joe turned off the motorcycle's engine, grabbed the skull, and wrapped it in burlap.

His great uncle, Atsa, stepped outside the hogan and smiled. "Ah, Shadow-talker. It's been a long time."

Joe embraced Atsa tightly. "It has."

"What purpose has brought you here?" He gave a gentle nod toward the wrapped skull. "Is it this?"

"Yes, Uncle. I need to meditate and seek guidance from the Spirit World about what I must do with this."

"A dark chindi has attacked you?"

Joe nodded.

"And it seeks rest. *Why* did you disturb its grave?"

"It was by accident. My brothers and I were digging for artifacts."

Deep creases furrowed on Atsa's forehead. "How did they react when you discovered the skull?"

"They wanted me to rebury it."

"And yet you chose to keep it?"

Joe eyed his uncle with shrewd interest. "Have my brothers visited you?"

"Not in many years. It's a shame they did not come with you today. They could help you with this matter."

"If they haven't been here, how did you know that I had a skull?"

"I sense these things. Its presence is mighty."

Joe smiled. His uncle was a more powerful Shaman than Joe with many more decades of spiritual experience and visions. Atsa's name meant the Great Eagle, full of power, wisdom, and strength. His attunement to the earth and the spirit world enabled him the understanding that Joe would eventually achieve should he continue to devote his life search to their bestowed gifts of knowledge.

Atsa smiled through his sun-aged wrinkles. "Odd that you'd come today."

"Why?" Joe asked. He gently tucked the wrapped skull under his arm.

"Last week a terrible storm crossed the valley," he said. "Lightning struck that Foxtail Pine tree. I gathered needles this morning with great urgency. Now, I understand why. You were coming. Let me prepare the sweat lodge. Shall I call your cousins to join you?"

"No," Joe replied. "This is one I must do alone."

"Alone?" Atsa shook his head. "Against the chindi? No, that is too dangerous. It's best to be in company during such a confrontation."

"Not this time."

Atsa studied Joe's face for a few minutes, staring long and intently. Finally, he acquiesced a nod. "Very well. At least, let me get the ceremony prepared for you."

Joe helped his uncle raise the dark blanket door of the sweat lodge. The small lodge was made out of red mud and stood about four feet in height, almost resembling the top half of a hornet's nest. Joe carried several melon-sized stones and laid them on a large log in the fire pit, which was about four feet from the door. Then he gathered dried kindling and stuffed it beneath the log.

It had been a while since Joe had visited the lodge. He was looking forward to what revelations the spirits brought him.

Atsa sensed the chindi and seemed to believe it to be a bad omen, much like Owl-hunter had first pointed out to Joe. And yet, Joe had never felt this. He knew the skull had a purpose for being found.

Burying it and hiding it from the world wasn't something he felt he should do.

But why did his brother and uncle believe the skull must be buried?

There was only one thing Joe knew he must do. He must seek the guidance of his ancestors and whatever they deemed best, he would obey without question or protest. This was how he lived his life. Disobedience brought disharmony and uncertainty.

AN HOUR PASSED before Atsa had the fire prepared.

He mixed water, cedar, and pine needles together, and then he motioned Joe inside the sweat lodge. He handed Joe a pitchfork and reminded him where to place the heated stones to impede the north wind to ward off sickness. After completing the task, Joe ducked and entered the lodge. Atsa dropped the blanket door behind him. Darkness surrounded Joe. Only the glow of the rocks was visible. Heat radiated from the stones. Because of the low four-foot high ceiling, the warmth immediately surrounded Joe.

Joe unwrapped the skull and set it in his hands. He closed his eyes and began his first chant. His other senses heightened. After several minutes, Joe poured some of the water mixture onto the stones. Steam rose quickly. The aroma from the needles brought the sweetness of spring. The cleansing moisture drifted through the air and clung to Joe's skin.

Warmth pulsed from the skull into his fingers. The heat traveled through his hands and radiated up his arms. He felt no alarm or any threat. No attack. The peace-filled power eased slowly through him until it reached his core. Dizziness overcame him for a few brief moments as this unknown energy connected with him.

Outside the blanket door, Atsa chanted along with Joe. Apparently his uncle sensed the urgency that weighed on Joe's soul.

Joe waited and wondered if what Atsa sensed might actually reveal itself to Joe. He had no anxiety about being alone, nor did he have any sense of dread. Joe's great uncle sensed an unwelcome presence around the skull, but Joe didn't detect anything formidable about it. In fact, Joe perceived something quite the opposite.

Destiny.

Finding the skull had not been an accident. It was fate. This was something only meant for Joe.

The fire crackled. The fragrant steam fell into a heavier mist on Joe's sweaty skin. The outside sounds quieted. His soul lightened.

With eyes closed, Joe let his mind drift, searching and hunting for the answer. The unseen power vibrated softly through his body. The skull, whatever once occupied it, tapped into his brain neurons.

Joe's head tilted upward. A rush of vivid colors splashed through his mind. Chills covered his skin even though the lodge was nearly ninety degrees. He knew he was about to enter his vision quest. Answers would be revealed.

Still chanting, Joe's body swayed as if he danced to slow music. He allowed his soul to drift and be carried to wherever the power beckoned.

A tall man came into view in this netherworld where his soul journeyed. Blurry at first, but slowly refining, he finally made out who the person was. He was puzzled to see the man holding and admiring the alien skull with great interest. It wasn't what he expected.

Peace settled over Joe. He couldn't bury the skull. That wasn't its rightful place. The skull needed to be delivered to the man in his vision. Joe had only met this man one time before and didn't really know him, nor did he understand why the skull insisted it be given to him.

Joe had no other choice except to obey the vision. Otherwise, if his brothers were right and he was supposed to bury the skull, no vision would have come. At least not this vision.

Destiny had given Joe the skull and determined that only one other person should possess it. The reasons were not given, but the recipient was shown, and now Joe's journey was to find the man.

Dr. Helmsby.

Chapter 61

Kat nudged Lucian after the helicopter landed. His eyes opened. He rubbed them and shook his head. He turned to face her. She smiled.

"We've landed," she said.

"Damn. Already? I was sleeping pretty deeply."

"I know. You've snored for the past three hours."

Lucian wiped his chin. "And drooled, too, apparently."

Kat kissed his cheek. "At least you're not still feverish."

"That's a plus, I suppose."

Lucian stood and took his pack. He unzipped it and found his 9mm. After checking the clip, he slapped it into the gun before tucking it behind his belt. He took another gun, did the same quick inspection, and tucked it inside his boot.

Kat took her gun and placed it into her shoulder holster. Then she pulled on a thin vest jacket to conceal the weapon.

Tim Felson opened the rear side door of the helicopter. He was a large, retired Air Force pilot with silver hair. He could fly almost any plane or chopper. His hands were huge and menacing, but his warm smile reminded most people of their grandfather. He spoke softly, slowly, and with a gentleness that eased folks into conversation without the slightest intimidation. Few people ever witnessed the man angered, and those that did, never dared to arouse that side of him again.

Felson had been a close friend of Kat's father in the service and like an uncle to her whenever he visited. After her father passed away from lung cancer, Felson checked in on her from time to time. She was thankful he did, and he always insisted that if ever she needed his help, he'd be there. Like now.

"You needn't worry about a big welcome reception here," Felson said, extending his hand to Kat to help her step down.

"Why?" Kat asked.

"Damn landing strip isn't much more than a corn field."

Lucian stepped from the helicopter and looked around. Thin sheets of fog were growing thinner. He looked at Kat. "I thought we'd be able to rent a car."

Kat looked across the large fields and shook her head. "I did, too. Tim, this is it?"

"Ma'am, you both have weapons. Not much chance landing in a larger airport and getting through security without causing a big stir. Then you'd have unneeded attention."

Lucian nodded. "Agreed. Kat, call Mitch and let him know we've landed and that we're trying to get transportation to find them."

"Okay, sure."

"Come with me," Felson said to Lucian.

Lucian followed him to a small private plane near the fuel pumps. A small hanger was behind the plane and pumps. Felson walked to the door and peered through the window.

"No one's here," he said.

Lucian glanced at his watch. "It's still quite early."

"Yep. Probably trains people how to skydive or offers pilot flying lessons. Not a big operation here."

Felson turned the doorknob. It was unlocked. He entered and Lucian followed.

Inside the small hanger, Lucian noticed a motorcycle in the midst of three small airplanes. He smiled.

"I think we could use that," Lucian said.

Felson nodded. "I'll be here if the owner returns. I'll explain that we had an emergency and that we'll pay them for using it."

"Thanks."

Felson shrugged. "Don't mention it. It's not like I'd leave you here."

"I know. But we don't have time to wait for him to show."

"Could be hours or not at all, depending upon his schedule."

Lucian inspected the motorcycle, found the key still in the ignition, and then he checked the fuel level.

Felson stepped beside him. "I don't know what you and Kat are here for, and I don't want to know. All I know is that she needed a chopper ride, and I am always more than happy to oblige. But do one thing for me."

Lucian looked up at Felson. "Sure, what?"

"Keep a close eye on her."

Lucian smiled and nodded. "I always do."

"I imagine you do, but after her father passed away, I made a solemn promise to him that I'd ensure her safety. But, as you can see, I'm getting old and no possible way I could even attempt to keep up with you two."

"Say no more. I've dedicated my love and life to her. I'd died before I let anyone harm her."

A broad smile crossed Felson's face. "As would I."

"But, for what it's worth," Lucian said. "She's one tough lady. One of the best with a handgun, and she'd have never been recruited by the FBI if she wasn't capable of taking care of herself."

"Yeah, but she's like the daughter I never had. Once upon a time, I thought I might settle down and have kids, but the military kept me occupied so I never did."

"Sometimes life gets in the way."

Felson nodded and grinned. "Yep. And sometimes your country needs your expertise."

"So do friends."

Lucian pushed the motorcycle toward the hanger door. Felson opened a small set of double doors to let Lucian pass through.

Kat stood outside with the cellphone to her ear.

Lucian smiled inside and out at the determination set in her eyes while she spoke. No one looked more beautiful. For such a peaceful morning, he feared the outcomes might become bleak. Danger awaited them, and with his deteriorating health, he wondered if he could keep his promise to Felson and himself.

Although he did feel a lot better, inside his body struggled to survive. With his current physical weaknesses, he didn't want to confront whoever had attacked Mitch and murdered the others in this town. But he had to do what was necessary to right the wrongs. This might be the last time he carried out such a mission.

Chapter 62

Cassandra awoke when Mitch's cellphone buzzed. She glanced around the garage. The lantern burned where Sheba had placed it, but the morning light was shining through the cracks in the pull down garage doors.

Mitch talked on the phone. The swelling around his eye was almost gone but a dark shade of black and purple outlined it well.

At first, Cassandra thought that Sheba had abandoned them during the night. She didn't see her anywhere in the room. One car rested about four feet in the air atop an old hydraulic lift. Feet dangled off the rear of the car.

Sheba sat on the trunk of one old car and watched the doors. She had kept her word and stayed up all night keeping watch. She couldn't fault Sheba for that. Perhaps it was time Cassandra allowed her heart to trust another person.

From this angle, the young lady looked so fragile and innocent that she understood how easily Mitch had fallen for her and wanted to protect her. Cassandra found that she wanted to wrap her arms around the girl like a loving mother and let her know that everything was going to be okay.

Only things *weren't* okay. Alicia was still gone.

"Sheba?" Mitch said.

Sheba turned and smiled at him. "Yes?"

"Kat and Lucian are here," he said.

The world on Cassandra's shoulders seemed lighter. Hope was nearby.

Sheba hopped off the car. Her feet hit the concrete with a solid thud. Clouds of dust puffed around her shoes.

Mitch rose to his feet. "They have a motorcycle and want to know how to find us."

"Where are they?"

"A small landing strip in the middle of a grassy field."

Sheba thought for a minute. "They aren't too far from us if they headed west through the fields. This garage is on the first street they'll intersect once they reach the blacktop."

Mitch relayed the message. He pressed the phone to his ear for a few moments. "They're on their way."

He ended the call.

Sheba smiled. "I suppose we should get ready to leave."

Mitch nodded. "So you know where the landing strip is?"

"Yes. I run through those fields at night sometimes. Alpha has visitors land at that landing field from time to time for meetings."

"Oh?" Mitch said. "Who?"

"Other doctors and scientists."

"Why not meet at the major airports?"

"He's very discrete with his research projects."

"Why did he need you?" Cassandra asked.

"Because of what I am. In case he felt threatened, he could use me, but he has never requested me to change or attack."

Sheba led them to the front door.

Mitch looked at her. "Did you feel Alpha's presence any last night or this morning?"

"No. It'd take him a long time to find me here."

"Why?"

"A fairly large population here, so he'd have to search for hours. I think he'd get too tired to pursue for the amount of time it would take to find us."

Sheba opened the door. The brightness was minimal against the dispersing fog.

"How will we leave?" Cassandra asked. "If they have a motorcycle, there are five of us."

"We'll figure that out when they get here," Mitch replied.

"No, that's not something we need to worry about," Sheba said.

"Why not?"

"We go underground through the tunnels," Sheba said. "We can't risk Parker finding us."

Mitch sighed. "Okay. How long will it take them to arrive here from the landing field?"

"On motorcycle? At least fifteen minutes."

"Good. Then we don't have long to wait."

BROCKTON KNOCKED LIGHTLY on Kyle's bedroom door. "Are you awake?"

"Yes."

"Mind if I come in so we can talk?" Brockton asked.

"If you must," Kyle said like a spoiled teenager.

Brockton opened the door. Kyle sat at his little desk and stared at the computer screen.

"What do you want?" Kyle asked. His words came slow and stammering. "More experiments?"

Brockton smiled and shook his head. "Have I overburdened you that much?"

"Many times."

"I'm sorry that I was overzealous. I know there's so much you can do. More than what others can do."

Kyle offered a lazy shrug. "I'd rather be . . . normal."

"I only need one favor, Kyle. No more experiments."

Kyle turned and faced Brockton. "What?"

"Can you locate Dr. Helmsby? Please? Lucian's life depends on it."

Kyle nodded slowly. "I know. I've already been looking."

"Really?"

"Of course. Lucian is a good friend of mine, and look at me, I don't have too many."

"You always have me."

"I know," Kyle said, playfully rolling his eyes. "And you enjoy nagging."

Brockton chuckled.

Kyle smiled. "I talked with Morton. He doesn't know where Helmsby is, either. He will ask Daniel and get back to me."

"That's good."

"Do you think Dr. Helmsby is in danger?"

"I truly don't know. I hope not."

"I've been reaching with my mind, but I cannot sense where he is."

"Maybe Morton will know something."

"Maybe."

KAT DIALED CARPENTER'S NUMBER.

"Kat?"

"Yes."

"Is everything okay?"

"We're in Salem, Oregon."

"Why?"

She explained about the odd murders and that Mitch had been abducted by what seemed to be a woman shape-shifter.

"Keep me informed, especially if anything might be associated with Idris or TransGenCorp."

"I will," Kat said.

"And Kat?"

"Yes?"

"Did you ask if Lucian could help us with finding Matthews?"

"No. I've not had time. This came up suddenly. Since it involved Mitch, we had to come help him."

"I understand."

"Once we get things situated here, I'll mention it to Lucian."

"Okay, Kat. You say this woman's part wolf?"

"Yes."

"That's what Typhis' sons were, too."

"That's right."

"I'll catch the first flight out there."

"Why?"

"Whoever created this woman might well be the person that we're looking for. Alpha. Anyone mention that name?"

"No one yet, but we've just arrived."

"I'm heading there. Call me if his name's mentioned."

"Sure thing, Mike."

Chapter 63

Joe drove the motorcycle to the hospital where Lucas was being cared for. He hoped Lucas could give him information on how to contact Dr. Helmsby, but when he went into Lucas' room, the bed was empty. The sheets were wrinkled and the warming blanket pulled back.

A nurse stepped in behind him.

Joe turned. "Where's Lucas?"

"They moved him," she replied.

"Why?"

"He lost consciousness. I believe he slipped into a coma, and they've taken him to the ICU to monitor him."

"Will he be okay?"

"I'm not certain. Are you family?"

Joe looked at the scar on his palm. "We are brothers."

The nurse studied him carefully and slowly shook her head. "You don't resemble one another at all."

Joe shrugged. "There's always diversity within families. I got the good genes and the looks."

A warm, caring smile crossed her face. "If you'll go to the waiting room, I'll see what I can find out. Okay?"

Joe nodded. "Thanks."

WHEN THE MOTORCYCLE APPROACHED, dread and relief over-shadowed Cassandra at the same time. She wanted to believe that Mitch's friends had arrived, but at the same time, witnessing all the bizarre things over the past couple of days and weeks, she worried that perhaps someone else had intervened and arrived in their stead. Or worse, Alpha controlled them and he'd use them to kill her and Mitch. She wasn't able to be opti-mistic. She figured her dream for hope would sour into a bitter nightmare.

Mitch reluctantly stepped outside the garage door and peered around a rusted pickup truck at the fence where the motorcycle idled for several moments before the engine shut off. A grin spread across his bruised face and he waved, indicating that his friends had arrived.

Sheba hesitated to step outside and allowed Cassandra to go first. Sheba's eyes showed fear and uneasiness.

Mitch pulled open the cut section of the chain-link fence. It rattled and jangled, but Lucian and Kat squeezed though.

Kat smiled at Cassandra. Cassandra looked at Kat and marveled. Kat stood a little over five feet tall and Cassandra wondered how this small woman planned to help find Alicia. She didn't understand why Mitch had raved over his boss like he had. She had expected a much taller and more muscular woman than Kat.

Lucian gave Mitch a firm handshake and a quick bro hug. After he inspected the bruises on Mitch's face, he frowned. "Looks like you've had it a bit rough."

Mitch responded with a slight grin. "It could have been worse."

Kat came to Cassandra. "We're going to find your daughter."

Cassandra couldn't hold back tears. Kat pulled her close and hugged her.

"It's going to be okay," Kat whispered. "We do stuff like this all the time."

"You don't know what you're going up against," Cassandra said.

"We've gone against worse," Lucian said.

Sheba stepped out from the garage. "Not like this, you haven't."

Lucian placed his hand behind his back, just a few inches above his gun. He glanced at Mitch. "Who is she?"

"That's Sheba. She's going to help us."

"Isn't she the one—" Kat said.

Mitch nodded. "Yes. She did this to me."

Lucian shook his head. "You're more forgiving than I am."

Cassandra wiped tears and choked while trying not to laugh. "He has issues with infatuation."

"I like to give people the benefit of the doubt," Mitch said, looking away.

Lucian laughed. "Generally, you don't do that with your face."

Mitch changed the subject. "But what Sheba says is correct. We're going against someone who is powerfully dark."

"In what sense?" Kat asked.

"He attacked me mentally by projecting himself into my thoughts and my brain. It was the most excruciating pain I've ever experienced."

"Telepathically?" Kat asked.

"Yes. Like Kyle and I communicate. But Alpha's power is stronger. He can inflict pain and even control a person's actions."

"Really?" Lucian said.

Mitch nodded. "And he was using his power to make Sheba transform into her wolf form."

Lucian's eyes widened. He gazed at Sheba and studied her. Sheba refused to look him in the eyes.

"I thought something was different about you."

"She has good control over it," Mitch said. "But Alpha almost overpowered her and made her change."

"Alpha?" Kat asked.

Sheba nodded. "That's what he's always called himself."

"And he actually made you begin to change with his mind?" Lucian asked.

"Yes."

"Interesting," Kat said. "I've seen Kyle use mind control only once. It was a bit frightening to know someone can wield another's mind to do his or her commands."

Mitch smiled. "So Kyle can do that, too?"

"I believe he only did it because our lives were endangered. A man was going to shoot us, and somehow, Kyle made the man turn the gun back on himself. Excuse me, but I need to call Carpenter."

Lucian frowned. "Why?"

"Because he's looking for Alpha."

"He knows about him?" Lucian asked.

"He believes Idris worked with him."

Lucian nodded and looked at Cassandra. "Does Alpha have your daughter?"

Cassandra shook her head. "No."

"How are you certain?" Kat asked.

Mitch said, "When he attacked me, he insisted that he wanted to find Alicia. He doesn't have her."

"Okay," Lucian said. "What clues do you have that might help us find her?"

"You'll think I'm crazy if I tell you," Cassandra said.

Lucian smiled. "Try us."

She explained the catlike creatures and how often she had seen them before Alicia disappeared. Then she explained how the cats had saved her life in the cemetery and that they protected her and Mitch from Sheba in the tunnels.

"Then that's where we need to go first," Kat said.

"The tunnels?" Sheba asked.

"Yes."

Chapter 64

Sheba led them into the underground tunnels.

"This is amazing," Lucian said. "From the surface I'd never expect something like this under the streets."

"There is a labyrinth of tunnels under the city. A few have collapsed, and most people have lived their lives here and not known about them," Sheba said.

Lucian and Kat pulled their guns. Mitch held the flashlight.

"Take us to the last place where you saw the cats," Lucian said.

Sheba pointed. "It's about fifty feet that direction."

"And then what?" Cassandra asked. "You're not going to kill them, are you?"

Lucian shook his head. "That's not my plan. The guns are in case Alpha sends others after us. The cats, I believe, are on our side. Besides, Morton would never forgive me if I shot a cat."

Kat chuckled. "Don't even breathe that aloud around him."

"Who's Morton?" Cassandra asked.

Lucian raised his right hand and placed an index finger to his lips. "Something moved up ahead."

Mitch lowered the light but didn't turn it off. "We're definitely not alone."

"What did you see?" Kat whispered.

"Not certain. Let's hold here for a few moments to see if it approaches."

The flashlight shook in Mitch's grasp.

"There!" Lucian said, pointing. "Put the light there."

Bright green eyes glowed when the flashlight beam struck them. Three large black cats stood and showed their sharp teeth. Low growls rumbled in their throats.

"Damn," Lucian whispered. "They're the size of cougars."

"But they're not the only ones here," Mitch said.

"How do you know?"

"I sense others."

Lucian frowned. "Humans?"

"Perhaps. Or something more paranormal. Troubled spirits."

One cat uttered a low guttural growl.

Sheba took a couple of quick steps backwards. "I told you."

"No," Lucian said. "Don't back away. Any sign of fear and they might rush us."

Sheba stood still and closed her eyes.

"Cassandra," Lucian said.

"Yes?"

"I want you to step ahead of us."

"What?"

"Trust me. I don't believe they want to hurt us, and especially not you."

Timidly, Cassandra stepped between Lucian and Kat. A few seconds later she braved a few steps forward.

The cats watched her approach. The center one showed teeth for a second and promptly sat down. The other two lay down on the damp earth floor and exposed their bellies while playfully rolling on their sides and batting at one another.

"What are they doing?" Cassandra asked.

"Showing submission. Or they're young cubs."

Cassandra glanced at Kat and Lucian. "What now?"

"Talk to them. Ask where your daughter is. Just don't be afraid. They aren't agitated and aren't threatening us."

Cassandra took another step closer. The sitting cat stared solemnly, unmoving.

"Easy," she said, taking another step. She reached her hand out ahead of her. "Easy. Do you know where Alicia is?"

The large cat gave a partial roar and licked its lips.

"Can you take me to Alicia?" Cassandra asked.

The cat stood to all fours, forcing Cassandra to stop moving. She swallowed hard. The cat stepped toward her. She took a deep breath.

"Don't run," Lucian said. "Stand your ground."

The cat walked to her and placed its large head beneath her extended hand and nuzzled it.

"See?"

Cassandra exhaled a sigh of great relief. She knelt in front of the cat and placed both hands on its head, rubbing and petting its ears. The other two cats, apparently jealous, came to her as well.

"Where's Alicia?" Cassandra asked.

The leader of the three turned and darted into the shadows. The other two cats followed a bit slower.

"Let's go," Lucian said.

"Even me?" Sheba asked.

"Especially you."

Chapter 65

They followed the large cats through the main tunnel for about a quarter mile before entering a small, barely visible, side passageway. This tunnel was narrow with much cooler pungent air and ascended a fairly steep slope.

Lucian walked close behind Cassandra. Both he and Kat had holstered their weapons. He shone the light ahead of them.

"These tunnels are all over the city?" Lucian asked, looking back.

Sheba nodded.

"Where does this one lead?"

"I'm not certain. I've not been in this one, but it seems like it's heading toward the center of the city."

Noise rumbled overhead. The sides of the tunnel vibrated.

"A car or truck?" Kat asked, looking at the ceiling.

"There's probably a street above us," Lucian said.

"At least there aren't any rats down here," Cassandra said, following the steep narrowing path.

"Not with cats for guides," Lucian said.

The steep tunnel leveled. The lead cat slinked through a small hulled out opening in a brick wall. The other cats entered as well.

Cassandra stared at Lucian. Her eyes widened with doubt and apprehension.

"I think we're here," he said.

She put her head through the opening and squeezed her body through the narrow crevice.

Lucian hurried after her. He didn't want to leave her unprotected, but he believed the cats meant them no harm. He didn't fear them, but he did worry about what else they might encounter on the other side of the wall.

The cats sat and waited for all of the humans to get into the small room. Their tails swished back and forth.

They stood inside an old abandoned building. Most of the windows were covered with boards or painted over. The green painted walls were peeling. Ceiling tiles sagged.

"Where are we?" Lucian asked.

"An old business office, I think," Sheba said.

Cassandra shook her head. "Why would they have my daughter here?"

"I guess we'll find out soon," Kat said.

The large cat scampered down the hallway and rounded the next corner. When they caught up with the feline, they saw a fourth cat standing outside a room. Its ears backed upon noticing them and it hissed. The lead cat growled at the guard and placed its paw upon its nose. The guard cat lowered its head in submission before turning and entering the room. The other three cats followed.

Lucian took Cassandra's hand. "Come on."

Cassandra peered into the room. Seated on the old couch were Seth and Alicia. They were playing checkers.

"Alicia?" Cassandra said softly.

Alicia's eyes widened. "Momma?"

She smiled broadly and leapt up off the couch and ran to her mother. They hugged one another tightly. Cassandra kept whispering over and over how much she loved Alicia.

Through her teary eyes, Cassandra noticed the man standing in the room.

"Why do you have my daughter?" she asked, releasing Alicia and pulling her around behind her.

"Hey, I'm on your side. I only took her to protect her."

"If that is true," Lucian said, "why didn't you tell Cassandra what was happening."

"I couldn't."

Kat studied the man with narrowed eyes. "Why not?"

"Because everyone in the city believes I'm dead."

"Dead?" Lucian asked.

"Yes. That's why I sent the cats to help Alicia and Seth escape. I was going to send them for Cassandra and Deidre, too. If anyone discovered I was alive, I'd never get close enough to stop Alpha."

Sheba stared at him while he spoke. In an instant she smiled with curiosity. "Tom?"

"Sheba!" Tom grinned and hurried to her.

She wrapped her arms around him and squeezed. "I thought you were dead."

"That's what they led everyone to believe."

Lucian looked at Kat. "I'm confused."

She nodded.

Sheba told them a condensed version about Gloria and the cemetery prank.

She glanced at Tom. "Alpha has Gloria."

"So she's still alive?"

"Yes."

"But Jill is dead," Sheba said.

Sadness hollowed Tom's eyes. "Dead?"

"She killed herself."

"Damn. What about Beverly?"

Sheba sighed. "Alpha has her locked in the asylum. She's drugged most of the time so she never speaks or even acknowledges me when I visit."

"He lets you see her?"

"He doesn't know that I do. I use these tunnels and sneak in sometimes to see her."

"But Gloria is still alive," Tom said. "Do you know where he keeps her?"

"No. I've only seen her once. Alpha uses Gloria to blackmail me."

Tom shook his head. "We tried to get Gloria before we escaped, but a couple of guards had moved her to an isolation cell. We should have rushed them, but they had guns. I couldn't risk any of us dying."

"So the others are alive, too?"

Tom nodded.

"Where are they?"

"I'm not certain. They went their own direction."

Sheba frowned. "Why?"

"I don't fit in with them. They are like you," Tom said.

"Part wolf?"

"Yes."

"How?" Sheba asked.

"Alpha did weird experiments on them. Injections and surgeries. None of the stuff worked on me. After we escaped, they resented me because I wasn't like them, and they left me behind."

"How did you know about me being part wolf?" Sheba asked.

"The night of the prank. We watched you enter the manor with Gloria and the others, but something bad happened. There were a lot of screams. The next thing I knew Jill and Beverly ran out of the manor cellar. You chased after them. You had changed into whatever it is you are. They ran fast to get away from you, and then you reverted into a young woman. Seeing that scared the hell out of us, so we headed out another direction. Some men stopped us and forced us into their van at gunpoint. That night was the first time I knew anything about Alpha. He took us to the asylum and locked us up. He showed us newspapers where the police reports showed us dead. Experiments started happening not too long after that."

Sheba said, "I never knew you were there."

"Almost three years."

Lucian cleared his throat. "How long ago did you escape Alpha?"

Tom shrugged. "About five years ago."

"And you never went to the authorities?"

"No."

"Why not?" Kat asked.

"Alpha would kill them," Sheba said.

"That and he controls some of the policemen," Tom said.

Cassandra nodded. "That's true."

Kat turned and faced her. "How'd you know that?"

Cassandra kept one arm around Alicia's shoulder and looked at Kat. "After I reported Alicia missing, Officer Parker came to my house, questioned me, and hardly fifteen minutes after he left, two men showed up with guns and tried to kill me. Later, Parker killed his partner and told the news reporters that I had shot and killed him."

"So we can't go to the police," Mitch said. "They weren't too happy about my poking around here either."

"I believe they were responsible for Deidre's death, too," Cassandra said.

Tom nodded. "They're directly responsible."

"Why didn't you do something to save her?" Cassandra asked. "It seems as if you knew."

"I tried, but from my understanding, they weren't supposed to make their move that night." Tom said. "For some odd reason, someone had read my thoughts and moved in earlier than I expected."

"Alpha probably did," Sheba said.

Tom shrugged. "I don't think he did. I never felt his approach. Not even a subtle touch. That's why I don't understand it. My guess is that he doesn't know I'm here."

"Why did the cats take Alicia without taking me?" Cassandra asked.

"The cats knew you feared them. They didn't have any time to waste trying to earn your trust. They had to move fast and that's what they did."

"And had I died?" Cassandra asked. "What then? Seth is without his mother, and Alicia almost lost me. Did you plan to take care of them until they were old enough to be on their own?"

"If it became necessary, yes."

Cassandra frowned. Her lips narrowed as she spoke, trying to rein in her anger. "Your cats killed the two men that were trying to kill me. Why didn't they kill Parker?"

"We still needed Parker alive," Tom replied.

"Alive?" Cassandra said. "Why?"

"Because he was the only one I know who could lead us to Alpha."

"Parker is dangerous."

"After I beat the shit out of Parker last night," Sheba said, "he'll try to kill me on sight should we run into him."

Tom shrugged. "Now that we have you, Sheba, Parker is expendable because you know where Alpha is. If we cross paths with Parker, we take him out."

Sheba smiled. "With pleasure."

"These cats," Lucian said, looking at Tom. "Where'd you get them?"

"They were a new project Alpha started when we had escaped. He only had two. They were cubs, so I grabbed them and tucked them into a bag and carried them with us. These younger ones are their offspring."

Sheba frowned. "I've never seen Alpha experiment with any feline projects."

"Nope," Tom said. "And you probably won't. These are another reason Zack and the others abandoned me."

"Why?" Kat asked.

"The same reason Sheba feels apprehensive around them. She has canine genes and the cats sense it. They are in direct opposition to one another. Enemies in the wild."

Kat stepped closer to one of the younger cats and rubbed between its ears. "But they seem more perceptive than most animals."

"They are." Tom nodded. "I won't say that I can read their minds or they, mine, but we do have a mental sense of communication. I guess that sounds odd. Perhaps a little crazy."

"No," Cassandra said. "Alicia has that connection with them, too."

Tom glanced at Alicia. She nodded and smiled. "I knew about them for several months."

"Perhaps that's why they were determined to rescue you so eagerly. They really like you."

Alicia grinned. "I love them."

One of the cubs moved beside her and nuzzled her hand.

Cassandra smiled. "They're the first animals she's been able to pet."

"She's gifted," Tom said.

"I know," Cassandra replied. "Why do you have her and Seth hidden in this abandoned building?"

Tom pointed at the walls and ceiling. "This is an old steel vault. The building might have been a bank long ago, but the reinforced steel walls and ceiling are thick enough to keep Alpha from seeking these children with his mind power. This is the safest place I could think to keep them."

Lucian said, "Then Cassandra you need to stay here with Alicia and Seth while the rest of us go after Alpha."

"No argument here," she said.

"I'll have two of the cats stay here," Tom said. "The rest will help us through the tunnels. They can detect Parker or any others that Alpha might send after us."

"Are you sure we'll be safe here?" Cassandra asked.

Kat nodded. "You're a lot safer here than out in the tunnels or the streets. Excuse me, but I need to call Carpenter. I never got the chance earlier."

"Why call Carpenter? We can handle this situation ourselves," Lucian said.

"He's already on his way here. I promised him if I heard anything about Alpha I'd call."

Lucian frowned. "Why would he come for this?"

Kat nodded toward Sheba. "Because of her and if we stop Alpha, he wants him taken into custody."

Lucian shrugged. "He may arrive too late."

"I know, but I told him that I'd call."

Chapter 66

"Kat?" Carpenter said. "I'm aboard a Learjet. Should be there in an hour."

"An hour?"

"Yes. Testing out our newest sonic jet."

"I wanted to inform you that Alpha's here," she said.

"Good. On my way. I called the local police in Salem and informed them of the situation and that I'm in transit now."

"You did what?"

"The local authorities there have been contacted and will help."

"Damn."

"What's wrong, Kat?"

"Some of these officers are working for Alpha."

"Shit, sorry, Kat. Never considered anything like that."

"Neither did we," she replied. "The shifter woman's at odds with the police and Alpha. I believe they'll shoot any of us on sight."

"Keep low until I get there. I'll contact more authorities outside of Salem to help."

"Thanks." She disconnected the call and sighed. "I guess."

KAT WALKED to where Tom and Sheba stood with Lucian and shook her head.

"What's wrong?" Lucian asked.

"Carpenter's on his way, but we have a problem."

"What?"

"Seems he contacted local police and informed them that he was coming here."

"Damn," Lucian whispered. "That means Alpha will be ready for us when we move."

"In a way that might be beneficial," Sheba said.

"How?" Kat asked.

"Alpha will post more security around himself, which means that we could get Beverly out of the mental hospital without ever being noticed."

Tom nodded. "That'd be the best way to get her."

Lucian shook his head. "We can always extract her after we get Alpha."

"I know, but the longer Alpha's security waits for us to attack, the more impatient they'll become. They are more likely to make mistakes once their anxiety rises."

"You have a point there," Lucian said. He looked at Kat. "What do you think?"

"We rescue Beverly and evaluate what we do after that."

Sheba smiled. "Follow me. I know which tunnels will get us there the fastest."

Chapter 67

Louisville, Kentucky
Center for Infectious Diseases

DR. HELMSBY PLACED the petri dish into the storage rack, removed his rubber gloves, and straightened his glasses. He jotted some notes into his journal.

He was happy to offer his genetics knowledge and research to the CID in their current attempt to find a new drug to combat the ever-evolving strains of influenza. But that wasn't the only reason he had accepted the job.

The high security clearance allowed him to feel a bit safer from Grayson's reach. Although Grayson had never directly threatened him, Helmsby believed Grayson was one to retaliate. Resigning from the lucrative offer Grayson had given was probably considered a snub, or at least, that's what Helmsby believed.

In normal circumstances Helmsby would have done extensive research on the alien DNA gratis. Such an opportunity yielded a wealth of scientific discovery that, even now, he regretted leaving. But situations with Grayson weren't normal. They were strained by intimidation and Grayson's power and wealth. Helmsby never felt comfortable around the tycoon. Grayson was as dangerous—if not more—than Idris had been. Helmsby couldn't look at Grayson without being reminded of Idris and those memories shook him to the core.

The more reports Helmsby read on Grayson's work projects, the better he understood how few people liked Grayson's ethics when it came to establishing his place in the scientific world. He was a volatile conceited man who wished to have the world view him as a celebrity, even though he was a proficient scientist and entrepreneur. Regardless of how he tried to convey himself, Grayson never got the public to meet him eye-to-eye.

Fewer people liked Grayson because his greed superseded his passion. Some hated him because of his ever-growing name and media exposure. Establishing human colonization projects on Mars should have brought raves from the majority of people on Earth, but with Grayson's name tied to the projects most viewed them tarnished since the public was soured to hear anything associated with Grayson Enterprises.

Helmsby closed the journal and almost jumped when he turned to find Yvonne standing behind him. She wore her security guard uniform and smiled. He marveled at how she moved stealthily and closed in behind him without making a sound.

"Sorry," she said. "I didn't mean to sneak up on you."

"Oh, it's okay." Helmsby shook his head and chuckled. "My mind was somewhere else. I didn't even hear you come in. Making your rounds?"

Yvonne nodded. "Actually, I was sent to discuss something with you."

"What?"

"The security chief received a phone call earlier from a Bennie Dunlap with the FBI."

"The FBI?" Helmsby said, loosening his shirt collar.

"Yes. Seems they're trying to find you. He wanted to know if you'd call him back. He didn't tell him that you're working since you are under the radar here."

Helmsby removed his glasses and rubbed his eyes. "What do you think I should do?"

"You should probably call him back. It's highly unlikely Grayson would have spies within the FBI. Too many of them despise him."

"I know," Helmsby said. "But Idris had people in high places, too."

"True, but Grayson isn't Idris. He's more interested in money than revenge."

"I don't know. He was ready to kill Steven Matthews. I imagine he could have done it with his bare hands."

Yvonne smiled. "But Matthews double-crossed him. You didn't. You changed your mind. Everyone's entitled to do that, regardless of the situation."

"I *feel* like I may have double-crossed him, too. That contract was very binding. I'm surprised that he let me walk away."

"Bob, let go of your paranoia. You're only working on an unnecessary stomach ulcer. Grayson admires you a great deal. He was straightforward about that. You want to know why I believe he will never harm you?"

Helmsby frowned. "Why?"

"Because deep inside he hopes you'll reconsider and come back to Grayson Enterprises to work for him." She placed her hand over his heart. "And I'll bet deep in here, you really would like to go back to research the alien DNA. Am I right?"

Helmsby looked away, but he couldn't stop the smile spreading across his face. "You're right. I'd leap at the chance to analyze that DNA, but knowing what all Grayson does and what he stands for, I cannot sacrifice my morals."

"Good. You're every bit the man I believed you to be when we married." She handed him a small slip of paper. "Here's Bennie's phone number. Think it over, and if it feels right, call him. Now, if you'll excuse me, I must get to my rounds."

Yvonne gently kissed him on the lips and headed out the door. Helmsby stared at the number and his brow furrowed with worry. Regardless of what Yvonne believed, he didn't know if she was right or not. What if Grayson wanted him dead?

DANIEL SAT AT HIS DESK. His cellphone ringtone played. He looked at the number, didn't recognize it, but his curiosity convinced him to answer.

"Dan?"

"Helmsby?" Daniel asked. "Did you come out of hiding?"

"Not yet," Helmsby replied with a chuckle.

"Where are you?"

"Ah, Dan, I'd rather not say right now."

"Why not? Is there a problem?"

"I'm not certain."

Daniel shook his head. "Seems a lot of people are trying to find you."

"Really?" Helmsby asked in a near whisper. "Who?"

"Kyle relayed a message to Morton about Lucian dying."

"Dying? So his body is shutting down?"

"I think that's probably it."

"Why would he want my help?"

Daniel replied, "They hope you can reverse his condition."

"Sadly, Dan, there's nothing I could do to help him. The enhancers *are* his only life source. Once his body rejects those or they fail to work, I'm afraid there's nothing more we can do."

"That's sad to hear," Daniel said.

"Who else has called for me?" Helmsby asked.

"A man with the FBI named Bennie Dunlap."

"He called here a little while ago. Do you have any idea what he wants?"

"You haven't talked to him?" Daniel asked.

"Not yet. I didn't know if he's legit or not. What did you think about him when you talked to him?"

"He seems like a decent person."

"What did he want?"

"He wants to talk to you about what research Grayson had you doing."

"Why?" Helmsby asked.

"He didn't elaborate anything more than that. Why don't you talk to him and find out."

"Are you certain he's actually with the FBI?" Helmsby asked.

"I believe so. He mentioned Carpenter."

"I don't know that I should call him."

"Why not?"

"Because what I worked on for Grayson was top secret. Grayson forbade me from telling anyone. I signed a contract agreeing to uphold the confidentiality. And if I tell anyone, especially someone within the FBI and Grayson finds out, my life will definitely be in danger. Yours, too."

"Mr. Dunlap sounded like a quite harmless, elderly gentleman," Daniel said.

"Sounded and *being* are two different things, Dan. Don't forget how we were deceived at my research center by two imposter clones."

"I know. I understand your paranoia."

"It's *not* paranoia."

Daniel shook his head, trying to remain patient. "Look, he's already called where you work, right?"

"Yes."

"Then he knows where you are, so I would go ahead and call him if I were you. Otherwise, he'll probably show up where you work."

"I suppose you're right."

"Good to hear from you, Helmsby. I'll relay the message to Morton that there's nothing you know that will improve Lucian's condition should Kyle contact him again."

"Okay. Thanks, Dan."

"But do us all a favor."

"What's that?"

"Brainstorm for awhile and see if you can think of something. I know you love exploring genetics possibilities."

"I'll give it some thought after I call Mr. Dunlap. Should I discover anything that might add longevity to Lucian's life, I'll call you back."

"Thanks," Daniel said, ending the call.

Morton sat on the desk, staring at Daniel. "Well?"

Daniel shook his head. "Sorry, but he doesn't think there's anything that can be done."

Morton released a small sigh. "I'll tell Kyle."

"Sorry," Daniel said.

"Death comes for us all. Some sooner than others."

Morton hopped off the desk and strolled out of the office.

Chapter 68

Davis parked the white van in the rear parking lot of the apartment building. Lydia slid open the side door and climbed out. She tucked her 9mm behind her back and crossed the parking lot, heading for the rear lobby door.

Davis opened the left rear door of the van. Two men hurried out and followed him down the side of the building to a lowered fire escape ladder. They climbed to the second floor.

Lydia gave a solemn stare at the woman behind the desk before she headed through the stairwell door. She took the steps and pulled her gun. At the second floor door, she eased it open and peered into the hallway. Approaching from the other end of the hall was Davis and his men.

She moved down the hall where they had stopped.

Room 212.

"In there?" she whispered.

"Yes."

Lydia clicked off the safety. Taking a step back from the door, she kicked right beneath the doorknob. The wood split and the door caved inward. She rushed through the door with her gun raised.

Matthews turned in surprise, reached for his gun on the desk, but before he got it, she fired. The bullet struck his gun and spiraled it off the edge of the desk. She was across the room in seconds and pressed her gun to his neck, backing him to the wall.

Beth screamed and ran for the hallway. Davis grabbed her arm and twisted, dragging her down to the floor.

"You son of a bitch! Let her go!" Eric yelled, rushing from the bathroom and heading for Davis with his fists raised.

One of the men behind Davis fired and struck Eric in the chest with several rounds. Eric's eyes widened. He clutched his chest and looked at the blood leaking through his fingers. He sank to his knees and fell forward.

Dead.

Beth sobbed, watching his body grow still.

"We've not done anything wrong," Beth said. "You didn't have to kill him. They offered us money if we allowed them to do drug experiments on us."

"You should be more careful whom you take money from," he said, pressing his knee into her back.

Davis took handcuffs from his back pocket and cuffed her hands behind her back. Tears flowed down her face into the thick carpet. He motioned his two gunmen to seat her against the wall.

In the other room, Lydia stared into Matthews' eyes and pressed the gun harder to his neck.

His jaw tightened.

"Do it," Matthews whispered. "Pull the trigger. Kill me."

Lydia smiled. "You don't get off that easy."

His eyes widened when he met her harsh gaze.

Lydia lowered the gun and backhanded him in the face with the butt of the weapon. He cried out and fell to the floor, holding his face.

"Dammit, Lydia! Do you realize how much plastic surgery costs? Hmm? Perhaps you and I can come to some sort of financial agreement?"

Lydia ignored his offer. She swung a hard kick into his gut that lifted him off the floor and flipped him over onto his back.

Panting and wincing in pain, he stared up at her. A large red mark spread across his cheek where she had struck him. Blood leaked from one tear where one of the surgery incisions had almost healed. "I get that you're angry. You hate me. What I did was unethical. I realize that now.

But, I was foolish in what I attempted, but let's let bygones be bygones, huh? No one needs to die."

"Oh, you're going to die," she said, looking down at him. "But it'll be very slowly."

Matthews shook his head and laughed. "A woman clone scorned."

Lydia gritted her teeth and kicked his ribs hard. His ribs snapped with an unpleasant sound.

He cried in pain, rolled over to his stomach, and tightened his arms to his sides to protect his midsection. He coughed and blood trickled from the side of his mouth.

Matthews wheezed to breathe. "How'd you find me?"

"Grayson."

"That arrogant bastard sent you? Typical that he always makes others do his dirty work for him. How much is he paying you? I'll double it."

Lydia shook her head. "No, I was coming for you anyway. I would've found you. He just made my search shorter by pinpointing your location."

She placed her gun on the desk, grabbed Matthew's shirt collar, and yanked him to his feet. Placing her right hand around his throat, she pressed him to the wall and lifted him about a foot off the floor. Her eyes narrowed and her fingers squeezed tighter.

"Today, you die," she whispered.

Matthews' face reddened. His eyes bulged. Choking gasps struggled to get past her tightening grip.

She squeezed even tighter from all the anger growing inside her. Veins swelled on Matthews' forehead and neck. He tried in vain to pry her fingers loose with both hands, but he couldn't wrest free.

"What the hell?" Davis yelled from the hallway. "He should be dead."

Lydia glanced over her shoulder and saw Davis and the two gunmen scramble backwards out into the hall. Davis pulled his gun and fired several rounds into Eric as he stepped past Beth. Each shot jolted Eric for a moment, but he kept moving forward.

Two gunshots echoed from the other side of the room.

Lydia turned and saw Mordia shoot the two guards behind Davis. The two gunmen took headshots and dropped to the floor, dead.

Lydia lowered Matthews. He collapsed on the floor. Lydia sprinted toward Mordia.

Mordia swung around to shoot Lydia, but Lydia moved faster than

Mordia expected. Lydia lunged low, catching Mordia around the waist and picked her up. She flung Mordia over the couch.

Mordia landed on the glass-top coffee table. Glass exploded into tiny shards and rained down on the carpet and couch.

Mordia grunted when her back struck the bottom of the table. She rolled to her side and didn't move.

Eric continued walking toward Davis. Davis stopped shooting because the bullets had no effect.

Davis turned and stepped over the dead gunmen. He hurried for the outside hallway while Lydia turned her attention from Mordia to Matthews.

Matthews scooted backwards across the floor. His face was crimson. Blood streamed from the gaping face wound. Gasping for air, he took deep breaths and was trying to put some distance between himself and Lydia. He tried to speak but only a hoarse sound came from his mouth.

Lydia grinned a sadistic smile. She took slow steps towards Matthews, enjoying the look of terror in his eyes.

Matthews put his hands out before him in surrender.

"Pleading for mercy?"

He offered a weak shrug.

"Not today." She stood over him.

Lydia grabbed her gun off the desk, loaded a round into the chamber, and aimed at Matthews' forehead. He closed his eyes tightly, still holding his hands up in surrender.

In her rage, she was ready to pull the trigger, but the whispering in her ears stopped her.

Lucas?

"Don't, Lydia. Don't become what he is."

Her finger loosened on the trigger.

"How?" she whispered.

"I've been searching for you," Lucas replied.

Lydia shook her head, trying to sort through this strange hallucination, but she remembered when she was unconscious that Lucas had found her before. Joe had told her how to whisper into the wind, but this didn't seem the same. Lucas sounded weak, hurt.

"Where are you?" she said quietly.

"Hospital. Coma."

The words shot through her. Remorse for not going with him to help Joe weighed upon her.

For a few moments, Lydia forgot where she was. The sound of crunching glass should have alerted her, but she didn't hear it. Matthews moved, and she looked down at him. She drove the sound of Lucas' voice from her mind, allowing her anger and rage to quash her remorse. She held the gun with both hands and aimed at Matthews again.

Before she pulled the trigger, she glimpsed movement from the corner of her eye. She turned. Mordia stabbed Lydia in the back with a needle and pushed the stopper.

"You damn bitch!" Lydia seethed.

Lydia slapped Mordia across the face with the gun. Her neck twisted with a sharp crack and the impact slung Mordia around. Her limp body dropped to the floor.

Lydia faced Matthews again. Her vision blurred. The room spun. She gripped the edge of the desk.

Matthews backed into the corner and using the wall for support, he forced himself to his feet.

Lydia staggered. Her knees buckled. Instead of allowing herself to drop to the floor, she fell forward onto the desk. She held the gun, tried to aim it, but her fingers numbed. Even with all her focus on trying to make her fingers tighten, squeezing the trigger was impossible. The gun loosened in her grip and slid onto the desk. Her eyes closed.

Chapter 69

Matthews took a couple of steps toward the desk. He placed his hand on Lydia's gun and picked it up. He took two deep breaths and exhaled through his mouth. After wiping his face with a handkerchief, he pulled away the white cloth and noticed a thick crimson line of blood. He was bleeding badly.

He walked over to Mordia and knelt beside her. Checking for a pulse, he found none.

"Dammit," he whispered.

Matthews staggered to a large mirror on the wall and looked at his face. A long flap of skin along his cheek resembled flesh of a fileted fish. Detached, it hung loose. Blood oozed.

With Mordia dead, he wondered how he'd get his face repaired.

Anger washed through him. He gritted his teeth and stared at Lydia. He marched to her unconscious form. He wanted to shoot her, to kill her, but she deserved a worse punishment than death. He almost smiled, but the pain stopped him. He could use Lydia for his original plan to make clones from her and use them for assassins. She'd be trapped forever. Not dead, but she'd never be a threat to him again.

With the barrel of her handgun, he flipped her blonde hair from the side of her face and smiled. When her face wasn't controlled by anger, she was very attractive. He leaned down to whisper his triumph in her ear.

An instant later, he was struck from behind. Pain reeled through his head. He dropped the gun and turned to see Jimmy holding a tall brass lamp stand. He swung again.

Matthews dropped to the floor, writhing in pain, holding his face with both hands.

Matthews was losing consciousness.

Jimmy stared down at him with a broad smile. "You damn asshole. How'd you like that?"

IN THE OUTER hallway Davis emptied his clip into Eric, but the man continued to pursue. The bullet wounds didn't bleed. The man didn't seem to have any blood and was somehow still alive. The woman he had handcuffed mentioned drug experimentation, but surely, this wasn't what Matthews had done. Then again, perhaps it was.

Thinking back, he remembered Matthews' attempt to overtake Grayson Enterprises with his undead corpses, but why would he use the same serum on living humans? What was he attempting to achieve? Grayson needed to know.

The gunshots only angered Eric. His eyes were strangely alert but held a strange red around the pupils. Apparently Eric's drive came from a vindictive need to get even for Davis' attacks.

Davis holstered his gun. He decided the best thing he could do was fight the man since Eric didn't possess a weapon.

Davis swung a hard right into Eric's jaw, knocking Eric back a couple of steps but it didn't deter him. At first glance, Davis assumed Eric's frail-looking body and stature would make this a quick, easy match to win. He found out differently.

Eric came at Davis. Davis punched him over and over. The man didn't stop coming. He expressed no pain. The blows went unnoticed.

Davis swung again. Eric caught his fist with one hand and then grabbed Davis' shirt with the other. He hoisted Davis into the air and threw him toward the open apartment door. Davis rolled when he landed and rushed into the apartment.

He grabbed a gun from one of the dead gunmen, crouched low, and waited.

Eric stepped around the doorway. His eyes searched for Davis.

Davis fired two rounds through Eric's right knee, which severed his leg in half. Eric tumbled forward and immediately pulled himself across the floor, still determined to reach Davis.

Davis took both sets of handcuffs from his dead partners and dove on Eric's back. He yanked back Eric's arms and cuffed his wrists together. Although the arms were secure, he wasn't certain being restrained would hold him down long. Eric continued rolling side-to-side, trying to find a way to right himself.

Davis got up and headed to the desk. Jimmy stood over Matthews' body and slowly set the lamp on the floor when he noticed Davis.

"He's out cold," Jimmy said.

"What happened to Lydia?" Davis asked.

"Mordia sedated her."

Davis shook his head. He took Zip-tie handcuffs and restrained Matthews' wrists.

"Check on Mordia," Davis said.

"She's dead."

"One less problem for us then."

Jimmy shook Lydia, trying to wake her. Her body was limp, lifeless. "She'll be out for a while."

"Get her on the couch."

"You're leaving her?"

Davis shrugged. "No, but with all the gunfire, the police will be here soon. Matthews is the one we wanted. Lydia beat his ass pretty badly. Not sure how we can get them out of here unnoticed."

"I can carry her over my shoulder," Jimmy said.

Davis looked at Matthews.

"I don't know if I could carry him all the way back to the van."

"We could use the elevator."

"Still have to get them through the lobby. Two unconscious people will arouse immediate attention."

Jimmy bent over Lydia, wrapped his arms around her thighs, and propped her over his shoulder. After a few moments of adjusting her weight, he stepped cautiously to the desk and grabbed his laptop briefcase.

Davis gave Jimmy an odd stare.

"I'll take her as far as I can. Perhaps we go through the first floor hallway to avoid the police when they arrive."

Sirens wailed outside the building.

Davis shrugged. "Sounds like we have nothing else we can do."

Chapter 70

Although Lucian was covered in sweat, the dark tunnels grew colder the closer to the asylum they came. His head throbbed with constant pain. He was thankful the darkness prevented Kat from seeing how much he was suffering. He held the flashlight low, so the light didn't reflect his facial expressions while he lit the path ahead of Sheba.

His energy was escaping him. Breathing became more difficult. The temporary strength serum Brockton had injected faded much faster than he or Brockton had anticipated. For whatever reason, his body refused to fight to survive and disregarded outside medicines or remedies. His DNA was unraveling at a rapid pace. Most certainly, Time's hands on Lucian's life clock were coming to a halt.

"Are we getting closer?" Lucian asked.

"Not much further," Sheba replied. "After we cross beneath two more streets, we should be there."

They trudged forward with water splashing beneath their feet. Lucian fought to stay behind Sheba so Kat wouldn't suspect his health was degenerating, but his leg muscles grew tighter, making him almost limp to keep going.

They passed beneath the second street. Their path was as wide as a two-way street but nearly inaccessible from a cave in.

"Be careful through here," Sheba said. "Part of the tunnels collapsed a long time ago. The place where they keep Beverly is an area actually closed off from the rest of the hospital."

"Why?" Kat asked.

"Possibly so he can do his experiments without being interrupted or discovered," Sheba replied.

"Damn," Mitch said. "Did you feel that?"

They stopped walking and Lucian aimed the flashlight back in Mitch's direction.

"What was it?" Lucian asked.

"Cold spot."

"The whole place seems cold to me," Lucian said.

"No, this is different. It is intensely cold. Something paranormal."

"Like a ghost?" Kat asked.

"Or a spirit," Mitch said.

Sheba said, "I told you this area is like that. A lot of haunted grounds in Salem. No one has proven otherwise. Part of the hospital is known to house ghosts."

Tom shone his flashlight across the tunnel. "Sheba's right. I've noticed a lot of unusual things while crossing through these tunnels. I've not seen anything but I definitely don't feel *alone*."

Lucian sighed. "Let's stick to rescuing Beverly."

"Not a believer?" Mitch asked.

"Don't plan to convert any time soon," Lucian replied.

One of the large black cats stopped beside Lucian and rubbed its head against his leg. He scratched between its ears. It made a deep purring sound before heading through the rubble where Sheba stood. Turning the light onto the large blocks and broken bricks, Lucian shook his head. The short distance was filled with enough obstacles to drastically slow down their pace.

"How do you expect us to bring Beverly through this?" Lucian asked.

"We won't," Sheba said. "She'll need a wheelchair to get around if she's still drugged. She always looks like she's in a trance."

Lucian climbed slowly over and around the rubble. Each step forward seemed more difficult than the previous one.

After a half hour of getting through the pile of cluttered stone, they reached a narrow side tunnel.

"We're here," Sheba said, heading through the tiny opening.

Lucian followed, along with the others in single file. The wet walls glistened in the glow of the flashlights. The old steps were smooth stones set in place well over a hundred years before.

"A lot of intricate hidden tunnels," Lucian said.

Sheba nodded. "Yes. If you don't know your way around, you can get lost."

The stairwell spiraled upward and light filtered in after the second turn in the steps. They were above ground. The air no longer smelled musty but held the scent of disinfectant and bleach.

Lucian leaned against the left wall of the stairwell for support with each laboring step. Kat placed her hand on his back.

"Are you okay?" she asked.

"I'm fine."

Kat frowned. "You look as bad as the other night."

"I'm okay, Kat. Really."

Sheba motioned for them to be quiet. She stood at a rusty door. Green flakes of paint piled at its base. Sliding her hand into her pocket, she removed a key, placed it in the lock, and twisted. She placed her hand on a door handle of a rusty metal door, turned, and pulled. More paint chips fell to the floor like green snowflakes when the door opened.

The smell of bleach and disinfectant grew even stronger.

An old janitor closet.

A nasty mop and bucket set near an old floor drain. Bottles of various cleaners set on rusted dissolving shelves that might crumble at any time. Brooms, trash bags, and dustpans littered the floor near the large sink.

Sheba stepped past the janitor tools that time had forgotten and opened the other door. She peered out and pressed the door closed again.

"Guard," she whispered.

"Making rounds or stationary?" Lucian asked.

"Headed this way."

Lucian eased past her and placed his hand on the doorknob. The guard's hard sole shoes clacked on the tiles. He was coming closer. Since this hospital wing was closed off and seldom used, Lucian hoped the element of surprise was in his favor.

When the guard stepped beside the janitor closet door, Lucian yanked open the door and grabbed the man from behind.

He wrapped his arm around the man's neck in a tight chokehold.

"Easy, just relax," Lucian whispered. "Don't fight it."

He held tightly until the man grew limp in his arms. Gently, Lucian lowered him to the floor.

Lucian leaned against the wall and took several deep breaths.

Kat stepped beside Lucian. Her brow creased from her concern. "Are you sure you're okay?"

He returned a serious stare but said nothing.

"Okay," Kat said. "You have me worried."

Sheba grabbed the man's keys and his security keycard. Tom grabbed the man by the feet, slid him out of the hallway, and into the closet. Then he pushed him through the other door and locked it.

"We don't need to worry about him coming after us when he awakens," Tom said, dusting his hands off on his pants.

Kat glanced at Sheba. "Any idea how many guards are along the hallway?"

She shook her head. "I don't think we'll run into any others right now. This isn't a high security place."

Kat pulled her gun and smiled. "Well, just in case."

The hallway was dark. Only one fourth of the overhead lights were on. The place was eerily quiet.

"I could see this as a place where ghosts could hang out," Mitch said.

Lucian shook his head and walked past him.

Sheba took quiet steps, nearing the turn in the hallway. She peered around the corner and motioned the others to follow.

"Her room is the second one up across the hall," Sheba said.

Lucian pulled his gun and stepped into the adjoining hallway. Kat stood behind him with her gun drawn. The hallway was empty.

Chapter 71

Mitch had watched Lucian take down the guard and wondered why fatigue had overcome Lucian so quickly. The guard wasn't a large man. He wasn't even strong enough to resist Lucian's hold. The man barely put up a fight. But Lucian looked wiped and worn. He certainly didn't look like the man who had interviewed him a few weeks ago.

Along the dark tunnels, Mitch had felt the presence of others. Invisible beings. They didn't seem threatening, but they were there. Watching.

Mitch had been in a lot of places where similar presences revealed themselves, often ignored by passersby, which let him know that he held some type of connection with those from *the beyond*. He thought it was ironic that this Salem was as *possessed* as the one in Massachusetts, but for different reasons.

Spiritual unrests were uncanny similar, but the other Salem's haunts came from the persecutions of innocent people. This Salem? He wanted to do more research to discover why some spirits ceased to find peace.

Sheba hurried to Beverly's door and pushed it inward. Tom and one of the cubs followed her inside.

Kat and Lucian entered the room.

Beverly sat in a wheelchair facing a large window that overlooked a grassy patch with large oak trees. She didn't blink, just stared straight ahead. An I.V. drip was inserted into her left arm.

Sheba placed her hand over Beverly's. "We're going to get you out of here, so you can get better."

Beverly never responded to Sheba's voice or her touch. Mitch studied Sheba's reaction. She truly believed Beverly was in a sedated state, that she'd wake up, but it was obvious to Mitch that something more affected the young lady. And that troubled him.

Tom stared into Beverly's eyes and shook his head. "What'd they do to her? I don't think this is due to drugs."

"What do you suspect?" Kat asked.

He shrugged. "Surgery? Or maybe she had an accident and fell. Major brain trauma."

Sheba frowned. "Don't say that!"

Kat and Lucian observed that Beverly didn't respond to Sheba's outburst. Her eyes never moved. She didn't jump or move. She simply sat like a limp statue.

Tom lifted Beverly's right arm and let go. Her arm dropped without any resistance. Apparently he was keen enough to perceive the same prognosis Mitch had.

"Sheba," he said. "I'm sorry, but I don't think there's anything we can do for her."

Sheba growled. Her eyes narrowed. "No! *Don't say that!*"

"She's not in there," he said softly. "I know it's hard to accept, but she's gone."

Mitch placed his arm around Sheba's shoulder and squeezed. Tears formed in her eyes. He pulled her closer and looked into her sorrow-filled eyes. Shaking his head, he showed his remorse.

"We can't leave her here," she said.

Kat said, "For now, I think it's best. After we stop Alpha, we'll come back for her and take her to another hospital to be examined."

Sheba said, "You promise?"

Kat nodded. "Yes, dear."

Lucian headed for the door. Mitch followed. Once Lucian stepped into the hallway, he stopped and leaned against the wall. Before Kat entered, he righted himself, trying to keep his composure. He glanced at Mitch for a moment and looked away. What was he hiding?

"How many people work in this wing?" Lucian asked.

Mitch shrugged.

Kat shook her head. "I'd like to find out, so we'd know more about what's going on. It's strange they'd only keep one patient here, and for what purpose? Seeing how her condition is?"

"Let's find out," Tom said.

Following the hallway, they came to a nursing station but strangely none of the computers were on. The phone buttons were dark.

"No one is here?" Kat said.

"Surely someone checks on her," Lucian said.

Sheba frowned. "We saw the one guard. A nurse has to be on staff somewhere."

Lucian stopped at the desk, propped his arms across the top, and slowly shook his head. "Doesn't seem that anyone has been at this desk recently."

A door slammed down the hallway. Footsteps approached their direction. Lucian pulled his gun.

A gray-haired nurse walked with a roll of paper towels tucked beneath her arm, oblivious of their presence. When she stepped around the corner and headed toward the desk, Lucian aimed the gun at her. Her eyes widened.

She dropped the towels on the floor and gasped.

"How did you get in here?" she asked. "This is a secured area."

"We're here for Beverly," Kat said.

The nurse frowned. "Alpha didn't send you."

"No," Kat said.

"Without his permission she cannot leave."

Sheba's eyes shifted, becoming dark and outlined with gold. She stepped toward the nurse but Mitch grabbed her hand and shook his head.

Kat read the nurse's badge. "What's wrong with Beverly, Ms. Rowe?"

"Are you related to her?" Rowe asked.

"No."

"Then I can't tell you anything."

Sheba jerked free of Mitch's hand and pinned the nurse against the desk. Long claws emerged from her hand. She pressed them against Rowe's throat. "She's one of my best friends. You better tell us or I promise, you won't speak again. I'll cut your tongue out."

The nurse's wide eyes glanced from Sheba to Lucian.

Lucian smiled and shrugged. "Don't look at me. I'm not going to stop her."

"Okay," Rowe said, slowly raising her hands in surrender. "Alpha tested some type of drug on her."

"What exactly?" Tom asked, stepping closer.

Rowe shook her head, and glanced at him in surprise. "I recognize you. Did you work here?"

"Not voluntarily," he replied.

"Oh." She swallowed hard. "You were one of the boys that escaped . . ."

Tom nodded. "What drug did Alpha use on Beverly?"

"The same thing he used on you boys, but it did *that* to her. It didn't change her like it did your friends."

Kat gently pulled Sheba away from the nurse. "Why's she being kept over here, away from others?"

"Alpha let her parents believe she'd died. He feared a lawsuit for malpractice."

Lucian frowned. "He'll fear much worse shortly."

"He'll kill all of you." Rowe seethed. Her aged facial features tightened, making her look like an unflattering old crone in dark, twisted comics. She no longer appeared to be an innocent, feeble elderly woman. The warning in her voice made Mitch believe she might cast some sort of curse upon them, but her boldness retreated when Sheba stepped around Kat. Rowe cowered and closed her eyes.

Sheba grabbed the woman by the collar and lifted her off the floor with one arm.

"Don't," Rowe said, choking. "Please."

"Sheba," Mitch said.

"She'll contact Alpha if we don't do something with her," Sheba said.

Tom shook his head. "No, she won't."

Sheba lowered the woman slowly.

"I'll leave one cub behind with her," he said. "She won't move an inch. Well, if she does . . ."

The large cub walked over to Rowe and snarled with a low, menacing growl. The nurse shook. Her hands trembled. The cat wrinkled its nose, revealing its large, sharp teeth.

"I guess you'll stay put, won't you?" Kat asked.

Rowe nodded and rested her back against the side of the desk.

Tom placed his hand on the cat's massive head and looked down at the nurse. "Don't move a muscle and you'll be fine. He's not eaten in a while."

She nodded, closed her eyes, and hunched down to make herself appear smaller.

Lucian motioned to the side door. "It's time to get Alpha."

Chapter 72

Lydia awakened on a narrow bed inside Grayson Enterprises. After rubbing her eyes, she looked around the room. The white floor, ceiling, and walls lead her to believe that she was in an infirmary. Mordia stabbing her with a needle was the last thing she recalled.

"Good to see you're awake," Grayson said from across the room.

She squinted because of the bright fluorescent lights. "Where am I?"

"In one of my recovery rooms."

"Where exactly?"

Grayson smiled and came to the edge of the bed. "This is one of my wings at Grayson Enterprises where I do research and experimentation."

Lydia massaged her temples. Everything remained blurry. "What about Matthews? Where is he?"

"Come," Grayson said, extending his hand to her. "I'll show you."

Lydia took his hand and set one foot on the floor to stand. Her leg wobbled. Grayson looped his arm with hers to steady her.

"Easy. They sedated you with a powerful drug."

"Where's the bitch that drugged me?"

"Both Jimmy and Davis said that you killed her with one punch."

Lydia shrugged. "I was quite pissed."

"Obviously."

"What happened? How'd I get here?"

"Actually, you were quite lucky that Davis and Jimmy got you out without the police taking you into custody. They broke into an empty apartment on another floor and hid until the authorities cleaned up the area. I made a few calls to keep the police off your trail."

"Who'd help with that?" she asked.

"Money does a lot of things," Grayson replied. "Some people love money more than they honor duty. It gets me by during times like this."

Lydia shook her head.

Grayson led her to the outer hallway and to a large window. On the other side of the glass were two doctors dressed in surgery scrubs. Matthews lay facedown on an operating table. The doctors were placing a metal chip at the base of his skull.

"What are they doing?" she asked, frowning. "I want him dead."

"Some things are worse than death," he replied.

"Meaning?"

"I have other plans for Matthews."

Lydia shook her head. Her eyes narrowed. "No. *You* promised me. You hired me to kill him."

"No, I asked if it became necessary, would you kill him? You insisted that you had no problem with it. Just . . . his death isn't *necessary* at this time."

"Damn you. I want him dead."

"Before you storm off in a rage, listen to my proposal."

Lydia yanked her arm from his and leaned against the glass. Still frowning, she crossed her arms. "Okay, what?"

"That chip they're implanting is a Sleeper Chip."

"So?"

"It's attached to neurons and sends signals to the brain. When one of these is activated, the possessor does exactly what he or she is programmed. They have no control of what they do. They do only what's demanded of them."

"And what will you expect Matthews to do for you?"

Grayson smiled. "I'm sending him to mine in Olympus Mons on Mars."

"Mars?"

"I'm on the ground floor to establish a thriving Martian civilization. I have over one hundred miners all programmed and controlled by these chips. It's a degrading job really, especially for someone like Matthews."

"I'd enjoy the thought of knowing his disgrace," she said with her voice rising. "But he won't *even* be aware of it!"

Grayson gave a slight nod. "Well, there is that downside."

"Oh, there's a plus?"

"Actually, yes."

"What would *that* be?"

"His labor will weigh upon him, day by day, and the grinding work will slowly kill him."

"Will he feel the pain?" she asked.

"No."

Lydia frowned. "He tried to kill you and take over your empire. I thought you wanted him dead, too."

"I do . . . did."

"Then let *me* kill him. How can you be satisfied knowing he's alive?"

"Immediate death doesn't please me, Lydia. Knowing how his life dwindles daily does. Besides, his labor is putting money into my pockets. He's investing in my company. That is something I know he'd hate above everything else. The sad thing is how brilliant he really is and how he and I could never get on the same page."

"You're ridiculous."

Grayson laughed. "In what way?"

"He won't know what he's doing. How can you take pleasure in it?"

"Easy. It's like I'm harboring this huge secret from him, which in a sense, I am. He's not in control. I am. I *own* him."

"Like a slave?"

"That's a harsh term, but in his case, I like it."

"And what about the other miners? Are they your slaves, too?"

"I wouldn't leak that to the media or dare even hint that is what I'm doing, but I suppose that is the proper slant."

"It's unethical."

Grayson shrugged. "They're hardened prisoners that were convicted of the most brutal crimes. I'm doing society on Earth a favor."

"I can see your justification for them, but not Matthews."

"Give it some thought. I think you'll understand my reasoning for keeping him alive."

"Any way you can film his degradation?" she asked.

"Of course. I plan to view footage of his labors each day to relish over the fact that he will never overtake or outdo me."

"I want to see that, too."

Grayson nodded. "Not a problem."

"Now, if you'll excuse me," she said, brushing past.

"Where are you going?"

"To get some air."

"I hope this isn't going to discourage you from working for me. You're the best at what you do, and I really want you here."

Lydia smiled evenly. "I need some time to collect my thoughts. But, I'll be back."

Grayson folded his massive arms. "You'll work with my security team?"

"Depends on the money and the service needed."

"The pay scale is far more than anyone else would ever give you. I need someone with your expertise that can get into places undetected. Can you do that?"

Lydia recalled the invasion at her farmhouse and how, like a cat, she had snuck in unseen, silently, and took out the three hired mercenaries without having a shot fired in return.

She nodded. "Like no one else."

"Great," Grayson said. He extended his hand. "Welcome aboard."

Lydia glanced at his hand, and then she looked into his eyes and at his devious smile.

Firmly, she shook his hand. "Thanks."

Lydia turned and walked away.

"You're still leaving?" he asked.

"I have things to do. They won't take long."

"Very well."

Chapter 73

Lydia seethed. Almost immediately after Lydia left Grayson, Davis approached her.

"You okay?" he asked.

"Fine."

"You look . . . disgruntled."

She kept walking a brisk pace. "I imagine so."

"Why? Because Matthews is alive?"

Lydia stopped and faced him. "What do you think?"

"I understand. Anyone would be pissed about the situation."

"Apparently not Grayson."

Davis nodded. "Once you've worked for him a while you'll understand his peculiar way of thinking."

"That's doubtful. He hired me to carry out an assignment, which I had planned to do anyway, only for him to turn around and keep the bastard alive."

Davis handed her a cellphone. "Here."

"What's this for?"

"In case I need to contact you."

Lydia handed the phone back to him.

"I don't need this," she replied.

"We may need to get in touch with you."

She frowned. "Where's my bike?"

"Basement parking. Stan drove it here after we boarded the plane, remember?"

Lydia shook her head, trying to remember. Some memories were still fuzzy, possibly because of the sedative. "I won't be gone long. Besides, the only reason you're handing that to me is so you can trace my steps after I leave. If Grayson's that paranoid, perhaps he should hire someone else. I've put up with enough bullshit for one day."

Davis opened his mouth to speak, but Lydia sprinted away, leaving him alone in the hallway.

She entered the elevator and after the doors closed, she looked at her reflection on the shiny silver doors. For a moment, she barely recognized herself. She was bent by rage. Her eyes reflected the darkness of her soul. Shaking her head, she thought about how close she had come to killing Matthews. Her finger was squeezing the trigger. So close. But Lucas interrupted her at the worst possible time.

"Dammit," she sighed. *How had he known?*

Hearing his voice had *not* been her imagination. She knew it was him. She had heard him before. But the timing . . . his exactness for speaking, wasn't mistimed. It was like he had been sitting on her shoulder and voiced his opposition to temporarily hinder her actions. Him knowing her heart frightened her but didn't dissuade what she was determined to carry out. She wanted Matthews dead and not in the manner that Grayson wanted. Somehow she hoped to a way to exterminate Matthews before Grayson shipped him to Mars.

Lydia exited the elevator at the basement parking garage and hurried to her Nighthawk. She needed to drive, to clear her mind, and readjust. Although she was certain Lucas was in a hospital somewhere, she was not going to seek him out. Their relationship was over. She wanted to return to that forest where the strange hybrid human had thrown a rock at her. Getting there would take half a day of driving, but that didn't matter. She needed to know what he was and why there seemed to be so many living in that underground cavern.

They were the reason she'd been compelled to settle there with Lucas. With him in the hospital she could scope out the area without the fear of encountering him. Should she see his face or hear the love in his voice, she would find leaving harder to do. But as perturbed as she was, she feared she'd shoot Lucas without a second thought. She could no longer hold herself to any intimate relationship. And as much as she despised Idris for creating her, she couldn't fight the urges erupting inside her. She was everything he had wanted. Perhaps more. Perhaps she was far worse than he had ever estimated her to be.

Chapter 74

The nurse stepped into the waiting room where Joe sat. She smiled when he opened his eyes and saw her.

"Good news," she said. "Lucas is in and out of consciousness, but the doctor believes he's coming around. So hopefully his condition continues to improve and you can visit him in a few hours."

Joe smiled. "Thanks. You've been very helpful."

"If you'd like," she said, "I can call you by cellphone should you need to do some things outside the hospital instead of waiting."

Joe shook his head. "No, thank you. I will wait."

"You really love your brother," she said.

"With everything that I am," Joe replied.

***

LUCIAN SHIVERED when they edged their way through another dark underground passageway. His shirt was soaked more from sweat than the moisture dripping from overhead. He leaned against the wet rock wall, fighting the nausea crawling through his stomach and trying to creep its way out. The last thing he wanted was to vomit with Kat around. He could no longer insist that he wasn't sick. He'd have to do what Brockton told him to do. He'd have to tell Kat.

Tom trained his flashlight on the door.

Sheba stood at the tunnel door with her hand on the handle. "We're here."

"Are you ready?" Kat asked Lucian.

"Yes."

Kat took out her cellphone. "I need to call Carpenter."

"Now?" Lucian asked. "Why?"

"To let him know we're going in."

"He'll tell us to wait. We don't have that kind of time."

"I know, but at least he'll know where to find us once he lands."

"Make it quick," Lucian said.

Mitch walked to Sheba at the doorway. "This isn't the same door as earlier, is it?"

"No. This leads into the basement where the heating system is at New Horizons," Sheba replied.

Lucian chuckled. "You certainly know your way around these underground tunnels."

Sheba shrugged. "I have lots of spare time. I love to explore."

"So," Lucian said, "Give me a brief rundown of the place. Where will Alpha be?"

"Second floor is where he stays."

"Surely he leaves," Lucian replied.

"Seldom does he go outside the facility anymore, except in what he considers emergencies. He tends to travel more with his mind."

"Like astral projection?" Mitch asked.

Sheba replied, "I suppose it's something like that."

"That's odd," Lucian said.

"No," Tom said. "His mind's where his power lies. He won't leave because he will become vulnerable. His strength is his mental power."

"It was a painful experience," Mitch said, rubbing the back of his head.

Lucian smiled. "If you say so."

"Don't underestimate him," Sheba said. "Just because you've not been exposed to his power, don't think he's weakened. We've been in a safety zone in the tunnels. Once we step out of here, it's possible he'll locate us fast."

"When's the last time you've seen Alpha?" Lucian asked.

"Over a couple of weeks ago. He's avoided me. Not sure why, but he turned down the several requests I've made to visit him in person."

"Was he behind the murders last week?" Lucian asked.

"Probably," Sheba replied, "But I honestly don't know for certain. Parker's been trying to make me believe I killed them."

"You didn't, did you?" he asked.

"I don't think so."

"But you're not certain?"

"That night escapes me."

Lucian nodded. "Do you think Parker was involved?"

"He has a dark side and likes to inflict pain, so yes, he probably had a hand in it."

"Okay," Lucian said. "If possible, we keep him alive until we can question him."

Kat joined them. "Carpenter says they will land in less than a half hour."

"That soon?" Lucian asked.

"Yes. He got the okay to get aboard a new experimental plane. A chopper is waiting for them when they land."

"That's good."

Lucian shone his light around. "Everyone ready?"

They nodded.

Sheba pulled open the door and stepped into New Horizons' basement. Lucian followed, pulled his gun, and tried to ignore the pain the surged throughout his body. If he were to die today, he wanted to make certain that Alpha died first. He didn't know that he even had that much time left.

Chapter 75

Carpenter sat aboard the plane. His cellphone vibrated.

"Bennie? Is everything okay?"

"I found Dr. Helmsby," he replied.

"Great. Where is he?"

"Working for the CID."

Carpenter smiled. "Right under our noses the entire time?"

"Sort of. For some reason he believes Grayson might harbor a vindictive grudge against him for leaving Grayson Enterprises, so Helmsby had insisted that his name not be listed on any search file engines when the CID hired him."

"Any validity to his suspicions?"

"Full investigations into Boyd Grayson and all his operations are underway right now. For other reasons, but I'm certain we'll find out if he is plotting to kill Helmsby."

"Keep me posted, Bennie."

"You know I will."

THE BASEMENT FLOOR WAS DARK. Only a few fluorescent lights were on. Rows of old heating units lined the floor. Rusted file cabinets were nestled in between the units, cramping the floor space. Layers of dust coated everything.

The metal duct network kept everyone from standing upright as they walked.

"Tight squeeze," Lucian said, glancing over his shoulder.

Kat smiled. "Not for me."

"Well, I'm not *that* short."

"Sometimes being vertically challenged has its perks."

Sheba walked up a dark flight of stairs to a door. She opened the door, which led to the first floor and peered out.

"How many guards do you think Alpha has waiting for us?" Lucian asked.

"Parker is the only police officer that frequents this facility. As for guards, I don't think he keeps more than a half dozen at New Horizons since he resides here. Maybe two on duty during each shift."

"Seems a bit overconfident," Lucian said.

"No. You still fail to realize how strong he is."

Lucian smiled. "You fail to understand who I am, too."

"I don't know you or what you're capable of," Sheba said. "But Alpha, I *know* what he can do."

Sheba started to step outside the door when Mitch grabbed her arm.

"What is it?" she asked.

"Alpha. Can you sense him?"

She closed her eyes for a moment, concentrating. She opened her eyes and nodded. "Yes. You?"

"Of course. That's why I stopped you."

Sheba gave a slight shrug. "We're in his fortress. Naturally, we're going to feel him. He's probably been searching for us after we escaped."

Lucian inspected each corner of the room. "Does he have security cameras in the hallways?"

"No," Sheba replied. "He doesn't need them. Trust me when I say he knows what goes on in this place. It's possible he already knows we're down here."

"I'll take your word for it," Lucian said.

Sheba faced them. "I'm going in. Is everyone else ready?"

They nodded.

"Should the worst of possibilities occur," she said, "It's been nice meeting you all."

She opened the door.

OFFICER PARKER STARED at his face in the restroom mirror. After opening his mouth, he ran his tongue over his teeth. Although they had repaired themselves, stabbing pain throbbed through his lower jaw. He rubbed his chin. His brownish golden eyes sparkled beneath the fluorescent lights.

"Parker," Alpha whispered into his mind.

"Yes?"

"We have unexpected company."

"Sheba?"

"Her and several others," Alpha said.

Parker grinned, bearing his teeth. "Where are they?"

"They came out of the basement a few minutes ago."

"I'll take care of it," Parker said.

"I'm sending the guards down, too."

A hurt expression crossed Parker's face. "You don't think I can take care of this?"

"There are five of them."

Parker shrugged. "I can handle them."

"You weren't able to handle Sheba alone."

Parker snarled his upper lip. "I would have killed her had you not instructed me otherwise. She hit me because I *didn't* shoot her."

"Don't debate me, Parker. This isn't open for discussion. Understood?"

A sharp prick of pain vibrated at the base of his skull. Parker was seconds from being knocked to the floor by blinding agony.

"Yes, sir. I understand. Sorry for speaking against you."

"That's better."

Parker sighed. "Do you still want her alive?"

"No. Kill all of them."

Parker checked the clip in his gun and smiled. "Not a problem."

Chapter 76

Sheba headed down the hall while the others followed close behind. Lucian checked the doors on one side of the hallway, and Kat checked the ones on the other side. All the doors were locked. None of the rooms were lighted. The hallway was lit but strangely empty.

Kat's cellphone vibrated in her back pocket. She pulled it out and read a brief text.

"Carpenter's plane has landed," she said. "They're in route."

"It's a shame he'll miss all the excitement," Lucian said.

Sheba neared the stairwell door. Instead of pushing it open, she pressed her back against the wall. She placed her index finger to her lips. The action and her faded makeup made her face resemble a mime.

"Someone there?" Kat whispered.

Sheba nodded.

Kat and Lucian aimed their weapons at the door.

Tom patted the cub's flank twice and pointed. The large cat slinked along the wall toward the door.

The door creaked open with a dull whine.

The cat pranced forward, barreled through the door, and seconds later a man screamed in anguish. Silence followed.

Sheba and Tom pushed the door open. The cat stood on the man's chest. Blood pooled on the floor around the man's ripped out throat.

Mitch stared down at the man and then to Sheba. "You know him?"

"He's one of the guards," she replied.

A gunshot echoed from the other end of the hallway. Lucian grabbed Kat around the waist and carried her into the stairwell. The bullet hit his left shoulder. He groaned.

Setting Kat inside the door out of the man's sight, he pushed the door closed and leaned against it. Blood saturated his shirt. He winced in pain.

"How bad is it?" Sheba asked.

Lucian shook his head. "I'll be fine."

Kat stepped closer and pulled his shirt open.

"It's okay," Lucian said.

She frowned. "It's bleeding badly."

"It'll mend."

Several rounds echoed in the hall. Bullets chipped at the steel fire door but didn't pass through. Another round struck the small square window in the center of the door. The glass split, but the inner mesh prevented it from bursting.

Lucian glanced through the glass and yanked open the door.

"What are you doing?" Kat asked.

Lucian aimed his gun and fired twice. The other guard dropped to the floor. Dead.

Lucian shrugged. "He was reloading."

"God," Kat said through clenched teeth. "Why do you have to do stuff like that?"

"So no one else takes a bullet."

Kat shook her head. Her eyes narrowed in anger. She examined his wound again. It was still bleeding. If it was healing, the process seemed longer than normal. She walked away and looked up the stairs.

Lucian wiped sweat from his brow and leaned against the door. His heart raced. The throbbing pain in his shoulder wasn't lessening. While Kat held her back to him, he peeled back the shirt and examined the bullet hole. The wound did appear to be closing, but he had lost a lot of blood. He closed his eyes to keep the room from spinning. When he opened them, Kat was standing in front of him.

He smiled. "Two down."

"Yes, but we still have Alpha to take down," Kat said. "We need you at your strongest. We should wait until Carpenter and his backup get here."

"Trust me. All will be fine."

Kat rolled her eyes and sighed.

The second floor door to the stairwell opened. Footsteps clacked on the tile floor. The door shut with a heavy thud.

"Someone's up there," Mitch said.

Lucian pressed his hand over his bleeding shoulder.

Kat raised her gun and angled herself to where she'd see the person's feet when they rounded the descending stairs. She waited.

Sheba crinkled her nose and sniffed the air. "Dammit."

"What?" Kat asked.

"Officer Parker."

"You can tell that from your sense of smell?"

"That and his horrid aftershave."

Kat grinned and steadied her weapon.

Parker's shoes thudded softly down each step. He seemed apprehensive about heading to the next level.

Sheba whispered, "Can I take him?"

Kat frowned. "He's armed."

"I know. He had a gun yesterday, too, and I hurt him badly without getting shot."

"When he comes around, I'll have him in clear sight. He'll have no choice but to surrender."

"He won't surrender, Kat. His pride is too hurt for that. You'd have to kill him. Besides, Alpha has probably given him only one thing to do and that is to kill us. He's afraid of me. That much is obvious, but he's terrified of Alpha."

Tom gave Sheba a harsh stare. "But what if Alpha is controlling Parker?"

Sheba looked away. "I didn't think about that."

"Isn't it odd," Mitch said, "That Alpha hasn't launched his own attack yet?"

"What do you mean?" Kat asked.

"Earlier I sensed his presence, but now, he's not detectable."

"He's hiding," Sheba said.

"Or baiting a trap," Mitch replied.

Parker's footsteps clacked on the steps above. Kat aimed, but Sheba rushed up the stairwell at him.

"Sheba!" Mitch shouted.

Lucian pushed himself away from the door, still clutching his shoulder. The bleeding had stopped, but he had lost enough blood to weaken him. He took two wobbly steps.

Gunfire echoed in the stairwell. Sheba growled and ripped at Parker, but he caught her in the gut with one bullet and then kicked her down the stairs. Kat fired two shots, but Parker rushed out of sight and upstairs. The door opened and slammed shut.

Sheba tumbled down the stairs like a limp doll until she struck Mitch's legs. He leaned down and turned her over. Blood flowed from the bullet wound in the center of her abdomen. Her eyes darted back and forth in confusion. Her hands shook.

Mitch sat on the step beside her and pulled her into his lap. He gently rubbed her cheek with his fingers while whispering, "It's going to be okay."

Kat shook her head. "It looks bad."

Mitch wrapped his arms around her and gently held her. Her body grew rigid, jerked. Her eyes suddenly shifted, darkened. Low guttural growls came from her throat. Her jaw popped. Her ears elongated like a wolf's.

"Mitch," Kat said, "Let her go."

Mitch eased her onto the step beside him and backed toward Kat.

Fur sprouted on her face and arms. Her body shook. Her transformation caused her to cried out in pain.

Lucian stared in disbelief. He remembered Typhis' son, but his changes never went this far.

Sheba's mouth lengthened with rows of canine teeth. She rolled over onto her stomach. Thick, yellow claws grew over her fingernails. Growling, she sprinted on all fours up the stairs to the door. She fumbled with the doorknob.

Kat turned and faced Lucian. "Are you ready?"

Lucian nodded. "As ever. When this is over, there's something I need to discuss with you."

"Sure," she said. She studied him a moment more. The concern on her face was evident, but due to the danger they were about to enter, she didn't pry like she normally would have. He had a feeling that she knew he wasn't well and he should stay behind, but duty called. She turned with her gun raised and headed after Sheba.

Lucian grabbed the handrail and started up the stairs. He wished he had told her that he was dying. And more than that, he wished he had told her how much he loved her.

Chapter 77

Sheba was through the door and rushing across the second floor by the time Mitch and Kat got to the hallway. Sheba ran on all fours, headed straight at Parker. He turned to fire, and she lunged into the air. She fastened her sharp teeth around his wrist and slung her head back and forth. Parker screamed. The gun dropped and spun across the floor.

Kat stood before Mitch and held her gun, examining their surroundings. This floor wasn't like the first floor. It didn't have a dozen rooms. The floor was open with a glassed in laboratory on one half and the other half was divided by a long blue curtain like those that divide the beds in an emergency room.

A steady beeping echoed softly from the other side of the blue curtain. Lucian stepped through the stairwell door. He turned his head from side to side and popped his neck. Some of his strength was coming back, but the dizziness had not stopped completely.

He checked his gun clip and slapped it back in.

Parker screamed.

Sheba thrust her knees onto his chest and pinned him to the floor. She flailed him with her sharp claws, striking his face, and ribbons of thin flesh peeled from his cheeks and forehead. She was more animal than human. Her rage and destruction was hard to watch. The wound in her stomach was no longer bleeding. She healed quickly.

But what happened next astonished them all—including Sheba.

The blue curtain swayed near its base. Inside the glassed laboratory a thin man moved. Kat aimed her gun at the man, but he didn't seem to notice. He was busy watching different monitors and writing down his observations.

Parker roared. He caught Sheba's wrists, growled, and slung her against the wall. She yelped like an injured pup and dropped to the floor. Shaking her head, she staggered to all fours, and then snarled.

But Parker was on his feet, prepared. His face contorted.

"Dammit!" Lucian said. "He's changing, too?"

Tom patted the black cub and it sprinted to stand beside Sheba. She and the cub lunged onto Parker and ripped at him with their teeth.

Lucian stepped past Kat. He leveled his gun out before him and walked toward the curtain.

"What are you doing?" she asked.

"Keep an eye on the man in that laboratory," he replied. "Someone is behind this curtain."

Kat turned and aimed the gun at the man. With all the noise and fighting he still had not turned to notice them. The walls didn't appear thick enough to be soundproof.

Lucian grabbed the curtain and yanked it open, revealing a hospital bed. He pointed the gun at the head of the bed. A man with silver hair lay sleeping, helpless. An I.V. drip hung near the side of the bed. The heart monitor beeped steadily. The man's heartbeat was strong even though his face looked thin and emaciated. He estimated the man to be in his mid-fifties.

Kat glanced from the man in the laboratory over at Lucian.

"Who's that?" she asked.

"I really don't know," Lucian said, lowering his gun. "Some old man."

Lucian turned toward Kat. "Find out who that is inside the lab."

She nodded. Keeping her gun held out at chest level, she moved toward the door.

Lucian looked at the old man. The man's eyes opened widely. He frowned at Lucian. His eyes were blacker than a devil's soul.

The man's hand rose from the bed. He extended his open palm at Lucian. An invisible force slammed into Lucian and knocked him backwards.

"Kat!" Lucian yelled.

She turned.

Lucian struggled to stand but the force pushed against him harder. A piercing high-pitched sound rose inside his head. The pain was unbearable. He tried to fight it, but it was too much. He placed his hands over his ears without any lessening of the noise or pain. The man was attacking his brain.

Mitch ran to Lucian but bounced back from what seemed an invisible barrier.

"That's Alpha!" Mitch said, pointing at the man in the bed.

"Lucian!" Kat said. She raised her gun and aimed at Alpha.

Alpha's other hand rose. He made a spinning movement with his fingers. Kat's hands turned against her and slowly, she aimed the gun at Lucian.

"Get down!" she yelled at Lucian, but he was frozen in place. He couldn't move.

She tried to move her finger off the trigger, but she couldn't budge it. Instead, it was tightening.

"Lucian, get down!" Kat screamed. Tears formed in her eyes.

She squeezed off one round.

Two.

Both bullets struck Lucian in the back. His body jerked. He collapsed to the floor and didn't move.

SHEBA BASHED her fists into Parker's face. She kept striking relentlessly. His eyes widened and became distant. He wasn't even resisting or fighting her off. He didn't seem to be fading into unconsciousness, but he looked like he was dying. She stopped hitting and sat back. His eyes closed and his head turned to the side. Blood oozed from the cuts across his face.

She looked at her bloody hands and took a deep breath. She resented Parker with a passion, but she still didn't want the guilt of killing him on her conscious. She backed away.

Parker's chest stilled for a moment. His breathing stopped.

Fear shot through Sheba like a blade of ice. She wiped her hands on her shirt.

Parker gasped. His body jerked erratically, and his breathing slowly regulated.

Relieved, she stood. The black cub slinked around her and walked upon Parker's chest. It pressed its sharp claws into Parker's throat until they sunk deep into the flesh. Blood welled up around the sharp-tipped claws and trickled down the sides of his neck. With a quick swipe, the cat tore through Parker's jugulars. More blood gushed. The cub raised its head, turned, and walked away.

Chapter 78

Tears streamed down Kat's face because of what Alpha had made her do. But he wasn't finished. She tried to drop the gun, to toss it away, but she couldn't. Alpha wouldn't let her. She remembered Kyle exhibiting this same power against the corrupt coroner and wished he were here to counter Alpha.

Her hands rose and she knew Alpha wanted Mitch dead. His desire to kill Mitch pressed into her mind. Her hands moved against her will and her aim centered on Mitch. Even if she looked away, she didn't think she'd miss. Alpha would ensure the bullet hit where he wanted.

Mitch focused his energy at Alpha like he had in their earlier confrontation. Instead of a broad attack, he shoved his mental energy like a narrow sharp dart, which somehow managed to penetrate Alpha's shield. With every bit of mental strength he had left, he struck.

The impact rattled Alpha enough for him to lose his control over Kat. Kat dropped the gun. She ran to Lucian and dropped to her knees. Sitting on the floor, she placed his head on her lap. She felt for a pulse. It was shallow as was his breathing.

"I'm so sorry," she whispered.

Mitch stepped toward Alpha and closed his eyes. He called upon his mental strength and prepared his next blow.

"You worthless fool!" Alpha seethed.

Alpha sat upright in the bed. Fury pulsed through him. Before Mitch did anything, Alpha sunk jagged tendrils of heated pain through Mitch's brain. He dropped to floor and wailed in agony.

Sheba and the black cub stepped away from Parker's shredded corpse. Tom motioned hand signals to the cub. It growled. The cub and Sheba leapt across the floor and headed for Alpha.

The black cub ran under the bed. Sheba rushed to the foot end. Alpha turned his attention toward her.

"You had everything," he said.

"I'd rather have my freedom," she replied. "And Gloria released."

She reached to grab his feet, but he turned his power toward her. She pulled at the invisible hands tightening around her throat. Her face reddened. She choked. Spittle formed at the edges of her mouth. The pressure he applied forced her mouth open. She panted to get air, but she couldn't. Everything in her vision turned black. To keep from falling, she clutched the bedrail and locked her elbows.

Her eyes pleaded for mercy.

"You'll have nothing," Alpha hissed.

A blast of gunfire reverberated through the room. Alpha clutched his chest. His eyes widened in horror. Blood leaked through his hospital gown. He glanced over to see Tom holding Kat's gun. Alpha gasped and slowly sank back on the bed. His body went limp.

The restraint around Sheba's neck unraveled. She panted for air and leaned across the bedrail to lie on the mattress. Tom rushed to her. Mitch crawled toward Kat and Lucian.

The heart monitor squealed a long, steady beep.

The laboratory door opened and the man hurried out. "What the hell have you done?"

Kat said, "Who are you?"

"Dr. Shelby," he replied. "Sheba, what have you done? Who are these people?"

Kat took Lucian's gun and aimed at Shelby. "We're here to shut down your operation."

"Why?" he asked with a gentle voice. "What have we done?"

"Attempted child abduction and murder," she replied.

"Murder?"

Kat nodded. "The two people last week. One child's mother."

Dr. Shelby shook his head and forced a gentle smile. "What proof do you have?"

The black cub slinked from beneath the bed, came up behind him, and growled.

Shelby stiffened.

"We have plenty of proof. A dirty cop over there on the floor. A mother that will testify to everything she has witnessed. Do you want more proof?" Kat asked.

Tom brought a clipboard over to Kat. "How about organ harvesting?"

"What?" Kat asked.

"That's why Alpha is in that hospital bed. He's had a heart and liver transplant. Want to take a guess where he probably got those organs?"

"Is that true?" she asked, looking at Dr. Shelby.

He paled.

Carpenter and a dozen agents entered the room. He aimed his gun at Shelby while scanning the carnage. Shelby turned and saw the gun in Carpenter's hand.

"Don't move," Carpenter said.

Dr. Shelby raised his hands and nodded.

Carpenter came closer, and noticed Kat on the floor with Lucian.

"What happened, Kat?" he asked.

"He made me shoot Lucian."

"Who?"

"Alpha."

Carpenter looked at Shelby. "This is Alpha?"

"No. Alpha's dead now. On the hospital bed."

Carpenter glanced around the room. "It's a damn bloodbath in here."

He walked over to the hospital bed, took out a small handheld device, and scanned Alpha's thumbprint. The information popped up on the screen.

"Winchester Hayze was Alpha?" Carpenter shook his head and walked back to Kat.

"You know him?" Tom asked.

"I know of him," Carpenter said. "He helped Idris launch TransGen-Corp. They parted ways and no one has been able to find him until now."

Tom shrugged. "No one will have to worry about him anymore."

Carpenter sighed. "Thankfully."

Lucian was getting colder in Kat's arms. She hugged him tighter and looked at Carpenter. "Mike, I think he's dying."

"How?"

"I really don't know, but he's not healing like he normally does."

Carpenter turned to his co-agents, and pointed at Shelby. "Take him into custody. Get more agents out here and tear this place apart. I want to know everything that's occurred here."

Sheba looked at Carpenter. "Alpha is keeping my friend Gloria hostage here. Can you find her?"

Carpenter motioned one agent toward Sheba. "Give him a detailed description of her. If she's here, we'll find her."

Sheba smiled and nodded. "Thank you."

Carpenter turned back to Kat. "We'll get Lucian to the helicopter and to a hospital where they can get him stabilized."

Kat sobbed, cradling Lucian's head in her hands. She feathered his hair with her fingers.

"Don't die," she whispered. "I need you too much. I love you."

Chapter 79

Inside the helicopter, Carpenter answered his cellphone.

"Lucian's critically injured," he said. "He did? Good. In transit now."

Fifteen minutes passed before they landed at the hospital helipad. Paramedics stepped aboard the FBI chopper and carried Lucian to a gurney aboard a medical chopper.

"What are you doing?" Kat asked, wiping her eyes.

"Hopefully saving his life."

"But where are you taking him?" she asked.

"You're going too. Get aboard. We have a bit of a trip to make."

"What about everyone at New Horizons? Aren't you going to stay behind and investigate?"

Carpenter smiled. "Kat, I've left everything in good hands. Top agents are there and more are on the way. I'm sticking by you and Lucian through all this. Okay?"

"At least let me know where we're going."

Carpenter hugged her tightly. He whispered in her ear. "Just stay beside him. Hold his hand. Let him know you're here. Don't worry about anything else."

The helicopter lifted and paramedics inserted an I.V. drip line into the back of Lucian's hand. One stripped open Lucian's shirt to examine his wounds. Instead, they found the two bullets had been pushed out, the holes were gone, and the bleeding had stopped.

Lucian was pale. His breathing remained shallow. She had never seen him look so vulnerable. She never believed he would be. Now, all her fear of loss settled upon her and attempted to paralyze her.

Kat wrung her hands. She took in deep breaths too quickly and began to hyperventilate.

"Easy, Kat," Carpenter said. "Calm down."

Kat took deeper gulps of air. Her eyes revealed her fear. She shook with hard sobs.

"She's having a panic attack," Carpenter said.

A paramedic tried to put an oxygen cup over her nose and mouth, but she knocked it away. She looked like a caged, frightened animal.

"Kat, it's okay," Carpenter said in a soothing tone.

Another paramedic grabbed a syringe and injected it into her thigh.

"What are you doing?" Carpenter asked.

"A sedative to help calm her."

Kat frowned, but Carpenter sat down beside her and draped his arm across her shoulders. Her eyes grew heavy. Her head bobbed side to side. A few seconds later, she collapsed against his chest. He kissed her forehead softly and gave her a firm side hug.

He looked at Lucian. The paramedics continued with the life support apparatus.

Carpenter whispered, "Sorry I thought the worst of you. Had I known the truth, we probably could have been great friends. You need to live so I can properly apologize to you."

He took out his cellphone and dialed a number. He did have a few favors he could call in and hopefully make some things right. Provided Lucian lived.

ASLEEP, Joe sat in a waiting room chair. The cloth-covered alien skull was tucked between his side and the chair. The nurse gently shook his shoulder.

He opened his eyes and smiled.

"Lucas is awake. You can go in and see him," she said.

Joe grabbed the skull and stood. He hurried through the door. Lucas lay on the hospital bed. His face was gray. Dark circles shadowed his eyes.

"Glad that you're awake," Joe said. "You had me worried."

Lucas forced a smile. "I'm awake, but I hurt all over."

"That's understandable considering how badly we rolled down that hillside in the SUV."

Lucas noticed Joe holding the cloth-wrapped object. "Is that it?"

Joe nodded. "Yes."

"Mind if I hold it?"

Joe glanced toward the door to make certain no one else was in the room and that the door had closed. Carefully, he unwrapped the skull and placed it into Lucas' hands.

"I'll be," Lucas said. "Definitely not from this world."

"No, bro, it's not."

"Wonder why it was out in the desert?"

"No idea, but I need a favor," Joe said.

"Anything."

Joe told Lucas about the sweat lodge vision and that he needed to talk to Helmsby.

"I've not talked to Helmsby in a long while," Lucas said. "The only person that I know who might have his number is Daniel, but I don't know what happened to my phone."

Joe reached into his back pocket. "Here. I took it while you were unconscious and recharged your battery."

Lucas took the phone. Squinting, he dialed "1."

Chapter 80

"Hello?" Daniel said.

"Hey, Dan."

"Lucas? You okay? You don't sound too good."

"Recovering, but I'll be fine."

"From what?" Daniel asked.

"A long story but I'll tell you when I see you."

"What's up?"

"You heard from Helmsby recently?"

Daniel laughed. "Everyone keeps asking me that. It's not like I've ever kept track of him."

"Well, *have you* heard from him?"

"Yes. Why?"

"Joe has something that he needs to give to him."

"What?"

"I really shouldn't say over the phone since you never know *who* might be eavesdropping but it's important."

"Helmsby called me earlier, but he refused to tell me where he was."

"I wonder why?"

"After all he's been through he's always acting insecure and paranoid. But I do have the number of someone who knows where he is. Got a pen? Write this down."

AT FIRST BENNIE couldn't believe what Joe had told him over the phone. He thought someone was pulling a hoax. But if Joe actually had what he said he possessed, Bennie didn't want anyone *outside* the FBI getting their hands on it. Helmsby seemed like the logical choice to analyze the alien skull, but Bennie wasn't certain how Joe had come to that conclusion.

Bennie contacted the FBI agency nearest Joe and put in a request to have Joe and Lucas flown to Helmsby's laboratory in Kentucky.

AN AGENT NAMED Perry Milton walked along the hallways with Sheba to inspect the rooms. Her heart raced. She desperately wanted to find Gloria. Each door they opened led to either a medical tech lab or an empty observation room with an examination table.

"We've checked almost every room," Perry said.

"She has to be here somewhere. I know she is."

"We'll keep looking."

Perry opened the next door and found a woman sitting on the edge of the bed, holding a boy on her lap.

"Who are you?" he asked, placing his hand atop his holstered gun.

"Jen," she said nervously. "This is my son, John."

"Why are you here?"

She explained how Blake had killed her husband, Doug. When she returned home, Dr. Shelby and Blake had taken her and her son at gunpoint.

"Come with us," Perry said.

"No," she replied. "Blake's out there. He'll kill us."

"We have agents scouring the place. You're safe with me," he said.

Jen slid off the side of the table and cradled John against her chest even though he was half her size and weight.

Perry placed his hand on the doorknob and turned.

"Wait," Sheba said.

"What is it?" he asked.

"Someone's out there."

Perry frowned. "How can you tell? I don't hear anything."

"Trust me," she said, smiling.

Jen's eyes widened. "It's him, isn't it? It's Blake."

"I think so." Sheba looked into Perry's eyes. "Allow me."

Perry stepped aside. Sheba opened the door and slipped out, shutting the door behind her.

Blake frowned when she glanced his direction.

"What are you doing in there?" he asked, placing his hand on his gun.

Sheba smiled playfully and tugged down at her skirt. "Looking for you."

"Me?" he asked surprised. "Why?"

"Well, look at you," she said. "All those times panting over me and asking me out, and now you're all nervous because I'm looking for you?"

"I'm not nervous."

"You certainly don't seem as interested in me as before."

"Oh, it's not that. I . . I just didn't expect to see you *here*."

"I can leave if I'm bothering you."

She turned to walk away.

"No," Blake said. "You've really changed your mind? You *want* to go out with me?"

"I'm considering it. If you ask me properly."

Blake relaxed his hand on the gun. "But I remember you quite enthusiastically said that you'd rather have maggots dancing in your brain than even sit at the same table with me."

"I get poetic like that from time to time."

He ran a hand through his hair while looking her over. "What happened?"

"What do you mean?"

"You have blood on your jacket."

Sheba ignored the question and walked to the other side of the hallway opposite the door where Perry, Jen, and John were. She pressed her back against the wall and lifted her skirt to just beneath her panties.

"What are you waiting for?" she asked. "You gonna come closer or run?"

A lustful smile crept across his face. He took two steps toward her when the door behind him creaked open. Before he could turn, Perry stuck the gun against the small of Blake's back.

Blake reached for his gun but Sheba snatched it. She rammed it into his gut and smiled.

"I still prefer the maggots," she said. "I truly couldn't stomach doing *anything* with you."

Perry cuffed Blake. Another agent entered the hallway. Perry motioned him to take Blake away. He insisted that Jen take her son and go with the agent as well.

Chapter 81

On the next floor the hallway was dark. Doors were spaced six feet apart on both sides of the hallway. Each door had a square window centered four feet above the floor. He peered through the first one on the left side of the hall. A young man sat on a narrow cot. He leaned forward, propping his elbows on his knees and rested his head in his hands like he was in deep thought or had lost all hope.

A small sink and toilet were also in the room.

"Damn," Perry said. "These are prison cells."

Sheba stepped on tiptoe and peered through. "Gloria must be on this floor."

She hurried from door to door and about midway down the hallway, she said, "Here she is!"

Before Perry reached her, Sheba had kicked the door in.

"How the hell did you do that?" he asked, examining the door's latch. "The door's made of steel."

She shrugged.

Gloria lay on her bed with her blanket pulled to her chin. Her eyes were closed. Her chest rose and fell.

"Gloria?" Sheba said softly.

Gloria slowly opened her eyes and looked at her.

"It's me. Sheba."

Gloria rose and slid into a seated position beneath the blanket.

"Alpha said that you were dead," Gloria said.

"No. He lied."

"Then why haven't you come to see me? Why'd you let him lock me in here?"

"I've been trying to see you," Sheba said. "Alpha wouldn't let me. He kept promising that I'd get to see you. And he ordered me to do things or else he'd kill you."

"How'd you find me?"

Sheba told Gloria in short detail how Alpha was killed and that the FBI had come to rescue them.

Sheba edged closer, but Gloria's eyes examined her with skepticism.

"It's okay," Sheba said. "I'm not going to hurt you."

"But, you turned into a wolf-like creature. I saw you."

Perry frowned. "What?"

Sheba sat on the edge of the bed. Gloria pulled the blanket tightly beneath her neck.

"I saw you," Gloria said. "You aren't human. You can't be."

"I'm different, Gloria, but I'm not going to hurt you. You never need to be afraid of me. I promise. You're my best friend."

Sheba extended her hand to Gloria. Gloria timidly took it.

Sheba smiled. "Come on. Let's get you out of here."

Standing, Sheba helped Gloria to her feet, and then she hugged her close.

"I've missed you," Sheba said.

"I missed you, too."

———

BY THE TIME the helicopter landed at the CID in Louisville, Kentucky— a few hours later—Kat had awakened. Kat held Lucian's hand, but he was too weak to keep his eyes open. He dozed in and out.

Two security guards met the paramedics and took Lucian and the gurney off the helicopter.

"Bring him to Dr. Helmsby's laboratory," one guard said. "Follow us."

HELMSBY SMILED at Kat and Carpenter in the hallway, but his smile was soon replaced with concern when he saw Lucian's gray complexion.

"He's worse than I imagined," Helmsby said.

Carpenter frowned and shook his head. Kat wiped her eyes.

"But let's see what we can do for him," Helmsby said.

The paramedics stopped the gurney in the laboratory and glanced at Helmsby.

"The next room, please," Helmsby said. "There's an examination table I've had moved in there so we can evaluate him."

He glanced at Kat. "I'll do whatever I can for him, Kat."

"Do you perform miracles?" she asked.

"Sometimes."

She cocked a brow.

Helmsby smiled. "Morton. Just think of him. If he's not a miracle of sorts, I'm at a total loss."

Kat offered a slight smile. "That's true."

Helmsby clapped his hands together with a loud smack. "Let's get started."

After the paramedics placed Lucian on the examination table, they took the gurney and left.

"What can we do?" Kat asked.

"First, you need to undress him down to his underwear. I have some things I need to gather before examining him."

Kat nodded. Looking across the room, she gasped.

An incubation chamber stood against the far wall.

"You're not going to put him in *there*, are you?" she asked.

"Unfortunately, I don't have many options."

"But why?"

"I will explain, but for now—" Helmsby took a syringe from his pocket. He thumped it and pushed out the air bubbles. He injected Lucian.

"What's that?" Kat asked.

"Something to boost his energy. Nothing more."

Lucian opened his eyes.

"Why must he be placed in that chamber?" Kat asked.

"Kat, his body is shutting down. If I don't temporarily suspend him, he'll die. While there may be a chance that I can reverse his genetic flaws, there isn't any way I can reverse *death*."

Helmsby walked to the chamber and punched in commands for the computer.

Kat stared at Lucian. He gave her a weak smile.

Chapter 82

Lucian wore only briefs and lay beneath a thin sheet on a cold gurney. Sweat beaded from his pores and drenched the sheet in spite of the frigid room temperature. His body spasms intensified. Kat leaned over with tears in her eyes. She placed one hand on his forehead and gripped his right hand with the other.

"Don't cry," Lucian said in a weak voice. "I'm not going away."

She looked at the incubation chamber. Thick liquid slowly filled the glass walls.

"You may not survive this," she said.

"I certainly won't live if Helmsby doesn't try it."

Dr. Helmsby walked to the side of Lucian's bed. He thumped a syringe to get the excess air bubbles to rise to the top. He pushed the plunger and squeezed out the remaining bubbles.

"Lucian, this will hurt. It'll probably feel like ice entering your bloodstream."

Lucian forced a smile. "Can't be worse than the pain I'm experiencing right now."

"The incubation chamber will cryopreserve your body until I develop a cure for your condition."

Kat wiped her eyes. "How long will that take?"

Helmsby shrugged. "I don't know, but I promise I'll work around the clock to find a cure to correct his genetic flaws."

Carpenter stepped into the room.

Lucian raised his head, smiled, and eased back onto the gurney.

Carpenter stepped beside Kat.

"I guess you'll be relieved now," Lucian said to Carpenter.

"About what?" Carpenter asked.

"Justice is finally served."

Carpenter shook his head. "Lucian, there's no justice here. I know the truth."

"That being?" Lucian asked.

"You never killed Godfrey, the guards, or the other senator."

Lucian nodded slowly. A frown crept across his brow. "So they finally told you?"

"Yes," Carpenter said. "I met with Godfrey in private. I cannot understand why you'd keep me in the dark about this."

Lucian shrugged.

"Kat's eyebrows rose. "So it is true?"

"Yes," Lucian replied.

"Why didn't you tell me?" Kat asked.

"I couldn't. I had to protect Godfrey. If anyone knew . . ."

"And that's greatly appreciated," Godfrey said, stepping into the room.

Lucian gave a weak smile. "Good to see you."

"How are you holding up?" Godfrey asked.

"Not too well, apparently."

Godfrey squeezed Lucian's shoulder. "You're in Dr. Helmsby's hands now. He'll figure out something. We'll provide him with whatever resources necessary. For what you've done, and Carpenter, you're both heroes and heroes should be honored. At all costs."

Godfrey turned to Carpenter and offered his hand. Carpenter hesitated for several seconds before shaking the senator's hand.

"Again," Godfrey said. "I'm sorry that situations like ours presented themselves the way they did. It appears everything is on track now."

Carpenter gave a slight nod and watched Godfrey head for the door.

At the door, Godfrey paused to look at Lucian. "See you on the other side."

Lucian nodded.

Godfrey left the room.

Kat smiled at Lucian, then turned to face Carpenter. "You don't seem too happy."

"I'm not happy with how they kept all this information from me. I'm glad to know Lucian has been on our side from the beginning," Carpenter said. With sad eyes, he looked at Lucian. "I'm sorry to have pursued you with as much aggression as I did."

Lucian forced a grin. "It was all part of the plan. You were doing your job."

"It's never been a part of my procedure to harass an innocent man."

"Well, since they told you and Godfrey has come out of hiding, it means we must be close to ending the rogue scientists." Lucian coughed violently until his face flushed red. When the coughing subsided, he took a deep breath.

Carpenter looked at Helmsby. "Is he going to be okay?"

Helmsby shrugged. "I don't know yet. I probably won't know for quite some time."

"There must be something we can do," Kat said.

"Research first," Helmsby said. "Solutions follow."

"Have they captured Matthews yet?" Kat asked Carpenter.

"No. What's worse is that Lydia has disappeared, and we still have had no way to contact her," Carpenter said.

Lucian said. "She'll find Matthews."

"I suspect that's what she's attempting to do."

"And when she does," Lucian said. "She'll kill him."

Carpenter sighed. "I've no doubt."

Helmsby took Lucian's right hand and helped pull him into a seated position. "Kat, help me walk Lucian to the prep chair."

Lucian stepped gingerly onto the floor. Kat wrapped Lucian's left arm around her shoulders to support some of his weight. He walked like an elderly man. Without their assistance, he'd have fallen.

After he sat down, Carpenter pulled some folded papers from his jacket pocket. "I have something you two need to sign."

"What?" Lucian said.

"These are official adoption papers granting you sole guardianship for Paul and Paula," he replied.

Tears flowed from Kat's eyes. "How?"

"I called in a few favors. Everything's legal." Carpenter said, winking at them.

"Thanks," Lucian said with a weak smile.

Kat threw her arms around Carpenter's neck and squeezed tightly. "Thank you *so* much!"

"It's the least I could do," he said.

Helmsby stepped beside Lucian. He took slender plastic tubes and coated them with clear lubricant.

"This won't be pleasant," Helmsby said. "Try to remain still."

Helmsby slid a tube in each of Lucian's nostrils. He then taped electrodes to Lucian's chest and his temples. A few minutes later, he inserted an I.V. needle at the back of his left wrist.

"What are these for?" Lucian whispered.

"We're taking every precaution to keep your body monitored at all times. This procedure is hazardous, even for you."

Kat squeezed Lucian's hand.

Helmsby smiled at her. "Are you ready?"

Lucian nodded.

Helmsby took a syringe. "Give her one last kiss before we put you under."

Kat pressed her lips against Lucian's. She wrapped her arms around his neck. He pulled her tightly around the waist.

She leaned back and looked into his eyes. "I love you. Helmsby's going to fix you. I'll be here when you awaken."

Lucian smiled. "I love you, too."

Helmsby injected the needle and pushed the sedative into Lucian's bloodstream. "You have about five minutes before you're out, so let's get you inside the chamber."

Lucian nodded and pushed himself to his feet. Kat tucked her arm under his and led him to the narrow metal stairs at the side of the chamber. He took each step with care, using the handrails for support. At the top of the stairs, he sat down and placed his feet into the warm nutrient-based substance.

Helmsby stood on the stairs behind him. "Before you plunge into the liquid, insert the mouth piece."

Lucian gave a weak nod. Helmsby knelt beside him and connected the I.V. tube to the rig. He then attached rubber-coated wires to each of the electrode attachments and moved the bundled wires over the top of the tank.

Helmsby clasped Lucian's shoulder. "You're ready. The sedative should kick in soon."

"Thanks, I guess."

Lucian lowered himself into the tank. Helmsby sealed the door shut. The liquid was at Lucian's waist. Kat stood at the front of the tank with her hands pressed against the glass. Lucian positioned his feet and put his right hand against hers.

Tears made Kat's mascara run.

The warm liquid filled the tank. Lucian's eyes closed a few seconds before the nutrient-based fluid reached his nose. The heart monitor showed a decreased rhythm in his heartbeat.

"He's asleep, Kat," Helmsby said.

Carpenter squeezed her shoulder. "I'm sorry."

Fighting tears, she turned and pressed her face against Carpenter's chest. He wrapped his arms around her, resting his chin on top of her head.

"I can't go through this again," she said. "I can't survive this."

"He's not dead," Carpenter whispered.

"He's *not* with me, either."

"I know."

Helmsby cleared his throat and walked to them. "I have an idea that just might work."

"What?" Kat asked.

"The notion is absurd, and you'll probably object to submitting Lucian to such a test, but I believe it might actually reverse his condition."

"What is it?"

"You remember the assassins Steven Matthews manipulated?"

"Those damned zombie-like creatures?" Kat asked.

"Yes. Matthews incorporated a mutant gene that regenerates dead tissue."

Kat frowned. "You can't turn Lucian into something so hideous."

"I'd never do anything like that. But if I could somehow splice the regeneration trait into Lucian's cellular makeup, it should be enough to reverse his condition."

"How could you without transforming him into something similar to them?"

"Kat, Lucian's telomeres are too short for his cells to properly divide and replenish themselves. I'm assuming that the enhancers are no longer working. I need to confirm that with Dr. Brockton. But if we add Matthews' regeneration trait, we'd eliminate Lucian's need for enhancement drugs. The regeneration agent will keep his cells healthy and alive. Just like the ones Brockton took from GenTech."

"He'd become immortal?"

Helmsby rubbed the stubble on his chin and smiled, entertaining the thought. "I can't guarantee that he'd become immortal, but he'd be stronger and healthier than he has been in the past six to seven months."

"Can you guarantee he won't look like those zombie men?"

He smiled. "Now that I *can* guarantee."

Carpenter frowned. "How?"

"The men Matthews used were corpses that he reanimated. Lucian's alive, so his appearance won't be compromised. He's already a genetic miracle. In fact, his ability to heal from serious wounds is nearly the same as the regeneration trait. The flaws he suffers are from being the clone of Lucas at age forty."

Kat folded her arms and looked at Lucian. "Did you discuss this with him before he went under?"

"Unfortunately, no. The idea hit me just minutes ago. But you're his wife. You'd have to make this medical decision for him."

"Damn," she whispered. Her eyes revealed her confusion.

"Take some time to think it over," Helmsby said. "A few hours or even a day, if necessary."

"You really believe this will work?"

"I see no way it can fail."

Kat walked to the chamber and pressed her hand to the glass. The strongest man she'd ever known floated helplessly. She couldn't bear losing him, but she couldn't justify allowing machines to keep her husband alive, either. That kind of desperation weighed heavy on the soul.

Already she missed the warmth of his eyes, the strength of his embrace, and his soothing voice whenever she was troubled or alarmed. She had grown used to sleeping beside him. Until he was cured, she didn't believe she'd have a peaceful night's sleep.

"Do it," she said.

Helmsby smiled. "Call Dr. Brockton."

"Why?"

"I need some of those tissue samples he stole from GenTech."

Kat turned. Her face paled. Her heart dropped. "He doesn't have them. He destroyed them in an incinerator. He feared they'd fall into the wrong hands if he didn't."

"Call him," Helmsby said. "If he's every bit the scientist I am, and I suspect he is, he saved some of those tissue samples."

Kat took her cellphone from her back pocket and hit autodial. "I hope you're right."

Chapter 83

Kat stepped outside the laboratory. She wiped away hot tears, waiting for Brockton to answer. Several rings later, he finally did.

"Hello? Kat?"

"Yes," she said, sobbing.

"What's wrong? Are you okay?"

"I'm fine. It's Lucian."

"What happened?"

She tried to answer but instead, she cried even harder.

"Kat?" Brockton asked. "Is Lucian still alive?"

Kat took a deep breath. "Yes. We're at Helmsby's lab."

"Okay, that's good. How is Lucian?"

"Helmsby has placed him into an incubation chamber."

"What? Things are that severe?"

"Yes," Kat replied.

"Has Helmsby mentioned anything that might help Lucian?"

"He has an idea, but he needs your assistance."

"Anything," Brockton said. "What does he need?"

"He needs those tissue cultures that Lucian took from GenTech."

"Why?"

"He thinks they'll reverse Lucian's aging processes."

"Kat, you know I incinerated them."

Kat sobbed and wiped more tears away. "I know. That's what I told Helmsby. But—"

"But what?"

"He seems to believe you kept some of them somewhere."

"Why does he think I kept some of them?"

"Helmsby said that if you're as much a scientist as he is, you would have."

Brockton chuckled.

"What's funny?" she asked.

"Apparently he knows me pretty well."

"So you did keep some tissue samples?"

"Of course. But I never thought there was a way they'd help Lucian. Otherwise I might have experimented with them."

Kat allowed a brief smile while wiping her eyes. "How long would it take for you to get them here?"

"Where are you?" Brockton asked.

"Louisville, Kentucky."

"Louisville?"

"Yes."

"It shouldn't take more than six hours at the most."

"Great."

"Kat?"

"Yes?"

"Hang in there, okay? I'll bring these immediately. Between Helmsby and myself, we're going to find a way to have Lucian around for a long time. Okay?"

"Okay. Thanks."

Kat disconnected the call and returned to the laboratory. The tears returned when she saw Lucian in the chamber. His suspended body looked lifeless in the fluid.

"Well?" Carpenter asked.

Kat beamed a smile in spite of the tears. She nodded. "He kept some of the cultures."

"See?" Helmsby said. "A good scientist *always* keeps samples. How soon will he have them here?"

"About six hours."

Helmsby smiled. "Perfect! Now, why don't you and Carpenter get something to eat or some coffee? Get out of here and let you attention focus on something less stressful."

Carpenter put his arm around Kat's shoulders and gave a tight side hug. "He's right. Being in here isn't good for you."

"I promised Lucian I'd be here."

"I know. But getting some food and coffee won't take too long. We can come right back."

Helmsby nodded. "It may still be a day or so before Brockton and I can formulate a serum to bring Lucian out of his induced comatose state."

"That long?" she asked.

Helmsby shrugged. "Or longer. Some things are best not rushed. Our analysis must be thorough so we don't actually do more damage than good."

"That's true," Carpenter said.

Kat closed her eyes. Tears crept down her cheeks. "I . . . miss him so much."

Carpenter nodded. "I know you do. But, at least he's still alive, and they are closer to finding a reversal to his condition."

Kat nodded. "I know. Things are more optimistic than fifteen minutes ago. I probably need to eat."

"That a girl," Carpenter said. "Come on, let's go."

She glanced at Lucian and walked alongside Carpenter. When it came to prayers, she was a loss for words. Her continued hope had faded, and she didn't know how she'd cope with the ache in her chest. All she knew was that she needed Lucian more now than ever before.

Chapter 84

Helmsby checked the monitors on the incubation chamber. Then he turned on the flow pump that filtered the nutrient base fluids surrounding Lucian. He loved challenges, but never one that involved life and death situations with friends or family. Remorse struck him. He recalled Margaret's failed battle with cancer and his inability to find a way to treat her. And even though Yvonne played a key role in helping his heart heal, he was still unable to accept his loss and failure.

Footsteps clattered through the hall. The echo indicated more than one person, and they were headed his direction. When they stopped at the doorway, Helmsby turned around. His eyes widened with surprise. He rubbed his tired eyes, looked again, but he had seen correctly the first time.

"Lucas?" he asked.

Lucas nodded.

"Why are you here?"

Joe stepped into the room.

Lucas said, "You remember Joe?"

"Ah, yes, we met briefly at Grayson Enterprises. How'd you find me and why are you here?"

"Show him, Joe," Lucas said.

Joe walked over and placed the wrapped skull onto a lab table. He smiled at Helmsby's interest.

Joe picked up the skull, unwrapped it, and set it down. The white bone gleamed under the fluorescent lighting.

Helmsby gasped. "I'll be damned. Where'd you get this?"

"An archeological dig near our ranch."

Helmsby leaned close to the skull and marveled. "What do you plan to do with this?"

"It's yours," Joe said.

"Mine? Don't tease."

Joe nodded. "I'm not. I insist that you have it."

"As much as I greatly appreciate such a gift, this is worth a fortune."

"I imagine so."

"Then why give it away?"

"It's what my ancestors insisted I do."

Helmsby gave Joe a brief inquisitive glance.

Joe continued, "There is a reason for me to have found it. A young woman was killed by men trying to steal this. They even tried to kill me. When I consulted my ancestors, the vision I received showed you holding this. There is no questioning what I was shown. This is yours. They want you to have it. Perhaps you'll uncover the mysteries surrounding it."

"I'm speechless, Joe, and for me, that's a rarity. Thank you."

Joe smiled and nodded. "You're welcome."

Helmsby held the skull and grinned. The moment was exactly the image Joe had seen in his vision.

"You know, I've been kicking myself for leaving Grayson Enterprises and now, with this, I never have to hold that regret again."

"Grayson is not a good man," Joe said.

"I know."

"Perhaps this is why you were to receive this. For your good moral standing."

Helmsby looked across the room. Lucas stood at the incubation chamber and looked at his clone.

"What happened to him?" Lucas asked.

"His short life has run its course," Helmsby said. "That is, unless I can find something to extend it longer."

Lucas studied his mirrored self. It was remarkably eerie to see what was essentially himself glassed inside a life support system.

"Anything I can do to help?" Lucas asked.

Helmsby straightened. "That was the last thing I expected you to ask."

"Why?"

"It's no secret how outraged you've been having a clone."

Lucas sighed. "I know, but with all the losses I've had in life, especially recently, there's no sense allowing his life to fade if there's anything I can do."

"Brockton should arrive in a few hours with something that might help, but it's no guarantee. One thing you might do though."

"What's that?"

Helmsby shrugged. "Part with some of your blood so I can harvest stem cells and transplant them into Lucian's system."

"That will work?"

"It gives me an alternative if the other doesn't."

"Sure, I'll do it. How much you need?"

"Half a pint at the most."

"Sure."

Helmsby smiled. "There's something you need to know. And it might forever change your view of Lucian."

"What's that?" Lucas asked.

"He didn't kill Senator Godfrey or those other men. It was staged."

"Seriously?"

Helmsby nodded. "Godfrey was here earlier. Now, let's steal some of your blood."

Chapter 85

A few hours after Lucas donated the blood and he and Joe left, Brockton arrived. He carried an ice cooler and knocked on the side of Helmsby's open lab door.

"Yes?" Helmsby said.

"I brought the cell cultures," Brockton said.

Helmsby straightened his glasses and met Brockton at the door. Helmsby extended his hand. "Good that you've finally arrived."

Brockton firmly shook Helmsby's hand. "Thanks."

"Come on in and make yourself at home."

"Where is Lucian?" Brockton asked.

"In there," Helmsby said, pointing.

Brockton shook his head. "Damn. I hate to see him in such a condition."

"Me, too. How long has he been showing symptoms?"

"A few months, but it had gotten worse during the past week. I tried to get him to tell Kat how serious his health issues were."

"So the enhancers stopped working?" Helmsby asked.

"Yes, for a while now."

"I had assumed such. He's made it longer than I originally believed."

Brockton nodded. "I know."

"Where's Kyle?"

"Stayed at home. Refused to come."

"Really? Who is staying with him?"

"No one," Brockton said.

"So his progress has advanced that much?"

"Other than his disfigurements, he copes well and could venture out in public if he wanted."

Helmsby placed his hands on the cooler lid. "Do you mind?"

"Not at all. Take a look."

Helmsby opened the cooler and took out a petri dish. He chuckled and shook his head. "I told Kat that you were too good a scientist to incinerate all these tissue cultures. She didn't believe me."

"She told me."

Helmsby took the dish to one of the electron microscopes and set it on the stage. He adjusted the ocular and peered through the eyepiece.

"Damn, Matthews is a genius, but in a more frightening manner than we are," Helmsby said with a wide grin.

"Insanity sometimes runs parallel with genius."

"Often they are paired."

Both scientists laughed.

Helmsby stepped away from the microscope and motioned Brockton to look.

"What do you think?" Helmsby asked.

"If we do what I believe you're suggesting, we're crossing a bridge that leads to Matthews and Idris' demented playground."

"As long as it's a short stay."

Brockton nodded. "Agreed."

"If this doesn't work, Lucas donated blood we can use for stem cells."

"Seriously? Lucas did that?"

Helmsby nodded. "So we do have a choice. Should we attempt the stem cells from Lucas' blood first, which may only last for a few days or weeks? Or use Matthews' wicked stem cells that continually replenish themselves?"

"I know it sounds unethical, but I believe we should use Matthews'. Because, as you suggest, Lucas' cells might not last long and it would be too dangerous to subject Lucian to the chamber a second time so soon."

"I agree. I know it's late, but are you ready to get started?"

Brockton smiled. "Of course."

Chapter 86

Two days later

KAT STARED through the glass at Lucian. She had barely slept a few hours for all her worrying. Her heart ached. She wanted to hold him.

Lucian floated in the chamber. His limp body looked lifeless. Had it not been for the various monitors providing data about his health status, she would have thought he had died. The greenish liquid made it impossible to see if his complexion had returned to normal.

"Good morning, Kat," Helmsby said, stepping beside her.

Brockton joined them.

"How much longer will you have to work before the serum is complete?" she asked.

"Oh, we're ready," Helmsby said. "We plan to test it now."

"Really? Today?"

"Yes."

Kat smiled. "How long before we see any positive results?"

"Under typical situations, Kat, stem cells can take several months to work."

Kat's smile faded. "That long?"

"Emphasis is on *typical*," Helmsby said. "With Matthews' research cells, they *aren't* typical. In fact, their growth progress has been too quick for me to believe had we not charted their growth progress over the past two days. Between their rapid growth and Lucian's remarkable metabolism, who knows how long this will take?"

"But do note," Brockton said. "That there may be side effects. It may not work at all. There is always that chance, too."

Kat said, "I understand."

"Is this a chance you're willing to take?" Helmsby asked.

Kat looked at Lucian. Tears wet her eyes. She took a deep breath. "My choices are limited, aren't they?"

"Yes, they are," Brockton said.

Kat wiped her eyes. "What do you think, Brockton? Is this worth the risk?"

"If I was in Lucian's place, I'd beg that someone try this on me."

"Then do it."

Helmsby took the syringe and walked up the steps to the I.V. He inserted the needle and pushed all the stem cell serum inside the bag.

"All we can do is wait now," Helmsby said.

SEVERAL HOURS PASSED. Kat never took her eyes off Lucian. She wanted to be the first person he saw when he awakened. She wanted him to know she had never abandoned hope, even though many times she thought hope had escaped her mental grasp.

But after more hours went by, nothing seemed to have changed.

Lucian remained still. The life monitoring machines indicated nothing new.

She watched Lucian and caught a reflection of herself in the glass, which startled her. Her hair was unkempt. Dark circles weighed beneath her haunted eyes. She barely recognized herself.

Where had she allowed her independence to retreat? Before Lucian, she had savored the strength of being her own person and not relying on another for anything; that is, not until love had knocked her feet out from under her and sent her into a romantic cartwheel where her path no longer remained singular. But looking back, she wouldn't trade the companionship with Lucian for what she had back then. She had found new strength and the joy in sharing life with someone else that held similar interests. That bond had not weakened her. Instead, it had actually made her stronger.

Fear of losing the one true love in her life made her more vulnerable than anything else life had ever dealt her. Should Lucian die, she faced a new path that she didn't want to explore.

"You have to wake up, Lucian," she whispered. "Please."

Helmsby stepped into the laboratory and saw her standing at the incubation chamber, so he made his way to her.

"Kat," he said. "You should go rent a hotel room and get some sleep. This kind of process . . . well, let's just say, it takes a lot of time. Days, weeks, who knows?"

Kat closed her eyes and shook her head. "I want to be here when he wakes up."

"I understand. But stems cells, even these uniquely specialized ones, take some time to attach and take root. Once that process initiates, his recovery, provided this works, will be rapid."

"I hope so."

Helmsby offered a reassuring smile. "I have some things to work on in my office with Brockton. You really need to get some rest. Your anxiety will only weaken your immune system. Don't you want to be at your best when Lucian wakes up?"

Kat nodded. "I do. Give me a few more minutes alone with him, and I promise, I'll go get a room, shower, and get some sleep."

"Sure. I'm in the next room if you need anything."

Helmsby walked away.

Kat watched until Helmsby was gone, and then she stepped closer to the glass. She pressed her hands and forehead against the glass. She tried to see his eyes, but his body stooped forward in a position where he faced downward.

"I need you, love," she said. "Paul and Paula need you, too. They need both of us."

Tears heated her eyes.

Lucian stiffened and his body jerked. Bubbles pushed out from around his mouthpiece. His eyes opened. He stared straight at Kat.

"He's awake!" Kat shouted. "Dr. Helmsby! Brockton, come quick! Lucian's awake!"

Brockton and Helmsby rushed from their side room office and hurried up the stairs to the incubation chamber. Helmsby pulled open the chamber door. Gallons of the solution sloshed out and trickled down the steps.

"Hurry," Helmsby said. "We have to pull him out of the tank so he doesn't drown."

Brockton stepped down into the chamber and lifted Lucian high enough to get his nose above the solution. Helmsby grabbed Lucian's right arm and pulled him to the edge of the stairs. Brockton and Helmsby carefully pulled out the plastic tubing and unhooked the I.V. needle.

Lucian gasped and choked for air. Helmsby placed his arms around Lucian's chest and tugged him up while Brockton pushed from behind. Solution dripped off his wet body. His breathing stabilized.

He looked down at Kat and smiled.

Her body shook. Tears flowed. She hurried up the stairs and wrapped her arms around him.

"How do you feel?" Helmsby asked.

Lucian took a deep breath. "Awake, and a lot better."

Kat loosened her hold and pulled back. She looked into his eyes and frowned.

"What's wrong?" he asked.

"I don't know. Your eyes look *different*."

"How?" he asked.

"They're not the same color."

Helmsby looked at them, too. "Hmm. There's a black ring around your irises."

"Really?"

Kat nodded. "Yes, that's the difference. What does it mean?"

Helmsby shrugged. "I don't know."

Carpenter stepped into the laboratory. "Well, good to see you're out, Lucian."

"Thanks."

"Helmsby, is he going to be okay?" Carpenter asked.

"Right now, his prognosis looks good. We'll do a few tests, but I think he'll make a full recovery."

Kat took Lucian by the hand and led him down the steps. She looked at Carpenter. "How did everything turn out in Salem?"

"I was asked by Mitch to give you this note."

Kat took the note and read it. She laughed. "He's staying in Salem for a while to be with Sheba?"

"Appears that way."

Kat read on. "He says that although he hasn't see any spirits in the haunted areas, he does sense their presences and wants to conduct further investigations."

"I think he's attracted to her, too," Carpenter said with a broad grin.

"I don't doubt that," Kat said. "What about Cassandra and her daughter?"

Carpenter smiled. "We've decided to take them into Witness Protection after their testimonies against Dr. Shelby are made in court. She is adopting Seth, too. Since they don't have any other relatives, the change won't alter their lives that much."

"That's good."

"Tom vanished in the underground tunnels after he led us to Cassandra and Alicia. Those strange cats did, too."

"Odd," Kat said. "So when will they have to testify against Dr. Shelby?"

"Shelby goes before a federal judge today to have the hearing set."

Brockton brought a bathrobe for Lucian after Kat helped towel him off.

Carpenter smiled. "So how soon before we go get those twins?"

"As soon as Helmsby lets us leave," Lucian said.

Helmsby chuckled. "A half hour is all I need. That is, as long as you promise to come back in a few days for me to finish my research on your results."

Lucian nodded. "No problem."

Kat hugged Lucian and smiled. "I can't wait until we get Paul and Paula. We'll spoil them rotten."

Chapter 87

Dr. Shelby and his attorney sat down in the courtroom, waiting for the judge to appear.

Several benches were filled with eager onlookers and a few others were also awaiting their arraignments. Reporters sat inside and dozens more waited outside the courthouse for a chance to interview people.

Shelby's attorney leaned close to his ear and whispered, "The best thing you can do is plead guilty."

"Guilty?" Shelby asked with a stunned expression. "Why the hell should I do that?"

"You've done what you could at New Horizons, but I no longer have any need for you."

"No more projects?"

"*None.*"

"But you're Alpha's brother. He'd expect you to carry on."

"I'm finished. Done."

"But you're—"

His attorney smiled. "I know. I'm Omega."

"You *have* to keep working."

"No, I don't."

"Then I'll let the world know *who* you are."

Omega slipped his hand into his leather satchel. A few seconds later, he jabbed a syringe into Shelby's thigh. He pressed the stopper and shot the potassium chloride into Shelby's bloodstream. He dropped the syringe into the side of his satchel.

Within seconds, Shelby clutched his chest. His face flushed red.

"My client's having a heart attack," Omega said, helping Shelby lay down on the floor. "A doctor? Anyone here a doctor?"

People gathered around, but before any specialized help arrived, Dr. Shelby was dead.

LYDIA WALKED the forest path where she had shot at Lucas days before. Any remorse she had felt for leaving was gone. She crossed the cascading creek with a long roll of rope slung over her shoulder. She realized why she had told Lucas they needed to live here. Whatever had beckoned her lived here, deep beneath the forest floor.

She found the spot where the creek disappeared beneath the ground. Unlooping the long rope, she tied one end to a massive pine tree trunk. Then she dropped the rest of the rope down into the hole. Placing thick leather gloves on her hands, she descended the rope as fast as possible. When her feet touched the ground, she turned on a huge flashlight.

The light met dozens of glowing wolf-like eyes. They all gathered around her, sniffing and growling. The leader stepped before her. A tall, grayish wolf-like man. He studied her for a few moments and bared his teeth.

With lightning speed she struck his jaw and knocked him backwards. He rolled and came sprinting at her on all fours. She kicked and planted the toe of her boot beneath his chin. He reeled backwards and landed on his back.

The rest of the pack eased closer with narrowed eyes and snarls on their faces.

The leader rubbed his jaw and shook his head. "Who are you and what the hell do you want?"

"I'm Lydia. I'd like to join your pack."

He stood slowly, still rubbing his jaw. Blood leaked from his lips and he smiled.

"How'd you know where to find us?" he asked.

"For months I've felt your presence. I had this inner tugging that kept calling me to come in this direction."

Extending his hand, he said, "I'm Tobias. Why do you wish to join us? You're human. We're escaped lab experiments from New Horizons."

"Then we both have something in common. I was created in a lab, too."

"Then, my lady, you most certainly may stay."

Lydia smiled. For once in her life, she believed she might have found the place she could call home.

About the Author

Leonard D. Hilley II grew up a quiet, shy kid with an inquisitive mind. Learning to read at an early age, he fell in love with books. He read every book he could get his hands on and stacks of dark comics about ghosts, monsters, and creepy things that stalk the night.

Like a lot of boys, he caught beetles, wooly bears, butterflies, and had an ant farm. When he was ten, his interests in science increased even more after seeing a professor's insect collection. Soon he set out on his quest to build his own collection. He also learned to rear butterflies and moths to obtain perfect specimens. He learned botany, gardening, and set his goal to become an entomologist.

At eleven, he saw Star Wars. His imagination soared. Soon after, he discovered Roger Zelazny's Chronicles of Amber. Six months later, he had written the first draft of a novel. A novel he later discarded, but the characters stuck with him. Years later, these characters came to life in Shawndirea, which Hilley intended to be a novella for Devils Den. The characters, however, refused to be ignored and took the opportunity to unveil Aetheaon in their first epic fantasy. Lady Squire: Dawn's Ascension was quick to follow.

Shawndirea was Hilley's farewell to butterfly collecting, and those who have read the novel understand why. He has taken Ray Bradbury's advice to heart: "Follow the characters." He does. He follows, listens, and take notes—often never knowing where they're going to take him, but he's never been disappointed in the results.

Hilley earned a B.S. in Biology and an MFA in Creative Writing to combine his love of science and writing.

Sci-fi Titles: Predators of Darkness: Aftermath, Beyond the Darkness, The Game of Pawns, Death's Valley, The Deimos Virus.

Epic Fantasy: Shawndirea (Aetheaon Chronicles: Book One), Lady Squire (Aetheaon Chronicles: Book Two), Frosthammer (Aetheaon Chronicles: Book Three), Shadowfae (Aetheaon Chronicles: Book Four), and Devils Den.

UF/PR: Succubus: Shadows of the Beast (Nocturnal Trinity Series: Book One), Raven (Nocturnal Trinity Series: Book Two), A Touch of the Familiar (Nocturnal Trinity Series: Book Three).

YA UF/Paranormal: Forrest Wollinsky Vampire Hunter; Forrest Wollinsky: Blood Mists of London; Forrest Wollinsky: Predestined Crossroads.

CPSIA information can be obtained
at www.ICGtesting.com
Printed in the USA
BVHW032204070419
544894BV00001B/28/P